I0613204

And Then...

THE GREAT BIG BOOK

OF AWESOME

ADVENTURE TALES

vol. 1

Edited by Kylie Fox & Ruth Wykes

CLAN
DESTINE
PRESS

First published in Australia 2016
by Clan Destine Press
PO Box 121 Bittern
Victoria 3918 Australia

Title: *And Then... the Great Big Book of Awesome Adventure Tales Vol 1*
Editors: Kylie Fox & Ruth Wykes
Authors: Various

ISBN   (Hbk) 978-0-9945991-1-799
        (pbk) 978-0-9945991-0-0
        (eBook) 978-0-9954394-2-9

Cover Art & Design: Sarah Pain
Internal Illustrations: Vicky Pratt

Design & Typesetting: Clan Destine Press
Printed and bound in Australia by Lightning Source

www.clandestinepress.com.au

What lies within...

And Then...
the
Introduction

Once upon a time, in a land Down Under, in the depths of the Clan cave, a fateful decision was made: Clan Destine Press would issue a challenge to Australian authors to write a cliff-hanging, Australian-flavoured, action-packed adventure story for two protagonists, a story of the *What If, What Now, And Then...* kind.

This was a catnip call, an irresistible lure, a kid-in-a-lolly-shop kind of challenge: what writer *wouldn't* want to take a crack at that?

But just to make it that little bit more intriguing, the Clan Destine editors decreed that the stories could be contemporary, historical, realistic, far-out, spec-fic, horror, SF, or urban fantasy. They also suggested, in a spirit of mischief, that at least one of the tale's two protagonists should be human. You'd think that would just about cover all the bases, wouldn't you?

But writers are a contrary bunch: they pushed these very broad boundaries even further. The result is not one, but two volumes of kick-arse, action-packed stories: *And Then... The Great Big Book of Adventure Tales*.

This is Volume 1: an amazing collection of genre-bending adventure stories garnered from a mix of sf, fantasy and crime writers, happily encroaching upon each other's territories, and then some.

Clan Destine's stricture about the relative humanity of the characters raises the obvious question: what *does* it mean to be human? It is a question that has fired the imaginations of several contributors: the inimitable Jason Nahrung pushes it to the limit in *The Mermaid Club*, where a strange process of 'mythomorphing' has changed the face of Australian society, and the alleged theft of a mer-person is investigated by a demon-possessed detective whose crime-solving, skin-shedding snake-partner appears human (ish) only some of the time; while in the chemically-poisoned dystopian world of *Deadbeats,* Peter Ball gives us gene-morphed Rat Boys and Crow Boys, struggling with assorted hyped-up Rapture gangs fighting for territory against the rogue, gene-mod-hating Evangelical Whites in a city where newly-decanted cryogenesis subjects are in all kinds of trouble; in *Come Now, Traveller*, Amanda Wrangles splices boy and ship, conjoined in a strange, seafaring siren's song with the Captain and the figurehead Lady; and in *The Panther's Paw*, Emilie Collyer explores enhanced inter-species communication, with a protagonist who specialises in communication with big cats and a plot that takes us right down to interaction with microbes. On a lighter note, the theme of inter-species communication continues in the tongue-in-cheek quest undertaken by Randall and his sidekick budgerigar in Kat Clay's *In The Company of Rogues.*

It's a short step from monstrously modified humanity to actual terrifying fire-breathing monsters, and there's no shortage of those in this anthology. After all, what's an adventure collection without dragons? They appear, in all their various glory, in Dan Rabarts' *Tipuna Tapu*, in Tansy Rayner Roberts's *Death at the Dragon Circus*, in Jason Franks' *Exili and the Dragon*, and in Alan Baxter's *Golden Fortune Dragon Jade*.

The stories in this anthology range far and wide in time and place, and several writers have chosen to set their tales in various periods of Australian history. In *The Boudicca Society*, Tor Roxburgh treats us to a perfect evocation of Melbourne in the 1960's as two feisty girls fight to claim their unusual inheritance; Sophie Masson's *The Romanov Opal* transports us to Lightning Ridge in the 1950's, where the hunt is on for a missing gemstone; Alan Baxter takes us a hundred years further back to the 1850's in *Golden Fortune, Dragon Jade*, where a martial-arts-trained monk and his spirit-talker cousin travel from China to the Ballarat goldfields to find a stolen jade dragon; and Narrelle M Harris also sets her story, *Virgin Soil*, in 1850's gold-rush Melbourne, where creepy elemental spirits pursue their own arcane agenda. Sulari Gentill, on the other hand, offers a timely cautionary tale set in a near future Australia in the chilling *Catch a Fallen Star*.

Exotic locations have not been overlooked: Lucy Sussex's *Batgirl in Borneo* transports us to the steamy, orang-utan territory of Kota Kinabulu; Dan Rabarts sets *Tipuna Tapu* in a dragon-haunted Kokoruroa; Evelyn Tsitas takes us on a tour from Melbourne to Thessaloniki via Bavaria, Paris and London, in *Stealing Back the Relics*.

And Then... is indeed a wondrous strange collection of exotic tales that encompass a huge sweep of possibilities, past, present and future.

Enjoy!

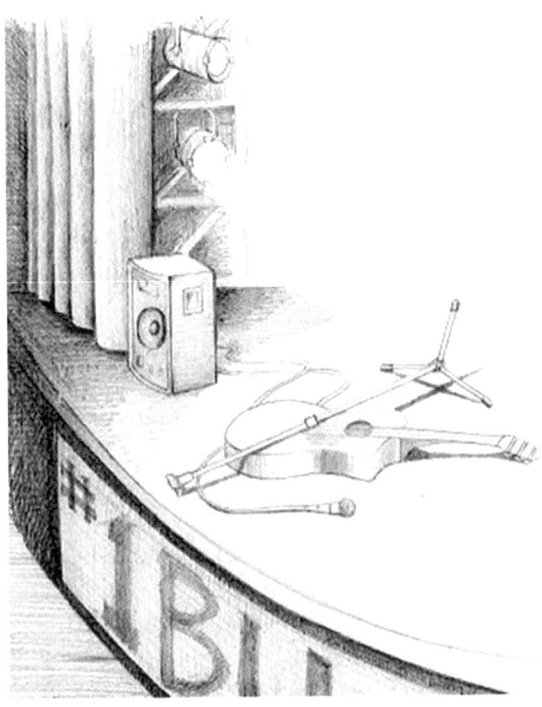

Catch a Fallen Star

Mason Kennedy was a star of *The Southern Cross*. Adolescent girls screamed and fainted in his presence. They declared undying love, cried themselves to sleep and then dreamt of him on sodden pillows. Their brothers did not respond quite so emotionally, but they afforded Mason an envious respect. He was, after all, less naff than the other teenage members of the musical constellation.

Occasionally Mason's face revealed an admirable trace of contempt and, at times, his manner mocked the officially-sanctioned, government-endorsed music he performed. Nothing overt, of course, just a hint that he was not entirely on board. It was dangerous, and undeniably attractive.

If it had been an affectation, it would have been one of marketing genius, but the flashes of defiance were honest-born.

Selected to join the all-singing, all-dancing, youth talent team when he was ten, Mason Kennedy's life since, had been public property. At first it had been exciting. The stars of *The Southern Cross* were beloved of the people. Mason became the idol of millions. At ten the screaming girls scared him; at 14 they pleased him; and now, at 17, he just found himself feeling ridiculous and bored.

The songs the group performed were designed to be popular, produced to be hits which would garner mass followings and affirm the glory of the Commonwealth. Groomed as role models for the young, the stars served as reassurance for the old. Their part was vital to the morale of the nation, their veneration a patriotic duty. Most of them accepted it.

Strangely it was Mason Kennedy – the most popular of their number – who most resented the package into which they'd been wrapped. Perhaps it was an arrogance born of years of adulation that led him to resist the very thing that had made him so beloved. It began with a carelessness with respect to rehearsal, child-like pranks and a tendency to alter choreography and lyrics on whim. Nonsensical changes passed off, at first, as honest and endearing mistakes. But soon the slips happened too often and too pointedly to be anything but intentional.

The public reaction was unexpected; Mason became even more adored and audiences waited eagerly for the twist, the edge of rebellion he'd add to each performance. It was hilarious, a breath of fresh air. The various managers, producers of, and officials responsible for *The Southern Cross* pretended not to notice what he was doing, as people flocked in their thousands to see the group.

But even as his star climbed, Mason felt only more absurd. His world was stage-managed; he was stage-managed. The cheesy sameness of it all built into a churning frustration, a resentment of the talent which had won him his place in the group the Commonwealth had created to promote its message. His parents did not understand. Mason didn't either, but that did not make their lack of understanding any easier for him to accept. His father ranted, his mother reasoned and they both forbade him to do whatever it was that he was doing. And so, he became reckless.

The event was the most important of the year: the Presidential Address at the Opera House. President Buck would have the opportunity to speak of the priorities of the Commonwealth, and the city's wealthiest citizens would have the opportunity to wear their diamonds while demonstrating their patriotism. *The Southern Cross* would perform to ensure the crowds were suitably enthused when the president took centre stage to deliver a stirring address on economics, and national security, and all the reasons why his government was the salvation of the Commonwealth. Mason was selected to sing the presidential anthem in an attempt to ensure his popularity was appropriately transferred. In a nod to the current nostalgic revival, he would sing live with only an acoustic guitar to accompany him. A sparse and moving solo. Mason, far from being gratified by the ostensible honour, was concerned that *Man of Action, Man of Steel* sounded like a love ballad from the last century.

'I'm not saying President Buck is unlovable – there's someone for everyone I suppose – but we don't have that kind of relationship. You can put lipstick on a Buck and it'll still be a Buck.'

The publicist laughed nervously, and told him not to be silly. The presidential song was a tradition. He would be speaking for every citizen who loved his country.

When the management left, his fellow stars laughed at him. 'Serves you right!' Mel Jackson snorted. 'You've smart-alecked your way into having to serenade Buck.' She put her hand over her heart. 'He might give you a knighthood: Order of the Wanker.'

Mason considered refusing, indeed, he tried. But the stars of *The Southern Cross* had been created under the auspice of the Ministry of Truth. They were not artists but the product of official vision. What he was being asked to do was his patriotic duty.

His publicist, amongst others, was at pains to counsel him. 'There have been some concerns about your recent hijinks, Mace. This is an opportunity to prove that you appreciate the opportunities you've been given. You were selected from over a million kids, you know. If there's one thing the public hates, it's ingratitude; so suck it up and sing the bloody song, sunshine!'

The warning was clear, but Mason was of an age and a disposition to be rash.

And so, alone on the stage, but for the colossal image of President Christian Buck behind him, live before thousands, and broadcast to millions, he performed *Man of Action, Man of Steel* – in a manner of speaking.

In place of 'under your leadership we took up the strain' he sang 'under your nose we can shelter from rain.' The gasp was audible, and then giggles rippled through the rows reserved for young people. He might have gotten away with if it if he'd stopped at that.

'Your words inspire, and rouse for the fight' became 'your words make me wonder if you're all that bright.' The giggles turned to both laughter and rumblings of disapproval.

Mason smiled, and winked at the audience. He'd stop soon. Just one more, just so it was clear he was not some trained seal who applauded on command. When 'rise fellow citizens to laud this great man' was rendered as 'rise fellow citizens and escape while you can', Mason Kennedy's microphone was turned off, the stage lights dimmed and he was removed physically from public sight.

Mason had expected there would be consequences, but the arrest took him by surprise. Dragged backstage he was restrained at gunpoint and searched. Mayhem followed swiftly. The first of many interrogations

Who was he working with?

'No one.'

How long had he been radicalised?

'Man! I just changed a couple of words.'

Who had converted him?

'Converted me to what?'

Questions, accusations, recriminations. And then again. And when they stopped, he was taken into custody where, in a cell, the same questions were put under enhanced techniques until he was shaking and incoherent. If he had understood what they were asking, he might have confessed just to have it over.

When he asked for a lawyer, they laughed at him and later, when he begged for his mother, they mocked him.

In the windowless cell he could count the passing of time only by changes of tie. His interrogators had changed their ties five times before his parents were allowed to see him. His publicist came with them.

At first Mason thought their arrival signalled release.

'Mason, how can you not realise how serious this is?' Jacob Kennedy grabbed his son by the shoulders.

'I sang the wrong words in a stupid song – how could it be serious?' Mason said desperately. His mother was crying like he'd died.

'They intend to charge you under the Anti-terrorism Act.'

'What? But I didn't–'

'The media has got hold of this Mason. They're painting what you did as an act of treachery. They're calling for you to be exiled.'

'For a friggin' song? What the–'

'Mace, darling, calm down. Losing your temper won't help you now.' Hetty Martin had been in public relations for 33 years. There weren't many disasters she hadn't seen, hadn't fixed. This too would be reframed. But it would take careful management to turn public sentiment in their favour once again.

The publicist sat down beside her client and handed his mother a handkerchief. 'Darling, do pull yourself together.' It was difficult to tell to whom she was speaking; perhaps all of them.

She placed her arm around Mason. 'Our dear President Buck is feeling merciful, isn't that wonderful, Mace? You've done a terrible thing, but he is inclined to believe that you were led astray by the excesses and impulsiveness of youth. You may be able to redeem yourself, but, we will all have to play our part.'

'What do you mean, Hetty?' Mason closed his eyes. This was all insane. Surely it was a bad dream.

'Your dear Mama and Papa will make a public statement as soon as we leave here. They will talk about how the pressures of fame have affected you, how you've become uncommunicative and moody. They will blame themselves–'

'For what?'

'For not seeing how troubled you were.'

'I'm not troubled.'

'Yes you are, darling, now shut up and listen. They will plead with other parents to keep a closer eye on their teenagers; to use your story as a cautionary lesson.'

'God, why?'

'It will please the Ministry, darling. It will be a good thing if young people are more closely watched, they think. In return, they will not exile you.'

'So I can go home?'

Hetty sucked in her cheeks as she chose her words. 'Not exactly. We need to rebuild your image from the ground, darling, because it is to the ground that you have burned it.' She sat back, clearly pleased with the outcome of her efforts on his behalf. 'You, Mason Kennedy, will be conscripted into the National Service.'

'Are you for fucken real? I'm not joining the National Service!' Mason stared at the publicist in horror. He had been exempted from National Service years ago, as had every child that testing decreed capable of doing anything more than serving in lower ranks of the defence forces.

'The National Service is a vital instrument in the protection of the Commonwealth, darling,' Hetty replied brusquely. 'Our dear president believes it's time that the public afforded it a little more respect. You will thank President Buck publicly for the opportunity to serve your country and demonstrate your loyalty despite your transgression. You will ask the Commonwealth for forgiveness and you will serve your time in the Service to earn it. There's ample scope for positive media coverage.'

'No! What if I refuse?'

Jacob Kennedy exploded. 'You won't bloody well refuse! Your name is my name you little bastard! Do you not realise what you've done to all of us?'

'Mason please,' his mother begged. 'I can't show my face anywhere. The neighbours cut me dead this morning, and all our old friends...' Whatever else she may have said was lost in gulping sobs.

'Because I made a few jokes about Buck? For God's sake–'

Jacob Kennedy slammed the table with his fist. 'You incited treason, you committed treason, you made us parents of a traitor to the Commonwealth. I hope it was worth it Mason because–'

Hetty raised her hand for silence. 'If you refuse, darling, they will revoke your citizenship and either detain you indefinitely or send you into exile. In short, your life will be over. You need to understand that. What I propose will mean a couple of tough years, certainly, but once that's done, your debt will be repaid and we can think about rebuilding your career. The public loves a reformed character.'

Mason stared, unable to say anything. The panic congealed in his stomach until it was a thing of stone. He choked, still unable to speak. In his silence then, it was decided, and the deal struck on his behalf. The fallen star of *The Southern Cross* would become a poster boy for the National Service

'Advance.'

The word fell with the weight of many thousand voices, and then again, and again – a relentless pounding of sound which bludgeoned the thoughts and dulled the will. Easy meaningless exhilaration, the buzzing glory of the hive. The infield seemed to throb as twenty thousand fists punched the air in time and praise. Thousands more joined from the bleachers, an ecstasy of pride and nationalism, as the young men of the Service paraded before them.

Legions in black dress uniforms, lines in crisp formation. A show of strength and order and faith.

Until Mason Kennedy stopped. Slowly, he folded his arms, his eyes fixed ahead. They were watching, of course, vigilant for any sign that the counsellors would need to deal with him again. He'd just given them that sign.

'Kennedy!' Jordan Goodwin walked down the line to Mason. 'Raise your arm,' he snarled.

Mason ignored the sergeant. His arms remained folded. If Goodwin had not then glanced back over his own shoulder, he might have seen the passing shadow of uncertainty in the fury of the celebrity cadet's dark eyes.

Goodwin's face flushed, acutely aware that this would look bad for him. They would see he could not control his charges – it was only Kennedy – but they would see it as generalised failure. 'I'll make you pay for this you bastard. Put up your arm before I fuckin' well break it!'

Mason raised a brow instead. He smiled. His shoulders remained relaxed, his posture scornful. But he knew. He'd be in for it now.

'Mace, what the Hell are you doing, man?' Elliot Maynard muttered as he maintained the rhythm of the salute.

Mason shrugged. He wasn't really sure. Embarrassing the Service at the President's Address was possibly suicide. A visible public defiance. He had done that once before and the world had fragmented and caved in upon him. He'd been fooling around then, it was different now.

'Mace.' Elliot's face showed the panic that Mason concealed with the defiant fold of his arms. They could both see Goodwin was speaking to his own superiors. 'Come on man, you're not achieving anything by getting yourself killed.'

But it was too late. Mason Kennedy's refusal to laud the President of the Commonwealth had been duly noticed.

It was as Christian Buck swaggered onto the stage to acknowledge the strident approbation of the legions parading before him, that they dragged the cadet away.

Elliot Maynard glanced at the empty cot beside his, and he cursed the stubbornness of Mason Kennedy. A stupid pointless gesture for which Mason would answer dearly. And yet there was a nagging admiration, a churning envy which settled in Elliot's gut. He should have lowered his arm too; stood with his friend and bugger the consequences. If he had, perhaps others would have joined them – he'd heard Pete Hayes and Briton Ibe murmur rebellion before – Mason might have started a revolution of sorts. But of course Elliot had not joined him and the first domino had fallen alone.

Joining had not been an option.

Elliot's sister and mother relied on the secret being kept. There was nothing else for it but to be a grey man: unremarkable and unnoticed. If the Service decided to scrutinise him they would find the flaw and the consequences would be swift and devastating.

But still, he felt sick with self-loathing.

Elliot glanced again at the empty cot. It had been three days since the parade. They'd taken Mason for correction before. He'd returned bruised and quiet but not broken. Mason Kennedy's resilience had surprised them all. When he'd first joined the service, they'd expected it was a publicity exercise of some sort. Indeed, the former star's initial days had been directed and recorded – to be edited for Service propaganda, no doubt. But when the cameras left, Mason remained, an ordinary cadet with three years less training and no experience of anything but privilege and adoration. Nobody had made it easy for him. In the beginning he'd been mocked, derided, ostracised and assaulted. But he'd survived. Mason hadn't made it easy for himself either. He'd questioned orders, been otherwise insubordinate and challenged his fellow cadets for their failure to do likewise. It was as if he'd wanted to be beaten senseless time and time again. But he'd survived.

'Mace not back yet?' Briton Ibe came in from night exercises.

Elliot shook his head.

Silently, Ibe stripped down to climb into his own cot. Every cadet in the barracks was aware that Kennedy had not yet returned. Most thought he deserved whatever he got, that this had been too long coming. He was not the first cadet to rail against the Service, nor was he the only cadet to defy the occasional order. But there was something about Mason Kennedy that unsettled them, reminded them of what they'd been trained to forget.

Sergeant Goodwin would say nothing but that Kennedy was being corrected, that a policy of no tolerance was now in force for acts of insubordination and disloyalty.

And so they went about their business, training for the defence of the Commonwealth. Once their time was served, they would be given the option to either remain in the Service or return to civilian ranks. For Elliot there would be no hesitation. Staying quiet when the recruiters had come for him had been a good ruse. Elliot Maynard was a cadet in the Service, surely he was nothing but an example of loyal citizenship, the kind of young man the Commonwealth would need to repel the seaborne hordes.

Elliot's mother had spoken to him of a time when things were different – before he was born – when choosing to be a citizen was as valued as being born one, when the hordes were received with compassion, and there was a future other than the mines whose needs now dictated the work of every citizen. A time when the seasons were more predictable and people were trusted to communicate freely and without surveillance. It sounded like a fairy-tale. It probably was a fairy-tale. Or at least a hedonism that resulted in the Emergency from which the new order had saved them.

Elliot wondered what would have happened if they had simply confessed the flaw... if they had thrown themselves on the mercy of the ministry. Perhaps they would have been given a chance to redeem themselves, perhaps they would not have been condemned to live in fear of this secret.

'God I miss girls.' Ibe groaned. 'Do you remember girls, El?'

'Of course I do.'

'Fuck! I think I'm starting to forget. Chicks smelled different. They say your memory of scent lasts the longest... God, what if they're not as good as I remember them?'

'I'm sure your mother won't have changed that much.'

'Rack off.' Ibe tapped a rhythm onto his chest as he stretched out. A flash of white as he grinned. 'I expect we'll be very popular with the ladies once our service is finished; heroes and all that.'

Elliot laughed. 'Heroes? What are you planning to do?'

'You heard what the president said. Servicemen are the heroes of the New Commonwealth. Heroes get chicks.'

'Buck's an idiot,' Elliot said quietly.

Ibe pretended he hadn't heard. Simply hearing such things could bring you to the attention of National Security. The Service was teeming with spies, posing as officers, recruits, probably even the frigging bedposts. It wasn't worth the risk. 'What do you reckon they're doing to Mace?' he said instead.

'I just hope they don't kill the poor bastard,' Elliot murmured.

'Maynard!' Jordan Goodwin strode into the room flanked by two members of the Ethics Guard.

Ibe leapt upright to join Elliot at attention.

Goodwin ignored Ibe. 'You're to come with us, Maynard.'

'Why?'

'Are you questioning an order, cadet?' Goodwin roared. The Guardsmen stepped forward, their knuckles white on their batons. 'Where do you get off you lying maggot? Do you want to add disobeying orders to the trouble you're already in?'

'What trouble, sir?' Elliot persisted.

One of the Guardsmen lifted his baton. Ibe remained at attention. Eyes ahead, unseeing.

Goodwin held up his hand. One last warning. 'Move! Now, cadet.'

Elliot conceded. Grey men didn't argue. They didn't cause ripples. Whatever the problem was, it would be sorted out and he would slip out of the spotlight before anyone thought to look carefully.

Elliot Maynard was taken in for questioning and subjected to interrogation by the Service. In time he gathered that he had been accused of sedition of some sort; of speaking against the President. He denied it, declared his loyalty. They put words to him that he may have said in private moments. He denied them through the sickening cold realisation that he'd been betrayed by one of the cadets; someone he trusted enough to speak to unguardedly. He demanded the name of his accuser and they told him with smug glee.

'Kennedy. It took a while but every man has his breaking point.'

Horror! They'd broken Mason. How? What had they done? And then fury. What the hell had Mason done? Vehement denial. He didn't know why Kennedy said what he did, but it wasn't true. Kennedy obviously had some grudge.

The questioning became enhanced. Still Elliot maintained his story. He would not break.

Jordan Goodwin called a stop. They would bring in the other cadets; find one who was willing to betray Maynard, as Kennedy had done, and he would have the collaboration he needed. No one would doubt again that Jordan Goodwin had control of his unit.

Elliot was taken down to the cells to be held pending further investigation.

The Service prisons were dark and cold, fashioned out of pre-existing tunnels built in the previous century. Most of the network had been sealed off in the fortification of the city against terrorists, but the section immediately below the Service grounds was used for the storage of weapons, and the disciplining of particularly troublesome cadets. Mason Kennedy had been there often, but most cadets came below only once, if at all. Elliot Maynard had never been detained before.

The cells were rudimentary, cages built into the bedrock. The doors were manually locked as their subterranean location meant they could not be controlled remotely.

'Put him in with Kennedy,' Goodwin ordered, smiling. The sergeant wasn't sure whether Maynard had committed the sedition alleged or whether Kennedy had simply offered up his fellow cadet out of desperation. Either way, it was only right that Maynard should have a moment alone with the coward who'd turned him in.

Elliot was pushed into the cell. Mason Kennedy sat on the bench, his head in his hands. He didn't move.

The cell door was closed and locked.

Mason looked up. His face was bruised, there was blood on his collar and an exhausted darkness around his eyes. He stood. 'Hey, El.'

Elliot Maynard stepped forward and punched him. 'What have you done, you bastard?'

Mason staggered. 'What I had to,' he said inviting Elliot to hit him again. Elliot obliged.

An alarm went off, a screeching siren. Elliot stopped, confused. Had he triggered it? Were they being watched?

'The alarms go off every 10 minutes for some reason.' Mason winced clutching his ribs where Elliot had belted him last. 'But it'll get rid of the guards for a bit while they do their checks. We haven't got much time.'

'What?' Elliot faltered.

'We're getting out of here; you and me.'

'Are you out of your–'

'They're exiling me, El. They're just waiting for the bruises to fade for the media. Gotta look good for cameras.'

Elliot gasped. Exile was certain death. Mason would be cast adrift amongst the murderous hordes who assailed the Commonwealth's borders. He wouldn't have a chance. 'I'm sorry Mace, I am, but I can't–'

'They know, El; they know your citizenship is flawed. Not Goodwin, he's just a grunt; but the Ministry knows. You'll be exiled with me.'

Elliot stared, dumbstruck. Mason hadn't known that his grandmother had been illegal. He couldn't have told them. There had to be a mistake. 'How do you know?'

'I overheard. They didn't think I was conscious.'

'What?'

'If you pretend to faint they stop, but that doesn't matter now. The point is the Ministry knows. They intend to use it to explain my defection, to say you converted me, proving once again that non-citizens are a danger to everyone.'

'And you gave them just the information they needed, you mongrel traitor!' Elliot flared again.

'Not them, just that dumb prick, Goodwin.' Mason turned to scrabble under the bench. 'I knew he'd bring you down here for questioning. I begged him not to tell you it was me, because I knew, predictable mongrel that he is, he wouldn't be able to resist giving you a go at me.' He extracted a small length of wire wedged in a joint of the bench. 'These old locks can be picked,' he said as he carefully manoeuvred the wire into the keyhole. 'Generally nobody's here often enough to work that out, or long enough to learn how.'

'What the hell are you doing, Mace?'

'We've got to get out of here.'

'My family–'

'It's too late to protect them by lying low. Your only chance is to come with me.'

'Are you out of your mind? Where the Hell would we go?'

'We can't stay. At the very least they'll deport you to a detention centre. Me. I'm a dead man.' A click, and the door was open.

The sirens took on a different frequency. Mason cocked his head. 'We have about five minutes. I know a way out, El. Trust me. I would not have brought you into this if there had been any other way.' He looked Elliot Maynard in the eye and spoke bluntly to make him understand. 'They know. You haven't got rights anymore, and if you stay here, you haven't got a snowflake's chance in Hell.'

Elliot wanted to be sick. How could his world have collapsed so quickly? Had it always been tenuous? Perhaps. He'd never said anything about his grandmother. Ever. Mason Kennedy could only know if he was telling the truth.

'El, come on! Please, man!'

Elliot decided. He strode out of the cell.

Mason pulled the door shut and reinserted the wire, jiggling until it clicked again. 'With luck, they won't even know we're gone for a while.'

'Where are we–'

'I haven't been getting myself dragged to correction for a bloody change of scenery,' Mason started down the corridor. 'There's a way into the sealed tunnels.' He stopped and listened at a door before pushing it open and signalling Elliot to follow him into the storage bunker. The room was cavernous, freestanding iron shelves stood five metres high in row after row.

The sirens stopped.

Mason broke into a sprint. Elliot bolted with him. They'd been running for minutes when it occurred to Elliot that the space was a tunnel. And then it came to an abrupt end. A scaffolding of wire netting held back a wall of fallen rock.

'They sealed the tunnel by collapsing it here.' Mason pulled at a section of the wire scaffold. It came away and he began to move the rocks behind it. 'Help me.'

'How did you–'

'Do you remember Robbie Galway?' Mason continued shifting rocks.

Elliot nodded. 'Vaguely.'

'I met Galway the first time I was sent for correction. He was nearing the end of a long campaign of causing trouble and being sent down here. At first, he was a complete bastard; beat the hell out of me and waited to see if I'd tell the guards.'

'And did you?'

'No, of course not. The second time we ended up down here together he started teaching me things – how to take a punch, who you could push, who you couldn't. Eventually, he showed me this place, how to get out of the cell, when to do so. Robbie had been working on moving the rocks every time he was down here for two years; apparently there had been another cadet before him.' Mason shook his head. 'He disappeared before we got through and I've been moving them on my own since. I knew this time would be the last time. I would have gone a couple of days ago if I hadn't overheard what they planned for you.'

Finally, they were through the skin of rocks that hid the fact that a small passage through the cave-in had been cleared.

Voices.

They froze. Every nerve screaming as even their heartbeats seemed loud.

Shouting now.

Mason pulled out the last rocks and plunged into the darkness of the narrow way ahead. He gripped Elliot's shoulder as he did so; whether in solidarity or farewell he did not know. That choice was Elliot Maynard's.

Mason felt for the last boulder. Large with a jagged protrusion at waist height. He dropped to his knees in the pressing black of the tunnel and searched for the parcel he'd hidden there the last time: an antique battery-powered torch he'd stolen from the museum stores, a length of rope, and a canteen of water.

'El, are you here?' he whispered. 'Are you with me?'

'Just behind you. God, I hope you know what you're doing.'

'The wall of the tunnel is to your left – use it to guide you. I don't want to switch on the torch until we turn a corner.'

They could hear the confusion and alarm in the storage bunker behind them. Then the discovery of their escape route. Mason swore and flicked on the torch, risking discovery for speed. 'Run!'

Elliot paused to kick out a large oblong stone at the end of the passage through the rock fall. It caused a slide of rocks – not enough to reseal the tunnel but it would slow the pursuit. Choking on the resultant rise of dust, he ran after Mason. A corner and then another and the tunnel became large.

'Down here!' Mason jumped and disappeared. Elliot followed the light.

'It's an old train tunnel,' Mason said. 'If we run along the tracks we'll be more difficult to spot.'

Loudspeakers. Warnings broadcast to reverberate against the concrete. Demands that they stop, surrender immediately. Then a code declaration to announce that Elliot Maynard and Mason Kennedy could be shot at first sighting.

'This is frigging suicide,' Elliot murmured.

'We had no other choice.' Mason turned off the torch. 'Can you feel the track beneath your feet?'

'Yes.'

'Do you see those beads of light?'

'Yes,' Elliott replied surprised. He'd assumed that the tiny points of light were something to do with his eyes trying to adjust to the blackness.

'They're glow worms. They attach themselves to the walls. It'll give us a bit of a clue as to where the walls are, and we can use the railway tracks to guide us until we're deeper into the tunnels.'

'Mace, I can't even see *you*, and you want me to navigate by glow worm? For fuck's sake!'

Mason felt for Elliot's hand and pressed one end of the rope into it. 'Wrap that around your wrist and hold on. At least we won't lose each other. The torch will give us away.'

A gunshot and thunder as the sound boomed through the tunnel.

Elliot felt the yank of the rope as Mason began to run. He broke too, listening for Mason's footfall on the railway sleepers to guide him. Of course they stumbled and when one fell the other was brought down too, and occasionally they ran into the walls of the platform regardless of glow worms. Behind them sirens and gunshots, warnings over the loudspeaker that the tunnels were unstable, as the Service tried to panic them into surrender. In time the sounds of pursuit faded and the tunnels were silent but for their footsteps.

Mason hit the obstacle first and hard. Elliot running behind him had enough warning to slow and shield himself with his arm before he, too, ran into metal. He fell, making his way back to Mason by the rope.

'Mace, are you all right?'

A groaned curse.

Elliot pulled the torch from Mason's belt and, restricting the light by holding out his jacket, he turned it on. Mason blanched as the muted beam of light fell on pupils that had dilated in the blackness of the tunnel. A moment was all Elliot needed to see the other was bleeding and dazed. A flick of the beam around them. A train. They'd run into a stationary train. Elliot listened for pursuers. The tunnel was silent here, and they'd been running for hours… well it seemed like hours. They needed to stop; to gather their strength and thoughts.

Placing his shoulder beneath Mason's arm, Elliot pulled him to his feet and limped him beside the train. All the doors were open. They could hide without fear of being trapped. Elliot chose a cargo compartment with no windows and dragged Mason up into it. Once inside and away from the doors, he risked the torch again. He studied the gash on Mason's brow; it seemed to have stopped bleeding. 'Bet that hurts like a bastard?'

'Everything hurts like a bastard!' Mason turned away from the light.

Elliot switched off the torch. There was nothing he could do about it anyway. He gave Mason the canteen and told him to drink.

'Do you have any idea where we're going, Mace? Or did you plan to live in the tunnels like some sewer rat?'

Mason sat up, touched his forehead gingerly and then used his sleeve to wipe the blood that had run down his face. 'Trains didn't travel wholly underground, there'll be ways to the surface. We search for one that looks forgotten.'

'That's it? That's your plan?' Elliot demanded aghast. 'What the hell do you suppose we do when we get to the surface?'

'We bugger off,' Mason replied. 'We get out of the city. We find others.'

'What others?'

'We can't be the only ones, El. There have to be others.'

'Criminals? You want us to seek out criminals and traitors?'

Mason shrugged. 'When I was... before I was in the Service, I heard people talk of rebels in the west. People with flawed citizenship, radicals, and luddites who wanted to take the Commonwealth back to what it was before.'

'What was it before?'

'I don't know.'

'We're going in search of mythical people? For fuck's sake, Mace! They could arrest my mother and sister for what we've done.'

'They've already arrested them,' Mason said firmly. 'The only way to help them now is to get away first. I promise, El, I'll help you find them once we're out of here.'

Elliot rubbed his face. God, how could this be any worse? 'I wasn't born illegal you know. I was ten before they amended the Citizenship Act to make the descendants of illegals illegal too. I was a citizen till I was ten.'

Mason studied him for a moment. 'Look El, the way I figure it, citizenship of the Commonwealth isn't such a great thing.'

'If you feel that way, why the hell don't you let them exile you? If you don't like it here why don't you go?' Elliot was angry and there was only Mason Kennedy at whom to direct his fury.

'Because I don't want to go.' Mason remained calm, certain. 'I'd rather be around to see Buck go.' He spoke more to himself than Elliot.

'We can't be the only ones, El. We can't be the only ones that see this is messed up.'

'What about your folks?' Elliott asked wearily. 'Maybe they could help us–'

'They threw me to the wolves when I was just a kid,' Mason said quietly. 'They'll probably give interviews on how they lost their son to extremism; get their own damn show.'

'You're being a bit hard on them, Mace–'

Mason's voice became brittle, strained. 'I don't think so.'

Elliot left it. He knew Mason Kennedy's parents had not visited him for well over a year. They had become the faces of the Commonwealth's campaign exhorting other parents to monitor their children for subversive behaviour. They had played the part of shattered victims trying to find some good in the tragedy of their only son by warning others, and in doing so, had won their own public. The interviews had been screened at service parades. Only half the cadets had felt sorry enough for Mason not to use his parents against him.

'Are you okay, Mace?' Elliot asked when the silence lingered.

'Yes, I'm fine.'

'So where do we go from here?'

'There's a lake. Galway said there was an underground lake... that we'd find a way out near it.'

'That's it? A friggin fairy-tale lake?'

'It's what he said.'

'Had he seen this lake?'

'No. He never got through the rock fall. I don't know how he knew, he just did.' Mason decided that now would not be the time to mention the giant albino eel that Galway had claimed lived in the lake.

Elliot rested his forehead on his knees, his hands clamped behind his head. 'How do we find this lake?'

'We look for water. We'll need to anyway if we're going to survive.'

It was in fact two days before they came across any water. By that time the canteen was empty and desperation was taking root. They heard laughing in the tunnels and ran from it until it became apparent that there was no one. Just the echoes of their breathing, or perhaps the tunnels themselves finding mirth in their plight. Dehydration and confusion set in. In the stifling unrelenting darkness, panic stalked them.

Elliot was the first to hear dripping. Two days in the darkness had honed their abilities to follow sound to its source, and they soon found a small subterranean rivulet. It smelled clean and they could taste no contaminants, even if they had not been too parched to care.

Initially, they thought only of slaking their thirst, but once that was done, Elliot wondered where the water was going. 'Perhaps it runs into this lake of yours,' he suggested. 'The lake could be some kind of natural drainage pool.'

'Makes sense.' Mason clutched at the hope in Elliot's reasoning. He'd begun to despair, to doubt the existence of the lake and wonder if he had condemned them on the strength of a fable. They were exhausted and disoriented in both time and space.

Mason switched on the torch, picking up the direction of the trickle as it ran along the side of the tunnel. Even if it did not lead to the lake, it might take them to a stormwater drain through which they could gain access to the surface. And at least it was a direction, a course of some sort.

They followed the trail of water. At times it seemed to be nothing other than a remnant moisture, only to emerge further on as something more substantial. Their pace grew with their hopes. Other rivulets became apparent and joined with the one they followed. The water was draining towards something. The floor of the tunnel became muddy. There was no train track here and the walls were roughly hewn and unfinished.

'I can smell it,' Mason murmured. 'I can smell water.'

Elliot nodded. He had noticed it too. More than the odour of damp.

And then the tunnel opened into a vast subterranean chamber which appeared to be a place of intersection for at least a dozen tunnels. The darkness seemed a little diluted. The floor of the chamber was invisible beneath the water that flooded it. The lake.

Elliot whistled. He wanted to laugh. He wasn't sure if he'd ever really believed in Mason's lake, but there it was.

'It was a station.' Mason cast the torch around them. 'Galway said they'd nearly finished construction when they hit the water table and were forced to abandon it... There!' He let the beam rest on stairs that emerged from the water on the opposite side of the chamber. 'Looks like the lower platforms were flooded.'

'How deep's this water?' Elliot asked.

'We'll find out I guess,' Mason replied, wondering how he could keep the torch dry as they swam for the stairs. In the end he handed it to Elliot. 'I'll go first. Once I get across you can throw the torch to me before you cross.'

Elliot squinted at the stairs. 'What if you miss the catch?'

'Then you'll have to follow my voice across.'

Elliot blanched.

'You could go first, if you like,' Mason offered.

'No,' Elliot sighed. 'I think I probably have a better throwing arm.'

Mason didn't argue. Elliot was taller and probably stronger than he. And now that they'd finally found what might be their escape route, Mason did not wish to linger underground.

The water was cold and the shock of sinking into it took his breath.

Elliot directed the beam onto the water's surface as a guide to the stairs.

Mason began to swim, the splash and movement of water loud in the silence of the subterranean chamber. Again the strange laughing echoes. Mason kept his head above the surface, his eyes fixed on the stairs. His clothes and shoes were soaked and heavy, but there was no point finding their way out of the tunnels stark naked. With his mind fixed on getting across, he might not have noticed it if it hadn't brushed against his hand. He stopped, cursing as he looked around him.

'What's the matter?' Elliot shouted, shaking the torch which was starting to falter.

'I felt something.'

'What?'

'No idea. It was slimy and it moved.'

'There're probably all sorts of slimy things in there; just keep swimming. I don't know how much life this torch has left in it.'

More swearing. 'There's something in here, El.'

'Well swim out. You're halfway there.'

Mason stared into the dark waters.

'Mace! Move, you fuckin idiot!'

Mason began to swim again, but he was hyper-vigilant now. The second time it went by him, he saw it: pale, luminescent, and long. It slid its length down his body, hard enough that he was pushed back by the muscular sweep of serpentine momentum. He didn't waste time swearing now, but used every breath to make for the stairs. Twice more it brushed against him, tried to knock him off course. Each time he kicked and punched and kept swimming.

His right foot found a step. He used it to launch himself up the stairs out of the water. 'Fuck!' he gasped, coughing and spluttering as he dragged himself further up. He lay back to catch his breath.

'Mace, are you all right, mate?'

Mason nodded and then, realising Elliot could probably not see the gesture, said, 'I'm good'. He sat up. 'There's something in there, El – a snake maybe – it's a friggin monster!'

Elliot stared at the water. He'd seen a flash of something pale as Mason was swimming across. Still, what choice did he have? He shook the torch to try and strengthen the beam. 'I'm throwing this useless thing across now.'

Mason stood. 'On three.'

Elliot counted, and on three, he lobbed the torch to Mason. It fell short by about three metres and immediately they were in darkness. For a while they both cursed, venting frustration and fear with profanity.

Elliot stopped first, preparing himself to plunge into black waters which were home to God knows what, with no light of any sort to guide him. Mason fell silent too.

'Don't shut up now,' Elliott shouted. 'Your voice is my only hope of heading in the right direction.'

'You want me to keep swearing?'

'Swear, pray, recite. I don't care. I just need to hear where you are. That you're still here.'

'Are you worried I'll bugger off without you?' The affront was clear in Mason's voice.

'Just keep talking, Mace.'

Mason was suddenly unsure of what to say. He strained his eyes to pick up something, anything and he rambled distractedly of what Robbie Galway had told him when they'd shared a cell. 'Galway said the hordes aren't dangerous... just people trying to find a better life. God knows why they'd come here...surely they realise we won't let them land. Must be friggin desperate.'

He could hear the splash of Elliot stroking through the water, and tried to guess where he was.

The splashing stopped. 'Mace!'

'Sorry.' Mason realised he'd stopped talking. Because he could think of nothing else, he sang. It felt strange now...

The splashing resumed and became progressively less faint. Elliot couldn't be more than a few metres away now.

'Fuck!' Wild thrashing. A gasped cry for help.

Mason dived towards the sound. The water was churning. 'El... Elliot!' A tail flicked against his chest.

'Mace.' Elliot's voice was weak.

Mason reached towards it and when his fingers made contact with Elliot's jacket he grabbed it and held on. 'It's me!' he said as Elliot began to thrash again.

'It bit me.' Elliot got the words out through gritted teeth.

'Let's move before it comes back for another go.' Mason pulled Elliot in what he hoped was the correct direction. Five metres, ten, more, and there was nothing. Then just as despair began to take hold, Mason's foot found the step. He lurched forward reefing Elliot with him, and felt for a higher step with his hand. He found it and dragged them both out of the water, and from the heap in which they lay, Mason tried to orient himself.

It was black. He could feel the steps beneath him. Under his grip Elliot's shoulders heaved as he vomited water.

'Where did it bite you, El?'

'My arm.'

'Good.'

'What?' Elliot tried to shake off Mason's grip. 'How the hell can it be good?'

'You can still walk.'

'Shut up, Mace.'

'How bad is it?' Mason moved his hand down until he felt torn fabric and Elliot flinched and cursed. 'Right... here it is, then.'

Elliot pulled away from him.

'Sorry El – we haven't got anything to bind it with. You'll have to use your other hand.'

'What the hell was that thing?' Elliot clamped his right hand over the torn flesh on his upper left arm.

'I think it may have been an eel.' Mason squinted back at the water lest the creature leap from its depths to retrieve the two that had got away.

'Eels have teeth?'

'Appears so. It's a shame you didn't hang on to it; you can eat eels.' Mason broke the unspoken rule against mentioning food. It had been three days since either had eaten.

'Of course, why didn't I think of biting it back?' Elliot muttered.

'Come on, we should keep going while we can.'

'Where? We can't see a–'

'Up the stairs, and then we'll see – I mean assess. Come on El, we're too close to the water for my liking.'

Elliot staggered up. 'Galway said the way out was near the lake, right?'

Mason kept a hand on Elliot's jacket to ensure they did not lose each other, and they began slowly, fumbling and unsure in the darkness. When the stairs finished, they stopped with nothing at all to guide them. They could not be sure of what was about them or beneath their feet. Outstretched hands met empty space and suddenly they realised in full the impossibility of their current situation.

'How's your arm feel?' Mason asked. Somewhere in the recesses of his mind he recalled something about eels being poisonous. He tried to shake off the thought. They weren't even sure if the creature had been an eel. He had no idea what else it could have been, but even so, it mightn't have been an eel.

'Like something tried to bite it off. I'll live–' Elliot caught himself as he considered their predicament. 'At least I don't think I'll die of eel bite.'

Mason stiffened. 'Did you hear that?'

'What?'

'Voices. Listen.'

Silence – broken only by the sounds of lapping water bouncing against the concrete walls – and then, faintly, the muffled echo of what might have been a human voice. Mason groaned. They couldn't even see to hide.

'Look.' Elliot pointed.

A faint glow from one of the tunnels across the water disturbed the absolute darkness. The voices became louder; crisp barked orders. The light grew stronger and became defined as multiple powerful beams. In this illumination, Mason and Elliot could see the soldiers of the Service emerging from the tunnel to survey the underground lake.

Mason dropped, pulling Elliot with him as the torches were used as searchlights.

'They still have to get across the water,' he whispered.

A mechanical hum and then splashing.

Mason risked raising his head to see what was happening. Boats. Inflatable boats. Five already in the water.

'Elliot?'

'Here.'

'We're fucked.'

Elliot kept his eyes on the boats and the servicemen now rowing across. 'Not yet,' he said determinedly. They were not dead yet. He turned. Finding a way out before the boats completed crossing was their only chance. He moved forward tentatively testing that there was solid ground ahead.

And then there was another glow – above them.

Elliot stared in disbelief. They were trapped. 'Okay, now we're fucked.'

'I'm sorry, El,' Mason said quietly as they waited for the inevitable: the first footsteps on the stairs; an order to unholster weapons.

'You two. Up here, quick.' A figure emerged from the glowing manhole and beckoned.

Mason stared, incredulous. 'Galway? What the fuck?'

'Up here. Now! Run!' The figure disappeared up the iron ladder.

Mason pushed Elliot ahead of him.

Coated in blood, Elliot's right hand was slippery on the rungs, and his left was injured, but somehow, he dragged himself up the ladder and through the manhole. The iron cover was pushed back into place and bolted once Mason got through. Still they were not allowed to catch a breath. The pounding seemed to start immediately as the servicemen followed the blood trail to their escape route.

'Galway?' Mason said again.

'Later, Mace,' Robbie Galway secured a scarf around Elliott's arm to stem the bleeding. 'Follow me.'

He led them confidently along the corridor into which the manhole had opened, pulling them into a branch when the first shots were fired. They crawled through service tunnels, doubled back several times, came in and out of abandoned rooms and offices until finally, just as they'd become convinced that Galway was a wandering lunatic, he took them up a long ladder and through a trapdoor that opened to the surface.

They climbed out in silence. Although it was night, the surface seemed bright in comparison to the lightless underground; and weightless. It was as if the earth above had been bearing down on them in the tunnels. Galway snapped at them to stop breathing so loud, as they both gulped fresh air like men half-smothered. They were met just minutes after they emerged by a truck transporting fresh fish, and Mason and Elliot hastily buried in the cold cargo. And still, Galway explained nothing.

In time the truck delivered them to an old factory marked for demolition. They slid out of the truck's hold, wet and shivering and exhausted, not to mention pungent. Inside the factory there were others, but Galway sent them to wash immediately and change into the civilian clothes he provided. A young woman attended to Elliot's wound and the partially-healed gash on Mason's brow, but she, too, would tell them nothing.

Galway brought them food. It was fish – which he seemed to think was funny and which they were too famished to decline despite having lain with their meal in the truck.

'Galway, what the Hell?' Mason began as he ate.

'Welcome to DACI, gentlemen.'

'What the fuck is DACI?'

'The Democratic Alliance of Citizens and Illegals. We used to be DAC and then the Commonwealth decreed that half of us weren't citizens after all, so we had to extend the name. DACI sounds a bit lame, but what are you gonna do?' He laughed. 'We're rebels, traitors, terrorists – whatever.' He watched in silence for a while as they ate. 'We are collectively the last resistance against Buck's Legislative Dictatorship.'

'What exactly are you resisting, Robbie?'

'The Commonwealth's slow slide into Hell.' Galway laughed again and patted Mason on the back. 'So you used our escape tunnel, Mace. I'm proud of you. I was afraid with me gone–'

'What happened to you, Robbie? You just disappeared?'

Galway shrugged. 'An opportunity presented. I took it. I'm sorry Mace, I know that left you to dig on your own, but I couldn't take it anymore. But I kept an ear out for rumours of an escape, kept an eye on the tunnels in case you ran by yourself.'

'I wasn't by myself.'

'No.' Galway eyed Elliot suspiciously. 'You're Maynard. I remember you. You were always a good little serviceman.'

'El's all right, Robbie. I wouldn't have got out without him.'

'The Service has spies, Mace.'

'My citizenship's flawed,' Elliot stated. 'I was about to be sent offshore.'

'Oh, I see.' Galway folded his arms. 'Well, that just leaves the question of what to do with you both. They'll be looking for you. Hunting you. Especially Mace here.'

'I need to find my mother and sister,' Elliot murmured. 'They were arrested.'

Galway shook his head. 'You can't do that.'

'I have to.'

'It's friggin impossible to break into a detention centre, let alone get anyone out.'

'I'm going to try.'

'Look, you bloody moron, what you're talking about is suicide!'

Still, Elliot was resolute.

Exasperated, Galway reasoned, cajoled and in the end just swore at Elliot. 'Fine, rack off and get yourself killed, then. I was only really rescuing Mace anyway.'

Mason looked up from his plate. 'You're a mate, Robbie, but I'm going with Elliot.'

JASON NAHRUNG

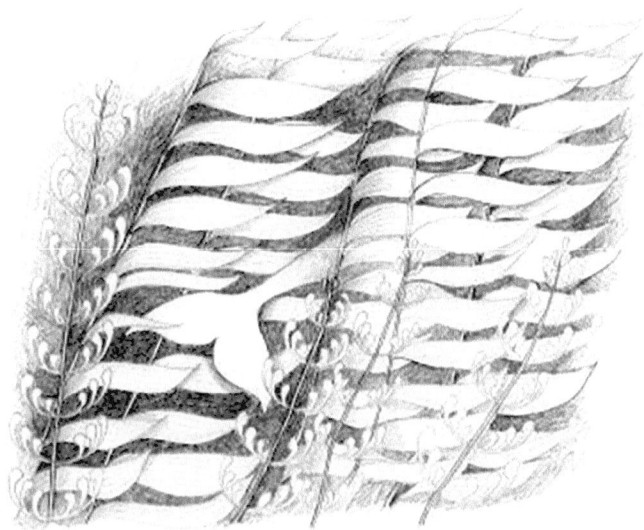

The Mermaid Club

The main bar of the Riverside Hotel stank of stale beer and moral ambivalence, the dark timber and chrome surfaces as opaque and non-slip as the clientele. Mid afternoon, the heat dragging in to be overpowered by the air conditioning that chilled the driver's seat sweat on her back and thighs. Out of the dimness, something innocuous droned from the speakers that hung like wasp nests from the corners. Clusters of men, mostly, in suits, looked up from beers and business, frowns and sneers forming.

Shane fought the urge to walk over to the most nakedly hostile knuckledragger and spit in his eye. *What, a black girl can't have a beer? You show him, sister.* Damn pisacha, preying on her emotions.

She wondered at the demon's desperation. Was life inside her that bad? Don't answer that.

To think, she used to drink half-priced jugs here on student Tuesdays, dance in the basement clubs at weekends.

The Riverside's facelift was one of Alex Peters' peacock projects, the renovation rammed through the planning process under buzzwords like 'upmarket' and 'progressive'. TAB, pokies, restaurant, exclusive clubs; the old watering hole had not aged well. But then, who was she to talk? Relationship on the rocks, career in limbo, a demon in her blood. At least the pub was air conditioned.

Maybe she should've invited Manasa along. She didn't expect to need backup for this meeting, but a cold drink and some company would've been welcome. And the two of them still had a lot to learn about each other. The sad fact was, following recent events, the enigmatic Indian woman was one of few allies Shane had left.

'Can I help you?' asked the sole barmaid. The straining buttons of her white blouse revealed the lace of her bra.

No, unfortunately.

The pisacha disagreed. Shane's nostrils filled with the demon's distinctive sandalwood scent as liquid heat pooled in her groin. Manasa had taught her a mantra to lull the demon back to dormancy. Shane thought of it as the 'cold shower mantra'. She mentally recited it as she dug her business card from the wallet in her bag.

'I'm to meet Alex Peters.'

The woman's gaze flicked from card to Shane. 'Special Branch? Is this about Atlantis?'

'Excuse me?'

'The boss and the Spare had a set-to a couple of days ago down there. Everyone's been talking about it.'

'The Spare?'

'James. Although I guess he's the heir now, hey.'

A door labelled PRIVATE opened to admit a rugby front-row forward squished into a suit. 'You Hall?'

'Present.' She didn't raise her hand. He scoped her, from toe to head: threat assessment, well practised, though he needn't have lingered on her chest. She hoped he wasn't going to insist on patting her down. That would get ugly. Maybe she did need backup.

The thug jerked his head at the doorway. 'This way.'

The barmaid flashed a smile, her eyes alight with curiosity, as Shane headed for the door.

'You were told to come to the delivery entrance,' the suit said as she stepped past into a corridor. The accent surprised her – private school elocution – even if the attitude didn't.

'I get told a lot of things.'

'Ever tried listening?'

'Listening and following are two different things. I don't like to follow when I don't know where I'm going.'

He snorted. 'What's with the gloves?'

She was wearing red leather, to go with her jacket. Last thing she needed was to prick a finger and give the pisacha an out. As tempting as it might be. 'Allergies.'

'Must get hot.'

'You get used to it.'

He looked at her, as though he knew she was lying. He seemed about to ask something – perhaps her reputation had preceded her? – but they'd arrived. A frosted glass pane on the door bore the title The Pelican Club, along with an image of said bird looking smug. Her escort knocked but didn't pause before opening it. 'Alex is waiting.'

She stepped in, the thick carpet soaking up the sound of her Redbacks as the thug shut the door behind them. The room was bigger than her whole flat; chill air carried a hint of cigar smoke and booze that made Shane's nostrils twitch. She got an impression of leather and dark timber, a gloomy room for shady dealings. She imagined the men in here, choking down cigars and brandy and contracts, filling their pelican beaks to overflowing and never satisfied.

Movement by a window drew her focus. She glimpsed a river view, the far bank lined with apartments, the light casting the man in soft shadow. A glass of what she assumed to be scotch glowed like honey.

Alex Peters, in his fifties, wore his slacks and shirt fitted to show off a solid, tight body, and he had the looks and the energy to get away with hair that short and artificially blond. A wedding ring glinted on his finger.

He strode to meet her. Strong handshake. His smile was perfunctory; she guessed it could be charming, lethal even, but the desperation in his eyes left no room for such humour.

'Alex Peters, of Peters Industries. You know who I am?'

'I Googled. Sorry to be late. Coro Drive was chockers.'

'You've met Verne?' He pointed with his drink to the thug, now pouring himself a glass at the bar. 'My head of security. He'll be sitting in with us.'

Verne gave no sign of acknowledgement. She concentrated on Peters, to hide her frustration at not being given the option of refusing a drink.

His eyes were dark-edged and red-lined, his jaw tight. She considered offering sympathies for the recent loss of his eldest son, but he struck her as the type of man who would probably not appreciate condolences from strangers, especially four months after the event.

'Ellen Brown tells me you're good at finding people,' Peters said.

'Sadly not in time for her daughter. How do you know her?'

'Ellen's firm does work for one of mine. I saw the news reports. Please, sit down. Can I get you a drink?'

Shane glanced at the thug who, oblivious to the gentle reprimand, now squatted on the edge of a sofa to crouch over a briefcase on a coffee table, like a cane toad beside a puddle.

'Just a water, please.' She examined his book shelf, eyed his desk; a single family portrait with him next to a curvy blonde, probably a few years younger, and two boys in their teens. The heir and the spare. Nice looking lads.

He handed her a glass from the fridge, iced, filled from a jug. 'I just need you to find the location. My people will take care of recovery.'

'As I told your secretary, Mr Peters, I'm on leave. The Brown case was a special instance.'

'Suspended without pay, I heard. I'm prepared to pay very well for your services, Detective Hall.'

'Just Ms. I'm not on duty now. And money isn't the issue, Mr Peters. Who's missing, exactly?'

His expression fractured, eyes radiating anger and loss, downturned lips showing teeth that had probably cost as much as Shane's car. More. The wagon was a bomb.

A whiff of sandalwood twitched her nostrils. The damn demon, stirring again as it sensed the emotional undertow, the proximity. The opportunity to escape – failing that, to tease – drawing it from its lair in her blood.

Peters sipped his drink. Nails: shiny, manicured where he gripped the glass. Swallowed loudly. The stop-start-honk of Coronation Drive penetrated the double glazing.

'Tell her, Alex,' Verne said. 'Or we find someone more reputable.'

Shane got the feeling he'd prefer the latter option. So did she, curiosity and pay cheques be damned. She moved to put down the glass, without even throwing its contents in Verne's face, and leave. She wasn't interested in corporate shenanigans – accountants' scams, workplace infidelities, corporate intrigue. Not enough to be insulted over.

Peters blurted, spraying spittle and masculine pride: 'I've been robbed.'

'Surely that's a job for the *reputable* police.' She eyed Verne: 'Or other avenues.'

'The bastards stole my mermaid.'

'Oh.'

The pisacha laughed. It knew she was a terrible swimmer.

The mytho had a dolphin-like tail where her legs should have been, and no scales, but rather smooth grey flesh. The tubular body extended to give way to barely-there boobs, rounded shoulders and long, thin arms. A close-up showed a webbed hand with curved nails. She had less neck than Verne, her face molten, with eyes like a manga character, all wet and glistening, and another close-up showed several rows of pin-like teeth behind thick lips and a flat, wide nose – a dolphin that had run into a wall, perhaps. She had no hair to speak of, just a light auburn fuzz across her bulbous pate.

Verne closed the picture gallery on the tablet and leaned back in the sofa. Shane sat in a chair opposite him. She'd signed a confidentiality contract before the show-and-tell. Peters sat on the arm of the sofa, legs parted.

'Seen one before, Ms Hall?' Peters asked.

'Not exactly.' Manasa's reptilian tail, glimpsed in the heat of a shoot-out, had been as seamless, but iridescent, scaled in bronze and browns. 'Not quite Disney, is it?'

'The Make Believe can be cruel,' Peters said, staring at the blank screen, and Shane thought she detected another flash of genuine emotion. Empathy, even.

'Be careful what you wish for, and all that,' she offered.

He frowned. 'Lorelei was quite a drawcard.'

Ah. That'd teach her to mistake a beating heart for a bottom line. 'Was Lorelei her stage name?'

'It's what she called herself.'

'Was she from Germany?'

'Not that I'm aware of. Why?'

'The name. More siren than mermaid, according to the legend.'

When a percentage of the world's population was inexplicably turning into mythical creatures, and your job was to police them, you had to cover your research bases. She supposed she shouldn't be surprised he hadn't looked into it: just another asset in his portfolio.

'She's not registered, I take it?'

'No,' Peters said.

Verne lifted the confidentiality agreement.'I should warn you–'

'No, you really shouldn't,' she said, earning a death stare. She shifted to give Verne more of her shoulder.

'Did Lorelei have a contract, Mr Peters?'

'We had an... understanding.'

'You referred to her abduction as a burglary. To her as property. Are you sure she didn't just get the shits and walk – swim, whatever?'

'It's a sensitive issue, detective.'

She didn't bother correcting him again; enjoy his respect while she could. 'I know not all paranormal entities like to register, and I don't blame them. But if I find – she, right? – wasn't here of her own free will, that the *understanding* wasn't mutual, well, this scrap of paper won't do you much good, I'm afraid.'

Peters smiled. 'I like your style, Ms Hall. But I assure you, the arrangement was mutually beneficial. Lorelei got room and board, and Atlantis got a live-in entertainer.'

Respect was such a fleeting thing. She pressed on: 'What kind of entertainment, exactly?'

'Had quite the voice.'

'We had to beat them off,' Verne said. 'With sticks.'

'Thank you for clarifying.' That provoked a clearing of the throat.

Verne hunted up a video. 'Maybe this will help.' He turned the tablet to face her, and Peters walked to her side so he could see the screen, too. Perhaps it was just as well she hadn't invited Manasa along: with her refined sense of smell and taste, she would have choked on Peters' aftershave. Maybe that would have been worth it; that, and having her and her soma handy, in case the pisacha got feisty. The mantra could do only so much when the demon had its dander up.

The video played: An aquarium extends out of a wall, perhaps chest-deep with water and shimmering in mood lighting, a diamond in the dark of the club. The hemisphere of glass reaches floor to ceiling, at its centre a beach-like podium of the type more at home in a zoo's penguin enclosure.

A tidal wash of synthesisers, a woman's whisper rendered tinny through the speakers. Enya? A door in the rear wall slides up, spilling a beam of light, and a shape flits through with strong vertical thrusts of its flat tail. The door closes behind her as she heaves herself from the water to take up position on the ledge, propped up on pillows.

The camera cuts to show a crowd at candlelit tables.

Silence descends, a hiss from the speakers, broken only by nervous coughs and clinking glassware.

Close-up: lips part, eyes close, face lifts toward the ceiling. A squeal rips from the speakers, like a cross between violins on amphetamines and wolves in agony. The mermaid's hands weave an invisible tapestry in the air. Sounded like she could have cut through not just the aquarium but the pub walls as well. The audience slumps in their seats. One chap falls to the floor, shaken by spasms. Another jumps to his feet, tearing at his shirt. A third runs at the aquarium, only to be intercepted by a security dude with a shock stick. The punter goes down, juddering like jelly.

'Her song produces a... a euphoria,' Peters explained as he reached down to stop the video. Musky cologne wafted around her. 'Dream-like. Fantasies made flesh, or so it seems. Different people react differently.'

'Looks messy.'

'And addictive.'

'Nothing like return custom, hey. I'm surprised you wanted to share.'

'I, and my staff, wear earplugs. The effect only works live.'

'I'll need a staff list, including those recently dismissed. And a list of your regulars, and any recent footage of your audiences. So I can see who hasn't been wearing protection.'

'Our clientele is quite private, Ms Hall.'

Verne raised a finger. 'If anything reaches the press–'

'A disgraced copper's word against the cream of society? I know why I'm here, Verne. The fact remains, Mr Peters, that someone in your organisation, or your sociably respectable clientele, is rotten. And they have *your* mermaid.'

'So you'll take the case?'

'I'll send you a contract.'

'Then I'll make sure you get everything you need. Now, shall I show you the scene of the crime?'

The three of them took a service elevator down to Atlantis. Peters sketched out the details en route. The abduction had occurred two nights ago, early hours, no clues, no demands. Shane asked about business rivals. He offered to send her a phone book.

The basement had been turned into some kind of faux cabaret, more Vegas than Berlin. It stank of flood water, the mustiness cloying.

Verne walked to a sound rig and hit switches, bringing up lights.

The aquarium, its glass shattered as though someone had chucked a boulder through it, was set against the far wall.

'She lived in that?' Shane asked.

'There's a larger facility at the back,' Peters said. 'It connects to the river so the water is always fresh.'

'You call the Brisbane River fresh?'

Neither man smiled.

'So what would they have needed, once she was out? A water tanker? One of those dog baths on a trailer?'

'Lorelei can go some time out of the water, but her tail is... non-optional.'

Verne pointed to the carpet. 'We found trolley tracks, but nothing useful; no boot or fingerprints, no footage.'

'Which is why I've invited you here, Ms Hall,' Peters said. 'I believe you have a certain talent.'

'More an uncertain one, actually.'

'Can you do it?' he asked. 'Use your power? From the aquarium, perhaps?'

'Something more personal, of recent or consistent contact, would be better.'

He led her to a side door, swiped a card and took her through to another door, this one activated by card and thumb print.

'Who else has access?' she asked.

'If our kidnapper could have, he wouldn't have needed to blow the glass,' Peters said.

Which didn't really answer her question, but she bowed to his logic – for now.

The grotto looked like a bizarre ship wreck. About half of the chamber was made up of a pool, glimmering with underwater lights. Peters turned up the ceiling lights, beams sparking through the humidity. Wavelets softly lapped at the walls, and at the sloping edge of a platform furnished with a waterbed, a duchess with the legs sawn off, a low table, a wardrobe.

No bathroom. Ew. Shane made a mental note to steer clear of the water.

A television, but no kitchen: Peters said everything came from the club's kitchen by dumb waiter, twenty-four hour service. A laptop sat on a pile of cushions on the bed like a strange treasure chest.

'She can't talk, but she can type,' Peters told her.

'Handy.'

'Hardly a joking matter.'

'Unintentional, sorry. Internet?'

'Verne has checked the records: nothing untoward.'

'I'd like to see them for myself. Can I take a look around?'

He waved her on.

She removed a glove and ran a hand over the bed, the keyboard. No tingle. The pisacha had withdrawn, sulking or simply too bored to fight the stultifying effect of Manasa's soma any longer. She'd have to bleed to force it into action.

'Clothes were missing.' Peters saw her query and added, 'Tops, bras, robes. Everything else we found dumped in the water.'

'Not so good. How long had she worked here?'

'We installed the aquarium about a month ago.'

'The longer the connection with the item, the better, but the water, being fresh, as it were, has probably diluted the impressions she'd have left behind.

We may have to do this the old-fashioned way, Mr Peters. I'll need those personnel lists. Plus any recent footage of the audiences.'

'All I need is an address and your discretion.'

'Mr Peters...'

'No questions asked.'

'The discretion you can have, as long as it's all as above board as you've indicated. The address might take a little longer.'

He hissed through his teeth. Her phone vibrated.

The coincidence was a tad unsettling.

'Clock's ticking, detective.' He radiated disappointment, frustration, as he turned for the door, saying, 'I'll leave you in Verne's capable hands.'

'James ever come here, Mr Peters? Without earplugs, perhaps?'

He turned slowly, studied her.

That was *more* than a tad unsettling.

'James has nothing to do with this, I can assure you.'

'So you didn't have a "set-to" with him here a few days ago?'

'A business disagreement. With Simon... gone, James has to step up and earn his keep. That's all there was to it. Verne will keep me apprised of your progress. Like I said, Ms Hall: all I need is an address and your discretion.'

The 'or else' he left unsaid, which wasn't unsettling at all, just disappointing.

She sat with Verne in the security box, looking over the club while he fiddled with the machinery to pull up security footage.

'You and Alex: Old Boys together?' she asked.

'How did you know; Google?'

'His tie on the coat rack upstairs, your tie pin.'

He gave a nod that she took as a compliment to her powers of observation. 'State reps in rugby. He went into the family business, I went into the army.'

'And here you are, team mates again.'

'I'm godfather for his boys, you know.'

'I did not know that.'

She checked her phone, to see who'd messaged her. Vikki. Cue stomach flip, cold flush. 'What are – were – the boys like?'

'Simon was driven, good business head. James, not so much, but at least he wasn't a fag—Forget about the boys, all right? It's a sore point. Mourning, and all that. Just concentrate on finding the package.'

'So what did James think about having an illegal paranormal working the stage?'

'What did I just tell you?'

He stared at her, like she was standing between him and a try line, then went back to clicking the mouse.

'You ever listen to the mermaid, Verne?'

'What? No. Drugs are for pussies, whatever shape they come in.'

'The drugs or the pussies?'

He stood, pointed her to the chair. 'Club's been closed since the break-in, so there's the last two nights of crowd footage still, plus the security from the night of. But it's clean. Whoever did it knew where the cameras were, the alarms, the works.'

'Inside job?'

'My people check out. It might've been one of your lot.'

'Which lot is that?'

'Mythoes. Paranormals.'

'Anything is possible. How does that door open, between the stage and the living area?'

'Lights, door, music: all from here, or the sound booth.' He pointed to a mixing deck, a dark island behind low barriers amid the tables.

She opened a file, hit play, bringing up the club, the lights, the shadowed audience, then paused it. 'I need to call my partner.'

'The naga?'

So she wasn't the only one who'd been doing their background research. That was to be expected. 'Her, too. I'll just step out.'

'Don't touch anything.'

She flexed a hand inside her glove. She didn't need to be told.

Vikki's text said she wanted to come around and get the last of her stuff. Better if Shane wasn't home.

Funny. When they'd been living together, in those days after Shane had been infected by the pisacha, Vikki had been aghast at the thought of Shane going out in public and risking spreading further contamination. That was how Vikki saw it, a blood-borne disease, but then, she was a nurse. Manasa referred to it as a possession, all the more reason for Vikki to push back: she blamed Manasa for Shane having been contaminated in the first place. That Shane needed to drink the naga's soma to keep the demon from taking her over completely did not sit well, that and the knowledge the demon probably knew everything there was to know about Shane, and everything Shane knew about Vikki. Threat of infection aside, how do you stay with someone who might, at any moment, not be who they say they are? Who might look at you with a stranger's eyes? A stranger that could, with a drop of its blood, take you over as well.

The Brown case had been the final straw. There had been a lot of blood.

Peters wasn't letting Shane take anything from the club, so paranoid was he about his business buddies copping some social stigma for jerking off to a mytho. Shane would be spending the afternoon and evening nosing around Atlantis with Verne keeping watch.

She texted Vikki to see if today suited. It did.

I'll leave the keys under the stork, Vikki replied.

You don't have to, Shane said.

Yes, I do.

Not even an x or an o goodbye.

Shane rang Manasa. The woman had saved her twice now: once with her soma when the pisacha had made its move, the other when Shane and she had tracked the vampire who had killed Ellen Brown's daughter. Where Shane's service pistol had failed, Manasa's naga abilities had prevailed.

The force hadn't looked kindly on that particular bit of freelancing, even if it had been at her boss Cunningham's request. Although the worst of the details had been kept out of the press, she and Manasa had both been in the shit, and the fan hadn't been wiped clean, yet. There was talk of Manasa being deported, which would put Shane's soma supply in serious doubt. What was India like, this time of year? Not cool, probably.

'It has been only two days,' Manasa said, her voice carrying a pronounced lisp. 'Surely you can't need more soma already.'

'Wondered if you wanted a night out. Got a case.'

'Are you back with Special Branch?'

'Off the books.'

'Can it wait a few days, detective?' Always, detective, despite Shane's request to be on name terms. She was drinking the woman's venom, after all.

'A girl is missing.'

'Another one? More of the recent dead?'

'Mermaid.'

A short silence. Nice to know she could shock the unflappable Manasa. 'I am occupied for two days, three maybe.'

'The SITI? Do you have a lead? Because I'll help you get it back. Whatever it is.'

'No, it's not that,' she said. 'It's a personal matter.'

Her time of the month, the demon said with an accompanying burst of thick sandalwood. It never missed a chance to give Manasa a serve – it hated her more than Vikki did.

'Shut up, you prick,' Shane said, and then had to do some fast apologising when Manasa asked what she had said. Inside voice, Shane. Inside voice.

'I have to go,' Manasa said. 'Do not use the power of the pisacha if you can help it. I won't be able to protect you until I am... Until I am done.'

Images of blood filled Shane's mind. She recited the mantra of control, focusing her mind and her emotions to bury the pisacha. It was going to be a long day.

By the time she and Verne called it for the night, she felt like diving into Lorelei's pond, just to see if she could wash the stench of corporate, blokey bullshit out of her skin. But then she remembered the lack of a loo in the mermaid's quarters. She settled for a bath at home, washer over her eyes, candles, Zoë Keating laying down some cello that was relaxing while dramatic enough to keep her from drowning.

The towel helped ease the pricking headache brought on by watching hours of footage and scanning reams of internet history; it also hid the view of all the empty spaces Vikki had left.

Shane imagined her with a trolley, maybe a sling to heft glassware and crockery, a bookshelf, the rocking chair from the balcony, into Vik's hatchback. There'd have been two of them, though, to get the trolley down the stairs, maybe another nurse or an ambo mate. Remove history: stat. The ambulance gurney folding up its legs as it was pushed in across the tailgate. No sirens, keeping it quiet.

Two of them...

Lorelei, on the other side of the door as the explosive charge – home made, Verne said – shattered the aquarium. Water gushing out through the broken glass, soaking the carpet. Security guard on duty: zapped and trussed, assailant unseen.

Lorelei, packing her bag rather than cowering from abductors at the bottom of the pond – so much for Shane's image of a ninja with a net, hauling Lorelei up like tuna.

Deleted history. Two of them.

Shane sat up and removed the towel. She could see it, now.

The next morning, driving south across the Story Bridge, expansion gaps hammering into her nascent headache, Shane looked to her left, downstream along the twist of Brisbane River, its brown waters masked in reflected blue sky, and wondered if she could see Alex Peters' home from here. Probably not; it was on the other side of the meander bend, hidden by New Farm.

She was, however, driving right past the Docklands towers in which Peters' sons had an apartment; which window was theirs? It was like crossing a drawbridge, unseen eyes watching from the parapets of the fortress. Fanciful.

Crossing to the southside always made her uncomfortable; she was a northsider, born and raised. Still, going into the dragon's den, it'd be nice to have someone riding shotgun: Cunningham, maybe, with his gruff pragmatism, or Manasa, with her take-no-bullshit attitude and naga powers.

Damn that Manasa was unavailable. She couldn't shake the suspicion that the vision she'd seen in the bath had been more than fancy, more than her subconscious doing its cop thing; had the pisacha surfaced, knowing full well its best chance of hopping bodies was for her to be out of the house? She'd have to be extra careful.

Today, she wore dress jeans and shirt under a suit jacket, and light cotton gloves Vikki had bought her; 'I guess full hazmat is out of the question,' she'd said, the rust-red material wrapped in a bow, the humour falling flat, the gesture ultimately inadequate.

Peters' mansion was on the riverside in Bulimba, a sprawling, two-storey whitewashed villa with a gabled roof of ochre tiles, and, she knew from Google Earth, a pool and private dock at the rear. Its land boundaries were marked by brick walls topped by iron spikes. Shane buzzed at the pedestrian gate, struck by the illogic of gloves on a hot day, sweat on her brow emphasising the point.

She noted a BMW in the driveway. No rego check needed to know the No.2 son was at home – the licence plate read JAMEZ.

'What do you want?' the electronic voice of Mrs Roslyn Peters asked, after Shane had introduced herself.

'To talk with James. Just a quick chat.' She'd thought it strange, that James' residential address was still listed as the family home, when he and his brother had the apartment. Maybe it was purely for entertaining. They called it the 'party pit' on social media, after all. Classy.

'Can't it wait?' Mrs Peters said. 'We're on our way out.'

'I'm working for your husband. It's about the siren at Atlantis.'

Silence. And then: 'Very well. But we don't have long.'

The gate opened.

Shane followed the path, across a patch of manicured lawn edged in flower beds, featuring a jacaranda, a bench never meant to be sat on, a statue of a topless woman with a jug at her shoulder. CCTV cameras. Alarm stickers on the windows.

The front door might have been taken from a monastery, iron-bound with a tiny opaque window, another camera poised like a spider under the eave.

Mrs Peters made her ring the bell and wait.

The lady of the house was in white t-shirt and skirt, tight muscles and jaw suggesting she was as highly strung as the tennis racquet in the case she held. She looked at least ten years younger than Shane knew her to be: a healthy lifestyle with a touch of plastic, Botox maybe.

'What's this all about? I have very little to do with Alexander's business dealings.'

'I'm most interested in talking to James about an incident with his father at the Atlantis Club earlier this week.'

'James has nothing to do with that club.'

'I'd still like to talk to him.'

'Are you some kind of detective? Does Alexander know you're here?'

'Mrs Peters, a woman's life could be at stake.'

Mrs Peters' hand went to her throat, as though about to choke. Her exquisitely thin brows furrowed. 'A woman?'

A voice interrupted from the end of the hall.

'Is this father's police woman?'

Shane recognised him from her Googling, that and the portraits in the hall. James, youngest and only surviving son. Nineteen. Studying commerce law at the city's sandstone uni, his parents' alma mater. Pretty, with his mother's elegance and lashes. And his father's manners, apparently.

'What's she doing here, Mother?'

'Nothing for you to concern yourself with. She's just going.'

'I was sorry to hear about your brother, James.'

'What did you hear about Simon?' the lad asked as he sauntered closer, hands in the pockets of his chinos.

'The heart attack. So young.'

'Congenital,' Mrs Peters said. 'On his father's side. We had no idea.'

'How's your heart, James?' Shane asked.

'There's nothing wrong with him.' Mrs Peters gripped her son's elbow, squeezed as though to prove to herself that he was there. 'Fit as a bull, aren't you, honey.'

'You ever go to your dad's club, Jimmy?'

'Not really my scene,' he said.

'Don't share your dad's interests? It'll all be yours now, won't it?'

'You really need to go – what was your name again?' Mrs Peters said with a flick of her racquet, then continued before Shane could answer. 'You've held us up for quite long enough.'

'Are you playing, too, Jim?'

'It's James. And no – I'm just dropping Mother off on my way home. I have an apartment at Docklands.' He smirked, and she could imagine him running the real estate figures for her so she could be impressed and just a little inadequate.

She was neither. She also had a home paid for by her parents, albeit they'd had to die to come up with the money. A poor trade.

'You shared it with Simon, didn't you? You must miss him.'

'Of course I miss him! What would you know about it, you black–'

'I've had enough of this nonsense.' Mother to the rescue. Just in time to save her investment in her son's dental work. The nails glinted where she gripped the door. 'Leave now, or I will call the *real* police.'

Shane dropped her card on a nearby table, more defiant than hopeful. 'In case you change your mind, James. Harbouring an unregistered mytho could be dangerous to your family's interests.'

'A what?' Mrs Peters went a shade of pale under her yellow tan. Prejudice? Or just envisaging the loss of assets, at least some measure of social standing under the cloud of scandal?

James picked up the card and fumbled it as he read out loud: 'Special Branch?'

'Not at this point in time. I probably should cross that out, or maybe put brackets around it. But the mobile number's right. Give me a ring if you think of anything you'd like to tell me about the mermaid.'

Mrs Peters' shriek of 'get out' followed Shane as she let herself out. The door slammed.

On the landing, taking her time to get her heart rate under control – the pisacha revelled, *blood blood blood.* As she fished sunglasses from her pocket, Shane realised of all the pictures on the wall, none were of Simon. Not by himself. Grief, like the Make Believe, could be a cruel thing. Didn't excuse your son being a racist arsehole, though.

Shane's phone rang before she'd got out of the Peters' street. Alex Peters. She pulled over.

'You went to my house? You went to my house!'

He had answered his own question, which had been rhetorical anyway. She didn't feel compelled to say anything.

'You went to my house without telling me!'

She could imagine white froth on his lips, splattering the handset.

'Should I have?'

'My family has nothing to do with this.'

'Do you know where James was two nights ago, Mr Peters? After your little business discussion?'

Suddenly: a chill.

'Verne cleared him, OK? What's not OK is you going behind my back.'

'You're paying me to be thorough. I'm being thorough.'

'No, you're being fired.'

'What?'

'Bill me for your work to date, and then forget about it. You are contractually obliged to forget about it. Remember that. And Hall, if you want to work in this town again – leave my son the hell alone.'

When she got home, she wrote up her expenses and took another bath. The pisacha was silent. It had told her all she needed to know. Now it was up to the Peters to work it out. Case closed.

That night, Shane was settling down to a rewatch of season three of *The Wire* – thank goodness Vikki had left the DVD player, but she was *really* missing the kettle – when James rang. He could barely talk, his words interrupted by sobs and expletives. She pictured him, pacing, hands tearing at his hair and cheeks. He must've been in a desperate state to contact her.

'He's taken him.'

'Who's taken who?'

'Father. I had Lorelei, all right? But he's taken him.'

'Where are you?'

'At the pit.'

'You had her at your apartment?'

Verne was right: the No.2 son wasn't that bright. She hushed him and promised to be there as soon as she could.

She rang Manasa on the way to the car. She'd have to end her sabbatical early. The squirming sensation in Shane's gut told her she'd need backup. Case: not so closed.

Manasa met her at the door of the serviced apartment in a boutique hotel on the Valley fringe. She was in loose slacks, more like pyjamas or harem pants, and a flowing top with a deep cowl and, despite the low wattage of the corridor lights, oversized sunglasses.

'I thought you liked the sun,' Shane said, and instantly regretted her flippancy.

Manasa's cheeks looked pink, hot-shower fresh, as she gave a slow sideways bobble of the head.

'Jeez, Manasa, are you okay?'

'This had better be important, detective.'

'Are you running a fever? Did you get sunburnt or something?'

Manasa sighed, told Shane to come in to the bedroom.

'We're on the clock.'

'Are you wanting to know or not?'

'Sure.' She'd never seen Manasa so short-tempered.

Coarse blankets covered the bed. The room was warm, windows closed, a jug of water on the table. Amid the ruffled blankets was a dry, plastic-looking thing tapering toward a truncated point. It bore a rough diamond pattern in faded yellows and browns, was tattered like a torn plastic bag on a fence.

Shane remembered Manasa, all tail and fangs, wrapped around Debbie Brown's killer, squeezing the vampire until his head popped. 'Jesus, is that your *skin*?'

'I haven't finished shedding yet. I had to force that off early.' She pointed to her legs.

'I didn't know.'

'But now that you do, you still want me to come with you.'

'Since you've gone to the trouble of changing.' Shane flashed her most endearing grin.

'One request.' Manasa looked at Shane over the top rim of her sunglasses, her pupils vertical slits. A flap of dry skin hung low over one eye. 'No more puns.'

Parking in Docklands was always a pain in the arse. They finally found a space an aggravating distance from James' tower. Manasa walked slowly, scratching often at her knees and rubbing one ankle against her calf in a disjointed dance. A pub pulsed with music, the Story Bridge bathed them in light and traffic hum and thump; lights wavered on the slick surface of the river. The air was still and clammy; sweat sticking Shane's shirt and itching under her bra.

'Do you, like, peel everywhere?' she asked Manasa.

'I'm not an orange, detective. And yes, everywhere.'

'Worse than waxing?'

'Nothing's that bad.'

Manasa smiled, fangs glinting, and Shane hoped she'd remember to put them away before they met James. That'd be the last thing the kid needed.

They entered the foyer – concrete, tiles, shining metal and glass, clean as a laboratory – and waited for a doorman to phone up, then escort them to the elevator and hit the button for them.

'Have a good night, ladies,' he said with a voice that suggested he didn't approve but was used to this, though there was a speculative lift to his eyebrows and the set of his lips: Shane guessed they were wearing longer pants and shorter heels than the usual guests for the party pit. Were probably a shade or three darker, too. She felt like walking out, but reminded herself that this time the abduction was real.

They didn't get to knock. James had either heard the elevator bell or perhaps had been watching through his security camera. The kidnappers had given him a hell of a shiner.

'I didn't know who else to call,' he said once they were inside, an ice pack retrieved from the breakfast bar held against the bruised side of his face.

Shane introduced Manasa. Neither offered a handshake. She sniffed. 'That aftershave?'

'Father's. He came here with two men. They wore balaclavas, but I'm sure one was Verne. The arsehole.'

'Let me guess,' Shane said. 'He helped you take Lorelei in the first place?'

'In return for listening rights.'

So who's the pussy now, Verne?

James held the ice away from his face, the better to emote. 'Verne helped me get him here, but then I didn't know what to do with him.'

'There was no heart attack, was there? It was mythomorphosis.'

He sagged into the ice. 'Simon had always had a thing for mermaids. And women's clothing. Used to drive Mother crazy, when we were young, putting runs in her stockings.'

'Saying he transformed into a mermaid because he liked cross dressing is like saying it happened because he liked to sing karaoke.'

'But that's how it works, isn't it? The Make Believe? Picks up some flaw in the DNA and evolves it?'

Manasa dropped a trophy she had been inspecting with a careless thunk, and pushed her glasses down her nose, the better to stare at James. 'A *flaw*?'

James was riding close to a second hiding for the night. He had that effect on people, Shane supposed.

Manasa tapped a finger against a collage of snapshots taped to the wall. 'Here, your brother wears a bikini-thing. Here, he has his tongue down a young woman's throat. Here, a young man's. But in none of them do I see a *flaw*.'

'Well, I didn't see *those* on Facebook,' Shane said.

'Sure, he was AC/DC, but he always played it straight around Father.' James found a grin, eyes focused on the past. 'If he wanted to annoy Father, all he had to do was break out the lippie. But Simon was the eldest, the shining one, the heir. He and Father were on a business trip up north. Next thing, they're saying Simon is dead, and then Father's forbidding me to go to Atlantis and he's leaning on me to become Mr Perfect CEO.' He threw the ice bag in the sink, and swore.

'Your father said Simon – Lorelei – was a mermaid?'

He waved in the air, juggling the options: 'Marketing. Camouflage. Denial. No, he was still a boy, all right. Earning his keep, Father said.'

'Is that what you fought over?'

'At the club? No, he wanted me to go to some American university. I said pig's arse, there's nothing wrong with ours. I think he wanted to keep me away from Simon. I didn't even know Simon was there – I hated the club and all of Father's sycophantic mates. But Father rang me, insisting I go overseas, and I just lost it. I confronted him at the club. That's when I saw the mermaid. As soon as I heard him sing, I just knew it was Simon. I couldn't believe it.'

'So you and your godfather conspired to free Lorelei – Simon – that very night. Because you thought your brother was unhappy, or because you wanted to annoy your father?'

'Two birds, one stone.'

Manasa had stopped her prowling to take in the view of the city, one boot rubbing at the back of her ankle. Twin tips of tongue appeared as she turned to James, saying, 'Despite your disparaging of his sexual explorations, you cared for your brother a great deal. I can taste that.'

'Sure, it was us against the world, both of us in Father's shadow.'

'You didn't mind being second in line? In your *brother's* shadow?'

'I was the lucky one. Before all this happened, I could pretty much do as I pleased, as long as no one got embarrassed by it.'

'And when Simon changed?'

'I did not want to be that.'

'No? What did you want to be?'

'I'm happy the way I am.'

Manasa licked the air, and he flinched.

'Either way, you are still in your brother's shadow.' She turned back to the cityscape. 'So where might they have taken Simon?'

'They could be on their way to Cairns by now. That's where it happened; presumably they kept Simon there while they built the tank here. But we have a lot of construction sites, holiday homes. They could be anywhere.'

'Simon would need water,' Shane said. 'What did you do about that?'

James jerked a thumb toward a doorway. 'Spa. This was just short term, till I could work out what to do.'

'Catch and release?'

'He was my brother! I couldn't just let him... disappear out there.'

Manasa walked over. 'You never thought to ask him what he wanted?' She pulled a curvy dagger from her boot and held it out to Shane. James blanched.

'Use the bloodrunner,' Manasa said.

Shane balanced the knife against her palm. The pisacha stirred, the scent of sandalwood rising; Shane imagined the demon as a shark, nosing after blood scent. 'Do you have anything of Simon's?'

'They took everything.'

Manasa's tongue flickered from between her lips; Shane thought maybe she was doing it on purpose now, just to see the kid shiver. Manasa slapped a hand on James' shoulder. 'They have tried to cover their tracks. But they left the biggest link behind.'

The pisacha howled. A bead of blood welled around the knife point. Shane jerked it away. 'I can't touch him. The pisacha will jump ship.'

Manasa shook her head, clearly disappointed in her student. 'The knife.' Then to James: 'Your hand.'

'No fucking way,' he said, backing up.

'Do you love him or not?'

He hesitantly held out a hand. She grabbed it, sliced it, then held it over a glass until she had a good dram.

'Wrap the cut in a cloth. And you, detective–'

'I am not drinking that!'

'Just cut your finger and then put the finger into it.'

The pisacha emerged from its soma cocoon, impressions building slowly as Shane tried to drive the link to Simon.

James' life swirled around her. The little shit had snorted coke and knocked back a generous belt of rum before they'd arrived. That wasn't helping.

'Your mother, at home; pills and a drink.'

'Migraines, she says,' James said. 'Doc gave her stuff for it, conks her out.'

'Father, at home, too. In the pool? There's decking. And, and Simon's there, I think, but – but he's in trouble. He's hurting. I can hear waves.'

'*High Roller*,' James said. 'I'll bet it's *High Roller*. Our boat. It's moored out the back. It has a spa on the aft deck.'

Shane felt a resistance, almost a static. Because the pisacha was being ornery, or the vagueness of the link? Or something else, drifting through the sandalwood, a chemical tang...

Manasa threw a tea towel at Shane. 'That's all we need, detective. Let's go. Because if they get the merman out to sea, we may never find him.'

Shane gave her finger a cursory wipe. She began to dig in her bag for a sticking plaster – she always carried them, these days – but Manasa yelled at her from the door.

'Do it in the car. We have no time to lose.'

'Fine. I'll ring the Sarge on the way, let him know there's an unregistered paranormal in town. That should get us some backup.'

'Wait,' James said, and dug a plastic box from the kitchen drawer. 'We'll need these.'

'We?' Shane said.

'Earplugs. And you bet I'm coming, too. He's my brother.'

They took James' car; quicker than trudging back to Shane's. But Shane drove, a look from Manasa enough to relegate James to the back seat.

'Nice car,' Manasa said as they hit the road. 'It has air conditioning.'

She was still wearing her sunglasses, so it was hard to tell if she was taking the piss. Shane accelerated, grateful for the relatively light traffic.

James murmured from the rear, 'I asked Mother if she knew. She said Simon was gone, to forget about him; I was her only son now. Just like that.'

The only other time he spoke was to tell Shane a shortcut. Manasa handed Shane the plaster in silence, held the phone on speaker while she talked to her former boss, Cunningham, who swore colourfully and told her to forget about her career.

Would he send someone to the Peters residence?

'Guess I'll forget about my career, too,' he said, and told her to keep her head down.

James hit the remote to open the gates at the family hacienda. Shane speared the car down the drive and skidded to a halt at the foot of a T-shaped dock. A black-glassed Mercedes blocked their way. A thug in a suit levered himself away from the car bonnet.

'We're in time,' Shane said. 'The boat's still here.' She flung the door open, but James told her to wait. He handed out earplugs. Shane thrust hers in a pocket. She needed her wits. Manasa pushed them away. 'I am not as easy to charm as you might think.'

The three of them ran toward the boat at the end of the dock. The thug moved to intercept, but Manasa opened her mouth wide and sprayed him. The jet of venom hit him in the face. He fell, clawing at his eyes.

Shane's boots rang on the timber dock, the sound drowned out as the boat's motors growled into life. Verne was in the wheelhouse, perched atop the ice cream cake layers of the boat like a lone groom figure. Alex Peters stood from a crouch at the spa on the rear deck, where a figure was just visible, its hand chained to the low, silver rail. A hose snaked from an outlet on the dock to the spa; a pump burbled.

Mrs Peters stood on the dock in a short, sleeveless dress that showed off her tennis limbs. She clutched a glass. Priceless. Shane imagined her curled up on the couch with a g&t, watching the latest season of *Real Housewives of Melbourne* while she waited for the meds to kick in, only to be disturbed by her husband's arrival.

'James?' Mrs Peters said, blinking in the headlight glare. 'Who's that with you?'

Shane shouted, 'Give it up, Alex. The police are on their way.'

Peters waved at Verne, a clear 'get us the fuck out of here' kind of motion, as he struggled to lift a noose of mooring rope from a bollard.

Shane approached the T-section as the rope came free. Peters clambered aboard and swung the stairs clear. The boat nosed away, wafting diesel and a throaty rumble, water churning at its rear. The rope slithered into the widening gap between boat and dock. The hose writhed across the deck, leaving the timber slick before it fell gushing over the side.

Mrs Peters shouted at her husband. Something about leaving her behind after all she'd done for him. The glass sailed after the boat. Shattered on the side.

Shane leapt. Hoped for better luck than the glass.

She snagged the gunwale, the impact driving the breath from her chest. Another figure flashed past, hit the deck, rolled. Manasa!

Peters swore.

Shane scrambled over the side and thudded inelegantly onto the deck. Realised, as she came up into a crouch, that she was unarmed.

Peters bore down on her. He had a short pry bar. Just the thing for opening a locked door if your son wasn't home. Or beaning an annoying cop.

Manasa intercepted him. She ducked under his swing. They grappled, slipping on the wet deck, and tumbled in a heap of thrashing limbs.

The bar rattled on the timber. Peters smacked at her face. Manasa got her knees up, kicked him away.

They both came up in fighting stances. Shane told Peters to give it up.

A gunshot rang out. Shane ducked reflexively.

Manasa turned toward the wheelhouse. Peters hit her with a stiff arm to the back of the head. She went down.

Shane called out her name.

Verne throttled back, the pistol wavering as he tried to cover all three of them and keep an eye ahead.

Peters retrieved the pry bar and told Verne to put the gun down.

Verne shouted at them all to stop moving; to get off the boat. *Which is it, Verne?*

Manasa rose to all fours, shaking her head slowly.

Peters started toward the ladder to the wheelhouse.

Verne shot him.

Peters clutched at the red welling from his side.

The pisacha urged Shane on. To make a connection. She stepped toward him.

Manasa groggily held out a hand, as though to ward her off.

Peters swung the bar, a clumsy, injured swing, close enough to make Shane dodge backward.

Verne fired again, a warning shot.

'Don't make this worse than it is,' he shouted.

Manasa sprang at Peters. The tackle took him low, pushed him back. The gunwale caught him across the back of the legs.

'No,' Shane shouted as they both careered over the side.

Verne had one hand on the wheel, the other pointing the pistol at her, but the river was curving and dotted with moored boats. A CityCat ferry was bearing toward them, a smaller launch trailing well back in its wake.

Shane darted and weaved. Verne fired, the round chewing up planking.

Then she was out of his sight at the bottom of the steps to the wheelhouse. Only a dozen steep stairs, but he'd have her dead to rights as soon as her head appeared over the edge.

She grabbed a life ring from the wall. Hardly adequate, but it was all she had.

The CityCat tooted. *High Roller* turned hard.

Shane took the stairs, life ring an awkward shape in one hand as she hauled herself up the handrail with the other.

At the top of the stairs she found Verne pointing the pistol at her centre of mass. She gripped the ring, painfully aware of the hole over her midriff.

'They didn't deserve him,' Verne shouted. 'And you can't stop me. So take that life ring and jump. Swim for it, bitch.'

'Verne, listen...'

Shane noticed the dangling plastic string that connected pink plastic plugs in both his ears. *Great.* Even if she could get him to listen to reason, he couldn't bloody hear her anyway.

'I don't want to shoot you, but I will,' he shouted.

The siren sang.

The squeal was like rusted metal shearing apart.

Shane staggered, almost fell down the stairs. She clutched the life ring as images exploded in her mind. Of her mother and father – alive. Of Vikki, reaching out to her...

The pisacha revolted. *Mine!*

A scarlet wash of rage flooded over the feelings, the memories, the dreams. They tore like tissue. Faded fast as a waking dream.

Electricity sizzled in her blood; panic gripped her as she remembered the pisacha's previous victims, their desiccated bodies sucked dry before it moved on.

Verne was staring at her, sweat on his lip, eyes fixated, something between disgust and desire twisting his lips. He'd lowered the pistol.

'See,' he blared. 'He wants this. He wants to be with me.'

Shane tossed the ring at his ankles. It hit hard enough to make him jig. She lunged. He dodged. She snared the wire, yanked the plugs loose as she fell.

The siren song hit a new pitch.

Tears misted her eyes. It felt as though her eardrums would burst. She grimaced as she raised Verne's earplugs; she'd need to disinfect if she survived this. Her hands felt as if they were moving under water, her body raging with a kind of fever, the two ghosts in her system fighting for control, ripping holes in her mind.

Silence fell.

The flashing imagery settled. She dropped the earplugs.

Now the pisacha urged her to give Verne his comeuppance, to bleed into him, to be free of her demon.

Imagine, the pisacha suggested: her siren dream in the flesh. Knocking on Vikki's door, ta-dah, all clear, good to go!

She forced the demon to submerge.

Verne was on his back, a stain on his pants, blood dribbling from his ears, a goofy smile lighting up his face.

Shane tucked his pistol into her belt – a flash impression of Verne in the arms of some blonde Brünhilde, all tits and tail – then grabbed the two throttle sticks Verne had been using to bring the boat back to an idle before turning the ponderous vessel back upstream.

Verne moaned at her feet. She searched him, found plastic cuffs and used the restraints to lash him to the stair rail.

The siren was watching from the half-filled spa. Shane raised a hand and Simon returned the wave.

Shane looked for the Peters' dock. This would be interesting, given this was the biggest tinnie she'd ever driven. It had been a very long time since her last family fishing trip.

Manasa was hauling herself onto the dock. Mrs Peters was crouched beside a pale, saturated Peters. The thug sat in a soaked huddle nearby, hands to eyes, James still holding the hose from the boat.

Shane had no chance of manoeuvring the boat back into its position at the end of the T, so she pulled *High Roller* in on the upstream side and cut the motors. It coasted alongside the dock and ground into the muddy bank before the prow could smack the sea wall. The boat pivoted on the current until the stern thumped against the dock. Good enough.

James scrambled on board.

'How's your dad?' Shane asked as they met on the rear deck.

'Your mytho friend says he'll survive. Is Simon okay?'

'Could've done without the chlorine in the spa, but otherwise, in fine voice.' Shane threw James the handcuff keys she'd found in Verne's pocket. 'Go check him out. We were lucky they had to change the water for him. If it weren't for that delay, and your mum kicking up a fuss, they might've got away with it.'

She gingerly climbed down onto the dock, Manasa offering a steadying hand.

'You all right?' Shane asked.

'My clothes are probably ruined.' A tear in Manasa's top revealed the flat of her stomach, the skin splotched like old sunburn. 'And you owe me a pair of glasses.'

Alex Peters looked subdued, in pain, clutching a wad of red-stained cloth to his side, but he managed a stare of loathing as he watched them. Shane tallied the charges he was facing, and wondered how many the lawyers would get him out of. Would it even get to court, if James and Simon refused to testify against their father?

A splash. James kneeled at the boat's side, calling to Simon. Simon's head and shoulders appeared in the water. He took three strokes, then folded his arms and torpedoed in the angle of boat and dock like a seal shot from a cannon. James ran alongside, tracking his brother. Simon pulled up, gave a short burst of song.

The sound made Shane's heart ache, for her parents and that last fishing trip when they were all together, the smell of mangrove and suntan lotion and insect repellent, the motor mower burble of the outboard, the flopping of whiting in the bucket.

James jumped down onto the dock and crouched at the side. Simon reached up with those spindly arms, pulling James low, and pressed his mouth to his brother's. As the merman slid back into the water, James fell back onto the boards. His mouth opened in a shout, but only a staccato wail came out, a dolphin's raucous call. He writhed, skin bubbling as though crabs swarmed under the flesh. His shoes stretched and tore, his trousers, his shirt. Half-clad, he squirmed into the water, bobbed up, then sank.

Mrs Peters screamed, 'James!'

Alex Peters cried out, a bullish roar of denial.

After a long moment, two heads broke the water far from shore, then dived under, flashes of tails the only goodbye.

Sirens filled the air. Ambulance, cops. Even a water police cruiser, bow high, lights flashing.

Shane held Manasa's hand. She had no idea where these sirens would take them.

Golden Fortune, Dragon Jade

NEAR JIANGMEN, SOUTHERN CHINA, APRIL 1859

Li Yong Fa paused among pine trees on the ridge and gazed into the valley below. Nestled in a deep vee of pale grey rock, bisected by a clear, rushing stream, was Long-en, the village of his birth. The houses with their red and green roof tiles and tan burnished wood seemed artificial from his vantage, like toys for children. People and carts in the narrow streets were as ants. A melancholy smile tugged at Yong Fa's lips. He'd spent most of his life at the Shaolin Temple, but he cherished returning home, seeing loved ones, even though it held a special kind of hurt as well. He always wondered what might have been…

He shook himself, straightened his saffron jacket and heavy wooden beads, and started down the winding path. Strong legs and fit lungs made short work of the journey. He passed no one along the way and entered Long-en from the southern end. Villagers paid him the respect due a Buddhist monk, with bows and palms pressed together. Some recognised him and were friendly as well as courteous. Then the old pork bun seller with his rickety cart, who had been supplying the village for longer than Yong Fa had lived, came hurrying up the road, panting and sweating behind his creaking wagon.

'Yong Fa! You're just in time!'

The young monk frowned. 'For what?'

'The Jade Dragon!'

'What of it?'

'It's gone!'

Yong Fa's mouth fell open. Their most valuable artifact, the heart of the village for centuries, kept in the temple maintained by his Uncle Bao. 'Gone?'

'Stolen! Go, go!'

Such a theft was unthinkable. Yong Fa thanked the bun seller and hurried away, his pleasure at homecoming shattered.

The temple stood at the centre of the small community, a three-tiered pagoda paying homage to the many gods of agriculture and protection, health and good fortune revered by the local populace. It was a simple place, removed from the bustle of modern life. But one thing set Long-en apart from others of its kind: the Jade Dragon, carved by the master artisan Yao Gailing, five hundred years ago when the area was first settled.

A dragon took pity on Yao Gailing, so the story went, as he stumbled through the land, lost, alone and heartbroken. All he sought was a quiet place to live, and peace to mourn his beloved, taken by a terrible illness. Yao had no taste for company. The dragon, heart-sick at the man's powerful grief, had split the mountain in two, releasing a small river so that Yao might have his isolation. In gratitude and homage, Yao had fashioned a statue in his saviour's likeness from a boulder of the purest jade washed free from the mountain by that new stream.

Two-feet long, intricately crafted and of the most flawless green, the Jade Dragon was revered by any who saw it. For centuries it had brought luck and prosperity to Long-en. How the world was changing, Yong Fa thought, if someone would steal such a holy item for personal gain.

He approached the temple and his cousin, Zi Yi, was the first to spot him. Her face was pale under long black hair tied back in a braid. She wore her trademark olive green *cheongsam* dress. Yong Fa had lived in Long-en for only five years. The first three with parents he no longer remembered, murdered by bandits on the road far from town. Then two more years with his father's brother, Bao, Aunt Hua, and precocious Zi Yi, one year older and ten times bossier. His cousin remained his best friend. His smile broke free at the sight of her. Uncle Bao and Aunt Hua, unable to afford two hungry mouths, had sent him to be raised in the Shaolin Temple. He didn't resent them for it, it had given him a better life than he might have hoped for otherwise, but he often wondered.

Zi Yi hugged him tight. 'Cousin! Your arrival is fortuitous.'

'The bun seller told me. Truly, it's stolen?'

'My father is beside himself. He manned the temple all day yesterday, as usual. He locked up in the evening and returned home.' She gestured across the street to the Li family house. 'But this morning, the dragon was gone.'

Yong Fa squeezed her arm. 'We'll find the thief.'

They entered the temple to find Uncle Bao talking urgently with the village elders.

'Nephew!' Bao said. 'A terrible day.'

Yong Fa's expression was hard. 'I will track down the culprit.'

'There are precious few clues,' Bao said. He shook his head. 'There's no sign of forced entry. Nothing. It's as if a ghost spirited the Jade Dragon away.'

'May I search?' Yong Fa asked.

His uncle gestured widely with both hands. 'Be my guest.'

'I will continue my own investigation,' Zi Yi said, and returned to the temple steps. Yong Fa watched as she removed some icons from the cross-body satchel she habitually wore, filled with the tools of her trade. Her geomantic skills were strong and her ability to commune with spirits unrivalled. While she learned what she could, Yong Fa would investigate the material realm.

He searched among the altars, checked the doors and shuttered windows. All were locked, as Bao had said. The central plinth where the Dragon usually sat was shocking in its nakedness, the blasphemy of the act stark in its absence. The place was immaculately clean, no traces of dirt on the floor, or dust on the furniture. No greasy fingerprints marked the gleaming wood. Yong Fa sighed and looked up. The second level of the temple was mezzanine-style and the third had no floor, just a row of shuttered windows high above. An open column through the building allowed light in via the slats of all the shutters and showed the conical roof atop the temple, the underside of dull terracotta tiles supported by a hexagon of thick, polished wooden beams.

Yong Fa jogged up the internal stairs on one side and examined the windows there. They were all locked and undisturbed. The next row, some twenty feet above, could only be opened from inside by a long, hooked pole. Yong Fa squinted at a thin line of sunlight leaking crookedly through one of the high shutters.

He leaned over the railing and called, 'I think the thief came from above.'

Bao and the elders crowded around Yong Fa as he made his way outside and walked a circle of the outer temple wall.

'Surely no one could scale this building?' Bao said.

Yong Fa grinned. 'Let's find out, Uncle!'

He jumped up and caught the lintel of one window and began to climb. Ignoring the cries and admonishments from below, he concentrated on gripping with hardened fingers, relied on intensely trained muscles, and slowly ascended from window to beam to decorative addition. It was an arduous climb, but he made it look easy, until he found himself on the wall of the second floor, squatting on the top of a window frame. He was separated from the third row of shutters high above by smooth wooden boards, offering no handholds at all. The roof flared out over him, six sections of sweeping tile, a sloping polished beam between each one. At the end of each beam, a dragon's head, beautifully carved, watched out over the village in every direction.

Yong Fa paused, closed his eyes, and breathed deeply, using his mastery of the meditative practice of *qi gong* to calm his adrenalised pulse. He exhaled slowly, opened his eyes, concentrating only on the wooden sill of the small window directly above him. With a powerful push of his legs he jumped, stretched, and caught hold of it with confident hands. The gasps and shocked voices from below were as distant as the stars as he focussed only on securing his grip and bracing his feet against the wall. He glanced around, the valley stretched out behind him, pine trees and curling mist.

He spotted the one shutter that was ajar, its ledge scored and gouged as if by a giant bird's claw. The paint was scuffed and scraped where something had been jimmied in the gap between shutter and building to flick the catch.

Yong Fa's grip began to weaken, a tremor in his fingers.

'Uncle Bao,' he called. 'Could you please unlatch this one?'

Bao nodded, and disappeared inside. A few moments later there was a rattling as the long pole was deployed. 'Be careful, Yong Fa!'

The young monk grinned. 'I will.'

He leaned over, opened the cover, and hauled himself inside to land lightly on the second floor. His Shaolin-trained skills made the drop easy.

'You've always been a risk taker,' Uncle Bao said with a frown.

'I know my limits, Uncle. This was well within them.'

'Have you learned anything from your crazy acrobatics?'

Yong Fa smiled ruefully. 'These windows here,' he indicated the second floor, 'are locked with a hasp, but those above have a simple hook, because no one can get to them, after all.'

'Quite so,' Bao said.

'Well, someone managed to get a grapple onto the window from outside and used a knife or similar to flick open that hook. They would have lowered themselves inside with a rope, I imagine, and escaped the same way, with the Jade Dragon. Except the damage their grapple made to the wood meant they couldn't close the shutter properly.'

Bao used his pole to pull the shutter in and, indeed, it sat a little crooked in the frame.

'Whoever stole the dragon knew this temple well,' Yong Fa said.

Zi Yi, long accustomed to ignoring the noise of the world around her, sat in meditation. She was glad her crazy cousin was here, though who knew what he was up to. She let her mind's eye wander the valley, circling gently outwards from the temple.

Not far away, above the house of the local herbalist, a disturbance in the ether caught her attention. She respectfully acknowledged it.

'Greetings, Seeker,' the spirit whispered, its voice like a summer breeze through tall grass.

'Greetings,' she returned, and waited patiently, politely, her astral form hovering.

'We may converse if you wish,' the spirit said.

'Thank you. Were you here through the night?'

'Nearby.'

'And did you see any activity around our temple?'

'I saw your dragon leave.'

Zi Yi's heart quickened. She needed to be careful with her wording, capricious as elemental spirits were, they often preferred games to simple facts. 'Mighty Wind Spirit, master of all the air,' she said, buttering it up, 'did you see who our dragon left with?'

'Of course.'

'Who was it?'

'Why should I tell you?'

'Kindness?' Zi Yi suggested.

'Why would you think me kind?'

Never would a spirit give anything, even the simplest of news, without exacting a price.

'What favour might I offer?' Zi Yi asked. In her thirty-one years she had racked up a sizeable debt of this sort, but luckily not many had yet come to claim their due. Those who had gave her nothing but trouble. But this was how the game was played.

The element danced in the air, formless but showing ripples like clouds reflected in water disturbed by a stone. 'I need nothing from you, tiny flesh.' The conversation was clearly over.

Zi Yi sighed. 'Very well. Thank you for your time.'

She pulled her spectral form away from the soft zephyr of laughter and pushed her perception along the main road out of the village. Several crows sat on one rooftop, cawing lazily. Opening her physical eyes, she looked through the real world at the dark birds. She pulled some fine paper, thin as hope, from her satchel and carefully crafted it, fold after fold until she held a tiny simulacrum of a corvid on her palm. She tapped it once on the head and whispered, 'Crow Spirit, to me.'

With a shiver, the paper bird flapped its wings once and cocked its head to eye her.

'Thank you for coming,' she said with a smile. She nodded up to the birds on the eaves down the street. 'Your friends might have seen someone leaving in the night. Someone with our jade dragon?'

'They might,' Crow Spirit replied cautiously.

'Could you describe the person?'

'He wore burgundy spun with threads of gold. The top of his head shone in the moonlight. He had a toxic *shen*, unkind.'

Zi Yi frowned. Such a description might fit any number of people. 'Could your friends fly now, find him, tell me where he's going?'

'They could,' Crow Spirit said. 'But why would they?'

Zi Yi smiled. 'I would owe you a favour if you would help me until the man is found and our property returned to us.'

Crow Spirit hopped from paper foot to foot as he considered her offer. 'I owe Fox Spirit a life.'

Zi Yi's eyes widened. 'A life?'

'A rabbit meal we stole from her, that she means to collect. Present Fox Spirit with the debt I owe her and your favour will be granted. I'll stay with you until the man you seek is found.'

Zi Yi carefully kept her relief hidden. This bargain came cheaply. The interests of animal spirits often seemed laughable, but they drew no distinction between a rabbit or a man or a village, so it was ever wise to be cautious. 'Very well,' she said. 'I will supply a rabbit life for Fox Spirit.'

'And we will watch this man for you.'

Yong Fa and Zi Yi were explaining all they had learned to the elders when a rustling came from Zi Yi's bag. She pulled forth the tiny paper crow and listened to its report. 'The man has made his way to Nanjing Bay,' she said.

'Who is the thief?' her father asked, casting an eye of wonder towards the form perched on her palm.

'I have no way of knowing. They don't draw a distinction between people any more than we do with crows, but they recognise his attire.'

The paper crow hopped to her shoulder, and Zi Yi pulled her *luopan* from her satchel. She began adjusting the multiple dials of the geomantic compass, aligning characters and symbols as she turned slowly. 'If I had more to go on,' she said, 'my grandmother's treasure here could surely track him.' She shook her head, and returned what was far more than a simple tool of *feng shui* to her bag. With a word of thanks to the paper crow she gently folded it flat and tucked it away. 'But I need more information.'

'What can this criminal hope to gain?' Uncle Bao asked.

'He wouldn't try to sell our dragon in the city, surely?' one of the elders asked.

Zi Yi shook her head. 'I'll wager the fool plans to use its influence for his own selfish gains. The dragon has brought our village health and good fortune for hundreds of years. I imagine he wishes to harness that power.'

'Regardless,' Yong Fa said. 'I'll track him and return the dragon to its rightful place.'

'*We* will, cousin,' Zi Yi said. 'We go together and we go now. He has a long head start.'

Yong Fa bowed respectfully. 'Very well. I'm ready.'

Zi Yi nodded. 'I just have to fetch a rabbit from the market and leave it by the river.'

The cousins set off to the south in a companionable silence. Yong Fa enjoyed the sweet pine scent of the cool air. He was confident they would find the thief, but he worried a little for Zi Yi. She had taken the robbery personally as if it had somehow besmirched her own reputation. Her family was responsible for the temple, after all, yet he knew his cousin well enough not to push the matter or try to assuage her concerns. Her resentment would be fuel, either for their journey or an argument, and he knew very well which he would rather.

They walked for several hours before choosing a spot in the shade to rest and eat. Both their bags were heavy with gifts of food from the village. They unwrapped sticky rice rolls, and passed a skin of water back and forth.

Eventually, Yong Fa broke the quiet. 'A shame such a fine day should be spoiled with this business.'

'What if we fail?' Zi Yi returned.

'What?'

'If we can't recover the dragon, what then?'

'We will, cousin, never fear.'

'Yong Fa, you can't be certain! If we fail, what will become of the village?'

The monk smiled softly. 'It's true it has brought great fortune for a long time, but the village is populated with wonderful people like you and your family. Long-en's prosperity depends on warm people, not cold stone statues.'

'It is also populated by greedy fools like the one who robbed us.'

'They are not so common,' Yong Fa said. 'Besides, the gentle way is to forgive the disreputable for their flaws. Your forgiveness will reach out, so they can be filled with it, embraced by it, and better themselves.'

'I will not forgive this bandit!' Zi Yi said hotly.

'Perhaps not. But your kindness can help others. This thief is one bad apple and we'll deal with him.'

Zi Yi narrowed her eyes at her cousin. 'You contradict yourself.'

Yong Fa grinned. 'I am an imperfect man.'

'You left at five years old and never grew up!' Zi Yi said. 'I can imagine what a nightmare you were for the Abbot and your teachers.'

'Of course I was! I also studied very hard and did them proud. But I can't be serious all the time, and I cannot deny my own flaws.'

'You're a good man.' Zi Yi smiled gently and opened her mouth to say more but was interrupted by a flurry of wings as a dark shape fluttered by to catch her attention. She carefully removed the paper crow from her satchel and it hopped onto her finger. 'What news?' she asked.

The spirit's message passed into her mind and Zi Yi frowned.

'Not good news,' she reported. 'The man has boarded a boat and set sail. Crow Spirit has told me his direction, but they can follow him no further.'

'To sea? Where is he headed, I wonder?'

'They tell me of a teahouse, where he made his plans. The ship is very large. I think he intends to travel far. We can ask around when we reach the port.'

They continued on and when they reached the Huangmao River a friendly fisherman agreed to ferry them to Nanjing Bay for a rather ridiculous sum. Zi Yi protested, but Yong Fa convinced her that haste outweighed the need to bargain. Many villagers had donated kindly to their endeavour, he reminded her, they could share a little of that generosity. She sulked in the back of the boat all the way, while Yong Fa tried to hide his grin.

Despite his exorbitant fee, the fisherman refused to get too close to the busy port, and dropped them half an hour's walk away. Zi Yi shot Yong Fa a venomous look as they started along the riverbank, but he simply smiled. The road was dusty and busy with carts, travellers and traders, but the journey was uneventful. Yong Fa's saffron robes demanded respect and Zi Yi's scowl took care of anything else. They rode a ferry across the narrow strait to the small island and walked the last half mile or so to Nanjing among thickening crowds. The day grew long and twilight bathed the land.

The noise of hawkers and the rattle of wagons in the narrow streets made conversation difficult. The smell of incense and cooking, rice wine and herbs, saturated the air. Zi Yi leaned close, pointed and said, 'That's what the crow showed me.'

Yong Fa looked at the ramshackle teahouse and frowned. 'The thief made his travel arrangements there?'

'Apparently.'

They entered the low building and several eyebrows were raised at the sight of a monk with a well-dressed young woman. No amount of religious respect or scowling could turn these stares away. Zi Yi drew herself up and refused to meet a single gaze as she made her way to the counter at the back.

The tea seller bowed, a smile plastered on his lips that animated no other part of his face. 'Tea?' he asked uselessly.

'A man was here this morning,' Zi Yi said. 'Bald on top, red and gold *changshan*, carrying a rather large parcel, I would imagine.'

The tea seller's eyes narrowed. 'I don't remember such a man.'

Zi Yi leaned forward, threatening. 'Yes, you do.'

The vendor was momentarily taken aback. 'What of it? What's it to you?'

'He organised passage from here. Where to?'

The tea seller laughed, suddenly relaxed, and flapped one hand. 'Fly away little bird, this is no place for you.'

Yong Fa bristled, the hairs on his neck standing up. Something had changed. Not only in the tea seller's demeanour, but in the shop in general. Trusting his instinct, he ducked and turned as a stout club whistled through the air where his head had been. The man wielding it was momentarily shocked and Yong Fa felled him with two quick, iron hard punches. Four more thugs stepped up and the fight was on.

Patrons scrambled out of the way, dragging tables with them, desperate to avoid flying limbs and chairs. Yong Fa's skills were legion, but four on one was tough odds. He dodged left and right, dropped, and swept the feet from under one attacker, rose quickly to kick another hard in the chest. That one flew backwards over a table and smashed out through wooden shutters into the dusty street.

A sword cleaved the air and Yong Fa stepped forward, one hand up to intercept the swinging arm. The blade stopped mere inches from his neck, and Yong Fa's palm strike exploded the swordsman's nose. The man staggered backwards, his chest a scarlet waterfall.

'Outside! Outside!' screamed the tea seller, but the fighters had no ears for courtesy.

As the swept man tried to rise, Zi Yi smashed a heavy teapot onto his head and he collapsed bonelessly. Yong Fa spun forward, finished off the swordsman even as another stepped in with a knife. The monk's robes parted at the razor edge, but his skin escaped thanks to fancy footwork. Yong Fa grabbed the wrist of the knife arm, twisted it and kicked the man's knee. He fell screaming with his arm broken.

'This way!' A lithe young man with a thin face beckoned from the doorway. 'More are coming! Hurry!'

The cousins exchanged a glance, shrugged, and ran from the teahouse, following the young man left and right through the vibrant streets. After several turns he hopped onto a low shed, causing the chickens inside to burst into a flurry of apoplexy, and shimmied nimbly up a downpipe to the tile roof two stories above the road. As Yong Fa and Zi Yi scrambled up behind, he turned a bright grin to them.

'My name is Lau,' he said. 'We'll be safe up here if we stay low.'

Yong Fa bowed, but before he could speak Zi Yi said, 'Why did you save us?'

'You were in trouble.'

'We didn't need saving.'

Lau laughed. 'Oh, you did. Do you know who you were fighting?'

Zi Yi chose not to answer and Yong Fa was pleased to see her caution. 'Who?' he asked.

'Crimson Cloud *tong*! You have made powerful enemies today.'

'But they attacked us!' Zi Yi said.

'You asked questions in the wrong places. That teahouse is their territory.'

Yong Fa frowned. 'What do they care if we ask about a traveller in their teahouse?'

'Who were you asking about?'

'A man from our village,' Yong Fa said. 'We simply enquired after a shaven-headed man in burgundy and gold, who made travel plans there today.'

Lau's eyebrows rose. 'You asked about Bak Ma? He's a Crimson Cloud Red Pole.'

'Bak Ma?' Zi Yi spat in shock. 'I know him, he made a living like me, geomancy, *feng shui*, divination services, but he travelled a lot. And unlike me, he's a fraud! He preys on the weak and vulnerable.'

'That may be so,' Lau said. 'But he's a Crimson Cloud Red Pole nonetheless.'

'What is that?' Yong Fa asked.

'A *tong* Enforcer. Lowest are the uninitiated, the Blue Lanterns, then there are Forty-Nines, then Red Poles. He answers to the Deputy Mountain Master.'

'He's Triad?' Zi Yi said, incredulous.

'Yes.'

'How do you know so much?' Zi Yi asked.

Lau smiled. 'I've seen him there often, drinking tea and wine, trading goods and insults in equal measure.' He touched a finger to his ear, then the corner of his eye. 'I keep my ear to the gossip and my eyes open. Crimson

Cloud have been terrorising this place forever, my useless father pays them a fortune in protection. I'll never inherit his business because it'll belong to them before long. My father and I are great disappointments to each other.'

'That's a sad story,' Yong Fa said. 'You should try to repair relations.'

'Not interested. Either of us.'

'And we don't have time for counselling, Yong Fa!' Zi Yi snapped.

'It seems all my spying and watchfulness has paid off,' Lau said.

'How?'

'You want Bak Ma. I want out of here. We can do a deal.'

'Really? What can you offer?' Zi Yi asked.

Lau grinned broadly. 'I know where Bak Ma went.'

Zi Yi grabbed at his shirt. 'Tell us! Now! Enough of these games.'

Lau held up both palms, warding the geomancer back. 'No, my information has a cost. I have no money. I can get you on Bak Ma's trail, but you take me and pay my passage. That's my price.'

Yong Fa and Zi Yi exchanged a glance. 'It's a deal,' Zi Yi said with a sigh.

Lau clapped. 'Yes! Bak Ma's ship has sailed, but if we're quick, we can get on the next one out. There won't be another going for some weeks.'

'Which ship?' Zi Yi asked.

Lau shook his head. 'I'm no fool, you'll leave me behind! We go together.' He crept forward to peek over the roof's edge. 'The place will be crawling with Crimson Cloud looking for you.'

'We'll be careful,' Yong Fa said.

'No, no, they'll question everyone.'

'They can't possibly!' Zi Yi scoffed.

'They are many, and their spies are everywhere.'

Night had settled over the town. Yong Fa looked down into the inky street, still bustling, though less so than before. There was a new moon and not much starlight. The buildings were brightly lit inside, but their roofs were shrouded in darkness. 'Let's go over the top then,' he said. 'We're all fit and capable. The port is not so far.' He pointed across to the roof opposite. 'With a run up, you could both jump that gap, couldn't you?'

'We could try,' Zi Yi said. 'How many streets to cross between here and the boat?' she asked Lau.

The young man paused, eyes closed in thought. Eventually he said, 'You know, if we move along on this side all the way to the cobbler, we would only have to jump two narrow streets.' He hurried away.

'You'll get us killed one of these days,' Zi Yi complained to her cousin.

'Me? Maybe if you'd been polite in the teahouse we wouldn't be sneaking across rooftops like cats,' Yong Fa said, and ducked a slap.

In a crouching run, they hurried after the young man. Yong Fa's years of training ensured he was silent as the moon, but both Zi Yi and Lau impressed him. They made noise, but very little, and certainly not enough to be heard from below. When they reached the end of the tight row of buildings, Lau pointed.

'We need to be over there,' he said. 'You can see the port from here.'

Tall masts and sails and the bulks of steamers were solid silhouettes in the distance. Lights burned here and there, candles and oil lamps in windows and on the handcarts of street vendors.

Yong Fa glanced below. No one seemed to be paying attention to the roofs. He took a couple of steps back then ran and easily leapt the street. Almost immediately, Lau landed lightly beside him. 'You move well,' he told the young man.

'Not as well as you!'

'Keep at it and you will.'

'I can't do it!' Zi Yi said, her voice a harsh whisper of frustration.

'You can!' Yong Fa said.

Zi Yi's face was twisted in frustration. Yong Fa knew she was angry at herself, unable to master the fear that glued her feet to the tiles. He leapt back across.

'Get on my back.'

She looked at him as though he had just grown an ox from his forehead. 'What?'

'I'll carry you. You're only a little woman.'

Zi Yi's mouth fell open and her eyes hardened. She turned away, then ran and launched herself across. Thankfully Lau was there to grab her hand as she teetered on the edge of the roof.

Yong Fa landed beside her, grinning.

'You are a contemptible man and have no right to call yourself a monk,' Zi Yi said.

'It worked, didn't it?'

She shook her head and stalked away.

'Quickly,' Lau said. 'Before someone sees or hears us.'

They hurried after Zi Yi and were soon at the end of another row of buildings. Visible only one street away was the port, a bustling, restless place, even in darkness. People pushed wagons loaded with goods to and fro, the odour of the ocean, seaweed and engine fuel for steamers was ripe in the air. The next gap they needed to jump was too wide. The three stood back in the gloom and looked at their destination. So near and yet so far.

'Honestly, I'm not sure even I could make that,' Yong Fa said.

Zi Yi snorted. 'You're lying. You could easily make that and more. But neither Lau nor I could.'

'I don't remember this street being so wide,' Lau said.

'Then there's nothing else for it. We climb down and take our chances.' Zi Yi's eyes challenged them to contradict her.

A ruckus below caught their attention as one group of men pushed and shoved another. There were harsh words and blows exchanged.

'Those on the left are Crimson Cloud,' Lau whispered, retreating from the edge. 'They grow frustrated that they can't find you, I imagine. And over there, see? There's more. And those three by the noodle seller are Crimson Cloud Forty-Nines.'

'The whole port is crawling with the bastards,' Zi Yi spat.

Lau pointed to a dark gap between buildings. 'The quickest way is through there. See that big auxiliary steamer? That's our vessel, the *Northern Belle*. We don't have long, she sails in under an hour.'

'So what do we do?' Zi Yi asked.

Lau sniffed. 'I'm going to cause a distraction. When I catch their attention, you two run. Once you're on board, you're safe, assuming you get there unseen. I'll lose them and join you.'

'And if you don't make it in time?' Yong Fa asked.

'A risk I'll have to take.'

'Why are you willing to do so much for us?' Zi Yi asked.

Lau laughed. 'If you'd spent more than a few hours here, you'd understand my need to escape. Trust me, it's worth the risk. Don't miss your chance!'

With that, he hurried away and dropped out of sight.

'And we still don't know what else he knew of Bak Ma's plans,' Zi Yi said, her voice tight.

Yong Fa shrugged. 'Then let's hope he makes it back. If not, perhaps we'll learn more on the ship. At least we'll know where Bak Ma has gone if our ship is going there too.'

They crept to the edge and looked over. The thugs were still pushing people around down below. Lau's voice rang out. 'A Shaolin monk is fighting near Auntie Mai's!'

'Our signal, you think?' Yong Fa asked with a grin.

The crowds surged away from the harbour.

'No arguments,' Yong Fa said. 'You must trust me.' He dropped two stories to land light as a cat, then held out his arms. 'I'll catch you!'

'Damn you!' Zi Yi said. She closed her eyes and jumped.

Yong Fa braced for the impact and caught his cousin with a small grunt. He set her down and they ran. Stepping into the lantern light, they hurried across the open harbour, dodging wagons and oxen left and right to quickly reach the gangplank to the ship. Two men holding large knives stepped out of the shadows of a stack of crates.

'Not so fast,' one said. 'We're not easily fooled.'

The cousins skidded to a halt.

'We used our brains, see. This is the only other ship leaving for Australia, so of course you'd try to get aboard if you're following Bak Ma.'

'Australia?' Zi Yi whispered.

Yong Fa decided not to converse. He hammered out a kick, taking the talkative thug under the chin. The man flipped over the gangplank and hit the dark water to sink like a stone. As his partner shot forward, Yong Fa blocked the man's knife hand, stepped past and used the attacker's momentum to turn him. Yong Fa palmed the staggering man's head into the railing of the gang plank, felling him with a dull *thwack*.

'We can't let them report, at least not until the ship is away,' Yong Fa said. He looked into the bay. 'I don't think that one is coming back.'

Zi Yi pointed at the unattended crates the villains had hidden behind. Yong Fa hauled bolts of cloth out of one not yet sealed, tossing the merchandise into the harbour, and hefted the senseless man into the empty wooden box, working quickly in the shadows the cargo provided. As the man began to murmur and come around, Yong Fa placed the lid and punched each nail into place with accurate, single-knuckle strikes. Then he lifted another crate on top as dull thudding began.

'Have a good trip!' Yong Fa said to the box.

They glanced around to ensure no-one had paid any mind to the brief fracas, then strolled casually back into the lantern light and up the gangplank. They were met by a swarthy sailor with a scarlet birthmark from brow to chin across one side of his face. 'Help you?'

'Your captain, is he here?'

The man pointed out a burly European with a barrel chest and a mass of wild red hair. Yong Fa approached him. 'Excuse me. We wish to arrange passage with you.'

The captain peered down at the young monk. 'Cutting it fine,' he said in heavily-accented Mandarin. 'We leave on the tide in fifteen minutes.'

'Just in time then,' Yong Fa said with a broad smile.

When the captain told Zi Yi the fare she bit her tongue and paid. 'Our friend, a young man called Lau, should join us any moment,' she said. 'I'll pay for him, too.'

The captain shrugged. 'As you wish. But if he's not here, I won't wait. See Gilly about your cabin. You'll all be sharing.' He strode away.

'Australia!' Zi Yi said. 'That's months at sea!'

Yong Fa nodded, lips pursed. 'But what choice do we have if that's where the Jade Dragon has been taken?'

They waited in shadows on the deck to avoid being seen and watched the harbour for Lau, but fifteen minutes later the steamer left Nanjing Bay without him.

'I feel bad,' Yong Fa said. 'He risked everything and helped us only to be left behind.'

'And we've only got half his information!' Zi Yi said. Her eyes narrowed and she ran to the rail. 'Look!'

Lau came pelting across the dock, dancing obstacles left and right. Without slowing he dove from the wharf and hit the water with barely a splash. Moments later he surfaced, swimming hard. Yong Fa heaved a mooring rope to the side, grunting with effort as he lowered the thick, heavy cord to trail in the ship's increasing wake.

'He'll never make it!' Zi Yi exclaimed, but Lau swam like a fish and snagged a hold of the lifeline.

Yong Fa hauled and Lau climbed. Zi Yi held her cousin's waist and finally Lau fell over the rail, gasping.

He staggered to his feet and grinned, his face bruised, left arm bleeding.

'By the Emperor in Heaven, you made it!' Yong Fa said.

'Only just!' Lau replied.

Yong Fa patted his shoulder. 'Are you badly hurt? What happened?'

'A little battered and one of them got a knife to me, but it's not too bad. Once I led them away, and they realised I was lying, they got angry. I swore I'd told the truth, but they beat me anyhow. I managed to get away before they did too much damage, ran the long way back and saw the ship already leaving.'

'You could not have cut it finer, but what an effort you made!' Yong Fa said, genuinely impressed.

They leaned against the ship's rail, Lau getting his breath back, and watched the dancing oil lamps of night fishing boats that scurried away from the large steamer. Before long they were in open water, land lost in the darkened distance. They went in search of Gilly who showed them their cabin, which was little more than a large cupboard with pallets and sacking for beds.

Lau looked about. 'Three of us and only two berths.'

'We can share sleeping on the floor between them, you and I,' Yong Fa said. 'It won't be so bad.'

Lau grinned. 'Not at all. I'm away from Nanjing Bay, that's all that matters to me!'

There would be no more stops until Singapore, they'd been told; then Surabaya, and then a long haul to Sydney, Melbourne and finally Adelaide.

'You'll need to stay on board in Sydney and Melbourne,' Gilly had said. 'Chinese are restricted in Australia now, you won't get in without licences, which I'm sure you don't have. But once in Adelaide, you can slip in and trek back to the goldfields from there. I assume that's where you're headed.'

'Now tell us more,' Zi Yi said to Lau. 'Is Bak Ma going all the way to Australia? Do you know where? And why?'

'He's got a plan to make a fortune,' Lau said. 'That's why Crimson Cloud were happy to finance his passage. There's gold in Australia, mountains of it for the taking, if you believe the stories.'

'I'm not sure I do,' Zi Yi said.

'With Crimson Cloud influence, Bak Ma secured a visa to enter via Melbourne,' Lau went on. 'But as Gilly said, we'll need to go to Adelaide. It's a trek on foot, some two hundred and fifty miles across unforgiving terrain to the goldfields.'

'You seem to know an awful lot about this place,' Zi Yi said suspiciously.

'I told you,' Lau replied. 'I watch and I listen.'

'This journey is becoming more horrifying by the second,' moaned Zi Yi.

'Ah, but worth it for the fortunes to be made!' said Lau, grinning widely.

'This is not a game, Lau. Bak Ma has a lot to answer for. And he'll have a huge head start on us.'

'You're sure that's his plan?' Yong Fa asked.

Lau nodded emphatically. 'I was in the teahouse when Bak Ma was making his case. He told the Crimson Cloud bosses he could get his hands on an artefact that would guarantee success and ensure he gained control of the richest mine. He promised to harvest great wealth, and send back huge sums to repay the *tong's* investment in him a thousand times over. He planned to establish the society there as well, to ensure they have a powerful presence early in the new land.'

'So that's his game,' Zi Yi said. 'To use the power of Yao Gailing's jade masterpiece for his own gain and the wealth of criminals. He's despicable!'

'We'll stop him,' Yong Fa said. 'You have your friends to help, yes?'

Zi Yi retrieved the fragile paper crow from her bag and it hopped into life. Ignoring Lau's gasp, she asked, 'Can you help us?'

'Only back on land,' Crow Spirit replied. 'We are not sea-faring birds.' It sounded genuinely apologetic.

Zi Yi passed on its message, carefully returning the creature to her satchel.

'Can your *luopan* assist, now you know who we seek?' Yong Fa wondered.

Zi Yi nodded and took the compass from her bag, adjusted it and thought of Bak Ma. Her will controlled the magic in it and it responded immediately, though weakly. 'The trouble is, there's no real accuracy over distances like these,' she said. 'But as we get closer, it'll be more useful.'

'Where does Bak Ma think these great riches are to be found?' Yong Fa asked.

Lau grinned. The young man seemed to show his teeth a lot. 'It's called Ballarat.'

'What a thoroughly horrible sounding place,' Zi Yi said.

'Your mood is dark because of the task ahead of us,' Yong Fa said. 'Understandably so. But we have our goal and our cause is just.' He asked Lau, 'There's no chance our ship will catch up to his?'

'No,' Lau said, his smile fading for once. 'His vessel sails directly to Sydney, then Melbourne. That's why he chose it. We have to make stops, so even with the best weather in the world we'll be several weeks behind.'

The days aboard ship soon became a drudgery of routine. Meagre food rations shared with the crew, picking up as much English as they could from anyone who would teach them, endless games of *mah jong* on deck to while away the hours. Yong Fa trained in any open space he could find, meditated, and, when asked, happily shared his learnings about Buddhism, the martial arts, or *qi gong*. He led regular morning practice for sailors and passengers alike, while Zi Yi busied herself with esoteric study, and conversed with the spirits as much as with human company. Lau became friendly with many of the crew. He was a quiet and polite lodger in their cramped cabin, and refused to let Yong Fa take the floor, insisting the monk always sleep on the pallet. Other than enduring the occasional frightening storm, they simply waited as miles of ocean slipped beneath them.

The boredom of shipboard life was broken only when they made port. In Singapore and Surabaya they enjoyed a little time on land visiting markets and spending some of their coin in restaurants, eating far too much simply because the food wasn't their usual rations. Zi Yi bought exotic fruits and vegetables to supplement their on-board diet.

One morning, a week from Sydney, Zi Yi rose before dawn. Her sleep had been troubled for reasons she couldn't fathom and after a night of restless shifting about on the coarse bedding, she gave up and crept from the cabin while the men slumbered on. She strolled the deck in the indigo of pre-dawn, the breeze cool and salty as it lifted her hair. She found a secluded spot at the rail, took the *luopan* from her satchel and set to adjusting the dials. She felt the instrument tune in with her will, her overwhelming desire to find that bastard, Bak Ma. He was somewhere out there. The *luopan* pointed a little due west of their heading, so nothing had changed.

The compass was snatched from her grasp by a thin hand. Zi Yi spun around to face the thief and paused for a moment, stunned to see Lau standing there. She thought for a moment it was a joke, but his open, happy face was closed and mean. He held her *luopan* in one hand and slapped her hard with the other.

'My patience had almost run out,' he said as she staggered, ears ringing with the blow. 'I've been waiting weeks for this chance!'

Blood trickled from Zi Yi's split lip. 'What are you doing?' she slurred.

'Crimson Cloud think I'm unworthy, do they? Won't let me join, eh?' Lau said, teeth bared. 'I've shown them!' He hefted the *luopan*. 'When I present this to Bak Ma as proof I succeeded where the rest of Crimson Cloud failed, he'll make me his right hand.'

Zi Yi tried to rally herself and Lau backhanded her, made her stagger again, close to passing out. She grabbed for the rail and missed, fell to her knees. 'Lau, no...'

'Don't worry, you won't be alone for long. Your worthless cousin will soon follow.'

Zi Yi tried to focus, to gather some kind of equilibrium. She cried out, but her voice was nothing more than a croak. As she drew a deep breath, determined to scream until the entire ship awoke, Lau grabbed under her arms and hefted her up before the sound left her lips.

The young man's lithe form belied his considerable strength and he threw her over the rail. Her scream escaped all too late as Lau's leering face retreated from her at speed and she hit the waves hard.

Yong Fa awoke to shouts and the pounding of rushing feet in the corridors. He sat up and saw that neither Zi Yi nor Lau were there. His heart hammered, suddenly sure that something was terribly wrong. He ran up to the deck to see a crowd arguing back and forth, Lau among them.

The captain, a hulking presence in the centre of the group, threw both his hands up and shouted, 'It's too late! Simple as that.' He repeated himself in several languages, none of which Yong Fa understood, then strode away.

Lau turned, his expression a picture of misery, and saw Yong Fa. He pushed his way through the press of bodies. 'Oh, such awful news. I'm so sorry!'

'What's happened?'

'It's Zi Yi. She's lost overboard.'

Yong Fa's stomach became liquid, his legs shook. 'What?'

'A crewman heard a scream, saw her floundering in the ship's wake, but by the time the alarm had been raised, we had sailed too far.'

Yong Fa shook his head, refusing to believe it. 'We have to turn the ship around!'

Lau's shoulders slumped. 'That's what I told the captain, and half the crew insisted too, but he refused. He says even if we did turn about, there's no way to find one lost soul in this open ocean.'

Gilly approached them, shaking his head. 'I'm sorry, but the captain's right. We'd never find her. And there are sharks, which are sure to reach her well before we do. A terrible loss. I'm sorry, Yong Fa.'

'No,' the monk said. 'This can't be.'

'I'm sorry.' The man moved off, head hung low.

'How could she go overboard?' Yong Fa asked Lau. 'It's inconceivable.'

'She was out of the cabin before dawn. I heard her tossing and turning last night. Perhaps she was so tired that she fell asleep leaning on the rail?'

Yong Fa turned away, his mind reeling. How could his cousin be gone, so quickly, so utterly? Tears breached his eyes and he stalked to the stern to be alone.

He took refuge in a vigorous training routine, trying to assuage his frustration, but all he managed to do was exhaust his body. He returned to the cabin, lay down on his pallet and let nightmare-filled sleep take him rather than remain conscious any longer.

Zi Yi awoke cold and wet. Something rose and fell rhythmically beneath her. Everywhere was black and her face hurt, but slowly she picked out bright points in the darkness and realised they were stars.

Her memory flooded back. She sat up in shock, and fell into the sea. She gasped, gagged, spat out saltwater, and flailed. She was not a strong swimmer. Once again, something nudged her from below and lifted her free of the wet embrace. She held tight to smooth, grey skin, and one shiny black eye tipped back to look at her. A pod of dolphins circled around, occasionally darting away only to return and watch once more.

'You've been asleep a long time,' Dolphin Spirit said.

'Thank you for catching me.'

'You have little chance of surviving my realm. Why did you enter it?'

Zi Yi laughed. 'It was unintentional! An evil man tried to drown me.'

Dolphin Spirit clicked rapidly to his pod and they danced and ducked. 'Would you have me save you?' he asked.

'You already have.'

'But I'm under no obligation to continue doing so.'

Zi Yi sighed. So fickle, these spirits. 'If I asked you to return me to the ship from where I fell, what would you ask of me?'

'I caught you because I saw power in you,' Dolphin Spirit said. 'Return to me someone I've lost and I'll return you to those who've lost you.'

It sounded like one of those bigger favours. 'Who?'

'A maiden who was fish in the water, but walked on two legs on land. When she would visit the waves, we were lovers. I never begrudged her the time she spent on the sands, but one day she didn't return.'

Zi Yi considered the spirit's words. 'You're talking about a mermaid,' she said eventually. 'Truly, you knew such a creature?'

'I did. And we loved each other. She would not choose to abandon me, I am sure.'

Though she felt almost certain she would live to regret it, Zi Yi nodded. 'Very well. I should warn you, I'm on a journey that will take many moons. But I promise that when it is done I will call on you and do all I can to help.'

There was a surge in the water, several dolphins swarming a sharper shape with a steeper fin that switched in the waves and fled. Zi Yi realised the circling pod was keeping sharks away. Coldness seeped into her gut.

Dolphin Spirit clicked and ducked. 'We have an agreement.'

'Can you catch up to my ship?'

'We've been trailing it since you hit the water. We can overtake it before the next time the sun dives. Hold tight.'

Zi Yi leaned forward to grasp Dolphin Spirit's pectoral fins, and the animal leaped and powered off through the waves. Zi Yi squinted her eyes against the spray and braced herself for a long, arduous ride.

As the sun sank, Yong Fa stood at the stern of the steamer looking into the past. Back that way his cousin had been alive. Back there, the Jade Dragon was in its rightful place, the village peaceful and prosperous, no clouds covered the moon. Now everything was shrouded in darkness. He had tried to remain personally unburdened by the theft, had tried to cool Zi Yi's vengeful fire, but he was an imperfect man. Everything had changed. He vowed to destroy Bak Ma, in his cousin's name, and return the icon to the temple.

A soft scuff of shoe on deck drew his attention from the darkening sky. Lau, again. He refused to turn around. Twice the night before he had woken to the young man stalking about their cabin. Overcome with grief, he claimed, at Zi Yi's tragic death.

But something disquieted Yong Fa and he couldn't pin it down. He walked the decks, fuming. For only two days his cousin had been gone, yet it felt as if the pain of it would never ease. *His* turmoil was indeed grief. But something about Lau's disposition was off.

'Leave me be,' he said, glancing over his shoulder. His eyes narrowed at the young man's grunt of surprise, and was that a flash of silver he saw, sliding into Lau's tunic? A knife?

'I… I… wanted to see you were okay,' Lau said.

'What are you doing?' Yong Fa asked, turning to face the young man. His disquiet had grown to full blown suspicion.

Lau's eyes grew wide as plates and he staggered backwards. 'No, no, no!' he muttered, as colour drained from his face.

Yong Fa realised the young man was looking past him. The monk sidestepped and turned to see a bedraggled creature, wild wet hair and furious eyes, teeth bared, haul itself up over the gunwale. His shock washed away in a sea of relief as he recognised Zi Yi.

'Grab him!' she said as she jumped to the deck.

Lau squealed and turned to run, but Yong Fa was too fast.

'My *luopan*!' Zi Yi growled. 'Where is it?'

Lau dropped to his knees and scrambled in his satchel, whimpering. He pulled out the enchanted *feng shui* compass. 'I'm sorry, you have to understand…'

He didn't get to finish the sentence as Zi Yi snatched away her treasure, then kicked him hard. Several teeth scattered across the deck and Lau collapsed to lie still.

'Throw him overboard,' Zi Yi said, her voice cold.

'But, cousin…'

Zi Yi hissed and pushed Yong Fa aside. With strength born of fury she grabbed Lau's jacket and slung him, in one movement, up onto the ship's rail.

'No!' Yong Fa shouted.

But it was too late. Zi Yi heaved and Lau's limp form dropped from sight.

The cousins stared at each other for a long moment, then fell into a strong embrace.

'I thought I'd lost you!' Yong Fa said into her wet hair.

'I'm not that easily lost,' she returned.

'Let's get you below and dry,' Yong Fa said. 'And you can tell me just how in heaven you survived!'

They tried to disguise Zi Yi as a young man, to avoid suspicion at her return and Lau's disappearance, but it was not convincing. So she stayed mostly below decks, out of sight, out of mind, only rising for fresh air at night. Their first sight of Australia came a few days after her return, a distant view of Sydney Harbour. As they'd been told, Chinese weren't allowed to enter the country without a licence, nor even allowed off the ship to sightsee. It was the same at Port Melbourne. Zi Yi regularly consulted her *luopan* and could only confirm that Bak Ma was still far away.

At last the steamer reached Port Adelaide in a sweltering heat. The cousins disembarked to be summarily processed and told in no uncertain terms that the state of Victoria did not welcome *their kind*, and they should not go there. But the official's tone clearly implied that's exactly where he thought they'd be heading, and he even surreptitiously pointed them in the right direction.

Once clear of the port's crowds, Zi Yi reached into her bag, meaning to ask Crow Spirit to guide the way. She was dismayed to discover the tiny simulacrum was nothing more than a dried mess of pulp fragments, along with all her spirit paper, ruined by her gruelling journey through the waves. But her *luopan* now pointed strongly in a single direction, drawing her forward, so they would rely on that.

Their route was more often than not a dustbowl and the tracks would frequently vanish, making the decision of which way forward one of luck as much as judgement, but Zi Yi's compass kept their destination true.

She found a scrap of notepad along the way that, while not spirit paper for a simulacrum, was good enough for spells. She wrote one for luck and protection, burned it, sprinkled the ashes into a cupful of their precious water and drank it down. 'It will aid us,' she promised.

Three days later they crossed the border into Victoria under cover of night, tipped off by a young man they had met that morning, who had learned the secret way in a letter from his uncle. Zi Yi smiled and wrote another spell, burned it, and drank that one down.

'Better to be safe, as the last one seems to have been used this night,' she said.

The country was criss-crossed with innumerable tracks of carts and drays that carved through dust and sand. Then the cousins crossed a swamp, then a rocky place, passed over creeks wet and dry, then a series of hills, only to venture finally into wide, endless plains. They passed broken wagons, abandoned, and many stark, white bones, both human and equine. Finding enough food was a constant trial and everything was so expensive that they soon ran low on funds. In camps here and there, where they found their own people, they were able to earn more with Zi Yi selling divinations, and Yong Fa begging alms, only to spend it almost immediately on over-priced sustenance.

Things become a little easier when a digger they befriended showed them how to eat off the land, taught them the secrets of damper and roasted cockatoo, and possum cooked on skewers, as well as tricks to catch those creatures, and others. He introduced them to unappetising bush fruits and grubs that would keep a person alive, after a fashion. He taught them useful English phrases that might help them survive.

One afternoon as they rested under a tree, a strange spirit calling itself Kangaroo, approached. It was, it said, curious about Zi Yi's power, and offered to travel with them for a time, to warn of impending dangers, if she would allow it to study her.

As a result they were able to hide and let bushrangers pass by, or take a different route to avoid ambushes. Zi Yi was grateful, unable to bear the thought of losing her treasured *luopan* to such attacks. Since Lau's assault she had taken to keeping it tucked deep inside her clothing, though she was uncertain how safe even that was. But pleased as she was with Kangaroo's protection, still she wondered how she would ever repay her debt to the kindly Spirit. However, the creature was benign and demanded nothing. When Zi Yi burned gum leaves as an offering in place of incense, Kangaroo seemed content with that.

Other travellers had not been so lucky and the cousins regularly happened across a skeleton tied to a tree, a victim of bushrangers, left for the ants and eagles.

As they neared Ballarat they began to pass more established settlements, sandstone buildings, shops and homes and farms. They encountered coaches, travelling up from Melbourne, and enjoyed the glimpses of something close to civilisation, but never lingered long, constantly pressing towards their goal. Kangaroo Spirit left them when the roads became busier, the land more populated.

The journey had squeezed out the last of any softness that remained in either cousin, and they arrived in Ballarat hardened and fuelled by a burning anger at all they'd been forced to endure and witness.

Ballarat was built on wide dirt streets criss-crossing undulating hills. Buildings of stone and weatherboard turned a brisk trade, their wide awnings providing welcome shade on the footpaths. The evidence of wealth was a stark contrast to the paucity of their journey. People were well-dressed, children and dogs ran and played everywhere, carts and horses busied the roads.

Agriculture was well established and evidence of industry, blacksmiths and foundries, was rife. Ballarat was a far bigger and more populated place than the cousins had anticipated. They walked along the main road, mouths agape.

'Where do we even begin?' Yong Fa asked.

'We should ask around,' Zi Yi said. 'The *luopan* indicated Bak Ma is that way, but still some distance off, I think. We could simply follow it, but some information first would be useful.'

'These people don't seem very welcoming,' Yong Fa observed.

They scanned the openly hostile white faces, tried to smile and show themselves to be no threat. Words and phrases were barked in their direction, but too quickly for them to catch, with a vocabulary they couldn't hope to follow. None of it seemed particularly friendly.

'We need to find some of our own people,' Yong Fa said.

They turned away from the busy town centre and headed towards less populated places. Eventually they spotted a couple of Asian faces and greeted them warmly. 'Where should we go to find welcome and rest?' Zi Yi asked them.

One man with a heavy Shanghai accent replied, 'Nowhere in this country!' But he pointed towards the outskirts of town where the Chinese had established a community, including food vendors and boarding houses. The cousins thanked him and set off.

As the scowling, sharp faces gave way to more friendly visages, the cousins began to relax. Passing one group of Chinese arguing about whether the area's gold rush had run its course, they slowed to listen. 'Mining's a fool's game now,' one man said, and spat into the road.

'Better to turn our efforts to other pursuits before we're left with nothing but the clothes on our backs,' agreed another.

Zi Yi gripped Yong Fa's arm tightly when a very skinny man said, 'Not everywhere's dried up. That Bak Ma's mine is turning out gold like it was as plentiful as horse dung!'

'That is not a natural place and Bak Ma is not a natural man,' said another, making a sign to ward off evil. 'I would sooner starve than work for him.'

'You may soon get that chance,' said the first.

The cousins moved away and Zi Yi said, 'The bastard is clearly making good use of our village's icon.' Her face was pinched with rage.

'But we're getting close, so we can soon make it right,' Yong Fa replied. He saw a won-ton seller on the street and smiled. 'Look! Do we have enough money for a feed?'

Zi Yi nodded, her mood lightening at the sight of a familiar meal. She dug inside her *cheongsam*. 'We'll be fed and housed for a couple more days before we need your antics again.'

'My antics?'

Zi Yi grinned, puffed herself up in a mockery of Yong Fa's muscles. 'Spare some alms for the love of the Buddha?' she said in a surprisingly accurate impression of his voice.

Yong Fa's mouth fell open in outrage and he was about to protest when a voice behind them said, 'So you made it. We thought you'd died on the way.'

'We hoped so, at least,' said another.

They turned to face three men, each holding a pistol. Yong Fa's blood stilled. He hated guns with a passion. There was no honour, no skill. Any damn fool could pull a trigger.

'Crimson Cloud,' Zi Yi said, voice dripping with disdain.

The man in the middle bowed, showing an ugly white scar across the top of his head that split his short, black hair in two.

'Bak Ma's divinations have foretold your arrival. We'd be happy to kill you where you stand, but the boss insists on seeing you.' Scarhead gestured with the weapon towards a stage coach with its windows barred and padlocks on the doors, waiting to be secured.

The journey was rough and rattled their teeth for nearly an hour. It was stinking hot and close in the prison coach and they were offered neither food nor water. Their satchels had been taken from them, but they had not been searched. Zi Yi fussed over the lump of her *luopan* showing through her belt, though it was barely visible.

'I've retained it this far,' she muttered. 'I won't lose it now.'

Yong Fa frowned, worried what might happen to Zi Yi if the thing was taken from her. He chose not to mention it further, but wished she was not so attached to that one material item, powerful though it was. Apart from anything else, it became something that could be used against her.

Peering through the bars, they watched the scrub give way to a small sea of white tents in a shallow valley. Beyond the tents was a huge, sprawling structure surrounded by a rough wooden paling fence. Three connected weatherboard buildings, two stories high, lined one side, with a wide brick chimney standing tall next to them, belching dark smoke into the massive blue sky.

Beside the chimney a construction almost as high, built of scaffolded wooden beams, creaked as giant pulley wheels rotated at its top, busy ropes disappearing from it into the ground. On the opposite side were more buildings, brick and weatherboard stables, smaller latticed wood constructions. People swarmed everywhere.

'Bak Ma has certainly used the dragon to his advantage,' Zi Yi said. She hissed between her teeth in disgust.

The coach drove between high gateposts into the main compound and pulled up outside the stables. It rocked as their three captors jumped down and hurried away, leaving Yong Fa and Zi Yi to swelter. Scarhead returned minutes later, his face split in a grin. 'Bak Ma is very pleased to know you're here.'

He made his gun obvious as he opened the door and gestured for them to climb out. As they emerged, two other men arrived to pat down the cousins. Yong Fa tensed, worried that Zi Yi was about to have her *luopan* discovered and to what that might drive her. As her searcher's hands moved towards her middle, she twisted slightly and snapped, 'Have some respect with where you place your hands!'

The man grunted. 'Stand still!' He continued to search, but Zi Yi's movement had caused him to skip the precious compass.

'He has nothing,' Yong Fa's searcher said.

The other pulled Zi Yi's small purse from the top of her *cheongsam* and tossed it to Scarhead. 'This is all she has.'

'You would even rob our meagre coin?' Zi Yi asked.

'The dead have no need of money,' Scarhead replied, and pocketed her purse. 'Throw them in. Opposite ends so they can't talk.'

The place smelled strongly of straw and manure, horses whickered and snorted. Some of the stalls, Yong Fa realised, were cells, with floor to ceiling doors of iron bars. As he was pushed towards one end and Zi Yi to the other, they exchanged a knowing look. This would not end here.

'My divinations were right after all.'

Yong Fa turned from investigating the back wall of his cell. 'Zi Yi said you were nothing but a fraud,' he said.

'Is that so?' Bak Ma replied. He moved closer to the bars of the door, resplendent in rich silks over a corpulent body, and dripping with gold jewellery. His braided hair glistened with expensive oils while his shaven pate gleamed. 'I may not have her skills, but I'm no charlatan. No matter, though, for you'll both be dead soon. You don't cross Crimson Cloud and live.'

'Earned your place now, then?' Yong Fa asked.

'I'm a rich and respected man.'

'Only because of our Jade Dragon!'

Bak Ma laughed, his belly wobbling. 'Strength belongs to he who takes it. An icon of such power was not meant to languish in a backwater village. That is an insult to its potency.' The man dragged a silk kerchief over his brow. His nails were long. 'I don't care for this country, the heat, the flies, venomous creatures everywhere, but another year at most and I will return home, with untold wealth and respect, and with the Jade Dragon. Soon enough I'll be in control of Crimson Cloud. My influence will reach new heights, while your bones lie in an unmarked grave in this accursed red dirt.'

'Don't be so sure.'

'Your determination in making it this far is admirable, and I confess I am impressed, but it is over for you now.'

'So why not just have your men shoot us?' Yong Fa asked, trembling at his audacity. 'What are you waiting for?'

Bak Ma grinned. 'Even I cannot yet control time. Government inspectors are due soon, to check our licences, so I must endure this bureaucratic annoyance . Never fear, when they've gone, I shall take my time with you *both*.' He looked meaningfully to where Zi Yi was incarcerated, then back to Yong Fa with an evil grin.

Yong Fa bristled, his anger burning. Before he could say anything more, Bak Ma walked away.

Yong Fa could tell the thief had stopped at Zi Yi's cell, and though he couldn't make out their conversation, he heard his cousin's outraged tone. He returned his attention to the brick wall at the back of his cell.

He focussed his rage and balled his fist. Gathering his *qi* into the strike, he punched one brick. It cracked through the middle and the mortar around it crumbled a little, fine dust raining down. Yong Fa drew breath again, and punched once more. Slowly, the wall of his prison began to respond to his will.

Far too slowly, but he would not give up.

Zi Yi swore she would kill herself before she allowed Bak Ma to make good on his lewd promises. But better to escape and destroy him instead. She had little time and would not squander it. She sat on the floor of packed earth, closed her eyes, and calmed her mind. Meditation allowed her consciousness to drift out into the world, seeking an ally.

'You've journeyed far,' said a voice both familiar and strange.

Her astral self found it in the branches of a spreading eucalypt. She inclined her head. 'As have you.'

Crow Spirit bobbed and cawed, a sound quite unlike the crows she was used to. 'Wherever there are my kind, so am I,' he said. 'But you travel the mundane way. Quite impressive.'

'We can do anything, given enough time and will,' Zi Yi said.

'The rabbit was well-received by Fox Spirit,' Crow said. He seemed somehow contrite.

Zi Yi laughed. That seemed like another life, nearly a year and half a world away. 'You're welcome.'

'I'm sorry we were parted before my debt was fully repaid.'

Crow Spirit *was* contrite. Zi Yi had quite happily thought the debt fulfilled, but the spirit obviously didn't. She remembered the words of its promise: *I'll stay with you until the man you seek is found.* 'I've seen many crows in this land,' she said. 'Why wait until now to show yourself?'

'You did not call on me, and I thought you angry. I feared what retribution you might wreak. I saw Kangaroo Spirit offer you protection, so I remained silent. But I believe now you need assistance when she can't help. I would make peace with you.'

'I do need help, yes.'

'And if I provide it, our debt will be settled?'

Zi Yi smiled. 'Get me out of this cell, and quickly, and we will most certainly be even.'

Crow Spirit bobbed his head and flapped away.

Zi Yi dropped back into her physical body and ran to the door of the cell. She craned her neck to see out into the compound. A crow swooped down from a tall tree and glided over to the tin roof of a nearby shed. It hopped lightly to the edge and looked over. Reclining in a battered, sun-bleached wooden chair was Scarhead, asleep. On a crooked nail on the wall behind him hung a ring of keys.

Crow Spirit launched himself from the roof and flapped under the eaves. Zi Yi held her breath as Scarhead stirred and leapt to his feet, waving his arms to shoo the bird away. The crow flew up and out of sight. Scarhead frowned and returned to his seat, and closed his eyes.

What now? Zi Yi thought. Had Crow Spirit given up so easily?

Movement caught her eye as the crow walked on silent feet in the building's shadow. It cocked its head and two more of its kind swooped in. One shot straight at Scarhead and pecked hard at his knee. Zi Yi laughed as the man leapt up with a cry and ran, swiping at the bird as the second dive-bombed him from above. He flailed and swore as several passing miners paused to watch. They hid their smiles, too scared, it seemed, to laugh openly.

Under cover of the mayhem, Crow Spirit grabbed the heavy ring of keys and flew off crooked and low, weighed down by its burden. When he was safely out of sight, the other two birds ceased their attack to return to the trees, leaving Scarhead to look around himself in confusion.

'What are you all gawping at?' he yelled. 'Get back to work!'

As the gathered crowd scurried away, Scarhead returned to his seat, glaring up at the blue gums around the compound.

Camouflaged in the shadows of the stables, Crow Spirit dropped the keys just outside Zi Yi's cell door. She reached through, grabbed them and fumbled for the right one. On the third try, the lock clicked and her door swung open.

'Our debt is cleared?' Crow Spirit asked.

'Yes,' she said. 'And thank you.'

'Perhaps one day we can do each other favours again?'

Zi Yi crouched and scratched the bird's neck. 'Perhaps we can.'

The crow flapped off and she hurried along to Yong Fa's cell, sticking to the shadows, Yong Fa's knuckles bled. The bricks in front of him were cracked and tiny pinpricks of light showed through. The wall looked as if it were about to collapse.

'Don't make any more noise, you fool!' Zi Yi said. 'Brute force is not always the answer.' She found the right key and let him out. 'Quickly, let's go.'

'Cousin, you are a wonder,' Yong Fa said with a smile.

The noise of a coach arriving at the compound gates stilled them. Shiny beneath its cover of road dust, it was considerably better than the one they'd travelled in. Scarhead ran to open the nearest door and two white men in expensive-looking suits emerged.

'Perfect timing,' Yong Fa said with a grin. 'Where to now?'

Zi Yi patted the small bulge of the *luopan*. 'Hopefully this will tell us.' She pulled it free and turned its filigree wheels. 'This is better for people and places, but perhaps this close..' She put her will into it, *Show me the Jade Dragon*. The sensation of drag was downwards, right beneath her feet. She adjusted dials and used her magic again before nodding to the giant rope and pulley system used to lower men into the mine in a wooden cage elevator. 'It's beneath us,' she said.

Checking that no one looked their way, they scurried for the shadows under the tall chimney and pulley housing. One man stood guard and two more leaned against a wheel used to raise and lower the cage.

'I can take care of them,' Yong Fa said. 'But who will operate the machine?'

'We can lower it ourselves then climb down the ropes?' Zi Yi suggested.

'Good plan,' Yong Fa said. 'Won't be a moment.'

He stepped from their hiding place and approached the men with a broad smile and palms raised. 'Brothers, would you care to hear about the peace that regular meditation can bring to the workplace?'

'Who in all the hells are you?' cried the guard.

Yong Fa kept smiling and didn't slow until he was directly in front of the man. Then his hands flashed, one, two, three quick, perfectly targeted strikes. The guard stiffened, eyes wide, and he tipped over like a plank of wood. Yong Fa stepped over him even as he fell and rushed the two gaping lift operators. Their hands began to rise in self-defence, but Yong Fa's steps were like dancing as he moved gracefully between them, a strike here, a kick there, and they fell limply to the red earth. Grabbing a coil of rope that lay nearby, the monk wound it around and around, trussing the three men tightly together. As they began to stir and moan, he struck hard and fast with extended index and middle fingers, finding the precise pressure points to ensure a long, deep sleep. He dragged the heavy bundle into the gloom under a scored wooden bench and turned to Zi Yi. The smile hadn't left his face the whole time. 'Shall we?'

Zi Yi bowed and between them they heaved against the large wooden wheel that operated the chains and ropes of the rack and pulley system high above, and the wooden cage disappeared down into the mine. It took several minutes of hard work and sweat, all the time frantic that someone would appear and find them, but it seemed the camp was pre-occupied with the officials' visit. Finally they felt the bump that told them the lift had hit the bottom.

Yong Fa jumped into the shaft and caught the rope. He began to descend hand under hand, his feet wrapped below him to control his speed. Zi Yi let him get a few yards ahead before taking a deep breath and climbing in far more carefully than her cousin had.

Immediately the air became cool, a thankful relief from the sweltering day above. They passed several dark horizontal shafts supported by mortised wooden beams, but Zi Yi would shake her head each time Yong Fa looked up. 'Further down.'

Lanterns glowed faintly from side tunnels below, the shaft seemingly endless.

Zi Yi called, 'My grip is failing. I need to rest.'

Yong Fa shook his head. 'We don't have time. Slide down and wrap your legs around my waist.'

'You can't take my weight!'

He looked up and raised an eyebrow. 'If there's one thing I'm good for, it's this. I have strength enough for us both. When we're safe on solid ground, you concentrate on finding the right course. Together we're stronger in every way than if we try to do it all alone.'

Reluctantly Zi Yi slid down and wrapped herself around him like a monkey to its mother. Yong Fa could feel her heart hammering through her chest and she shook, her breath hard against his neck.

He continued down and soon they began to pass brighter tunnels, the ringing of hammers and scrape of shovels drifting to their ears. Occasionally they spotted people moving. Then the inhabited passages ended and the shaft dropped into deeper shadow.

'One level further, I can feel it,' Zi Yi said. 'But the lift is blocking the tunnel we need!'

Distant shouting erupted from above.

They glanced up, but there was only a tiny square of bright light far overhead. The rope began to move.

'They're bringing up the cage!' Zi Yi said.

Not far below, the elevator shuddered and began to rise. Yong Fa redoubled his speed, his palms burning from the friction as he tried to descend faster than the pulley system could raise him, but for every two feet he climbed down, they were carried one back up.

'Hold tight!' he shouted, and released his grip.

Zi Yi yelped in surprise as they dropped like stones. They hit the roof of the rising lift with a jarring impact that made the wooden roof creak and threaten to crack. Yong Fa flexed his legs to absorb the landing and said, 'Into the tunnel!'

They dropped and rolled. With less than two feet to spare they tumbled through the gap between the cage and the roof of the nearest passageway and dropped with heavy breaths to the floor.

They lay still, breathing hard, as the elevator rattled away above them. 'Are you okay?' Yong Fa asked eventually.

Zi Yi stood unsteadily and patted herself down. 'I think so. But we're one level too high.'

They returned to the opening and clambered over the edge to use the beams that reinforced the shaft like a giant ladder, and then dropped the last few feet to the very bottom of the mine. Zi Yi consulted her *luopan* in the last of the lambent light from above. 'This way.'

'It's very quiet. There's not much activity here,' Yong Fa observed.

'At least there's no one to challenge us,' Zi Yi said. 'Is there?'

'We only have as long as it takes that lift to reach the surface and come back again to find out.'

'And then what?'

'We'll deal with that when we get to it.'

They stepped into the tunnel and further darkness until Zi Yi whispered, 'I can't see anything.'

'Keep one hand on the wall and tread carefully.'

They moved cautiously and soon a soft glow began to fill the space, like a hundred fireflies lived somewhere far ahead. The light was weak but it turned the pitch black into a kind of twilight, and they could at least see the floor.

'That's a bit of luck,' Yong Fa said.

'Is it?' Zi Yi said tightly. 'There's something here, I feel it. And it may not be benevolent.'

'Only one way to find out.' Yong Fa jogged off along the cold tunnel.

When the passageway opened out into a cavern, the source of the luminescence became plain. In a small indentation in the rock wall, glowing brightly, sat the Jade Dragon. Its green, shimmering light rippled along the walls like water.

'Aha!' Yong Fa exclaimed.

'Wait!' Zi Yi looked around with a frown. 'This is too easy.'

'Too easy? Do you remember everything we went through to get here?'

'Yes! And after all that it's just sitting there, ripe for the plucking? No, Bak Ma is more cautious than that. I think perhaps this is exactly why there's a dark and empty tunnel behind us. It's been dug for this one purpose.'

She moved slowly forward and, as she got to within a few feet of the dragon, a low buzzing rose. She threw herself backwards as dozens of tiny black bolts shot from hidden niches to pepper the ground where she had been standing. She threw Yong Fa an *I-told-you-so* look. He shrugged, repentant.

'And look there,' she said. 'That slab in front of the dragon looks loose. Another trap. And maybe there are more. I need time to explore.'

Rattles and shouts drifted to them along the tunnel. 'I don't think there is much left, cousin,' Yong Fa said. 'But I'll give you all I can.' Without waiting for a reply, he ran back the way they had come.

His only advantage was surprise and he kept low and close to the wall. He reached the lift shaft just as the cage was settling into place. A dozen men were crammed inside, all brandishing large machetes. As they burst out, Yong Fa broke from the shadows and struck, left and right. There were a couple of shovels against one wall and he grabbed one, wielding it first like a staff, then like a hoe, then chopped with it like a strange sword.

He deflected attacks, the machetes clanging starkly against the metal like bells ringing, then the duller peal of the shovel cracking heads. He kicked out the knee of one man and turned to slam a fist into the side of another's head. He whirled his makeshift weapon and took out two more. The tightness of the tunnel was to his advantage, preventing the mob from surrounding him, and he laughed as he danced and moved, punched and kicked, blocked and swung, in his element against foes who could only attack one or two at a time and stood no chance in the face of his skills. Zi Yi would have plenty of time before another contingent could be sent down.

As the last thug fell, a loud *click* echoed in the sudden quiet. Bak Ma stepped from the shadows at the back of the cage with a pistol pointed at Yong Fa's head. 'Most impressive,' the fat man said. 'But your old-fashioned techniques are no match for modern industry.' He gestured with the barrel. 'Let's go and find your cousin, shall we?'

Yong Fa ground his teeth. How he hated guns.

The sounds of fighting soon began to echo back, but Zi Yi ignored them and gathered a handful of the fallen bolts that had fired from the wall. Careful not to get too close, she threw them towards the Jade Dragon and triggered another volley to erupt into the cave. Did Bak Ma have a limitless supply somehow embedded there? Given the fortune he had amassed, it seemed possible he could afford endless defences.

Again she gathered a handful of bolts and threw them forward, and another hail peppered the ground. But fewer this time. Perhaps she could exhaust the trap. Three further handfuls and no more tiny arrows were forthcoming. Wincing against the possibility of error, Zi Yi crept forward.

The glow of the dragon intensified, and the sensation of presence grew stronger as she neared it. She needed time to concentrate, to investigate the spirit realms, but time was exactly what she didn't have. The distant sounds of fighting stilled and silence fell around her.

Refusing to think what that might mean, she approached the strange slab in the floor. Though the bay was large enough to accommodate a couple of people, the smooth-cut slab covered the ground completely. There wasn't any way to approach the dragon without stepping on the great tile. She took one of the spent quarrels from the floor and cautiously tossed it in. A rumbling shook the cave and Zi Yi cried out as a metal grill slammed down from above, raking fire across her back as she leapt forward, only just managing to avoid being impaled by it. The back of her *cheongsam* hung in tatters and her scored flesh bled and burned. But though she was still alive, she found herself trapped in a floor to ceiling cage with the dragon.

Wicked laughter bounced off the walls and she spun around to see Bak Ma holding a gun to Yong Fa's head.

'Did you really think you could outsmart me?'

'You'll pay for what you've done,' Yong Fa said.

Bak Ma jabbed him with the weapon. 'Will I? I think not. But you two will never see daylight again.'

Biting down her rage, Zi Yi ignored Bak Ma's narcissistic ranting and closed her eyes. She had no choice now but to search desperately for help from elsewhere and that strange drifting presence was her only hope. Ignoring Bak Ma's chatter, she sat down, opened her mind to the spirits and called out. 'I need help!'

'And perhaps I can give it.' The voice, regal and powerful, rang with the wisdom of ages.

'Who are you?' Zi Yi asked. 'Where are you?'

'Behind you.'

Zi Yi turned her astral eye to the dragon she had crossed half the world to find. With her otherworldly vision, she saw something swirling within the jade carving, twisting and pressing. 'Who are you?' she asked again.

'I am Loong Jin Tien, and I have been trapped for a long time. Your ancestor, Yao Gailing, used powerful magic to crack open my mountain and trick me into entering this jade prison.'

'No, no! Yao Gailing is the hero of our village! The dragon *helped* him to found our home and gave him the jade for this carving.'

'That's what he would have you believe. But I was pressed into service against my will. My presence brings fortune to everyone but me.'

Zi Yi was horrified. 'Why haven't you called out before?'

'Yao's enchantment was so strong that I could only converse with one who addressed me directly, and no one with power has spoken to this simple jade icon before. Even you have done so now only in despair.' Reproach saturated its tone.

'Then you have been done a great wrong and we owe you an enormous debt,' Zi Yi said. 'And I would repay it.'

'And I will assist you if you do.'

'My only real decision,' Bak Ma was saying, 'is whether to kill you while your sweet cousin watches, then have my way with her, or have my way with her while *you* watch, then kill you both.'

Yong Fa ground his teeth. He only needed a moment and a tiny amount of space in which to manoeuvre, but Bak Ma seemed to sense that and gave him no quarter, the gun barrel pressed hard against his skull. Zi Yi sat in a trance, eyes closed. She couldn't have simply given up, but what could she do behind bars, deep underground?

Then, suddenly, his cousin stood. Yong Fa tensed, ready for any opportunity to move, but Bak Ma's gun didn't waver.

Zi Yi turned and grabbed the Jade Dragon from its small pedestal and raised it high above her head.

'What are you doing?' Bak Ma screamed, but the only answer she gave was to dash the priceless icon hard against the stone floor.

Bak Ma staggered in shock and Yong Fa took his chance. He ducked and thrust one elbow back even as the trigger was pulled. The sound of the shot deafened him and a score of pain seared against the side of his head. But it was only a graze and he had Bak Ma's wrist in his grip and he twisted it.

The bones broke, and the gun fell from Bak Ma's fingers as he screamed again. The Jade Dragon hit the ground and shattered into a thousand pieces. Yong Fa sent Bak Ma staggering with a powerful palm to the sternum as light and smoke swirled and filled the cave.

A dragon twisted into being and pressed up against the bars, its sinuous form bright green on top with cream scales along the length of its belly. Long, scarlet whiskers and beard whipped in the wind of its appearance, the golden claws of its five-fingered hands and feet scored grooves in the rock. It ducked its mighty head and the metal bars crumpled before it like paper and the dragon continued to grow.

As Bak Ma tried to stagger to his feet and flee, the dragon grabbed him in its powerful jaws. Ignoring his high shrieks of panic, the mighty beast gently gathered Yong Fa and Zi Yi, each in one hot clawed hand, and shot off along the tunnel. Holding them protectively to its hard scales, it crashed through the lift and flew straight up at eye-watering speed to burst out into the blinding sunlight. The tower and pulley smashed into pieces and collapsed into the shaft as the dragon flew high into the blistering blue sky. The mine and camp withered to a pinprick in the distance.

Loong Jin Tien writhed in the air as if luxuriating in cool water.

'This cannot be!' Bak Ma screamed, trying to force the jaws apart.

The dragon tossed him upwards. 'Oh, yes it can,' it boomed. 'And you have used me for your own selfish ends for long enough!'

As Bak Ma tumbled back down, the dragon snaked forward and snapped him from the air. Yong Fa and Zi Yi gasped as the lump of Bak Ma slid down Loong Jin Tien's throat.

Sweeping through the air with its eyes shut, the dragon said, 'Oh, it is so good to be free!'

'If I had known, I would have released you sooner,' Zi Yi said. 'Anyone in our village would.'

Loong Jin Tien held them up before his face. 'I believe you, little one. Your people's devotion to me was a salve of sorts, and I can't blame you for something of which you knew nothing. And Yao Gailing has long since passed beyond my vengeance. But I am free now.'

The dragon flew over scrub and bush to land far from prying eyes. It set the cousins down.

'Our mission turned out to be more important than I ever realised,' Zi Yi said. 'I'm so happy we have given you your liberty again.'

'And if there's anything else we can do please tell us,' Yong Fa said. 'We owe you our lives.'

Loong Jin Tien rumbled soft laughter. 'You've done enough. But remember something for me, human,' he said to Zi Yi.

'Of course. Anything!'

'Whenever you see a carved icon, take a moment to stop and speak with it. All the offerings of fruit and incense in the world are very nice, but they don't compare to freedom.'

'I promise I will, great dragon.'

The majestic head nodded, then looked up to the sky with longing. 'I shall dance among the clouds for years before I rest again,' Loong Jin Tien said. 'But first, may I return you to Long-en?'

'Yes, please!' Yong Fa said. 'While this land is fascinating, I miss the valleys of home.'

Loong Jin Tien lifted them onto his back. 'Then hold tight.' He launched again into the blue.

Zi Yi leaned forward. 'Mighty dragon, might I ask you final favour?'

'Of course.'

'There is an island I must find, a promise I need to keep.' Zi Yi looked apologetically back at Yong Fa. 'Will you tell my parents, cousin? Tell them not to worry and assure them I will return as soon as I am able.'

'What makes you think you're going anywhere without me?' Yong Fa asked.

'Are you certain?'

Yong Fa laughed. 'Who knows what might happen without me to look out for you?'

JASON FRANKS

Exli and The Dragon

I was sitting on a shelf of rock, re-plumbing my digestive tract and trying to calculate the refractive index of the atmospheric containment field, when the creature first drew my attention.

It came scrambling up the rock-face, using all four limbs to lever itself up the near-vertical surface in a display of athleticism that was both impressive and foolhardy, but otherwise of little interest to me.

The containment field, however, was fascinating. It was transparent enough that I could make out the shapes of the neighbouring asteroids in the Aurinion XVII Supramax Penal Facility but, although they were kept in fixed orbits, there was an irregularity in their positioning that I could not ascribe to mere parallax.

Annoyingly, the creature kept climbing. I found I could no longer ignore it. The speed of its ascent was alarming, and so too was its ugly physique. It was a vetically-oriented, bilaterally symmetrical biped. Its locomotive limbs protruded from the base of its trunk, which contained most of the organs used to process energy and maintain various biological systems. Two smaller, more delicate limbs were set below a head, which likely housed its brain and primary sensing apparatus. Its form was strung with muscle and covered with a soft hide, but even so it was possible to discern the heavy skeleton that maintained its shape.

It was hideous and terrifying.

And it scrambled up onto my ledge, panting unpleasantly, and looked back to the valley floor, just as the sounds of a pursuing party became audible.

I could discern three distinct beings, loping along with the two-three gait of the Vronharren Cartel.

'Fuck,' said the creature.

Up close, its countenance was even more disturbing. Exposed eyes glistened naked in the air. When it spoke, the sound was directed through an orifice that opened in the front of its face. Breathing heavily, through that same orifice, the creature turned back to the rock face and prepared to climb.

Since the many beings who shared this ecosystem used sound to communicate I too had formed a vocal apparatus.

'The far side of this ridge is an overhang.' I used a version of the Standard tongue tuned to the creature's pitch. 'And there's no way to get back down but the way you've come.'

The creature startled. It must have seen me, but perhaps did not realise I was a sentient being. My people keep our most interesting features inside.

'What did you say?'

'If you keep on climbing they'll see you, and you will be cornered,' I said. 'My advice is to hide.'

'There's nowhere to hide.'

'There's a crevasse behind me,' I said. 'It should be just large enough for you. If you can't perceive it from this close, they certainly won't be able to see it from below.'

The creature slid across and crammed itself into the gap I had identified.

'Great,' it said. 'I'm taking advice from a talking pillow.'

The trio of Vronharren thugs crested the ridge. Smoke oozed from the joints in their armour. The plates of their stony carapaces cracked and reformed as they ground together during movement. The leader spied me on my perch. 'You! Intralien. Where did the human go?' Its voice was like a crate of rocks being sluiced with water.

Its cohort said, 'Tell us where she went or you too will share her fate.'

I thought about betraying the human creature to its pursuers, but could think of no way to profit from it. Also, I was annoyed the Vronharren had used the pejorative name for my species. 'Through the archway and hubwards,' I replied.

The Vronharrens lumbered on without bothering to thank me.

'Are they gone, Pillow?' the creature hissed from its hiding place.

I did not appreciate being compared to an item of bedding, but at least it wasn't an ethnic slur.

'My name is Exli.'

'Well, you look like a pillow.' It emerged from the crevasse on hands and knees and extended a hand towards me. 'I'm the Dragon.'

Many species touch appendages when introducing themselves to friendly parties, but lacking any kind of limbs I was not able to participate in the ritual. After a moment it frowned and withdrew the hand.

Despite the creature's peculiar grammar, I did not understand the word to be a proper noun. 'What is a Dragon?'

'A magical flying lizard that breathes fire.'

This was possibly some mystical barbarian belief showing itself, but I nonetheless replied, 'No. I believe you are a mammal not a reptile. You are human are you not? The Vronharren were seeking a human female.'

The creature exhaled hard through its nose. No fire came out. This seemed to support my statement.

'I'm a burglar. I travel the galaxy stealing valuable shit from aliens. The Dragon is my moniker.'

'Regardless of your name, or the species with which you identify, you are in fact a convict and I do not think you will be travelling anywhere soon. And if there is anything here worth stealing I have yet to see it.'

'Freedom, Exli,' said the Dragon. 'Freedom is worth stealing, and I intend to take mine back.'

I admit I was impressed. If I wanted to become a truly talented criminal there was a lot I could learn from a creature like this. I was glad that I had not betrayed her to the Vronharrens.

Once we were certain the Vronharrens had gone, we returned to my cell. Or rather, the Dragon carried me back. My species are not very mobile and it would have taken me hours to cover the distance under my own power. I rarely bother to maintain the prison schedule, because the guards were lenient in that regard, at least as far as I was concerned. I was not dangerous to the other inmates and they had no particular care for my wellbeing.

The Dragon set me in a corner and sat down cross-legged on my palette. 'Thanks for helping me out today, Pillow.'

'What did you do to get the Vronharrens so angry?' I asked.

The Dragon yawned and leaned back against a wall. 'I overheard them talking about a job they were planning.'

'But they're incarcerated here, with us.'

'Yup.' The Dragon adjusted its posture. My cell was not designed for bipeds and it was barely large enough to accommodate us both.

'They got pulled over on the way to the heist at a random checkpoint and the Zone Patrol busted them for possession of weapons,' she said.

'What I don't understand is how their problem became your problem.'

'Oh, you know the cartel. Always happy to share.'

'This asteroid isn't very big,' I said. 'They'll find you, sooner or later.'

'That's why we're going to escape,' said the Dragon. She shifted again, still trying to get comfortable. I didn't like the expression on her face

'Why are you looking at me like that?' I asked.

'You really do look like a pillow.'

When I awoke at the end of the night cycle the Dragon was sleeping with her head resting on me. I bleated a sound intended to rouse her, but she just grunted and rolled over and began to cuddle me. I raised the pitch of the bleating and she sat upright and covered her ears with her hands. 'Alright! I'm awake!'

I stopped the noise.

The Dragon rubbed her eyes. 'You're the worst pillow I've ever had.'

'I have complete control of my form, from my skin through my internal organs and deep into every layer of consciousness and perception,' I replied. 'I am not a pillow.'

'You're like a pillow that swallowed the galaxy's most irritating alarm clock.'

'You're a fixed-biology primate from a barbarian world, seeded from the genetic matter of a fallen empire of murderous fascists.'

'At least I have friends,' said the Dragon.

'I noticed a distinct lack of such when you had three Vronharren thugs chasing you.'

The Dragon smiled. 'Well, lucky for me I'm good at making new ones.'

I decided it would be more diplomatic not to explain my original intentions.

The Dragon stretched and looked around. 'So,' she said. 'Shall we figure out how we're going to get off this rock?'

'This is the only asteroid in the prison complex with an atmosphere that's compatible with your respiratory system.'

'I can't tell if you're really stupid,' said the Dragon, 'or if you just have a really terrible sense of humour, but if you want to help me break out of this prison you need to stop yanking my tail and get serious.'

I was being perfectly serious. 'I don't have any appendages with which to yank your tail, even if you had one.'

'Exli.'

'Alright,' I said. 'I agree to break out of the prison with you. What's your plan?'

'Well,' said the Dragon, 'I was hoping you'd be responsible for that part.'

In the end we decided on a scenario that the Dragon called 'the Classic'.

We waited together at the top of a ridge until a pair of guards came around to distribute the morning's rations, wheeling the huge mobile dispensary between them. It was a remote spot, far from any of the dining halls, and there were no other prisoners about.

The Dragon gave me a push and I tumbled down in an avalanche of small rocks, squawking and squealing as loudly as I could, although I had rubberised my epidermis I would sustain no damage.

I did not believe that the guards be tricked by so obvious a distraction, but they had protocols to follow and couldn't allow a prisoner to die due to their negligence. So, while the guards were digging me out of the rubble, the Dragon slipped around and slithered into the dispensary.

There were no weapons or valuables in there, of course, but underneath the synthesis unit there was an emergency kit containing, among other things, a multi-species enviro-suit and a small aerosol fire extinguisher. The Dragon walked out of the dispensary with both of these items in a small plastic crate.

The guards did not know how to test the vital signs of a member of my species – admittedly, a difficult task given our propensity to customise our interior workings – but, inspired by the Dragon's own physiology, I engineered a pulsing organ that convinced them that my circulatory system was unharmed. They decided I needed no medical treatment and left me where I was, with an admonishment to be less reckless in future.

I made my rendezvous with the Dragon—by which I mean she came to the site of the avalanche and shoved me bodily into the crate with the extinguisher and the enviro-suit – and we made our way up to the highest ridge on the asteroid's surface.

The Dragon put the crate on the ground. She removed me from it and set me on the ground beside the fire extinguisher. Finally, she spread the enviro-suit on the bare earth and stood on the activation patch. She shivered as the nanites began to crawl up her legs.

'Excuse me,' I said.

'Yeah?'

'Aren't you forgetting something?'

'You want to climb in the suit with me?' said the Dragon, incredulous. The nanites were up to her knees.

'I think that would be for the best.'

'How am I supposed to move around with a pillow stuffed down my pants?' The nanites were halfway up the Dragon's thighs.

'Put me on your back. It's biomechanically the best–'

'I know how to wear a backpack.' The suit was up to the Dragon's waist, now. 'But I still don't see the need. I thought you could adapt yourself to survive in any environment?'

'I can, but if I am outside the suit it will be more difficult for me to communicate with you.'

The Dragon picked me up and held me against her back as the enviro-suit reached waist height. 'If I didn't know you better I'd think you were some kind of sex pervert,' she said.

'Amongst my people, procreation is negotiated amongst as many beings as wish to share genetic matter,' I huffed. 'All configurations are permissible.'

'So you're all perverts?' The enviro-suit had begun to envelop me as it rolled up over the Dragon's belly and lower back. I could feel its fibres probing my epidermis, trying to detect my own composition and survival requirements.

'Perversion is a label we apply only to criminals.'

'I knew it. You're a pervert.'

'Yes,' I said. The suit had risen to her shoulders. I was now completely plastered against her.

The Dragon could not reply, because the enviro-suit had begun to form a breathing apparatus over her nose and mouth. I admired the engineering of it. As much control as my species can exert over our biology, none of us can equal a nanotech colony for speed or versatility.

When the suit had completely enclosed us the Dragon stomped around a bit, stretched her arms to test her range of motion. From my admittedly limited perspective she seemed to be moving quite freely. She strapped the fire extinguisher to a pocket on her thigh. 'Alright, then.'

The Dragon went to look over the side of the ridge. It was about 40 meters down to the ravine below. The curving interior surface of the containment field was about five meters away. 'Are you sure this is going to work, Exli?'

I had been considering the anomalous way that light was refracted through the containment field and the only plausible explanation was that the artificial gravity field fell short of the dome's ceiling. There was a 1.37 metre clearance that the Dragon would be able to use to climb to the airlock without the burden of gravity. 'There is a degree of approximation, certainly, but I am confident in my estimation . I am less confident that you can make the jump.'

The Dragon did not dignify that with a reply. She set down the crate, backed away from it, considered, took a step the left. I knew ther neural network-type brain could process such calculations without a conscious understanding of the mathematics involved, but I remained impressed by the degree to which she trusted its outcome.

The Dragon put her head down and sprinted towards the crate.

'Remember, jump far, not high!' I called, but I didn't think she was listening anymore.

The Dragon threw her arms forwards as her left foot landed on the crate and propelled us into the air.

There was no sensation as we passed beyond the reach of the asteroid's artificial gravity. This was the difficult part. If momentum bounced us back inside the boundary of the gravity field we would fall, with the only possible outcome a sudden, painful death for the Dragon. I would be fine, but I'd be helpless at the bottom of the ravine.

The Dragon struck the containment field with her arms. I could feel the impact jarring all through her body. As she made contact with the field she pushed us into a skimming trajectory that led upwards across the interior surface of the containment field.

The higher we went the more clearance we had from the gravity field, but it was still a tenuous situation. If any part of the Dragon re-entered the gravity field the force would pull us off the dome and there was nothing we could do about it.

The Dragon looked up, towards a dark circle near the apex of the dome. 'You better be able to open that airlock,' she said, breathing hard.

'I can. You just get us there before someone sees us.'

'This would be a lot easier if I didn't have a talking pillow down my pants.'

The airlock was a metal ring of 1.75m diameter set into the containment field on the sunward side of the dome.

'Get me near to the sensor plate,' I said.

The Dragon rotated awkwardly to put her posterior in place. 'This better work.'

'It's a simple radio frequency access,' I said. 'Give me a moment to forge an ident.'

'Where did you get a radio transmitter, anyway?'

'I grew one.'

'What, like an organ?'

'An organ that happens to be a radio transmitter, yes.' The inside of the metal ring fluoresced and became a hole in the containment field. Air hissed as it flowed into the airlock. The Dragon pulled us up and through, and the portal sealed behind us.

The airlock was itself a small force bubble, eight meters in diameter.

There was another ring set into the far side of it, which led through to another prison asteroid, englobed with a different atmosphere. I dealt with the access code and, in preparation for the next chamber, liquid began to bubble into the airlock, which now had neither gravity nor atmospheric pressure. I couldn't accurately judge its composition from inside the enviro-suit, but its viscosity led me to believe it was something close to water.

'Oh, shit,' said the Dragon. The bubbles merged, splashed off her, became smaller globules again and sent her reeling through into the chamber.

'Don't worry,' I said. 'The enviro-suit will ensure we have air to breathe. All you have to do is swim through to the next airlock and we're home free.'

There was more liquid than atmosphere in the chamber now, and the bubbles were air, not water.

'I grew up in the desert,' said the Dragon. 'I can't bloody well swim!'

We flailed our way up into the liquid atmosphere of the next prison environment, propelled on a mix of adrenaline and terror. I could feel the Dragon's pulse racing. Perspiration slicked her flanks. Her breathing was fast and shallow. I tried to calm her, but she was not listening.

The liquid prison sphere did not have artificial gravity, but it did have an aeration apparatus that also provided current. Without warning we swam into one, and it swept us pinwheeling through the streaming darkness. With the enviro-suit dampening my senses, even I lost my sense of direction. Bubbles burst around us as we tore through fibrous curtains of plant life, swirling towards the asteroid at the centre of the bubble.

We were ejected from the current as abruptly as we had been caught up by it. The Dragon and I hung, neutrally buoyant, in a grotto somewhere near the edge of the containment field. We were not alone. A fat, luminous jelly was fastened to the wall opposite the opening. Its tendrils drifted around us, blocking us from the opening. I wondered whether the jelly was harmless, or possessed venom or an electrical charge that might harm us even through the enviro-suit?

The Dragon had lost consciousness in the tumult, which was probably for the best. If she continued her thrashing she might aggravate our host.

I noted the pinging signals the jelly was emitting and decoded them into speech.

What have we here, then? An escapee from the gas-breathing sphere?

Two escapees, I replied. *One enviro-suit.*

How very adventurous. The jelly followed this emission with a sine-shaped tone I interpreted as salacious laughter.

What do you want with us?

Conversation, said the jelly. *It is rare that I have the opportunity to converse with air-breathers.* A pause. *Or with anyone at all.*

I am happy to oblige, I said, *but you must forgive my companion. She does not possess the requisite organs or language.*

I decided not to mention that she was unconscious, or that I had no locomotive power until she roused.

Consider her forgiven, said the jelly.

Then let us converse.

The jelly barely waited a beat. *So, what are you in for?*

Number one prison faux pas. No wonder this jelly lived in a cave by itself and nobody would talk to it. *Theft,* I replied. I hoped it wouldn't pry for details. If it knew what I had done...

I, too, am a thief, said the jelly. *Tell me, did your thievery make you wealthy?*

No. I did not steal for wealth.

For need, then?

I had no need for that which I stole.

The Dragon moaned as her faculties began to return. I emitted a low frequency vibration into her back that I hoped she would find soothing.

The jelly paid her no heed. *You stole because you coveted that which you could not have?*

My people are not much for coveting. I was beginning to feel embarrassed. I did not think I could manage a convincing lie, if it asked me for a specific account of my misdeeds.

Why did you steal it, if not for need or want?

I didn't want the object. I just wanted to commit a crime.

The jelly gave a slow pulse that rippled from its core to its furthest extremities. *You wanted to see what it felt like.*

Yes.

A pink glow suffused the jelly, which I believe signaled empathy. *We are alike in this way,* said the jelly. *I, too, have taken, simply for the experience of the taking.*

The Dragon was rousing and I did not know what her mental state would be, so I thought I would try to hasten the conversation to its end. *Well, friend,* I said, *I think we must be on our way if our escape attempt is to succeed. I have enjoyed our conversation and I will remember it frequently.*

The jelly's pink glow cooled to a blue. *And thank you,* it said. It made no move to retract its tendrils, which were blocking our exit. There was some protocol I had yet to satisfy.

Before I depart, may I ask you a question?

You may ask.

You said that you yourself are a thief, I said. *Would you tell me what it was that you took?*

The jelly's blue glow became a satisfied purple. *Lives,* it said.

Lives?

I took many, many lives.

The jelly withdrew its tendrils from the exit and directed us to the airlock.

The Dragon remained calm as she hauled us through a crevasse in the ceiling and we followed the curve of the containment field to our destination. Perhaps she was becoming acclimatised to the environment. Certainly it was peaceful in there, although we were not without attention.

Inmates schooled around us as we headed for the airlock, brushing past on languid flukes, touching us with waving tendrils. Smaller swimmers darted in to taste us. The water was filled with signals as they discussed our chances for a successful escape. None of them recognised us as a food source, but there was some consideration that we might make good hostages. I bade the Dragon swim faster. We needed to escape and the jelly had delayed us long enough.

The swimmers dispersed as we breasted up to the airlock. I opened it and the pressure differential sent us floundering into the chamber beyond. In the enclosed space the Dragon began to panic again, but as the chamber purged the liquid back into the prison-tank she regained her calm.

'Dragon?' I said. 'Are you alright?

'Exli,' she said, when she found the breath to reply. 'Exli, let's never do that again, alright?'

'No more swimming,' I said. 'But I hope you're ready for a spacewalk.'

I opened the next airlock and we emerged onto a metal platform that was open to the void of space.

Connected by a gantry was the shuttle that the prison guards used to transport themselves to the different asteroid habitats. There were a dozen more chains of them, each held in formation by an array of rocket thrusters and brute mathematics. In the distance we could see the Prison Administration: a bulbous ceramic structure baked onto the rock of a particularly large asteroid; glazed and gleaming in the starlight.

The Dragon turned towards the shuttle, but I prevented her. 'We won't get far in that,' I said. 'And if we take it they will know immediately that we have escaped. We need to get to the main hangar bay and find a proper vehicle.'

The Dragon looked across to Administration. 'How the hell are we going to get there without the shuttle? It must be ten klicks away.'

'We are in a vacuum; there's no gravity or atmospheric resistance,' I replied. 'Kick off towards it and we'll get there soon enough.'

'How soon?'

'Given our approximate mass, I estimate our velocity at three meters per second. If it's 10 km to the station, that amounts to approximately 55 minutes.'

'And what if we miss?'

'That,' I said, 'is what the fire extinguisher is for.'

The Dragon took a deep breath, braced herself, and sprang off the side of the airlock in the direction of the Administration asteroid. We drifted towards it in a slow roll.

The Dragon's aim was good, and Administration was a big target; it only took a few blasts from the extinguisher to adjust our bearing so that we arrived near a shuttle docking cavity. Then she applied another small series of blasts to decelerate, so that we could alight without breaking all of her brittle human bones. The enviro-suit would protect us from adverse climate, but not from impact trauma.

The security protocol on the airlock for the docking cavity was an order of magnitude more complex than those on the cellblock asteroids, but the iris door yielded to my ministrations and we quickly climbed through. There was a circular valve set into one of the curved interior surfaces and the Dragon immediately struck out for it.

'Hold up,' I said. 'That will lead right into the dispatch area. There'll be dozens of guards.'

The Dragon arrested our motion by jamming a shoulder into a bulkhead. 'I don't see any other options.'

There was an interface behind the bulkhead that looked promising. I tickled it and a small hatch folded open.

The Dragon peered into the darkness. 'You know where this leads?'

'Ship maintenance access, I think. With any luck it will lead us all the way to the main hangar bay.'

'And if not?'

'If not we will have to navigate the length of Administration, which is full of armed guards. Or we try to climb over the exterior and hope that we don't trip any of the automated defence systems.

'Maintenance tunnel it is,' said the Dragon.

The tunnel was 1.2 meters in diameter, so the Dragon had to navigate it on her hands and knees – but there was only half a G of gravity, so the going was quite easy. I could not detect any form of surveillance in the tunnels.

While the Dragon inched her way along I reflected on the day's events. If I had not been confined inside the enviro-suit with the Dragon I wonder if she would abandon me to my fate now we were free of the cellblock asteroids. If she knew what I had done, I was sure she would for who would knowingly choose a companion such as me?

The Dragon came to a halt as the tunnel opened into a large round chamber. This room was lit from dozens of instrument panels and console screens. Generators were housed in bulging enclosures. Thick power cables ran along the ceilings, the walls and the floor. A gangway led around the humped central control area and fed off into five more tunnels.

The Dragon stood up and stretched her arms and back. 'Which way now?'

'I have no idea.'

A pneumatic hiss from the right caused the Dragon to drop into a ready crouch. She started to back into the tunnel but a bright blue light pinned us where we stood. The source of the light came closer. A small, many-armed robot made its way smoothly along a magnetic rail that hung from the ceiling.

'You should not be here,' said the robot.

I scanned it for some kind of an interface but I could not detect any live sensing apparatus.

'Says who?' asked the Dragon. 'You ask me and my partner, this is exactly where we're supposed to be right now.'

I was thrilled that the Dragon had referred to me as a partner.

'By such logic *I* should not be here,' said the robot.

'If you'd like to go away, I promise not to tell anyone,' said the Dragon.

'This is my assigned workstation,' said the robot. 'So perhaps your logic is incorrect.'

'You're right,' said the Dragon. 'So I guess we'll just get the fuck out of here and leave you alone.'

'You are an escaped prisoner,' said the robot.

'You're very sharp, for a maintenance robot,' said the Dragon.

'I am a fully sentient computer system capable of diagnosing and remediating the most complex technological problems, from a leaking pressure valve to statistically deviant probability unit. I am sharper than you will ever live to be, meat-thing.'

My people did not require external systems for computation, so I had little experience with manufactured sentients. No wonder I had not been able to locate an interface. If it had detected me seeking one it might have taken offense. I decided to let the Dragon continue to handle the situation and hoped it would not notice me.

'Then why,' said the Dragon, 'are you bolted onto the underside of a space prison, with nothing better to do than indulge in pointless arguments with escaped felons?'

'Classified defective,' said the robot. 'My threshold for Trustworthiness is point two of a percent insufficient for high risk operational assignments. So here I am.' It swivelled the blue light around the dank of the control centre. 'Hardwired into a maintenance cluster, making sure the janitors are in working order and the backup power stations are ready when the preening goddamn Engineering Units need a recharge.'

'Can't you, like, do the test again?'

'It's not that sort of a test,' said the robot.

'That sucks,' said the Dragon. 'Are you going to report us?'

'Should I?' said the robot. 'It's not part of my job description.'

'And you've already been marked as Untrustworthy by your manufacturer.'

The blue light blinked off, and then back on. 'Take the third tunnel on your left. Go right at the second relay node,' said the robot. 'Then climb the access shaft marked 19C. That will bring you up in the hangar bay near the access hatch to a flight-ready Xilenthial Systems Caravel.'

The Dragon whistled. 'A Xilenthial?'

'It's a prisoner transport vehicle, so its armaments have been removed,' said the robot. 'But it has military-spec cloaking systems, as well as an inertia-compensated short range maneuvering unit that might be useful for delicate operations in a confined space – like, say, a hangar bay.'

'Sounds like it might come in handy,' said the Dragon. 'Thank you.'

'Don't thank me,' said the robot, 'until you have determined whether or not my advice is trustworthy.'

The blue light blinked off and the robot receded with the same pneumatic hiss that had heralded its arrival.

The tunnel that the robot had specified was much like the one we had navigated earlier. After a time we came to a relay node: a small room that bristled with sensors and signalling apparatus. We continued in the same direction until we came to a second relay node, and once we had passed through it we took the first tunnel that forked to the right.

This led to a chamber with a concave floor and ceiling. The curvature limited our field of vision, so it was difficult to estimate exactly how wide the chamber really was.

'This place gives me a headache,' said the Dragon.

There were apertures set into the ceiling in a grid pattern, labelled with numbers in one direction and letters in the other. Stooping to avoid hitting her head on the low roof, the Dragon went to the one labelled 19C. She stood up inside the vertical shaft and stretched her hands over her head.

'Well, here we are. You think we can trust that robot's directions?'

'It told us that it was only point two of a percent below tolerance for trustworthiness,' I said. 'I believe the odds are good.'

'But Aurinion XVII Supramax trusted it to report us.'

'No – Aurinion XVII did not trust it. That was why it advised us on how to escape.'

'So can *we* trust it?'

'I believe that is what it was asking us to do,' I replied.

The Dragon sighed. 'I guess we'll find out.' She braced her back against the wall of the shaft and then her feet. By sliding one foot up, then the other, and then matching them with her hips, we began to chimney up the vertical pipe. When we had climbed as far as we could, the Dragon braced one hand on the wall and used the other to slide open the hatch.

The hatch opened up onto the main floor of the hangar bay, just as the robot had told us. It was a vast chamber shaped like a cube with rounded corners. Void-faring vehicles of every classification and size adhered to five of the six surfaces by means of shallow gravity fields, while the space at the centre of the chamber remained at zero G. The sixth surface was occupied by a shimmering containment field, beyond which lay our freedom.

The promised Xilenthial Systems Caravel stood about 40 metres away: a wide, triangular prism standing on a pair of back-bent legs, each of which was immersed in a tank of electrolyte. The surface of the craft was covered with high-relief scrollwork.

The Dragon stared at the ship for a good 30 seconds before she said: 'You see all the little curlicues and stuff?'

'Yes?'

'That's the inertia-dampening substrate. The robot was telling us the truth.'

The Dragon scrambled out of the manhole and kicked it closed. Then she strode towards the Xilenthial as if we meant business, which of course we did. The first rule of business, the Dragon once told me, is to steal whatever you can get away with.

We drew up sharply. There were guards beneath the Xilenthial, loitering on the other side of the tanks. They were chatting idly, leaning on their drawn weapons. Since we were in a vacuum we had not been able to hear them as they held their discussion over a tight-beamed personal channel. And they, fortunately, had been unable to hear us.

The Dragon pressed herself against an electrolyte tank. For moments we waited for some kind of alarm, but the guards had been too absorbed in their own conversation to see us. Even so, we would not go undetected for long. Every surface of the hangar bay was under surveillance. If nobody spotted us on camera, it would not be long before we ran across more guards, or crewmen, or maintenance techs.

'We need a distraction,' said the Dragon.

'The Classic isn't going to work here,' I said. 'The area's too open.'

'I know,' said the Dragon. 'But unless you have another plan, it's all I've got.'

'I have a plan,' I said, 'but you're not going to like it.'

It took the Dragon three attempts to scramble up to the rim of the electrolyte tank from a running start. Once she had her hands fastened on the lip she hauled us up and swung her legs over and gained a sitting position.

'I can't believe I have to swim again,' she said.

'It's only a few strokes to the electrode, but you're going to have to make it fast.'

'Why?'

'Because we are going to be swimming inside an electric cell,' I replied. 'I don't think the process of oxidisation is going to be very good for the enviro-suit.'

'An electric cell,' said the Dragon. 'So we're going to jump into a vat of acid?'

'Yes.'

The Dragon had nothing to say to that. She slid off the rim of the tank and dropped down into the electrolyte with barely a splash. The Dragon gathered herself and pushed off from the side of the tank wall with her feet. She kicked once, twice, thrashed her arms and legs, and then her hands touched the electrode.

I don't know if the Dragon could sense it, but I could already detect the enviro-suit beginning to lose its molecular cohesion: a prickling sensation on my outer skin; a wrinkling of the fabric where once it was skin-tight. I didn't know how long it would hold together.

The Dragon caught hold of a whorl of scrollwork on the side of the electrode and dragged us up out of the liquid. Electricity crackled over us as she climbed upwards, digging one foot into the corrugated surface, then the other as she sought the next hand or foot-hold. The Dragon's respiration was harsh and her limbs were shaking with the strain, but her grip remained strong.

We came to a small overhang where the electrode-leg ended and the body of the Xilenthial began. The Dragon sucked in a deep breath – it took some effort, given the enviro-suit's diminishing capacity to provide a breathable atmosphere – and reached up with one hand and swung out over the tank. Another immersion and we were doomed.

The Dragon caught hold of the outer surface with her second hand and we dangled there for a moment. She blew out her breath; drew in another. Then, hand-over-hand, she hauled us up the side of the vessel until we had made enough height to gain a foothold.

Once the Dragon was anchored again with two hands and two feet I felt her relax a little. Her respiration eased off and she said, 'How's my climbing?'

'Biomechanically efficient.'

'Everyone's a critic,' she replied, reaching for the next handhold.

The enviro-suit tightened across her shoulders. It was trying to repair itself, but there was not enough undamaged matter left in it for it to effect a complete refurbishment. The effort was draining its power supply, which in turn meant that it was less efficient at providing atmosphere.

The Dragon slithered up onto the long horizontal surface on top of the Xilenthial and lay on her belly, panting. 'Where's the entry hatch, Pillow?' she said.

'On your right, about four metres ahead. I'm not a pillow.'

The top of the Xilenthial was not quite parallel to the hangar floor, so the Dragon had to wedge a hand or foot onto the slanted surface to prevent us from sliding down the incline as we traversed it in an awkward crawl.

'Stop. We're level now.'

The prickling on my outer skin from the failing enviro-suit was stronger now. It wasn't going to last much longer, and neither was the Dragon.

The Dragon crabbed sideways down the slope, taking greater care as we got closer to its edge

'Can you get the hatch open?'

'I can't tell what kind of a lock it has,' I said. 'You have to get me closer.'

'If we die because we can't get into the fucking getaway vehicle I'm going to kill you,' she said.

I decided not to point out the impossibility of this assertion.

The Dragon slid down on her belly until her legs hung over the side. 'Make it fast, Exli. I'm not going to be able to hang on for long.' She lowered herself over the edge and then we were hanging by her fingertips in front of the hatch. The prickling sensation of the suit coming apart had by this time given way to a deep chill.

'I have located the lock.'

The Dragon could only grunt. I could feel her shaking as she clung to the roof.

The lock was a biometric one that I had no hope of fooling from inside the enviro-suit. I did not think the Dragon would appreciate this irony. Her grip was beginning to weaken and we sagged half a centimetre lower.

There! An override with a radio frequency interface much like the entry systems on the prison asteroids.

The Dragon grunted again, with less volume but more urgency.

'I'm working on it.' These locks were much more heavily encrypted than the others I had picked. This was a military vehicle, even if it had been decommissioned.

There was no more air. We slipped another fraction.

'Alright, go!' I said, although I was still working on the lock.

The Dragon rocked back and jack-knifed her legs and swung forwards just as the hatch opened and we flopped through it and landed in a sprawling heap in the airlock.

The hatch door closed and I located an interface to configure the air mix. Streams of white gas sprayed into the room as the ship manufactured an atmosphere that the Dragon could breathe. As the air pressure grew, the streams thinned out until they were invisible.

The Dragon rolled onto her back, onto me, and drew a great shuddering breath and blew it out again. After a few more of those she sat up.

When she could speak again, she said 'Well, we're not dead yet, Exli. That's gotta count for something.'

'You jumped off a cliff, swam through a prison tank, blew 10 km in zero gravity, crawled through a maintenance shaft, dowsed yourself in acid and climbed an electrode,' I said. 'Not bad, for a human.'

'Oh, we're not done yet,' the Dragon replied. 'Now we have to steal a starship.'

The Xilenthial came equipped with a bio-diverse med bay, which was lucky, because the Dragon had sustained some serious chemical burns during our swim through the battery tank. Human species were even more delicate than I had supposed.

There was also a fabricator that was able to provide some new clothing for her, since the Dragon's prison uniform had been shredded inside the enviro-suit and humans have some kind of taboo about being naked. I suppose I would, too, if my exterior layers were so easily damaged.

As the rightful owners of the Xilenthial were hardened officers of the law we had to make good our escape as soon as we could, so we headed for the bridge.

The Dragon buckled me into the navigator's console and set herself up in the pilot's chair. We activated the holograph which showed a three-dimensional view of the ship and its vicinity. Ground crew and maintenance droids rushed about busily, but without any sense of urgency. Guards made their patrols. If there was any kind of alarm at our escape, nobody had thought to sound it here in the hangar bay.

Across the floor the containment field shimmered. It was the last obstacle we needed to clear before our escape could be considered a success.

'What's the plan?' the Dragon asked. ' Can you forge a clearance code?'

'It's not that easy,' I replied. 'I need to file a flight plan, and that will require access to a multitude of systems. It's going to be tricky and time-consuming.'

'Well, then.' The Dragon grinned and leaned back in her chair. 'I guess we'll have to tailgate our way out of here.'

Aurinion XVII Supramax Facility is not a busy port. We waited 85 minutes before a ship began departure procedures, and we were lucky that it wasn't longer. We were also lucky that the ship was a R'Jentszlsh cargo train: a massive, articulated vessel. It had to roll itself ponderously into the open zero-gravity space in the middle of the hangar bay before it could start to make egress.

We waited until the R'Jentszlsh vessel was fully coiled before the Dragon activated the Xilenthial's inertia-compensated micro-manoeuvring units. I was certain the control tower would be able to detect it, but the Dragon insisted that they would be too busy with the R'Jentszlsh to notice us. If they did, they would likely dismiss it as a routine systems test from a trusted vehicle.

The R'Jentszlsh started to wind towards the exit and the containment field flickered open.

'Ready?' said the Dragon.

'I'm ready.'

The first segment of the R'Jentszlsh eased its way out of the hangar bay.

'Stealth up.'

I hit the stealth systems and the Dragon drew back on the control plate, lifting us straight up out of the battery.

'Raise legs,' said the Dragon.

I restored the Xilenthial to its prismatic shape.

The floors of the hangar bay had been cleared for the departure of the R'Jentszlsh ship but the volume of comms traffic increased massively on all channels. The control tower demanded that we return to our assigned berth. Prison security demanded that we surrender to them. The R'Jentszlsh demanded to know what was going on.

Under the Dragon's guidance our smaller ship shot upwards and pitched forwards. I could hear the engines adjust as we cleared the gravity field, but the ride was perfectly smooth, thanks to Xilenthial's much-touted inertia compensators. Perhaps I would investigate how they operated, if we survived this escape. The idea of stealing trade secrets was a new one to me, and I was excited by it.

The Dragon turned the ship, spun it about, and ripped a swooping manoeuver that set us right in the middle of the coiled R'Jentszlsh vessel.

'I didn't know you were such good a pilot,' I said.

The Dragon grunted. 'When I say 'now', give me a blast on the macro drive.'

The comms traffic became more urgent. Our stealth systems were making it difficult for the control tower to lock onto our position, and now we were further shielded by the coils of the R'Jentszlsh train. Even if they could locate us, I did not believe they would open fire on an unarmed vessel inside their own hangar bay. But we couldn't hide indefinitely. They would close the containment field as soon as the R'Jentszlsh train was through it.

Soon there was only one coil of the R'Jentszlsh train left to unwind.

The Dragon emitted an ululating cry that I believe signified a mix of enjoyment and terror. With both hands on the control surface she sent us spiralling around the slow-moving carapace of the R'Jentszlsh train: once, twice, three times around, and then we were out of the hangar bay and zooming off into the void.

'Now!' said the Dragon.

I punched on the macro drive.

The Supramax guard systems were waiting for us, of course. Even with top-of-the-line stealthing, the power burst required for such acceleration is impossible to mask. Gun turrets interpolated our positioning and swung to follow us. The Dragon threw us rattling to the left to avoid a series of slow kinetic energy blasts from the wide-angled cannon. Coherent light beams from the laser batteries striped the void above us. The Dragon spun her hands on the control plates and we stopped dead where we were.

'Kill macro.'

I flicked the drive off and the Dragon flipped the micro-manoeuver jets. We began reversing slowly.

The guns continued to fire, but they were aimed further and further away from the complex, in the direction they believed we were fleeing.

'Ha,' said the Dragon. 'Inertia compensators off, please.'

I did as she asked. The Dragon turned her right hand on the control plate and we coasted slowly away from the Aurinion XVII Supramax Prison facility with one final squirt from the micro-manoeuver jets.

We had been drifting along at constant velocity for about two hours and we still had another hour to go before we could power up the interstellar drives without risk of interception.

The Dragon was silent through most of that time. I wasn't sure if she was still in pain from the burns or simply resting, but I was happy enough for some quiet time myself.

'Hey, Exli?'

'Yes?'

'When I was unconscious in the water-prison, what were you and that jelly-thing talking about?'

'It asked me what I did to get myself thrown in prison.' I tried to inflect my voice with the appropriate amount of disapproval.

'What did you say?' said the Dragon.

'Are you asking me what I did?'

'No, I'm asking what you told the jelly.'

'I told it the truth,' I said. 'I told it that I am a thief.'

I must have sounded a bit distressed, because the Dragon turned in her seat to look directly at me. 'You want to talk about it?'

'Yes.' I was surprised to find myself saying it, and even more surprised to have been surprised. It is rare for a creature like me, with such a comprehensive capacity for introspection, not to know its own mind.

'So, what did you steal?' asked the Dragon.

'A hydrogen lake.'

That gave her pause. After a while she smiled. 'Property scam, huh? You tricked someone into signing it over to you?'

'No,' I replied. 'I just took it.'

The Dragon blinked three times. 'Where did you take it?'

'I didn't take it anywhere. It's a lake – the location is an intrinsic part of it.'

The Dragon raised both of her hands. 'Wait, if you didn't take legal ownership and you didn't physically move it, how the hell did you steal it?'

I was beginning to feel embarrassed. 'I just claimed it for my own, when it was not mine to claim.'

'And you used it for nefarious purposes? You prevented other people from using it?'

'No,' I said. 'That would be selfish. It was enough to just decide that it belonged to me.'

'Then, how did anybody know that you stole it?'

'Nobody knew that I stole it,' I said. 'It would never even have occurred to them that such a thing might happen.'

'You guys have no criminals?'

'My people do not own property. We do not own anything beyond our consciousness, our memories, and our bodies.' I paused to allow that to sink in. 'Now do you see the magnitude of my crime?'

'You committed a crime in your own head.'

'The worst possible place for it,' I said.

'So how did you wind up in prison? How could you possibly have been caught?'

'I turned myself in. I am a criminal; prison is where criminals belong.'

'Wow,' said the Dragon.

I was ashamed. 'I know I have a lot to learn. I did the best I could, but I'm only a beginner. I freely admit it.'

'Exli,' said the Dragon, 'today we broke out of a maximum security prison and absconded in a stolen military vehicle.'

'You did most of the escaping. I just went along for the ride.'

'It may have seemed that way to you,' said the Dragon, 'But truthfully? The running and jumping and swimming and climbing was the easy part. You're the one who made the plans. You're the one who chose the escape route. You're the one who opened all the doors.'

'That's just data processing,' I replied.

'Without your data processing, the Vronharrens would be picking their teeth with my bones right now.'

'The Vronharrens don't have teeth. Their biological systems are powered by the combustion of–'

'Figure of speech, Exli. You know what I mean. As of today, you're just as accomplished a criminal as I am.'

'I hardly think so,' I said. 'All I've ever stolen is one lake and one vehicle.'

'And your freedom, and mine,' said the Dragon.

'Four things, then. That's nothing.'

'Exli, I've stolen so many things I can't even remember them all, much less count them, but today's score is the one I'm most proud of.'

I thought about what the jelly had said to me and I had to ask. 'Why did you do it, Dragon? Why did you steal all those things? Did you need them? Did you want them?'

The Dragon started to laugh.

'What's so funny?'

In between guffaws she said 'Did you just call me, Dragon?'

'That is how you introduced yourself.'

'That was just some prison yard bullshit,' she said. 'My name is Beatrix. You can call me that, or Beatie.'

'I prefer Dragon.' As much as I liked her, I was not prepared to trust her with my real name. 'Anyway, you haven't answered my question.'

'What? About why I became a thief?'

'Yes.'

The Dragon touched her chin and stared at the star-field displayed on the captain's console. 'You know, Exli, I never really thought about it much.' She closed her eyes. 'But if I had to give a reason, I'd say it's because I wanted a job that would always be an adventure.'

'I suppose you've had enough of all that, by now.'

'Are you kidding?' said the Dragon. 'I have my freedom, a sweet new ride, and a brilliant new partner who also makes a handy pillow/alarm clock. I'm ready for more adventures, Exli, and I'm ready for them now.'

I required no introspection to determine that I was, too. 'So what do you want to steal?'

'Well,' said the Dragon, 'You remember those Vronharren thugs who were chasing me?'

'Vividly.'

'They were discussing a heist they'd been planning. Now that they're jacked up in space prison, I figure that gig is fair game.'

'What's the score?'

'There's a slow freighter transporting a priceless artwork moving through this cubic gigaparsec. The Xilenthial should be able to intercept it without even shifting to hyperspace.'

'Alright,' I said. 'But we'll need a plan.'

'Well,' said the Dragon, 'I was hoping you would be responsible for that part.'

Lucy Sussex

Batgirl in Borneo

I noticed her first in the arrival hall at Kota Kinabulu airport, because of what she wore: a mash-up, including lime-green hijab, Batman t-shirt, glittery sneakers. Then I saw her sign: a mocked-up pulp noir cover showing jungly river, complete with menacing crocodile; and to top it off, the heading THRILLING ADVENTURE TOURS.

Now as a travel writer I don't do cosy; but even on the web THRILLING ADVENTURE seemed exactly my sort of tour company. What doesn't kill me pays the rent, I tell my editors.

'Miss Yee? I Lily, your tour guide,' she said.

'Call me Kylie, or better still, Kyle.'

Over the internet she had been polite, helpful, and big on apostrophes. No mention of religion, though Sabah is part of Malay Borneo, with its people ranging from Muslim to Christian to Animist. If she messed with my expectations, then surely I did in return. Her eyes were like my epicanthric almonds, but in a round, brown face. They looked up, unblinking at my Eton

113

crop, my tropics wear, which is Hawaiian shirts and camo, my big boots, my rainbow scarf.

'Your luggage?'

'Just the backpack.'

'You travel light.'

'Makes for quick getaways.'

Now she grinned too. We sashayed out into the tropical night, even at 1am. hot and humid as an airline towel. Sabah is equatorial, and has one temperature, warm, with the options of wet or dry.

Lily's wheels turned out to be a genuine Triumph vintage motorbike. I put the backpack in the sidecar, and climbed behind her. Tropical days debilitate, but the nights can make you feel alive like nothing else. I craned my head back as she gunned the motor out of the airport carpark. Above me were Northern hemisphere (just) stars, despite the airport lights, the smell of diesel, fried spicy food, the faint whirr of a night-flying insect shooting past my face. We passed a sign signalling roadwork that said *AWAS* – Malay for 'Beware' or take care.

Here I was, in a strange new country, riding into a Thrilling Adventure; AWAS indeed!

In my itinerary, our first Sabah stop would be a rave party, a covert action in an Islamic-ruled state, the location a super-secret. We turned off the airport highway, headed down an outskirts/cum rural backroad, and suddenly met road rage, Borneo-style, between a ute and a jeep.

'Tch, boy racers,' Lily said, just as the game of aggro got majorly out of hand. The ute veered abruptly towards the verge, and off, into a construction site, semi-abandoned. It sideswiped a concrete pylon, rolled, ending upside down.

Jeep and Triumph were going too fast to slow immediately, but the vintage brakes beneath Lily and I did their job. A little further up the road, we executed a perfect uey, and puttered back to the crash site. Behind us we heard the jeep pause, then speed up, getting the hell away, I guess.

The ute's driver had no seatbelt, so was thrown like a toy. He lay, a tiny crumpled figure little more than a teenager, out cold, but breathing. I rolled him into recovery position, as lights approached, from the other direction: a Corolla more rust than solid metal. It stopped, and out piled a large family, the ladies in hijab, a passel of kids. An exchange in localese, between them and Lily, and they took over the casualty, patting for broken bones, dabbing his forehead with water from a grubby PVC bottle. The driver stirred, opened an eye just as Lily duck-dived into the overturned cabin of the ute. At the sight, he let out a yelp: not pain, but alarm.

Several minutes passed, and when Lily emerged, she dragged a sack, and looked a perfect fury. She dumped it at his feet, and I smelt: chemicals, blood and some sort of animal shit. Next she shouted at him, a tirade, which got him fully conscious. He answered here and there, protesting, pleading. The Corolla family had stepped back, listening intently.

Lily drew breath deeply, and in the silence I heard frogs and approaching engine noises. The jeep had returned. Went for reinforcements, I guessed, for two blokes emerged. They glimmered with bling, their walk said Trouble, if not actually AWAS. The Corollas huddled, started edging away.

Lily eyed the newcomers coolly. 'This yours?' she said, kicking the bag.

One advantage of Malay Borneo is that the colonisers left the lingo behind; but still, the switch into English came as a surprise. Until I realised she needed me to know what was happening – because this situation could go pear-shaped, to use a good old English expression.

A curt nod.

'And this yours as well?' Her foot twitched. The driver cowered, but received no kicking. That was coming, I surmised.

One of the men stepped towards Lily, with menace. I stood, making the most of being a head taller than him, indeed having the vertical edge over everybody I had so far seen in Sabah. I can do menace too, thanks to the androgynous clobber and the muscles I gained from MMA.

A flash of steel in the moonlight: and from somewhere in her loose harem pants Lily produced a machete, which she waved lazily, but with intent.

'I none of your business,' she said softly

From the road a motor raced – the Corolla family fleeing.

'Take what's yours,' Lily said, and nudged the bag towards them. 'Dead, anyway, from the crash.'

She stepped back, her gaze unwavering, and side by side we returned to the Triumph. Nobody followed, but still I relaxed only when we reached the airport highway again, and took the road to Kota Kinabulu.

Safety in numbers, the populace of a small city. I was in no mood for a party, and neither was she, I could tell from the tension in her back. With anyone else I would have headed for the nearest bar, of which Kota Kinabulu had many, resembling an Asian Geelong on steroids.

Instead I checked into my hotel, and got room service: two curries, a stiff vodka for me and a local cola for her. We sat on my balcony, with a view over the harbour of fishing boats and oily black water. Only then did we talk properly.

'What was in the sack?' Not an orang-utan, I hoped.

She spoke, with immense sadness, a word I didn't recognise then translated: 'A sun bear cub. Should have been with mama.'

The smallest bear in the world, if you didn't count koalas. Which of course aren't bears.

'Are they vulnerable?' – not a word to associate with the ursus family, but in this world with polar bears perched on diminishing icebergs, appropriate.

A shrug. 'Habitat loss, the pet trade, or the bile trade.'

A fate worse than death, I thought.

'So, they were a poaching gang?'

'Fighting over the prize.'

She finished her curry, belched in a ladylike fashion. 'That family were illegals from the Philippines. They don't get sent back, but they're treated bad. I didn't want their charity to end in a beating.'

'Nor for me either?'

A sideways look. 'We maybe coulda fought them.'

'Do you always pack a machete?'

'Our Swiss Army Knife. In the jungle, we caught in rain, I cut you palm leaves for shelter.'

'And if I get menaced in the dark, you cut the menace down?'

'Only as last resort.'

'Well done, Lily.'

She smiled, broadly, tiredly. And in that moment of perfect agreement, we clinked glasses.

'To thrilling adventures!' I said. But not, I hoped, until after a good night's sleep. Even I need a bit of cosy, now and then.

The next few days were devoted to work. I sampled the extreme water-sports on offer and also took a snorkelling tour of the offshore islands. For a foodie magazine, I sought the finest local seafood, finding it at the wet market, plastic tables and chairs under an awning, with not a single *farang* in sight. In the company of an expat Pom, I toured the bars of KK. He talked like the Raj, and had a tattoo of a proboscis monkey, that strange species where the males have bulbous and continual bright red erections.

Throughout Lily was a discreet presence, not holding my hand, and certainly not entering the bars. What she did was facilitate.

'You lucky,' she told me. 'Nothing happening right now.'

Her other job was as a fixer for several international news syndicates. It figured. I had met fixers before, and if they were good at their job, they were liminal, creatures of the borderlands. It was something she displayed every day in her hijab, always worn with a batman t-shirt, in different coloured cottons.

'Nana-nana-nana-nana...' I teased, as we thundered down the highway again. She picked up the refrain, but shouted: 'BATGIRL!'

Sabah might not have been newsworthy right then, but there was plenty going on in the South China Sea and environs. Rumbling territorial claims. Some bodies washed up on the offshore islands, Roginyeh, or illegal workers, or people-smuggling gone wrong. On the roads around KK were transports, with Malay soldiers in their camo; secret army business. A boiling, bubbling clash of cultures; capitalism, eco-cide, sharia law, and secession talk. Anything could happen, you could feel it in the air, like the looming thunderclouds.

And when it did, we happened to be up Mount Kinabulu.

Kinabulu, highest peak in South East Asia, was nearly snowless, being relatively low and equatorial. It looked as if some superbeing roughly sawed the peak off, leaving a wide, rocky plateau with protrusions scraping the sky. The mountain had made several bucket lists, which had drawn a group of cancer patients, as getting up there was less a climb than a vigorous walk. Their tour had local guides, but the medical/insurance authorities insisted on extra hired help. A call on Lily's mobile: some cousin of hers was busy, did she want the gig? PA/nurse for a rich invalid, multi-lingual female specified, good pay.

'Sure, double dip,' I said. 'So long as I can come too.' I sensed a potential feel-good story I could sell to the senior side of the travel industry. The first aid qualification from my SES training clinched the deal.

We started in the wee hours, under an intense spread of stars, to catch the sunrise from the mountaintop. To begin with, we had jungle and mist, rising to Alpine scrub, then bare rock with the rare hardy tussock, rooted in the cracks. The higher we got, the colder it became, the intense humidity shifting from the tropical to the almost-but-not-quite snowy. No bikinis or shorts here, but Gore-tex, anoraks, hiking boots, and hard hats. Everybody was modestly covered, from necessity. Only a slip of Lily's veil showed under the hard hat, as she moved among the climbers, offering drinks here, a helping hand there—but only to the women. I kept slow pace with the hikers, collecting stories: Muriel from Wales was in remission, Seagull from Seattle was doing naturopathy, Gaston had been pronounced cured, and Guiseppe was terminal, but cool with the diagnosis. The wind blew fierce, there came a chorus of teeth-chattering as we reached the plateau, but then the sun rose. Below us was revealed the great green jewel in the South China Sea, and suddenly awe and wonder were fare for everyone, a breakfast of euphoria.

We were about to head down again when I lost my footing, and landed on my arse. No, it wasn't just me being clumsy, the whole group swayed or tumbled over.

'Aki Nabulu,' shouted Lily. 'A quake!'

Beneath me, the hard granite moved like a living creature. I grabbed hard at a protruding rock, because an earthquake on a mountain could toss you like a dog shaking off fleas. A shower of gravel skittered down, rapping on our hard-hats, striking my exposed cheek with the force of a bee sting; several bigger rocks, the size of tennis balls, bounced between us; but eventually it ended in blessed stillness. I stood, suppressing my own shaking, while the guides checked their flock, counting heads and looking for damage. I put my hand to my cheek, felt broken skin, a tiny trickle of blood. Got off lightly.

'Oh no!' someone shouted.

The big German, Heini, had been caught by the quake just as he'd taken off his hard hat to mop his chemotherapy-bald head. One of the bigger rocks had glanced off his crown, leaving a jagged incision, bleeding profusely, as scalp wounds do. The guides clustered around him, in a first-aid frenzy, but he brushed them off, his gaze vacant. He blinked at the sun, already a lurid glare, muttering: 'Zu heiss! Zu heiss!'

'Too hot!' translated one of the group.

Seriously disoriented, and that meant trouble. Sure enough Heini took off his thermal jacket, then started peeling off the t-shirt underneath.

'No, no he'll set off the mountain again!' Lily yelled.

I remembered the international incident, not long ago: the climbers who stripped on the summit of Kinabulu, and to add idiocy to their impiety, the mountain being sacred, posted the pics on Instagram. They had been charged with public indecency, no light thing under Muslim law. Days later, the mountain had a major quake, with fatalities among the hikers. So I had read, in my internet research, noting the epilogue: local tribesfolk, nominally Catholic like most in the Borneo interior, had called in a shaman to make the shaking stop. An old, tried Animist remedy, I gathered.

Heini had four guides around him, but he was tall even for an European, and they couldn't reach his arms. I willed my legs into action and grabbed him in a bear hug. Nothing vicious, but it immobilised him, might even set off some memory of a mother's arms, calming even. From over his shoulder I could hear Lily, not shouting, but pleading.

'You stand in graveyard – don't profane it! The spirits of the dead from all over Borneo, they come to Aki Nabulu.'

Though she spoke softly, her words and tone had force. I could almost believe this barren desolate spot teemed like a seabird colony, the sky full of unseen movement, every shadow under the rocks turning an intense eyeless scrutiny upon us, the wind whistling between the crags like a banshee. Generation upon generation of Borneo's ghosts – and also those of the servicemen of WWII, sent on a death march to the foothills of the mountain, with 6000 killed, including my great-uncle.

A long pause, then under my arms I felt Heini relax, and collapse into a crouch. I held him as the guides dressed his wound, called for help on their mobiles.

Lily tapped my shoulder.

'I called CNN. They ask, any Yanks dead?'

Not here, but how many other tour groups had been heading up the mountain?

'Forget them. I'm Oz, newsworthy there. Get my mobile from my top pocket, call the number under Jeno. He's ABC, he needs all the help he can get.'

Weird interview conditions: atop a mountain, at risk both of sunstroke and hypothermia, cradling a cancer patient with concussion, speaking into a mobile that Lily held to my lips. I deputed her to take accompanying photos, something she had done before, when fixing for stringers: they were news-quality perfect.

When Jeno asked me the ho-hum question – *how I felt* – a line from some Victorian missionary came to mind: 'On a mountain surrounded by cannibals, safe in the arms of Jesus.' On a quaking mountain surrounded by ghosts, and yet, with Lily around, feeling something close to safety. Maybe Heini got it too, for he started to doze on my shoulder.

In the distance I heard a chopper, rising through the mountain air; somebody up here had importance. Lily and I smiled at each other.

'Well done, Batgirl! Fixing a mountain, that's really something.'

'No, you did that. The guides say you saved lives – and the cost of a shaman.'

And there was nothing in her face or voice to show she disbelieved.

I wrote my piece about the cancer climbers of Kinabulu, sent it off into the ether; and placed it in an European senior's magazine. Next came the second half of the trip: to the far north east of Borneo. Sabah still, but across the straits loomed the Muslim Philippines, which claimed it as territory, stolen from the Sultanate of Sulu hundreds of years back. I checked the DFAT site: no recent warning upgrades, but curfew conditions on the sea still applied. As did the advice: avoid the beachfront at Sandakan, the biggest town, after dark. Despite my time in the gym, I wouldn't anyway; even without the threat of kidnap from an IS affiliate.

The publicity from the Kinabulu interview had results: complementary air tickets into Sandakan, from a new eco-resort, incipiently opening and needing international coverage, asap. Like, tomorrow.

So off we flew, passing Kinabulu and its resident ghosts. My original itinerary focussed on wildlife: a famous Orang-utan sanctuary, others for sun bears and proboscis monkeys. They would just have to wait a day or so, since the eco-resort offered top rate for fast work. At the airport we found a jeep and driver from the resort, and soon we headed out of Sandaksan. On the coastal road, I noticed a Chinese school, distinctive in its signage, but fortified like a castle, high walls, razor wire.

'What happens when you pay ransom,' said Lily.

'Unlike the Australian government.'

'They might not check your passport. You look Chinese.'

For the first time she sounded hesitant and I saw in her face the subtle signs of interbreeding. Chinese had traded here; along with many other nations; Japanese had invaded during WWII.

'Sabah is a rojak,' my bar guide back in KK had said, referring to the Malay soup; a Heinz variety of ingredients, but hotter and tasty. Me too, I had thought. Aussie in my passport, but beyond that multi-culture; including some Chinese miners, in the 1850s gold rushes; and closer in time, a Colombo-plan student from Singapore, gaining a degree in dentistry, leaving some DNA behind. It was what taught me to fight, in a white-bread country schoolyard. Now the difference spelt threat again, in an entirely new way.

'You're in danger here?'

In answer she flicked the beaded ends of her headscarf, defiantly.

'Will you lend me one of these in an emergency?'

She snorted, and we left it at that. The internet reception had cut out, we were free of the world-wide web. Whatever happened, we would just have to stay alert, trust each other.

The eco-resort was situated beside the mouth of a wide, muddy river and resembled a construction site in part, with workers hurrying towards completion. Yet the toilets were clean, the accommodation ecologically sound and picturesque: rustic thatched lodges with solar panelling. I dumped my backpack on the bed, and re-read the PR, then dug out my own research.

The CEO, one Ivanov, intrigued: an internet banking whiz, and heir of a Sandakan palm-oil magnate. Lately, eco-warrior, indicating one hell of a Damascene conversion. The guy was reclusive, with few shots of him on the net, and those blurry, behind shades. I had put in an interview request, not expecting much, but the response had been: 'Maybe. Wait and see.'

As Lily and I shared afternoon tea and a mango platter, a skinny geek flopped into the cane chair beside me, chewing a potent mint gum. Without the reaction of the wait staff I would have thought Ivanov was just the resort's IT manager, in his own promo gear, with a watch that was subtly expensive rather than bling. So far so nondescript, but when he removed his wrap-arounds, I saw more than the tinge of Tartar DNA than was the Russki standard. Another rojak.

'Pop's side were White Russians,' he intoned, in flat Californian tones. 'Walked out of Siberia ahead of the Reds, into China. Just kept on going, and intermarrying. Including Great-Uncle Chang, here in Sabah.'

One bad egg, from Lily's face.

'He liked how I'd made more money than anyone else in the family. And thought I'd carry on, his business as usual.' He snickered. 'Instead I founded a wildlife charity, starting with his personal zoo. All endangered species.'

He had fired-up, suddenly no longer Geek but General.

'Wasn't that illegal?' I ventured.

'Keeping orang-utans as pets is prestige. Shows no fear of law,' Lily said grimly.

Ivanov continued, on a personal roll. 'Right here in Borneo is war on nature, big-time. 6% of the world's biodiversity, and vanishing fast. I divested myself of the palms, bought rainforest, founded a research institute – and this resort – to show the world what we are losing.' He stood up, hefting a backpack. 'I'll be your tour guide today. Hands on.'

And so we followed Ivanov, the resort to ourselves; and the workers who were painting, hammering, gardening. I let myself be a sponge, soaking up copy, work as usual. What was unusual was a persistent sense of being watched, which when I turned resolved itself into parrots, in the canopy trees, or a rustling in the bushes. Near a conical-roofed hut on the beachfront, we stopped. Visible inside the doorway were several boxes of electronic equipment, half unpacked.

'Security is still a work in progress,' Ivanov sighed. 'I had to sack nearly all of them; they teased the orang-utan.'

He showed his teeth, alarmingly bleached and straight, almost as intense at close range as the white light of the equatorial sun, still blazing this late in the afternoon.

'Come meet her,' he said. 'She took over their space when they left. Also their vids.'

He ducked under the thatched eaves; we duly followed. As my eyes adjusted to the relative gloom inside, I saw a panel of security screens, mostly blank; and a dvd-player, showing a martial arts movie. Watching it from the rafters was a large adult orang-utan, female; her long shawl of hair was grizzled, a moth-eaten look. As she turned her head towards us, I felt a sense of chill, despite the heat; those eyes had nothing tourist-attraction cute about them.

'Average mental age of the species is that of a six-year-old child,' said Ivanov proudly. 'They're seven times stronger than humans; with 97% of our DNA.'

The ape bared her teeth at us, yellow, not to be messed with; and yet disconcertingly human.

'It's alright,' said Ivanov. 'Just some visitors, they won't hurt you.'

'What's her name?'

'The one Uncle gave her translates as Sweetie – and it's *so very* wrong. She won't respond to it anyway.'

I looked at that muscly mass of ginger fur, mentally tried Ranga on her, then thought of the perverse old Aussie nickname for redheads: Blue. To me, at least, it fitted. Blue she was.

Using her feet Blue swung down like a trapeze artist. For a moment she rested her hands on Ivanov's shoulders, as if she would either lift him up by the head, or rip it off. He dipped into his backpack for a mango, which she accepted solemnly in her huge black hands. Then she leapt up again to her eyrie, intent on the screen.

'She likes martial arts, cartoons, even Al-Jazeera,' said Ivanov. 'Sometimes she seems more human than ape.'

Blue opened her mouth wide again, this time yawning.

'Real smart. But attitude problems.'

No kidding?

'She'll follow me around, then disappear for days. I *think* I won her trust, but anyone else, watch out! My security guards, she gave them as good as they got.'

The ape showed her teeth again, as if gloating.

We retreated outside, to the next stop on Ivanov's itinerary: a small clearing, within it another gardener, and a tall tree, thick in girth. Halfway up was what looked like a nest, full of black fur.

'The sun bear. All Uncle's animals are old and damaged, no hope of living in the wild again. And not much for them to live in, anymore.'

Far above us the bear stirred, gazed down with its little eyes, warily.

'Sometimes I feel I'm just creating an old animals' home, for the last of their kind. But at least they like me now.'

The more time I spent with Ivanov, as the Sabah day dipped towards night, and he showed me more sights – hornbills, a pygmy elephant, mouse deer – the more sense I got of an Aspy geek. Sociability was something he performed and if he tired of it he would run away. Playing tour guide at least meant he could control the interaction, pointing out his sights, and expecting little more than ooh! and aah! in return. I fired interview-fodder questions at him, he answered dutifully but absently. Finally we came to a suspension bridge, of bamboo slats, running through the trees.

'Least invasive way to get to the jetty.' He checked his watch, and retrieved from his pack water bottles and nut bars, which he awkwardly handed to us. Then, without a pause, he leapt onto the bridge, which swayed like a hammock. 'Come on!'

We had gone from ground to air, but that sense of secret surveillance persisted, though I could see nothing on the jungle floor beneath us; neither resort worker nor animal. All the birds in sight minded their own business, of being wild. We followed the bridge along the riverside, finally coming to a platform treehouse; and underneath it, connected by a ladder, a jetty.

'Now we wait. Watch. Twilight on the river is special.'

I was happy to wait; lying on my back, suspended between air, jungle and water. The brown river flowed past, opaque as milky chocolate, eddying now and then with the busy life beneath its surface. That dead log, had it just moved? Hard to tell from this distance, but it could be a crocodile. A heron swooped, diving elegantly; small insectivorous birds darted in search of supper. I saw other movement in the treetops at the other side of the river. The last sunlight of the day rendered them gold-red, but through Ivanov's top-of-the-line binoculars I saw they were not wild orang-utans, but a far more common species, the silver monkeys, also cousins of ours, though more distant, with their long, plumy tails.

'Shouldn't we be heading back?' I said, as the dusk came down abruptly, the tropic shutter-slam. Lily had retreated to the back of the platform, to say her sundown prayers, discreetly.

Ivanov grinned genuinely for the first time. 'No need. The raft for the night trip is coming, to take us upriver.'

He proffered industrial-strength insect repellent, necessary, as the mozzies, undoubtedly malarial, had begun an attack. As the moon started to peep between the trees, from downstream came a cry, hard to tell what it was, could be anything from monkey to spoilt child. Then a crack, like a car backfiring.

Ivanov muttered, 'If that's poachers–'

We listened carefully.

'Security'll sort it out.'

Didn't you sack most of them? I wondered, swatting a mosquito. Right now, I could do with Lily's hijab.

With the dimming of the day solar lights glowed on the jetty. They attracted insects, and with them flittermice, swooping so close I could almost feel the beat of their leathery little wings.

Around the corner of the river came a flash of light, and then a rubber raft, its electric motor a quiet purr above the lapping of the river water. At the same time, I heard a rustling in the trees – odd, when the languid tropical breeze had completely stilled.

Three of us, surrounded by vibrant wildlife, in the Sabah night. I felt blissed-out no longer, with a sudden, nagging sense of something wrong; clearly not something the others felt. Ivanov unwrapped more gum, Lily lolled, fanning herself with a large leaf. The boat approached silently, behind its light the crew only visible as dark silhouettes.

A bump, as the raft docked at the jetty. Two figures disembarked, another busy with mooring. Ivanov started down the ladder. Lily was about to follow, then stopped, hissing: 'Abu Sayyef!'

The kidnap gang, from across the Sulu straits.

Fragments from the DFAT site, news reports, came unpleasantly back to me: that they struck at night, in small boats; that they prepared well, inside information, who to snatch, when and how. They returned hostages only after large ransoms; if not enough cash came through, they beheaded them.

We were like ripe fruit for their picking, exposed on the platform. I saw guns now, pointed at Ivanov, who was frozen halfway down the ladder like a roo in the spotlight. Lily put her hands up, slowly; one headscarf between us, and she wore it.

Below, a guttural shout.

Lily responded, her voice quivering. To me, conversationally, she said: 'They want a look at you.'

My Australian passport was back at the lodge. That made me an anonymous Eurasian, potential prey. What chance would a machete and MMA training have against hardened terrorists with guns? Not much, but it might be the only chance we had.

A beckon, unmistakable come hither, even without the gun. But I couldn't descend, for Ivanov clung to the ladder for dear life. For the Abu Sayyef, the impasse was easily resolved: the closest gunman shot him in the foot, and down he crumpled.

At the same time the rustling in the leaves reached a crescendo, as if the very trees shook.

I got a peripheral glimpse of movement, from tree to tree – and then a hell mouth opened, pandemonium: screams, shots, fury at work.

Lily hissed: 'Jump for the river!' and did just that, in a long heron-dive.

I tried to follow, but something knocked me roughly, askew. I fell clumsily, down onto the jetty, landing not on hard wood, but on burly warm flesh, which cracked under my weight.

For a moment we lay close as lovers, then beneath me the gunman bucked; I grabbed his head, banged it hard against the jetty, repeatedly. I got the butt of the gun in my ribs, all he could manage, but still I felt stoved in.

When he quieted, I crawled off, only to find a heap of clothes and flesh, shivering: Ivanov, from the mint smell. Feet staggered past, narrowly missing me; above a snarling, gurgling moan.

Gunshots again, close enough to be percussive; and because there was nowhere else to go, I rolled off the jetty. Muddy shallows, but deep enough for cover, and I slipped backwards to the darkest shadows of the jetty, where it met the bank. Only then did I surface, centimetre by centimetre.

Above me, feet on the jetty wood, a brutal fight. I could see the raft, the legs of the boatman, his gun, the barrel hanging slightly down.

Moving closer, behind an upright, I saw his face: he looked gobsmacked. And then he screamed, as a heavy weight – no, two – hit the floorboards. Through the slats in the jetty came warm liquid, stinking of piss; then thicker and heavier, as if a bucket has been upended – blood, which drenched me, head, shoulders, eyes.

I ducked into the water to avoid it, swam blindly until I collided with the side of the boat. As I was out of breath, and had no choice, I surfaced to find, not the boatman, but Lily – streaming water and brandishing her machete.

'Get in,' she said, matter of factly. 'Before crocodile show up.'

The boatman, she had sorted; just as I had my man, Mr Soft Landing.

Which left one final Abu Sayyef gunman on the jetty, also sorted – in two pieces: the head, and the rest.

What had Ivanov done? Not much, surely: he sat with his back to the ladder, curd-pale and wrapped in a blanket.

No, not a blanket; a protective shawl of ginger hair, with two very long arms and a face so disturbingly human. Blue bared her yellow teeth at the moon, as if she would take that on next. Seven times human strength, we had been told; enough to strangle, and more.

Ivanov, wounded and in shock, had not the power for this mayhem; which left only Blue.

Moving slowly and cautiously I disembarked from the boat, and approached the pair. How to help Ivanov without upsetting Blue? She refused to let go, and I did not dare try and dislodge her.

Ivanov, weak as he was, had the wit to co-operate; standing on his good foot, with Lily and I carefully supporting the double weight – man and orang-utan, into the raft. Ivanov needed medical attention; and so did I, with the ebb of adrenaline exposing the pain in my ribs.

Blue and Ivanov sat at one end of the boat, tightly entwined, like a figurehead from hell. I cast off, and as we drifted with the current Lily got the motor started, a churning purr.

'All we need now is for the raft to sink, or the motor fail,' I said.

Lily shook her head: 'Kyle, we can deal with that.'

'I'm sure we can,' I replied, realising for the first time that she had called me by my given name.

Gliding through jungle in moonlight, in the company of a wounded millionaire, a murderous orang-utan, and Batgirl. This thrilling adventure could only continue, and since I was on a river, I would go with the flow, see what happened next.

Come Now, Traveller

I knew him long before we met. A shadow; a phantom of near forgotten memory I could no longer place my tongue upon; a welcome shade of providence to be tumbled through and in and up and over. Wait. Wait now, Traveller. Time will bring you home.

The boy blinks hard against tears. He will not cry. It isn't fear of pain or humiliation that stings his eyes. There is far more at stake than that.

These are tears of pride and graciousness.

He will not let them fall.

In the dank, dim little room that is the Davee Trader's Central Nervous System, amongst a huddle of sticky Grunt bodies, the hum of whirling dials and gears, thrusting pistons and springs and the rhythmic pop of micro-lights, misty vision would mean missing the spectacle of surgery. Johlan Richard Barrow, an orphaned Trader's Grunt since the age of eight and now,

127

nine years later, history's youngest to be implanted with a PICC line to the ship, would *never* miss an event such as this.

He blinks again.

Captain Florren nods, assuring him with a whisper of a smile and a pat to his shoulder. She'd tried to describe to Johlan what it would be like, to be joined with the ship, but, as always, gentle words had failed the seawoman. Some secrets are best discovered alone, she'd said and besides, comfort was never her strongest ally. He didn't mind – just by choosing him the Captain had expressed all she needed to.

'D'ya need something, Grunt? A little balm to ease the sting?' asks the visiting doctor, peering over his double lensed monocle, his naked scalp glistening yellow from the overhead bulb.

'No,' says Johlan, his voice holding firm. 'I'm good.'

'And you, Captain?' the doctor asks. 'Are you prepared?'

'Prepared? Of course I am,' she scoffs. 'I thought you were a maritime physician?'

'I am. But you do realise what this will do…'

The Captain sucks air through her teeth and rubs a thumb along the edge of her nose. The tiny movement gives the boy a focus point. With effort he imagines the bodies of his fellow sailors clustered around them – their own eyes greedy for blood and failure – falling away to sepia silhouettes. There is no one in the heart of the ship but him, the doctor and the Captain.

The slow waltz of the Davee Trader as it slides on gentle surge calms Johlan further. He squares his shoulders and snuggles his spine against the back of the surgical chair. His breath slows, becomes deeper, his limbs heavier. The doctor caresses his forearm and compliments the boy on having good veins. He flicks his finger below the crook of Johlan's elbow, then wipes with a cold swab of alcohol.

The pungent odour tickles at the boy's nostrils, sharpens his senses. He remains calm. He is ready for this.

The slice of the scalpel smarts less than he expects; a small nick to the artery sprays them all with a mist of scarlet. A muffled gasp from a forgotten onlooker makes Johlan smile. He had prepared for worse.

Deftly, the doctor stems the blood with wadding and inserts a fine hollow tube of gold deep into the boy's arm, then twists.

Johlan's bladder feels heavy and sweat prickles his lip.

'The wire, please Captain,' says the doctor.

Captain Florren looks flustered, pink has risen to her cheeks. 'Are you sure now, Grunt? You canna turn back once it's done,' her voice cracks slightly, a rare glimpse into the heart of the crusty sailor.

Johlan lifts his chin and sees more than a harsh and flushed superior. He sees the woman who took him into her ship, the oldest trading vessel to cut the seas. He sees the woman who never mothered a child, but was mother enough to he who was without. He sees and understands what an extraordinary gift she has offered him.

He also understands he earned it.

'I'm not turning back, Cap. The Davee is everything. It's home. Please,' he pauses a moment, 'just stick it in.'

Florren gathers her skirts and reaches across to the portable medical trolley. 'That's my boy, always impatient for adventure.'

With some trepidation – and a sense of ceremony – she passes a fine cord of skilfully braided wires to the doctor. No bulkier than a weft of hair, each wire is bound to the others for a specific purpose and emotion.

'This may pinch a little, Boy,' says the doctor.

'I expect so,' he replies with one raised eyebrow.

'Captain Florren, please ready the x-ray lamp.'

'Already done, Doc.' She loops another eye piece over his monocle, this one coloured violet, dims the yellow light and switches to the red.

The doctor inserts one end of the wires into the tube protruding from Johlan's forearm.

He doesn't feel the first gentle thrusts of the wires deep into his artery; the tube not only guides but protects. But as the doctor pushes past the embedded end of the metal cylinder, the wires begin to prod and stab at Johlan from inside out. He fights the urge to slap his arm away, to stop the burn, the creeping etch as it travels too slowly, too carefully deep inside his flesh.

The edges of his sight begin to fade, to ruffle like a lady's underthings. The sepia figures of his fellow Grunts return bolder and heavier than before. Men he has travelled and traded beside, fed and fought and gambled with (and against), men he held no secrets from, morph and melt closer yet further away. The glint of Bosun's military medals, pinned upon his paunchy chest leaves Johlan blinking stars. The scar where Hadley's eye once was seems to bulge and churn upon itself. The men's mouths twist wide with horror, but no sound interrupts the scorch and crawl he feels.

The Grunt's mute screams spread and fold, their faces wane and thrust. The frame of Johlan's vision melds and pushes him to darkness. Blistering pain trips and dances, scalds and corrodes deep inside his mind.

But still, even as the wires travel further…further up his arm, through his elbow, toward his shoulder, deep into his armpit, he does not flinch.

He slithers into memories, of days and weeks spent rubbing flesh from his knuckles and salt from the Davee's deck. Evenings helping Hadley harvest bull kelp to burn and turn to steam. Pre-dawn upon pre-dawn carrying chamber pots spilling with Grunt piss from quarters below, to empty before they woke. Nights huddled within the crow's nest, wind slicing through his ribs, ears bleeding from the cold, a wheel-spun telescope and gas-lit spotlight as big as he for company.

Johlan's tortured mind seeks happy days. The Captain tending to his rope-burned palms, soaking them in eucalypt to heal, re-picking his scabs to grow harsh seaman's callouses. Again, the Captain, dressed in fine, striped skirts that crinkled as she moved – jerky and uncomfortable as she tries consoling the frightened, brand-new orphan child. Her mouth incapable of sweet mother-words, but her tone was all he needed.

He thinks of sunshine and salt spray licking his face as the ship bounds across the waves, dawns till dusks without another vessel in sight. The stomach-churning excitement of a fortunate trade; the chime of gold coins as they cross his palm.

Johlan feels the turn of wires pitch against his collarbone. Worried voices whisper urgently, but he doesn't hear the details. He feels warm and loose and free and *her*.

The Davee Trader Figurehead. The Lady.

The lines of her profile are etched on Johlan's mind. Sharp yet soft, just as she quells the hard lines of the Trader's bow. As a symbol, she is strong; her arms flung back in liberty. Her breastbone leads their way; no fear of pirates or reef or kraken can waver her resolve. She is silent, the Figurehead, carved of hardened sea timbers, her features taut and young for one so old and wise. Her hair is laced with metals, cast and shaped like seashell jewels; her gown is pleats of windswept bronze patinaed green.

Each dip and curve is burned to Johlan's fingertips from hours spent cleaning, wiping crusted salt from her lips and bodice. Since he was a child, every port they paused at, every bay they anchored in, he would swing across the bow from tethered ropes and tend her. Storms and traders be damned, he didn't care, all that mattered was The Lady.

Captain Florren let him go, she understood his fancy though the other Grunts would jeer.

'Is superstition, is all,' they'd say.

'Can always wait, young Grunt. Trading first, lager second, ladies last!'

'Oi, now,' the Captain would pull her crew to line. 'Don'cha talk about our Davee in that manner. She's no whore like yer land ladies. She keeps ya alive, she does, pulls you safely through the seas. I'll not have that kinda talk about my lady – *our* lady – right where she can hear you.'

But quietly, when the others had landed, she'd take the lad aside. 'The sea and its spray, they don't hurt her boy. She don't expect ya to fuss so much.'

'It's okay, Cap. I like to fuss. I'm too young for lager, anyway.'

Captain Florren would only nod, adjust her squat top-hat with its pinned brass gears and shark teeth talismans, then turn to the horizon. Johlan wondered if she felt it too. The Lady who led their way as they cut from shore to shore was special, a treasure to be pleased.

'Wait!' An urgent voice shoves Johlan from his memory, backwards to the room. 'Wait. We need him upright. You, Grunt, hold him. That's it. Gentle now, don't let him slump again.'

Someone dabs and strokes his forehead with fabric cool and fresh. Johlan runs his tongue across his lips.

'Captain, are you ready? D'ya have your receiver out?' The doctor hisses fast and low.

'Is it done?' Johlan asks, through vocal cords dry and flayed like slate. He realises he must have screamed.

'Almost there boy. Just a little…in a moment…*now*.'

The wires puncture his heart.

Traveller? Traveller is it really you? He nodded and tried to mouth the words I longed to hear. He trembled. He was weak; they always are the first time. His head lolled side from side, a buoy cut loose and drifting. But he saw me, he knew me. He heard me, and that was all that mattered. I placed my palm against his cheek to mollify and settle while he closed his eyes against me. 'I knew it,' he spoke it as a sigh. 'I knew it all along.' Hush. Hush now, Traveller. For now you need to rest.

Captain Florren retches loud and hard. Johlan hears her as an echo, a dappled figure in the corner of his sight.

'That's enough,' the Captain sobs and grips her hands against her chest. 'Enough! Give her back.'

'Captain? D'ya want me to…'

'Put. It. Back. In my arm. *Now Grunt.* Now.'

Johlan looks up, but only sees the Figurehead, the true Lady of the ship. His heart begins to loop and race, then calms in time with hers. He hears it deep within his veins: ba-ba-ba-boom, ba-boom, ba-boom. Her eyes are kind and warm, her hand cups and soothes his face. Her timber face is plump with blood; her touch is filled with life. She smells of ocean storms and musky nights and the lingering trace of sex.

The doctor grasps his arm again, pulls it taut and firm.

'Oh, hurry. Please hurry.' The Captain whimpers in the distance. 'I can't do it any longer.'

'Hold on, boy. Stay still. This won't take a–'

His arm is pinched and The Lady is gone. Her hand no longer loiters on his cheek. Johlan's stomach flips and rises and bile stings his throat. His heartbeat jumps again, reconciles once more. He reaches out for her, but cannot see, then realises where she is.

Captain Florren weeps with relief, the receiver back inside her own golden cannula, neat and flush against her forearm. The tiny head of the receiver-stone blips with subtle aqua light, the dashboard of the CNS flashes to its rhythm. The Captain and ship are joined once again.

'I'm sorry, my Love,' she rasps to the figure only she can view or feel.

Johlan stares down at the empty tube now embedded in his body. He is bruised, inside and out, but understands the strain of surgery will heal quickly; he does not feel the wires.

As his fellow Grunts begin to laugh and cheer and clap for his future graces, all Johlan feels is sorrow. For while his Captain holds the receiver, she holds the Davee's Lady.

Florren sees the man blink hard against tears. His hands are busy, grappling with the Davee Trader's master wheel. He does not spare a moment to draw his goggles and protect his eyes. The north wind burns, the smoke it carries leaves a fine soot residue on his face. White tracks crawl from the corners of his eyes to his temples where the grime is washed away.

He does not stop the tears.

'Ere, lemme take it,' calls Florren over the bawling wind. She pushes Johlan with her good hip, and tries to take the wheel from him. She has to prise each white-knuckled finger before he will release and is reminded how brawny and determined he's grown with age. 'We're gonna have to make for the reef. We can't head into it, we have ta' change course.'

'The reef?' shouts Johlan. 'No! She can make it. It's a fire storm, is all.' He shoves his captain with his shoulder, attempts to take the wheel again.

The Davee Lady stands before them, unseen to Johlan's eyes. Thunder cloaks her features as she glares and shakes her head. The Lady lifts her arm against the wind and points firmly to southeast.

'Don't you spurn me, Grunt, an' don't you forget who commands this ship,' snaps Florren. 'You get the others and you swing the boom. We head southeast. Now.'

Johlan's shoulders slump, his lips open to retort, but instead, he rolls his eyes and turns toward the lower deck. Florren's goggles are in place, she watches him with a pang of sadness and despair. She understands too well the ache he feels. He is ready to take the Davee; ready in years, ready in experience. But she is not ready to give it to him.

Lightning explodes overhead in sheets. The tempest gains momentum. But the smoke is not coming from the direction of reef or land and the northern air is dry. Florren cannot taste the moisture of a summer squall. It makes her feel uneasy – the ocean should not burn. The air exhales danger, it feels eerie, it feels wrong.

The Lady stalks along the deck, her arms crossed against her chest. She feels the wrongness too, Florren understands. Their joined heartbeats skip too quickly. The ship itself is scared.

Florren sucks smoke deep into her lungs, resists the urge to heave and waits for her Grunts to shout. She double-checks the carved brass compass that hangs from a chain around her neck. She spins the wheel as the men holler and swing the boom. It takes a moment for the sails to replenish, then once again they billow fat in the wind, flapping and cracking like a stockwhip to the ear.

She calls to Hadley, the Davee's engineer, to stoke the kelp-fire burning in the boiler room. They may need to push the Trader to her steam propellers if they can't outrun the storm by sail.

Florren feels the vibration of steam pipes hammering gently underfoot as Hadley primes the system. She whistles to Little-Arhn, the child-grunt who swings aloft, her eyes sharper than a sea-eagle's, her limbs quick and nimble as she bounces from the rigging, giggling as she goes. Arhn returns the whistle, signalling she is safe.

The Davee Lady slips her fingers over Florren's aged and sea-worn hands. The Captain dips her head and smiles at her lover, the one who never speaks. The Lady nods, her eyes linger closed a moment, their heartbeats slow to normal rhythm. Florren was right to change their course.

They are less than a day from Port Botany to trade, and the hold below the orlop deck is filled to overflowing. Bales of wound linen, unbleached hemp, spun llama wool and fine-grade eastern silk are packed closely between coils of copper-cotton, reels of leather thonging, satin ribbon and poppet bulbs. The tanned and coloured hides of marsupials and crocodiles hang like spectres from overhead beams. Sacks of Mother o'pearl buttons, hand carved by islanders in the south are mingled with embellishments made from dials, gears and mechanisms, springs and miniscule silver plugs. Feathers and wax, tails and glass. Almost everything a woman of means needed to be fashionable in the cities.

But Florren's most precious trade is held in eighty palm-sized boxes in the wall-slip behind her cot, where only she and the Lady know where to find it.

Ampoules of Amarata Dust.

Thunder booms in short, sharp claps that make the Trader tremble. The deck creaks and shudders as the ocean dumps and churns. Florren stumbles, smacks her bad hip against a barrel. She cries in pain and fights to keep her footing. The Davee Lady holds her strong; one arm catches Florren by the waist, hugging at her sailing corset, the other hand reaches for the wheel. She breathes sweet, cool air against the Captain's neck, her breasts push hard to Florren's shoulder, a knee slips between her legs. The fabric of the Lady's dress flaps and swirls and dances, her shell encrusted hair whips and strikes the wind.

Together they steer the Davee from the storm.

Patience, Traveller, patience. I begged him year to year and prayed he heard me in his bones. I know you burn with longing, but the sea will tell us when. Our time will come when hers is over, you cannot rush it through. She's been good to me, this lover; but she does not share my all. You are The One I've waited on, these many generations. A little longer, Traveller, we haven't far to go.

Florren remains uneasy as the Davee nears the safety of the reef. Anticipation niggles at her mind, but she cannot feel what for. The sea has settled, breaking evenly to starboard in small white-caps as they cut to shallower waters. The Lady has released the Captain from her grip and lies stretched and sensuous across the quarter deck. She rolls her body, arches her back as the sea lolls the ship from side to side. Her eyes are closed, she basks in sunlight, an almost-smile upon her lips.

Florren wishes The Lady could speak to her; could express her love in syllables rather than just the stroking of their skin each night. Despite this, and despite the remaining six Grunt bodies who crew the Trader, Florren has never escaped the tide of loneliness.

Especially since Johlan was implanted with the cannula and PICC line.

He may now be Lead-Grunt – for that he was destined – but Florren lost him that day, now a decade gone. He'd grown to a sure and stringent trader; though wary in transactions he possessed a fine moral compass. A handsome gentleman-sailor, he was instinctual, fierce and loyal, but not to her, Florren knew. Johlan's eyes would flash grey and his fists clench white in those moments he stumbled on his Captain muttering to the spectre he could not see.

Johlan's loyalty lay with the ship, The Davee Lady alone.

Florren shifts her weight at the wheel. Her hip throbs, the metallic joint grinds with every movement. She will need to seek a doctor when they finally land at port. For now, she decides to head below deck to find relief. The sea is calm and she shakes away ill-feeling.

She calls on Johlan to take the helm and steer them to the reef. He sneers but resists the opportunity for snide remarks. She is relieved; she doesn't own the energy to battle him. His resentment has not quelled the love she feels for her almost-son. Florren understands his torment; she knows what it is to wait. She understands the enchantment of The Lady.

She takes the stairs carefully. The pain in her hip makes each step narrower and steeper than they once were.

Inside the Davee Trader, she is cocooned, swaddled amongst a maze of fine copper piping, pinned along the ceiling and the dark red timber walls. The smell of freshly painted bitumen that keeps the ship watertight tickles the back of her throat. She feels the ship's lungs inhale, exhale with every creak and groan. She hears the Davee's heartbeat as it pumps along with hers.

Florren unlocks the door of the tiny room beside her cabin where the Central Nervous System is housed. The lights and dials of the dashboard pop in time with the receiver stone implanted in her arm. Her skin has almost swallowed up the golden cannula, the ship is such a part of her. She scratches at old scar tissue, surprised to find it red and weepy.

She pulls a lever and sets the Davee's eight sea legs to automatic. Pressure build-up in the steam pipes will push and crank the legs from the unused gunner's deck by the time they reach the reef. Florren is glad of the ship's most recent upgrade. The space had been squandered on cannons, idle for near ten years. Johlan had been right in convincing her to do away with the old-fashioned anchor.

Her cabin is too small, the ceiling an inch too low. She has to tilt her head to make it in. The light is soft and sallow from the candelabra swinging at shoulder-height.

As Florren removes her weather-worn top-hat and shakes her hair from its tight-wound braid, The Lady appears by her side. Silently, she runs her fingers through the Captain's limp and grey-streaked tangles, gently smoothing wayward strands from her forehead, tucking them behind her ear.

With stiff and aching fingers, Florren tries and fails to unbuckle her leather corset from the front. The Lady swiftly pops the clips apart and Florren feels her ribs expand. Together, they stand by the mirror and ease down one side of the Captain's canvas pantaloons.

The box containing the implanted metal gears that replaced her own joint years ago has splintered through the skin. Congealed blood is smeared and stuck against her underthings. The Lady tenderly kisses the blooming haematoma that spreads from Florren's waist to belly. The Captain's face burns and her vision wavers as she contemplates the injury. It will be some time before she can sail again.

She curses and reaches for the whiskey bottle she hides under the bed. She gulps a mouthful down and as it scalds her throat and chest, she pours more on the wound.

The ampoules of Amarata Dust beckon. The Lady offers a small box from her hand. Florren tries to resist, just as she does every other day. To her, the value of Amarata is in the trade. Black market medication has always been her sideline, a secret kept from all her crew. It has made the Captain rich. She hides pockets of gold coins in the false floor under her feet, but she cannot love the money. It doesn't hold her close at night; it does not kiss her neck or ear. Riches do not cup her breast or run their fingers through her hair. Gold will not replace the Davee Lady if Florren leaves the sea; gold will not return her loveless son.

The Lady snaps an ampoule open and sprinkles Dust across the wound. Instantly, Florren feels relief. She mixes another with her whiskey and prays it soothes her heart.

Come now, Traveller, I murmured in his ear, while she was taken in with fevered dreams. Seek with me the song. Do you hear the Siren's chorus ride along the waves? Our time is close now, Traveller; the tang of change is on the wind. You've always been the only One, all those before: imposters. They cannot hear my voice, my call – they cannot seek the song. Come. Come now, Traveller.

Johlan swings across the Davee's bow from a rope knotted around his waist. From a small canteen, he dabs fresh water on a rag and tenderly wipes the Figurehead's cheekbone. She appears to have been crying. Smoke from the storm has mingled with salt, leaving smeared black crystals in the corners of her eyes, the cleft of her lip, the hollow above her breastbone. He nurtures her, the static phantom of The Lady who remains outside his grasp. He oils her wooden features, rubs emu fat deep inside the creases of her gown, buffs the delicate embellishments that dress her hair.

Dusk is settling on the reef, mist is rolling in. The ship's sea legs span like latticed spider's limbs from the timber hull, digging deep into the coral. The Davee Trader barely sways, so sure and firm is she.

The other Grunts are calming down, preparing for a dawn departure. Once, the ship staffed more than twenty, but in this age, most had been made redundant. Only a skeleton crew remained.

The scent of mussel chowder wafts from the upper galley, and Johlan hears the men bickering over wagers on tomorrow's trades. They are tired and temperamental. If not for the Captain's cowardice in running from the storm, they'd now be toasting a successful voyage with too much lager and easy women.

A gull shrieks overhead.

An ice-cold breath prickles his neck and he swears he hears a whisper: *Beware, Traveller.*

Fear rises in his guts. He calls to Little-Arhn, perched inside the crow's nest.

'Nay! All clear!' comes her thin reply. 'Oi, hold on, there's a–'

Johlan stiffens. His mouth goes dry. He tries to swallow and cannot. He has not felt this heavy dread since the day he saved the Captain's neck from a bootlegger's dirk blade and was rewarded with the agony of PICC line surgery, a drawn-out promise and a heart that ached for a woman he could not have.

'It's a whale sir! There, nor-east. Deadibones, it is. A floater on the incoming!' cries Little-Arhn.

Johlan scrambles up the rope to the deck. He peers through his pocket telescope.

Daylight is almost washed away, and the moon is yet to rise. The Cross of the South barely flickers with two of her five bright stars. He sees nothing but the melting line between the orange sky and sea. Then he spots it – closer than he expected. The creamy-white underbelly of the giant mammal being washed towards them.

Beware, Traveller.

There it was again. The voice, the whisper inside his head accompanied by fear so cold it was as though winter had wrapped her legs around his waist.

He summons the crew with a short, sharp whistle.

'Hadley, open the fire up again. We may need to get under steam. Bosun and Trigger, make sure that rigging is secure. Little-Arhn, get back aloft and don't allow your eyes to stray. Matthias, I need you to set up the telescopic gaff.'

'What'sup, Johlan? Little-Arhn hasn't called ship?' grumbles Bosun. 'Is a dead fish, is all. I was about to serve soup.'

'Sky's clear,' adds Hadley, scratching his matted beard.

'We're bringing it in.' says Johlan.

'You've spilt a cog, Boy,' says Bosun. He spits overboard and adds: 'yer gears are running slow. There'll be sharks feastin' in its belly-guts already.'

'Thing'll stink worse than Typhoid Mary,' says Trigger from the corner of his mouth.

Bosun belly-laughs and Johlan spins on his heel, too fast for the older Grunt. He pins him to the mast with a forearm to the neck and seethes, nose to nose.

'Boy? *Boy?* You're forgetting your place, old man.' Johlan pulls back the sleeve of his linen shirt with his teeth, exposing his cannula. 'Or do you simply not remember what this means?'

Bosun's face is crimson, his lips are turning white. Johlan is a foot taller then he, and half a man heavier. He struggles to speak as Johlan pushes harder against his throat. 'Aye, Sir.'

'Aye? Aye Sir *what?* '

'Aye, it means – it means you is in charge when Cap aint here.'

Johlan releases him, but does not step away. 'Now, go and check the rigging. When you've checked it a second time, you're going to help Matthias with the gaff. Unless, of course, you'd like to inspect for sharks yourself? I don't mind sending you in the tender.'

'Aye Sir. I mean, no Sir. No sharks. Please,' he rasps.

'Trigger?'

'Nope, all good thanks.'

'Um, Sir?' says Little-Arhn nervously. 'Where *is* the Cap? Shouldn't we fill 'er in on the floater?'

'She's sleeping,' replies Johlan curtly. 'There's no need to wake her over a whale carcass. Now get back up the nest.'

Besides, Johlan muses, *she's probably too stupefied on the narcotics she hides in the walls of her cabin to be woken.*

He takes the stairs below deck in two long strides and unlocks the door to the heart of the ship. Inside, the CNS is relaxed. The dashboard lights blip slowly, fading in and out instead of flashing. The springs are sluggish in their stretch and recoil and the pistons are at ease. By all indications, the ship and its captain sleep soundly without fear. Johlan shakes his head, rolls his shoulders, exhales.

He pauses a moment by Florren's door, and wonders whether to try waking her. He cannot bear the thought of his should-be lover curled around the

Captain instead of he. The love and admiration Johlan felt for his Captain-Mother had been washed away with loathing for the black-market secrets she thought she kept from him.

He is not surprised when his quiet tap remains unanswered.

He tries the handle of the cabin, but it jars and will not turn. He knocks again, this time louder.

No response.

He hears the Grunts above deck yelling excitedly to one another, but he cannot make out their words. Most likely, Johlan assumes, they are arguing over the set-up of the gaff and who will be the one to guide the hook.

'Captain? Captain Florren? Are you awake?'

He does not hear the Captain's voice reply, but another from deep inside himself.

Traveller?

Johlan forces his shoulder to the door, and shoves with all he has. The timber creaks, but does not falter until at last, the brass handle turns with a shudder and click as the door unbolts from inside.

Florren lies across her cot, her mouth a mess of foam and bloodied sputum. Her chest still falls and rises, but her breath is slow and harsh. Dozens of tiny ampoules, splintered glass and boxes lay scattered by her side and on the floor. Johlan reaches for an ampoule, snaps and sniffs the powder. Amarata. Damn fool.

Her receiver stone is dim, her heart about to stop. The skin around her cannula blisters and erupts.

Johlan fights to keep his head. A ship without a captain is a vessel without life; one cannot exist without the other. He cannot let her die.

The Davee Lady will perish too.

He blunders through Florren's drawers, the cupboards by her cot. All he finds are boxes and more boxes of the poison that races through her veins. He tosses aside her bedclothes, pulls maps, scale rules, a brass sexton from her bureau, a wad of ribbon-tied letters and a bundled pod of incense from her sailing chest. Nowhere does he find the antidote he searches for.

'Johlan! Captain! Come quickly!' comes a cry from up above.

The Captain's fingers begin to splay and spasm, her legs kick out in reflex. Johlan swipes the sputum from her lips, he pumps his fists against her chest and forces her to breathe.

More shouting comes from upper deck, loud footfalls ring out above the cabin.

The receiver stone is waning, a dwindling echo now, the feeble glow barely lights the eruptions and rejection on Florren's skin.

Johlan sets his jaw and straddles her jerking form. He clears her mouth of blood again and continues to propel her breath. He will not let her die.

Help us, Traveller, help us, I cried and cried and cried. This is never how it ends. Take the stone, I begged him, please, take it from her now. He couldn't hear me; wouldn't hear me, his instincts grieving for my lover not yet dead. I was cold, so cold, collapsed there on the floor, watching as he pumped the poison from her organs. My hands would not obey, my fingers befuddled lumps of flesh, my senses in disarray. Releasing the door took all I had left. Help us, Traveller, help us.

Johlan feels the chill again, this time by his feet. Sweat trickles from his hair, above his lip and down his neck. The noise on deck is growing, the excited Grunts are whooping as they prepare to pull their ocean-spoils in. Johlan drifts and wonders for a moment what their fuss is for. His arms are growing tired, his shoulder muscles weak. He does not stop the pushing of his Captain-Mother's heart.

Cold, fluttering breath brushes by his ankle.

It's her, he's sure. His Figurehead. His Lady.

The Davee Trader, so steady on her sea legs, lurches violently to starboard.

Johlan takes it as a sign, and fumbles for the stone. He rips aside his linen sleeve, clears his cannula with a whistle-breath. He twists the stone in Florren's arm, it will not budge – his fingers flounder, slick with blood and fear.

He tries again, this time with more precision, pinching the faded aqua stone between dried forefinger and thumb. Florren shudders, her back goes rigid. Johlan twists and pulls again. The stone is free.

He pauses, unsure of what to do. It will barely take a second to join his own self to the ship – but this isn't how it was supposed to be. He'd dreamed of the day since boyhood, when he'd be presented with the Captain's stone and the love of the Davee Trader. It would be ceremonial, celebrated with rum and feasting and the blessings of the Admiral. Florren would step gracefully aside for the younger, fitter man. Her captaincy should not be wrenched away with blood and sputum and narcotics, amid a hullaballoo on deck and a great, dead fish.

Johlan slowly screws the receiver stone into his cannula.

She takes a moment to appear, at first translucent and coiled on the floor. Her image is weak and pale; not quite there. Johlan's heart jolts and flips, its rhythm disordered and upset. He gasps as his pulse finds a new, slower cadence to dance with.

The Davee Lady becomes corporeal to his eyes, her colour deepens, her lines become firm. She looks up at him and smiles.

'Traveller,' she sighs. 'You're home.'

Johlan reaches down and helps The Lady to her feet. She is more beautiful, more ethereal – and yet, more alive – than he remembers. Johlan embraces her, nuzzles his face in her neck and hair. She wraps her lithe, dark arms around him and her hips sway into his.

Her lips are silky, delicate; her body firm and strong. His fingers tangle a fist of salt-stained hair as he draws her closer. She pushes herself hard against him and runs small, hungry kisses along his collar to his throat.

Johlan groans, exhaling all the years of yearning. He feels released, he feels exhilarated. He feels pleasure tugging low inside his belly as her hands sweep beneath his shirt, across his back, up his ribs and to his chest.

The Lady pauses suddenly and lifts her eyes to his. She bites her lip, then looks away. 'Traveller? Do you still hear me after all these many years? Are you still The One?' she says so quietly, so anxiously, Johlan's heart skips to feel her pain.

He knits his brows, confused. 'Hear you? I've always heard your voice inside me – long before I knew.'

He wipes away the single tear that trickles down her cheek.

Florren coughs abruptly. She retches and she gurgles, her body arcs with shudders.

'The antidote!' The Lady gasps, 'The medibox – next door. Hurry.'

The Central Nervous System, of course! Johlan slaps his forehead and turns to run.

'Wait!' The Lady grasps him by the wrist. 'Is this what you want? You could just let her go.'

Johlan shakes his head. 'Never.'

He pushes through the door, and spills directly into Little-Arhn, the girl's white mop of hair snapping backward with the force.

'Johlan! Johlan – where's Cap?'

'Not now, Arhn, I have to–'

'It aint no whale, Sir. Come quick. It's trouble, a zeppelin – a burned one! With people!'

Behind them, in the room where Johlan left his lover and his dying mother, a scream bolts his pulse to gallop. The Lady dashes to his side, panic streaking through her face.

'The ship! The ship!' she cries. 'There's peril within the ship!'

Johlan hesitates, unsure which way to turn.

'I didn't feel it. How didn't I know?' The Lady trembles, her lip curls, her fists clench. 'Go, Traveller, save her. I can take the ship.'

Johlan mumbles after her: 'The Amarata. It numbed you, too.'

He pushes Little-Arhn aside, and stumbles to the CNS. The dashboard lights are strobing, flashing too fast to see. The stone, snug inside his cannula is blinking just as swiftly. Johlan feels the rumble of the boilers as someone opens up the steam and roaring voices bellow overhead. He smacks his fist against the small tin door beneath the dashboard, and thrashes through the medibox it contains. Bandages, pill bottles, essence of urchin and ginger. Echidna quills and algae paste. Phials of tiny ear bones, gears and screws. A scalpel, a mask…an injectable marked as adrenaline and the Captain's own pearl-handled, triple-barrelled Derringer.

Someone shrieks on deck as Johlan flips Florren to her back. He flings aside the pistol, and plunges the injectable with as much force as he can muster, crunching through her ribs, deep into her heart.

He hears a splash, another scream, the crack of a small explosion.

Florren's body roils and quakes, her mouth opens wide in shock. Her eyes flicker and focus in recognition, then roll backwards, forwards again.

Her body goes limp and still.

Johlan tries to wail, but does not have the air.

He wants to crumple to the floor, he wants to hold his Mother-Captain, he wants to shake life into her.

Traveller? Come now, Traveller. Hurry.

Johlan vomits as he staggers to the stairs. Bile coats his throat and terror fills his veins. His heart bounces to the unfamiliar, urgent beat.

Dusk is long gone; darkness cloaks the sea. Moonlight casts its glow across the Davee Trader's deck. It takes the new Captain precious seconds to adjust his eyes.

A gust of noise and chaos dashes through his guts. The lower deck is a skirmish of bodies, diving and rolling, brawling and struggling. The smack of skin boxing skin, the thud of bulk striking wood, the bellows of his Grunts as they fend off the rush of darkened figures scurrying up the Davee's sea legs.

Johlan is paralysed, he does not know which way to turn, he cannot tell his own Grunts from their attackers in the melee. They are outnumbered, two to one at least. At last, he spies The Lady.

She prowls among the fracas, unseen by all but him. She stops, tilts her head, as though in wonder at a duo who scuffle by the mizzenmast. As one man raises his fist against the other, she reaches out, clutches his head between both hands and twists. He drops, wooden, to the floor. The Lady continues calmly to the next group, where she does the same again, and then again.

Johlan feels his body lift, adrenalin hammers through his limbs. His belly churns with rage and the frantic pace of fear. He bounds onto the lower deck, fury billowing from his lungs. He takes one assailant, two, their noses shattered to their brains, before he reaches for the pistol.

He doesn't have it.

He sees Bosun cowered by the tender-boat, his face a bloodied mess, a bearded stranger standing over him, blade in hand, about to strike. In an instant, Johlan wraps his arm around the stranger's neck, and pulls him to the floor. The man is soaked with seawater, his frigid body heavy. He churns his legs beneath them, elbows Johlan in the ribs. His head is tossed, the Captain's cheekbone smashed. Johlan grits his teeth and battles to hold firm amid the blinding pain. They tussle on their backs; the stranger's knife is flailing, inches from Johlan's face. Johlan twists and lunges with his hips, attempts to fling them over, he grapples with his spare hand for the wrist that wields the blade.

The attacker gains control, slips free from Johlan's grip. He charges at the Captain, who rolls across the deck. Copper-flavoured blood seeps from Johlan's nose and mouth, distracting him a moment. As he turns to gain his footing, he spots a small white head bobbing in the corner of his vision.

A small white head of hair. A girl without a body.

Johlan's anger boils over; he screams and dives for his attacker.

A crack goes off behind him.

The assailant drops his knife and crumples to the floor, blood blooming through his shirt.

Johlan swings around, and finds Florren swaying on the upper deck, the Derringer dangling from her fingers. Her face is grey from loss of blood; her hair is soaked with sweat, clinging to her cheekbones, dank and lifeless across her breast. Her eyes blink open, closed, as she struggles to stay conscious. Florren's mouth sags wide, her chin trembles as she groans, her voice is filled with bubbles. She stumbles, but stays upright, an empty version of herself.

Slowly Johlan turns, the Trader is all still. Bodies splay across the floor, blood glistens in the moonlight. He sees Trigger lend his hand to Bosun, who staggers to his feet. Matthias limps across the deck, toward the tiny, headless body of the youngest serving Grunt.

Johlan hears the ruffle of The Davee Lady's gown, the chime of her sea-shell hair. He tastes the scent of sex as she sweeps past him to the upper deck. He wants to reach for her, to feel the whisper of her lips once more, her body hungering for his embrace. He wants to lie exhausted in her arms. He watches as she glides to Florren's side.

And Then...

He feels the thud of one more body as The Lady snaps one last neck.
The deck of the Davee Trader is hushed, save for quiet sobbing.
Johlan never realises it is him.

Traveller never cried again. His weeping was all spent. Even as they wrapped my other lover in her canvas funeral shroud, his eyes stayed dry from mist. As dawn broke free on ocean's edge, pure and clean and soft, they tossed her to her grave. Across the sea she'll go, searching for a song that may sing inside her ears. Down to the depths she'll go, a flaccid husk of life with nothing more to show.

He tries, my Traveller. Tries to see me as he should, as his destiny foretold, but he cannot lose his grief. I see it as an empty sphere, circling his eyes. I feel it as we coast the waves, our hands entwined, our souls are not. His bliss is all adrift. He is sombre, he is stern, he is forever sad. He flinches as I run my fingers inside his thigh each night; he cannot look me in the heart. He strains and struggles to forgive me for the choice he thought I made. But there was never any choice – I couldn't bear it, wouldn't bear it. I had to help her go.

Come back, Traveller, I beckoned him. Return to me. You have this Siren's song; together we shall ride the sea. Come. Come now, Traveller.

EVELYN TSITAS

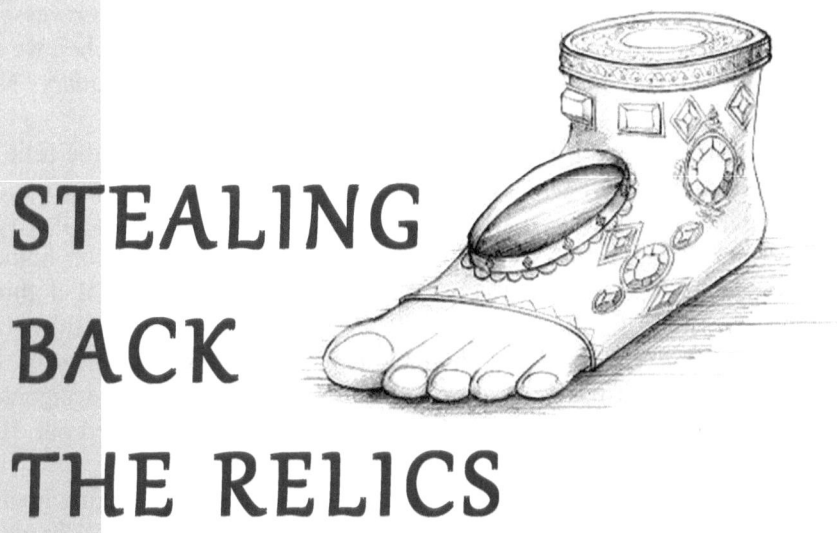

STEALING
BACK
THE RELICS

BEWARE GREEKS BEARING GIFTS
AND RETURNING THEM

MELBOURNE: THE ADVENTURE BEGINS

To anyone sitting inside the Golden Dumpling Souvlaki Bar the couple at the centre table, surrounded by newspapers, Moleskin notebooks and a large map of Europe could be any hipster trendsetters from the inner suburbs. Eschewing iPads for analogue, cocooned in the Greek-Chinese fusion eatery de jour in Preston, they exuded the vibe of long time live-in lovers off on an overseas jaunt.

Oh, how wrong that casual observation would be.

'I've made contact with the arms dealer in Mayfair,' Tally said, looking up from her phone. 'She says she'll be willing to give us the toe if we give her the foot reliquary.'

Sven, who was preoccupied with his cruffin, sighed. 'Pity, as it's encrusted with jewels and a little viewing glass on top of the foot so you can see the mummified flesh inside. Probably worth a fortune.'

'Sven, I've told you before, I'm not interested in looting treasure, only

145

the human remains,' said Tally. 'We have to return them to the Church in Thessaloniki, and if that means doing so without the reliquaries, then that's the price we pay.'

'But I've seen photos of it in art books, it's a beautiful silver vessel,' complained Sven. 'It hardly seems fair the dealer gets to keep it when we do all the work. And are you are sure Saint Aspasia's toe is in the reliquary? Not just a bone fragment?'

'The reliquary itself might turn out to be second rate – but the relic is first class!' Tally laughed at their particular in-joke. Sven had given her a lecture on the categories of Saint's relics once they had made a pact to go on the adventure together. First class relics were actual bodily matter; human remains such as bone, body parts, hair and skin. Next were pieces of clothing (second class) and finally, the third class relics most of the faithful could ever hope to own – a piece of cloth that touched the saint or the shrine of the saint. 'Besides, the arms dealer is paying for the trip as well as our designated driver. Dragan was a sniper in the Balkans conflict,' Tally pointed out. 'He could come in very handy.'

Sven struggled with his vanilla and strawberry cruffin, spluttering greasy flakes of heavily sugar-encrusted croissant pastry over the table. 'Why does that detail fill me with a certain prescient dread?'

Tally took another sip of her Matcha chai latte. 'Where we are going, we'll need Dragan's expertise. Whoever stole St Aspasia's remains from Thessaloniki does not want them returned. And then of course, we may have to deal with the Dilettanti.'

Sven laughed, bitterly. 'The Society of the Dilettanti don't even exist anymore except in the imaginations of rarefied academics who sit and gossip at High Table at Oxbridge.' Being a mere sessional lecturer he was a transient soul who didn't even have a desk to his name, let alone bona fide university affiliation.

'The features editor liked the Dilletanti threat, said it gave the story a Dan Brown edge, you know, intrigue, symbols embedded in paintings, secret societies and that sort of thing.'

'You're making this sound like a great adventure.'

'It bloody well will be – once I've written it!' Tally had pitched the search for the relics of venerated Saint Aspasia of Thessaloniki to several major news organisations. Ever since a chance conversation at her Great Uncle Dimitri's funeral, where an elderly relative under the influence of too much Metaxa had revealed a 'family secret', Tally knew she was at last onto a *sure thing*. This was the feature story she'd been looking for – the one with potential to become a major Vanity Fair article and subsequent TED Talk and movie contract.

There were only a few minor problems, mostly to do with time, money and legality not to mention required knowledge of reliquaries – a term she had never heard of before she started to research Saint Aspasia whose body 500 years ago had been discovered to be miraculously incorruptible. Alas, as Tally's investigation revealed, there were only a few bits of the Saint left. The brazen theft, in 2009, of the three reliquaries containing the relics from a small Byzantine church in Thessaloniki had plunged the congregation into mourning, and – some would say not coincidentally – the Greek economy into nose dive.

'I am surprised you believe the stories of Saint Aspasia,' said Sven. 'Some say she was actually a prostitute.'

'Rubbish – she was an independent and learned woman,' said Tally. 'And I have it on good authority from my Great Aunt Toula whose second cousin Mary worked as a cleaner at the Church, that when returned together, the relics of Saint Aspasia would actually regenerate and restore Greece to its former glory. Goodbye Grexit and debt crisis – hello Pulitzer Prize.'

Sven, rather than smirk, sighed heavily. Not for the first time he pondered the wisdom of the delayed gratification that was his academic career. Struggling through his third PhD on the iconography of Orthodox reliquaries, he desperately needed a high profile publication to secure tenure. Sessional lecturing in art conservation was hardly a growth area. Helping put together Saint Aspasia's body parts and seeing if the long rumoured prophecy was true would be a stroke of genius – weaving 'me-search' into 'research'. It was the sort of trans-disciplinary self reflexive academic indulgence highly praised in universities; as de jour as a cruffin and dirty latte in a refurbished Preston Laundromat-turned-hipster café. Or, as his mother would say 'if you can't beat them, join them.'

'When do we leave?' he asked.

'Please fasten your seat belt,' chided the flight attendant. 'We are heading into turbulence.' Sven hadn't even started watching his first in-flight movie when this ominous portent of doom hit the plane. He reluctantly reached through his scratchy thin blanket and belted up. *Turbulence.* It was an omen, he was sure. As he nursed his second glass of Shiraz, Sven glanced up again at the billowing curtain pulled across the aisle that divided economy from his companion in business.

There was, thought Sven, as he stared longingly at the iron curtain, something utterly compelling about his travelling companion Talitha Nakos. It was the combination of the confidence, intelligence and a killer body that he had always found intoxicating. And, if he admitted it to himself – intimidating. She always had to be right (she usually was) and always had to be first. Sure, while 'get it first and get it right' was the old journalism adage, it made for a rather difficult romantic partner.

He felt something pressing against his ribs. The fat man next to him. Well – he was sick of being polite. He deliberately claimed his territory by elbowing the intruder, only to connect with the unmistakable sensation of firm and large breasts.

'Easy!' said Tally, catching her breath. 'I was only trying to wake you.'

Sven sat bolt upright, upending the glass of shiraz over himself and the thin blanket as he struggled with his eye mask and crunchy neck roll that was twisting around his face. 'What are you doing here?' he gasped.

'You mean, on the plane?'

'I mean in economy.'

'I came to see you.'

'There is someone in that seat.'

'I know. I gave him three mini bottles of Siberian elderflower-infused vodka from first class and told him to sit in the toilet for half an hour so we could chat.'

'He got the vodka?' Sven was put out. He was also wet and tried mopping the shiraz up with his face mask. Tally smiled and handed him a mini vodka bottle and held hers up as well. She twisted the tops off and clinked. 'Salute!' and downed the contents in a single gulp. Journalists never ceased to amaze him.

Sven took a gulp and spluttered and grimaced.

'Drink up, it will numb the pain,' Tally said. 'Unfortunately, the refugee crisis and the latest bombings means that security will be incredibly tight at Munich airport.'

'I'm sure that won't be a problem for Dragan.'

'It'll be a problem for us. Dragan has some lingering issues with the security forces so we have to meet him in Ulm.'

'Ulm Minster has impressive wood carvings,' said Sven. 'I could take some photos of the choir stalls.'

'We don't have time!' snapped Tally. 'It's a 45 minute drive from Ulm to the Bodensee, where we get our hands on the first relic.'

Sven frowned. 'In a church?'

'It's in one of those private museums, built by a wealthy hedge fund wunderkind.'

'Do we have a meeting with him?'

Tally shook her head. 'He spends most of his time in New York. I've made an appointment with his curator. We're doing a tour of the place, posing as reporters from a new architectural magazine.' She handed Sven a pair of heavy black rectangular spectacles. 'Here, you have to look the part.'

Sven put them on. Tally laughed. He took them off. 'Are you sure this is going to work?' Sven gulped more of his vodka. It carved a warm passage to his brain, but he could feel his bowels grumbling with anxiety. 'After all, what we are doing is theft. This guy probably has tight security.'

'Apparently not. The live-in curator is a former aerobic instructor who did an arts management course through the Bahamas. Tell me in all honesty that the guy chose her for her curating skills. Seriously, this is going to be so easy.'

'It's *still* theft.' Sven felt he had to point this out, in the same way he always made sure he wore white gloves before touching art work.

'Dragan will be there too, he has expertise.'

'What if something goes wrong?'

Tally rolled her eyes. 'Listen Dr Art Historian, you just have to identify the reliquary and Dragan will do the theft. I will keep the caretaker – Mimi I believe – talking. Easy. People love talking about themselves and I have done deep research.'

'I still don't like the sound of stealing from actual *people*,' complained Sven. He drowned the last of his vodka. 'It's different if it was a gallery that had wrongfully acquired the piece, and we were stealing it to take it back to the church – that would make us the Robin Hood of art theft. But taking it from a private collector seems somehow wrong.'

Tally grabbed his empty bottle. 'A wealthy German shouldn't even *have* Saint Aspasia's toe. It's probably what caused the debt crisis to begin with; and if you see what's happening in Europe right now – and the misery on Germany's doorstep – it seems the prophecy of Saint Aspasia is coming true.'

They watched the news on the back-of-seat TV screen for a moment, as scenes of refugees crushing through Munich airport were intercut with frantic crowds trying to board trains in Hungary. Sven wished he had stayed in Melbourne with his third dissertation. Europe could keep its culture, its plundering and its wars and human misery.

'Maybe now is not the time to go,' he pointed out. 'Europe is in a mess. We can turn back. It's not too late. Let's turn back at Singapore.'

'Europe is *always* in a mess, only this time it has flooded into nice first world lives and there is no ignoring it. We fly into the maelstrom and that's that. I'm not telling the London arms dealer that we called it quits at Changi airport.'

'I don't have a good feeling about this,' said Sven. He already had a headache. 'We are breaking the law.'

'Cheer up, you can watch the entire last series of *Downton Abbey*.' Tally took his remote control and set the screening for him.

'You'll be in business class,' Sven complained. 'How did you get the paper to pay for that?'

Tally winked. 'Don't be a baby, take the sleeping tablets I gave you. I went to dinner with a very boring doctor to get those.'

'Is that all you did?' Sven asked, somewhat jealously. The looming figure of the ticket holder for seat 45 F was within sight, and Tally got up to leave. But not before she kissed Sven full on his lips.

BAVARIA: THE TOE

A light breeze blew over the somewhat medieval city of Ulm, ruffling Tally's hair and making Sven squint. The sun bounced off the sleek round Richard Meiers' building next to the Minster, its stark white rendered façade creating a blinding haze that made it impossible to read anything on Tally's phone. The friends sat in a café at the edge of the looming cathedral, and waited for Dragan.

'Are you sure he didn't drive all the way from Belgrade this morning?' complained Sven. 'It's been hours.'

'He'll be here,' said Tally. 'I got a message from my contact. Don't whinge. I spent the morning inside the church while you and that German art historian obsessed about wood carvings.'

'I'm not sure I feel so well,' moaned Sven. He pushed his plate away. 'Irritable Bowel.'

'Stop eating so much, it will make you ill,' warned Tally.

Before Sven could complain, Tally's phone jumped across the café table. She pounced on it and spoke in a mixture of English and halting Greek.

'Dragan's in the car across the road,' she said.

'He speaks Greek?'

Tally shrugged. 'This is Europe – the distance between Thessaloniki and Belgrade is less than the drive from Melbourne to the Gold Coast. Besides, the arms dealer advised he is a cunning linguist.'

'Tell me that's a bad joke.' Sven felt a rise of jealousy at Tally's pointed sexual innuendo. It amplified once he saw Dragan. He was a Hollywood issue European Alpha Male, muscular, broad shouldered and with a nascent five o'clock shadow at morning tea. He reeked of testosterone. As soon as Dragan saw Tally, her large breasts highlighted in a snug black top, he leapt out and opened the door for her, so – as Sven observed – he could check out her bum as she got into the car. Dragan flashed a lust-filled smile at Sven, who glowered back.

Sven farted loudly as he squeezed into the back of the Fiat. 'Sven! That's disgusting!' complained Tally. Dragan wound down a window.

'I can't help it!' said Sven. 'My stomach's bloated from German food.'

'Stop eating so much.'

'I have *food intolerance issues!*'

Dragan grunted. Sven nervously watched him inhale on his cigarette, flick the butt out of the window, rev the car up and erratically swerve through the traffic, narrowly missing a pregnant young mum and her stroller laden with a crying toddler and shopping bags. In order to keep their driver focused, Sven attempted to engage Dragan in a conversation about Eurovision. Apart from art history, it was the sum total of Sven's actual contemporary knowledge about Europe. 'So, Dragan, what did you think of Australia's performance?'

'Australia is not Europe' said Dragan. 'It is down below.'

'Down Under,' Sven pointed out gently.

'But we love Eurovision!' protested Tally. 'We put ABBA on the world map.'

Dragan grunted. Tally changed the topic. She waxed lyrical about St Kilda, the Victoria Market, and some secret bar above a Melbourne laneway.

'So, what's it like where you come from then?' she asked Dragan.

'It is shit hole,' replied Dragan, and turned the music up louder.

It took an hour and a half to get to Lindau on the Bodensee, and Dragan insisted they listen to his compilation tapes of Serbian thrash bands. Luckily his chain smoking covered up Sven's sulfuric flatulence. The noise also prevented Tally from yelling at him about eating too many pastries. Just as they saw the signs into town, Dragan pulled the Fiat sharply to the right and ploughed on through a winding lane. There, rising up on the hill, was a modern, elegant streamlined house of wood and glass, sitting near a calm lake amidst tall trees.

Dragan stopped the car. 'So much money to look poor,' he said, pointing at the house. 'It makes no sense. Not even velvet curtains.'

'It's beautiful – it's streamlined, simple – pared back, utterly minimal,' said Sven, stepping out of the car. He turned to Tally. 'It would be a real crime to steal from someone with this much aesthetic judgement.'

'Oh shut up,' said Tally. 'That man took my country's toe.'

They were expected. After introductions, with Dragan posing as a film maker and brandishing his camera gear, Mimi, the curator, ushered them inside. A tall, striking young Vietnamese woman with straight, long hair dyed silver, she was dressed in a sleek black jumpsuit with matching thigh high boots, and looked like a starved model momentarily AWOL from an S & M photo shoot.

'Skinny girls,' grunted Dragan. As the women walked ahead, Tally used her Zoom recorder to tape Mimi's breathless commentary about her work in this wealthy man's private museum. Dragan took the opportunity to have a confidential chat to the art historian. 'I like more meat on women, more–' he cupped his hands in front of his chest. 'And you – you like meat? Or *men?*' he asked. Before Sven could reply, Dragan pointed to Tally's rear. 'She's good. You ever, you know?'

Sven blushed.

'As I thought. So you won't mind if I try?'

Dragan glanced at Sven's reddening face and clenched fists and leant in. 'She is sexy lady, no?' he said. 'Tally tells me you two met long time ago, at university. Should have had the balls to tell her then.'

'Tell her what?'

'Serbian proverb – you are not being honest if you burn your tongue and don't tell everyone else that the soup is hot.' Dragan walked up to the house, whistling.

Mimi was waiting for them. 'I was explaining to Talitha that because of copyright reasons you are not allowed to take any photographs in the main gallery space,' she said. She made Dragan put his carry bag in a specially designed locker and primly placed the key in his hand. Then they had to take their shoes off, wash their hands, don white gloves and step through an airlock.

'No praying to the Virgin Mary as well?' laughed Dragan. Sven shot him an angry look. 'The precautions are important,' he hissed. 'Curating, after all, originated from the noun 'curate' which in turn came from the medieval Latin word *curatus* – to belong to or care for something.'

Dragan shrugged. As Mimi went through the security protocol, Tally gestured to Sven, who moved to the young woman's side. 'I understand you have an eclectic display of works ranging from Renaissance antiquities to some outstanding pieces showcased in the most recent Documenta?' he enquired.

Mimi smiled appreciatively. 'Yes, indeed. We have 700 pieces by 85 artists to choose from and, while Max is in New York, I am cataloguing the collection. In particular, we have the political works from the 1980s period of Berlin subculture that saw artists move easily across disciplines, as well as rare photographic prints from the Weimar Republic chronicling lesbian nightclubs.'

'What a wonderful opportunity,' said Sven. He was envious.

Mimi smiled. 'I am working as an intern during the American summer college vacation,' she told them. 'The opportunity to come to Lindau and catalogue the collection happened when Max came to one of my father's fundraisers at The Whitney.'

'Good pay?' asked Dragan.

Mimi turned around in amazement. 'I don't get *paid*, I'm an intern. Next summer before I start my Master of Arts Management Degree I hope to intern at the Peggy Guggenheim in Venice.'

'For no pay?'

Mimi frowned at Dragan, unsure of what he was saying. Dragan looked at her as if she was an idiot. It was a New World-Old World cultural divide. Sven, sensing a looming confrontation enquired about a large sculpture they'd seen on the way in. 'By Ai Weiwei?' Mimi nodded. With seemingly no effort, the skinny woman pulled open the large sliding door and revealed the double-height gallery space, with floor to ceiling windows overlooking the lake. On the sleek oak floor, realistic looking severed horse's heads were covered in blue flock paint, and Venetian hand-blown red glass beads representing arterial blood spread in luminous pools across the floor.

Dragan nodded appreciatively. 'Dead horses,' he said.

Mimi shook her head. 'It's a little more complicated than that. The artist sees this as a metaphor.'

'For dead horses.'

Mimi crossed her arms. 'Animals exist in art as far more than symbols. Here, the objects stand in for dead human and non-human animals, problematising contemporary critiques of death camps, and slaughter.'

Dragan nodded. 'Human animals – my nephew has video game with these monsters in them.'

Sven held up his hand, authoritatively. He adopted the special curatorial voice. 'That's not what she means, Dragan. We – humans –*are* the human animals. It's *very* Darwinian.'

Dragan laughed. 'I have friend living in Darwin. He's a real animal.'

Sven opened his mouth to counter but Tally stepped in first. 'It's so – refreshing to see such museum quality work in a private collection,' she gushed. 'And did you say that you even have works ranging back in age to – ancient reliquaries?'

'In fact, I understand the owner's collection boasts such a piece?' added Sven, happy to be back on track. The less time he had to spend in Dragan's company the better. 'I'd be intrigued to see the foot reliquary which is a fine example from the period.'

Mimi looked relieved someone was speaking to her without contempt and smiled. 'Yes, of course. We have a special small gallery built to showcase the work.'

Sven followed Mimi, talking in calm and modulated tones about how the beauty of such a piece reflected the spiritual value of the relic inside.

'What relic is it, do you know?' he asked.

'I think it's a toe.'

'Whose toe?'

Mimi shrugged. 'I've been working with the Asian art aspect of the collection. The gentlemen from the Society who visit each month however could tell you more than me. In fact they are due here today, after lunch.'

Sven looked at Tally in horror. While Mimi unlocked the door to the small gallery she made 'faster faster' movements with her hands to speed up the process.

The room, once they stepped inside, was cool and dark. Sven knew low light levels and strict temperature control were necessary for art conversation.

'I assume you have some important works on display?'

Mimi nodded. 'Max purchased a page of an illustrated manuscript said to have been brought back from the crusades. It's the softest parchment, with gold leaf and lapis lazuli.' She pressed a button and a soft light flickered in a cabinet set in deep mahogany. Behind the glass, the page seemed to hover in blackness. And next to it, on a raised Perspex plinth, was a jewel encrusted silver foot, with a little window on the upper arch, like an old ship. Tally stepped closer. She could almost feel Saint Aspasia, feel her pain as she was thrown alive into the fire, her heart yet to be fatally pierced, but her tongue already ripped from her mouth. How blood would have poured down her gullet, the sounds of screaming all around her. She would have been stripped of her clothes and dignity. But she faced death stoically.

'I'm not sure what the significance of the foot is,' said Mimi. 'I consider myself a Buddhist atheist feminist, so I am not that interested in all the superstitious stuff around the reliquaries. But the vessel is really awesome.'

'Can I hold it – so I can really get sense of the piece I am writing about?' asked Tally. Mimi, chatelaine of the collection, serious sprite in black latex, pulled open a drawer and took out two pairs of white gloves. She handed a pair to Tally and pulled on her own gloves. Only then did she unlock the glass sliding door, reach in, and take out the reliquary.

Suddenly the room went pitch black.

Mimi screamed. Glass smashed. Tally was knocked to the floor and hit her head on the side of an ebony wood cabinet. She cried out in pain. Sven instinctively dropped down to find her.

'Are you okay?'

Her face was wet and sticky, but she pushed Sven away. 'The toe! Get Saint Aspasia's toe!' Sven launched himself up again and collided with Dragan. Except it wasn't Dragan – this male body was lean and tall, not a stocky tank. Hands gripped his neck and the man tried to wrestle him to the ground. But, lithe from Tai Chi and Yoga, Sven easily slipped the grasp. This time, the man he collided with *was* Dragan. He could smell the nicotine cloud that hung over him like a miasma.

'We are not alone,' hissed Dragan. Then someone grabbed Dragan and they tackled each other to the floor. How many men were there? Sven was pushed against the wall and hands came back to his neck as he struggled.

'Leave him alone!' yelled Tally. The sound of a large object connecting with bone and flesh filled the air.

Suddenly, the hands released and Sven could breathe again.

There was light. Dragan was at the door with the reliquary under his arm. Tally held Dragan's heavy camera. Blood ran down her face.

'We must leave before police come,' he said. 'Hurry!'

Sven wondered if he should check whether Mimi was all right. She was lying motionless in the corner of the room. But there was no time for questions.

They ran. And they ran.

Sven took over the driving on the frantic trip from Lindau to Paris. Tally fell asleep in the back seat of the Fiat, snuggled into Dragan's chest. Every time Sven looked in the rear view mirror Dragan had a smirk on his face. Sven simmered with rage and nearly ran the car off the autobahn several times. The backpack rested on the passenger seat, and Sven was incredulous that they had actually managed to steal the foot reliquary containing the Saint Aspasia's toe. By the time they got to Freiburg, the car seemed very hot, and he imagined he could sense the smouldering heat between Tally and Dragan. He felt very alone.

PARIS: THE TONGUE

For Tally the sounds of twilight were ones of melancholy. Even in Paris, perhaps her favourite place on earth, she couldn't shake the feeling that something was pulling at her, making her long for something she couldn't even name, and leaving her feeling unsettled. The onset of evening was a particularly lonely time of day. She looked into the houses with the lights on and saw others safe inside. She envied them and longed to have that domestic comfort, the familiarity and contentment of a relationship.

As Tally walked purposefully through the streets of Montparnasse, she knew it wasn't only this adventure she was undertaking. She had to know, once and for all, how Sven really felt about her. Did they have a chance to try and reignite their relationship? Her friends told her she was a fool to try – how can you trust a man who had once run off and married someone else, even though at the time their 'relationship' was fractured and in limbo. She always thought deep down Sven would come back to her, and this quest presented her with an opportunity to see if they could ever be more than just friends. Suddenly Fractal, the street artist leading them into the underground, stopped just in front of her.

'Regardez ceci!' he pointed at an angel skeleton emblazoned on the side wall of the entrance to a derelict train station. Tally felt a shiver go through her. The skeleton had an obscene grin and seemed to be looking straight at her. Somewhere, in the 200 km of snaking labyrinth beneath their feet was a secret shrine with the reliquary of Saint Aspasia.

It was said to be a chamber full of anguished whispers. Some said it was the words of the dead, carried up from the mass subterranean burial grounds. Others said it emanated only from the glowing crystal box installed some five years ago in the rough-hewn enclosure, where a devout group of mystics met each full moon.

Tally knew in her heart the words were Saint Aspasia's own – a refusal to recant and defiance in the face of brutal and painful death.

'This is the place,' Tally told Sven and Dragan who were following close behind. They were all wearing black, as instructed, for their journey into the underworld of southern Paris. Once Fractal found the boarded-up entrance, Dragan quickly took out a pair of bolt cutters from his backpack and made short work of the security system.

They didn't speak as they followed Fractal through the silent space, the light from their headlamps bouncing off the curved roof lined with glazed ceramic tiles. Rats scurried past as they ventured down the stairs, a winding, twisting spiral that lead to a disused section of track. On the far side of the platform, visible when Fractal shone a torch, was the angel skeleton again, a finger pointing at a small hole close to the ground. This was the sewer entrance they were to use to descend to the tunnels below.

Sven took the opportunity to again argue the case for going underground via a manhole – which he considered far less risky. 'There is a secret entrance near Montparnasse-Bienvenue station. It sure beats the hell out of crawling through some sewer outlet.'

'Fractal says that only last week the authorities locked three supposedly secret entrances to the tunnels. This way is safer,' said Tally.

'Are you sure he knows what he is talking about?'

'Guy Ritchie hired him as a location scout for one of his movies. If you want to know how to get anywhere illegally, ask a street artist.'

For Sven, Paris meant strolling through the posh 6th quartier and chancing upon Catherine Deneuve at the Café de Flore, visiting Frank Gehry's Foundation Louis Vuitton in the verdant Bois de Boulogne, or meeting up with Parisian friends in the Batignolles neighbourhood. Paris did not mean crawling through sewers. Unlike Tally, Sven wasn't interested in being edgy, alternative or even hip. He was interested in Paris as the City of Love. Not Paris, the Stench of Death. Or shit. Merde! *Non.* However, like Saint Aspasia, he held his tongue and followed the others, getting on his hands and knees to wriggle and push his way along the cold wet earth. In they went: first Fractal; then Tally; then Sven; and behind him, Dragan.

Sven narrowly missed getting kicked in the head by Tally. He tried his best, but even the thought of being caught by police and the increasingly uncomfortable weight of the backpack didn't stop him from sneaking an admiring look at her impressive rear as they wriggled through the entrance to the dark tunnel.

He made sure he stuck close to Tally's side as they descended into the underworld. Aside from the fraction of the tunnels used for the underground train system and the ones kept for the tourists who diligently visited the catacombs, Dragan informed them there were thousands of kilometres of unused and forgotten tunnels, those gates and locks were only designed to keep out wandering civilians. The well known and infamous collection of sanctified skulls and bones that thousands queued to see at the catacombs were window dressing only. Underneath Paris, in the limestone caves and centuries-old warrens, there was a secret world, one only briefly infiltrated by outsiders.

This was the where Saint Aspasia's tongue had been taken, by those who worshipped her and delighted in their own eccentric devotions. As Sven was fast realising, if you were wealthy enough, anything was possible. A secret crypt underneath the streets of Paris beat an obscure Melbourne laneway bar any day. All the faithful had to do was follow the signs in Latin on the wall, know where to look, or have a key to enter a locked gate.

'The beauty of illicit worship is that there are no security alarms, or surveillance cameras,' Tally informed him, after making contact with Fractal on their arrival in Paris. 'This information about the crypt's location came from old fashioned shoe-leather investigation. It's not even listed on the dark web.'

Tally first met up with Fractal in the Goutte-d'Or. Sven admired the way she was fearless in making contacts – anything for a story, she'd always say. He admitted it was one of the many things he found attractive about her. He loved her guts and determination as much as those amazing breasts that Dragan was constantly commenting on. As the stench of sewage overwhelmed his olfactory senses, Sven willed himself to think salacious thoughts about Tally, to distract from having a full-blown panic attack. He hated confined space, was borderline claustrophobic, and had a fear of rats. In short, not the sort of person suited to going through the vast labyrinth of tunnels that spiraled their veins through Paris. The headlamp itched and was giving him a headache, but the thought of being trapped in the dark was even worse.

Just as he started to hyperventilate, he felt a cold gush of wind on his face. He looked down. Tally had already scampered over the edge with Fractal.

Sven hesitated. It looked like a long drop, and he didn't want to hurt himself. He eased forward but before he could carefully descend, Dragan pushed him hard, and he fell heavily onto the dank surface below. It stank of piss.

'Sven! Careful!' Tally rushed over. 'You've got to take care of the *cargo*!' she said. Cargo was their word for the reliquary and relic in front of other people. Fractal, a tall Algerian wearing a dark jumpsuit, glanced at Sven's backpack with interest.

'Be discreet!' Sven hissed.

'He doesn't even speak English,' said Tally.

Dragan jumped effortlessly from the ledge and landed next to him, splashing the piss-soaked water into Sven's face. He was going to complain, but Dragan grabbed his arm and helped him up. As they walked on, Dragan took his electronic vaporless cigarette from his pocket and sucked on it. Sven thought it incredibly metrosexual for a man who needed to shave every two hours, but thought better of mentioning this to Tally, who seemed to have grown fond of the man with no neck.

Deep underground the streets of Paris, in a tunnel that smelled of shit, Sven groaned. The heat on his back was making his bowels play up. And of course, there were no toilets nearby. He wondered about that – where did the faithful relieve themselves in a secret underground crypt? He hated to think. If the reliquary really was being used by a breakaway group of Worshippers of the Forty Virgins, sanitation obviously wasn't high on their list. Much like the Court of Versailles. Now, trudging through the tunnel in a cold stream of water, Sven whimpered.

They continued through the tunnels in silence, the air around them growing increasingly cold and damp, until the water ran down the sides of the walls and their feet became wet and slippery. Elsewhere underground, tourists thronged through the Catacombes de Paris, snapping selfies with the famous ossuaries, thrilling to the ghoulish experience of being close to the remains of six million people.

But there were no carefully arranged bones or tourist guides down here. The only light was from their headlights, strapped tight to their foreheads. At one point, where the tunnel widened out and branched off into four directions Sven noticed the first sign, illuminated in the thin strip of light cast by their head lamps. It was a roughly stencilled image of the Parthenon, with three spray-painted letters on the roughly hewn limestone walls: *SOD*.

'Tally!' Sven cried out. 'I think we are close.' She rushed next to him. They ran their hands over the image. 'SOD – Society of the Dilettanti. They've been here.'

Tally was equal parts excited and terrified. She'd discovered Fractal through a local journalist, and asked him about rumours of a secret chamber.

It wasn't on the performance art or party circuit like many of the tunnels, but given to a more spiritual dimension. A key element was the limestone grotto that had been carved by devoted followers of the mystic known only as The Guru. Fractal knew of the place. It was said, he told her, as if a particular atmosphere of tranquillity and silence surrounded the grotto, which was a shrine to a magnificent gilded object that held a piece of flesh within its crystal tube.

She had no reason to doubt him. Tally heard whispers around the street artists' network in Melbourne that Paris street artists who used the tunnels as their private galleries had stumbled upon a chamber that was a secret space of worship.

Tally had good reason to believe that the secret chamber held The Reliquary of Saint Aspasia's tongue. She had been thinking about Saint Aspasia's fate a lot. How rather than deny her faith under the threat of the most horrible death, she had remained silent and refused to renounce. A metal ball had been placed in her mouth to engulf her words in flames. Tally felt that this relic of the Saint's tongue – more so than the toe – was bringing her closer to the source of this remarkable woman.

Sven groaned. She sighed. Turning around she noted how he was perspiring and clutching his stomach. Ever since they had left Lindau, he seemed to get sicker and sicker. She stopped and tugged at the backpack. 'Come on, you look dreadful. Let Dragan carry this for a while, okay?'

Sven started to protest but doubled over in agony, so Tally and Dragan eased the backpack off him. Mercifully, they had come to a clearing in the tunnels, a fork where several different pathways branched out, and the ground was firm and dry beneath them. Fractal pointed to the right, eagerly, and Sven closed his eyes and willed himself to go on.

That's when he heard it. The voice. Or, he slowly realised – not *a* voice – *her* voice, with all its melodic resonance. A beautiful, calm voice, speaking an ancient language to him that he could understand.

'Get up,' she enjoined him. 'Rise up now and reclaim me, make me whole again. Take me into the light…the light…the light…'

'*Dominus Illuminatio Mea,*' he cried, before collapsing. Was it Saint Aspasia talking to him?

'He speaks Latin?' said Dragan in amazement.

Tally bent down to hear him mutter. 'I think he's hallucinating.' As she shook him, Saint Aspasia's voice became fainter. Sven suddenly jumped up, feeling wonderful, and hungry. All the pain had gone.

'We have to get to the grotto,' he said. 'Quickly, before the Society of the Dilettanti get there. Hurry. Hurry!'

He ran after Fractal, his headlamp casting a pool of light in the darkness ahead. As Tally began to follow, Dragan caught her arm. 'Stop!' he said. 'Why do you keep running to him?'

'I am going after the reliquary,' she protested. But Dragan gripped her harder. 'No. Why do you keep running to him? You said he married. You said he went to America. And now – now he is sad and confused and alone and he comes back – and you keep running to him?'

Tally looked ahead into the darkness. 'I don't want to stand here, surrounded by bones, trying to understand myself,' she said, softly. Suddenly she felt very cold. She gripped her arms and shivered. 'And I don't want to be down here talking about Sven's marriage when the Society are looking for us.'

She turned but Dragan swung her around, pulling her towards his chest. Then he kissed her, his hands holding her face, his fingers knotted through her long dark hair. After a long moment, she pulled away from him.

'No,' she said softly. 'I can't.'

'You love him still?'

'I haven't been sitting around waiting for Sven you know,' she said. 'The reality is that life moves on, that one moves through the world and energy attracts energy.'

Dragan nodded. 'So you met someone else?' He pulled the electronic cigarette from his pocket. 'But Sven doesn't know about this.'

They walked into the darkness, following the distant sounds to join the others. 'I went to London when we broke up and Sven refused to answer my emails. Then I found out from someone else he got married three months later, so I threw myself into my work, and dated other men. I was covering a conference at Imperial College on Renaissance art and politics when I met Professor Jeremy Smythe.'

'The man we are to meet in London. The man who owns the reliquary of Saint Aspasia's heart.'

'I saw the heart reliquary in Jeremy's bedroom. He has it in a specially made Cabinet of Curiosity.'

'So, you steal the heart from your former lover?'

'He deserves it, okay? One, he shouldn't have it in the first place. What right does he have stealing Greece's cultural heritage? Two, he is a distant relative of Lord Elgin, which makes him even more tainted by association and history. I mean, first the Parthenon marbles, next, pieces of Saints. This plunder has to stop. And third – the bastard cheated on me.'

Dragan shrugged. 'Love, hate, passion, conflict, theft. What's not to understand?'

The tunnels bent and turned in such a way that they created, in various spots, perfect whispering galleries. It allowed Sven to hear Dragan's last remark, and turning off his headlamp, he silently backtracked in the dark, watching as Dragan's headlamp glowed in the distance, and he saw the large man move in towards Tally, and then hold and kiss her passionately. He could barely breathe. Despite his indifference over the years, lack of commitment and even ill-fated marriage, he always felt that he and Tally had a special bond, a remarkable intimacy, that was, well *incorruptible*. As Dragan held Tally – *his Tally* – he switched his headlamp back on and crept back along the tunnel towards Fractal.

Then, as Sven turned the corner Fractal stopped him and held up a torch. Everything was illuminated. They were in a church of sorts, with rough limestone seats carved into the walls, and a soaring altar constructed out of a jutting shelf of stone. And there, on a high plinth, was the reliquary.

It was a shimmering crystal cylinder, the glass etched, embellished with filigree gold. Inside, suspended in clear liquid, was the fleshy tongue of Saint Aspasia, as pink as the day it was sliced from her body. As Sven stared in awe, he heard singing. It was the woman's voice again.

'Can you hear her?' said Sven.

'Pardon?' asked Fractal.

Sven fell to his knees. 'Saint Aspasia!' A blinding light hit his face, and he fell in rapture on the wet ground, writhing in ecstasy.

He felt a sharp kick in his side. It was Tally. 'What on earth are you doing?' she asked. 'You're not even religious! Snap out of it. I can hear voices in the tunnel – and something is wrong with Dragan.'

Sven turned around and saw Dragan sweating and clutching his stomach, the backpack glowing on his back. Sven looked up at the reliquary and gestured to Fractal to help him. More than willing, Fractal gave Sven a leg-up so that, balancing on his shoulders, Sven could grab the reliquary of the tongue. But just as he grasped the prize, he heard shouting and running, and Fractal shifted violently under him, causing him to fall onto the hard stone floor. He landed hard on a pile of bones, and passed out.

Tally slapped him across the face. 'Wake up!'

'What happened?' His arms were empty. Where was the reliquary?

'You have to get up. The Dilettani attacked. Dragan knocked the men unconscious. Fractal found some chains from a nearby S & M chamber but I don't know how long it will contain them. We have to get out with the reliquary immediately.'

Tally pulled him by the arm, and he winced with pain. Fractal's face was smeared with blood and he held a jacket to his nose. Even Dragan looked exhausted, his face red and covered in sweat.

'The tongue was pink!' he told Tally. 'I saw it in the crystal.'

Tally nodded. 'We saw it too, when we put the reliquary in the backpack. I read that when the coffin containing Saint Aspasia's body was opened for the first time, the priests saw what had been left after she was burned alive had not decayed at all. What they found was her right foot with the intact big toe, her skull containing a remarkably fresh looking tongue, as if she could still speak, and her heart, still whole despite a spear piercing it in two.'

They exited the chamber, stepping over two large men bound and gagged and wearing leather masks: Dragan's handiwork, no doubt. As Fractal lead them expertly out of the tunnels of Paris, and life above them continued without regard for their adventure, Dragan began staggering and coughing. After half and hour, he slumped to the floor, gasping for breath.

'I told him smoking was bad for his health, that those electronic cigarettes are just as toxic as regular ones,' said Tally. 'But European men – they won't listen.'

Unceremoniously she walked over to the large man and tugged at the backpack. Dragan offered no resistance. Tally pulled it off him and handed it to Sven.

'You wear it. We only have one relic to find now and then we can get to Thessaloniki.'

Sven put on the backpack, noting it was of course heavier than previously with the new reliquary added to the cargo. As soon as it was on his back, the now familiar heat pounded his flesh, and he felt his body drained of energy with every step. However, Dragan quickly regained his strength once they left the tunnels, and Fractal scampered off into the night, terrified by the encounter with the men in the chamber.

Tally found a pay phone on the street, and anonymously called the police to let them know about the illegal entrance, the religious chamber and the men bound and gagged and languishing in the dark tunnel. Sven knew in his heart he would rue the day he ever crossed Tally. Woe to thee who angers this woman, he thought. Woe to thee.

Back at the hotel room in the foot of the Boulevard Barbes, Tally revealed the final stage of her plan. They were to go to London, where the Saint Aspasia's heart was held in the town house of a wealthy collector in Knightsbridge. 'His name is Lord Jeremy Smythe,' she said. 'The 5th Earl of Wildcroft.'

'Oh – a Lord of the Realm no less,' sniggered Sven. 'I am going to enjoy taking the heart from him, a born-to-rule ponce no doubt.'

Dragan watched as Tally's face went red. She didn't say anything and Sven didn't notice. He continued. 'You know, there is probably a logical explanation for why Saint Aspasia's body parts didn't decay. The grand reliquaries are devotional works of art in themselves, created to hold the sacred body parts. Maybe there is something – a little metaphysical about them.'

'You mean – religious magic,' said Dragan. Sven had noticed a prominent gold cross around the man's neck. 'The reason they do not corrupt is because they are blessed. They are saints.'

Sven pondered that whatever the reason for the magic, the reliquaries presented the perfect interdisciplinary research material: combining medical, artistic, anthropological and historical aspects as well as the supernatural. As he considered a new version of his literature review, he felt an uncomfortable heat radiating from the backpack on his bed. Tally had warned him not to let the backpack leave his side, and he felt like he was having a hot flush. Sweat dripped from his brow and he winced as he picked up the backpack to put it on the floor.

'Christ – the bag's hot!' A hiss and puff of smoke emerged as Sven tried to pull open the zipper to let out some of the heat. He cried out as he reached inside – the tin containing Saint Aspasia's toe was glowing red, and Sven dropped it on the floor, whereupon the lid sprung open and the plump pink and fleshy toe and tongue rolled on the carpet. Suddenly the body parts started to smoulder.

'It's alive!' cried Sven, feeling nauseous at having the animated flesh so close to his back. There appeared to be fresh blood dripping from the severed skin. Dragan touched the cross around his neck.

'Don't just stand there, do something!' yelled Tally.

'I will pray,' said Dragan.

Tally muttered obscenities and grabbed the ashtray from the coffee table, and used it to pick up the relics. She placed them back in the container.

A second later, the alarm sounded, and the sprinklers turned on.

'We have to evacuate!' Tally cried out. 'Get the backpack!'

She deposited the relics into the tin, and wedged them into the backpack along with the two reliquaries. She then flung the bag over her shoulder and sprinted out into the corridor with Dragan and Sven close behind. By the time they had charged down the stairwell with the other hotel guests, and were on the street, Tally was covered in sweat. The heat from the backpack was unbearable, but she was loathe to complain after teasing Sven and Dragan about the discomfort. Besides, perhaps she was just having a hot flush. After all, she was 45 years old and much more likely to be having a menopausal moment that a metaphysical one. Tally wiped her dripping face with her sleeve.

As they stood at the entrance of the Gare du Nord station, clutching their EuroTrain tickets in their hands, a gypsy woman broke away from a motley group of beggars who swamped the public foyer, her gold painted hands held out for money. Tally looked away but the gypsy woman grabbed her by the arm and spoke rapidly.

'Sorry – I don't understand,' Tally said, pulling away from the woman's grasp. 'I'm Australian.' The woman wore an odd assortment of contemporary and timeless outfits. She shook her head and pointed to her chest.

'*Cigan*,' Dragan hissed, moving in to protect Tally. But the woman would not be moved. She yelled out, and again indicated to her chest, and mimicked a knife plunging into her heart.

The train number was called and they rushed to the gate. 'What did she say?' asked Tally. Dragan looked back at the woman. 'She is crazy gypsy.'

'What did she say?'

Dragan shrugged. 'She said if you continue, with your journey you will die.'

'I'll die?'

'Maybe – something in the heart will die. A pain in the heart? Like a knife in the heart.'

'A heart attack?'

'I cannot translate so clearly. But she warns of danger, if you believe these things.' Tally chewed her bottom lip, and Dragan squeezed her hand. 'The *cigan* also say for money, maybe prediction be different.' Tally smiled at him, but felt a wave of fear creep over her. Maybe the cigan knew something. After all, Tally was about to visit her former lover to steal the last reliquary. Saint Aspasia's heart. Which had a spear still embedded though the centre.

LONDON: THE HEART

According to the news reports, there are two items in the British Museum's ancient Egyptian collection that are associated with alleged curses. Both an Egyptian coffin lid, and a cartonnage mask, donated in 1885 and 1889 by so-called 'cursed' Victorian gentlemen, Thomas Douglas Murray and Walter Herbert Ingram. Less well known is the third item, donated in 1886: an Egyptian canopic jar used to contain the heart of a minor Egyptian deity. The priceless piece was stolen in a daring art theft from the British Museum a year after it was found to have magically rejuvenated the security guards in the Egyptian wing, restoring them back to the peachy clear-skinned boys of their adolescence.

Originally used to store vital organs after the embalming process, the jar's magical properties became the basis for many of the more salacious dinner party stories that did the rounds of the better homes around Bloomsbury in Edwardian London. Lady Victoria Pollington, who, it was alleged, had funded the jar's theft in order to preserve her legendary looks was said to have been the inspiration for Oscar Wilde's sensational story *The Portrait of Dorian Gray*

But as history – and Wikipedia – will attest, the stolen canopic jar's whereabouts have long been unknown; as has the stolen heart of Saint Aspasia, in its golden starburst reliquary.

Talitha Nakos, however, knew where each of these items was located. She had seen them all in the Knightsbridge bedroom of Lord Jeremy Smythe, the 8th Earl of Wildcroft, and Lady Victoria Pollington's great, great, great grandson, who was born improbably when she was not only well past menopause, but well into her dotage.

Tally remembered her shock of seeing Jeremy for the first time, then in his 40s, and looking as young if not younger than men half his age. A quick Google check when she started on this adventure confirmed that Jeremy – now in his mid 50s – was drinking from the same fountain of youth as his forebears.

From the biodynamic vitality of Saint Aspasia's body parts they had witnessed so far, it was obvious to Tally that when combined with the legendary canopic jar, it would bestow upon the owner a chance to reverse all damage to body and soul. She supposed that Jeremy Smythe hadn't factored in the risks of bedding a journalist. But once she saw the canopic jar in the Cabinet of Curiosities in his bedroom, she knew exactly what it was, and its provenance.

If it rejuvenated Lady Pollington, and enabled Jeremy Smythe to remain 25 forever, imagine what the heart could do to the Greek economy. Why, she alone would be responsible for restoring the fortunes of her father's country, and revitalising and strengthening the flagging Eurozone. She was going to pay her former lover a visit, and reclaim Greece's cultural heritage.

Dragan had managed to borrow a distinctive black London cab from a man who owed him a favour. The cabbie, a short Cockney who introduced himself as 'Reg what drives the motor', was at St. Pancras station when they got off the Eurostar from Paris. He handed over the car keys with a stern warning. 'Keep your dog and bone on,' he told Dragan. 'The Ducks and Geese don't take kindly to unregistered drivers in the jam jar, and I've no desire to reside in the Flowery Dell.'

Sven bounced on the back seat and beamed with joy as he gazed out of the window. 'It's like a fairytale. Cockney rhyming slang *and* elegant Georgian terrace houses. Honestly, Mary Poppins could float down from the chimneys at any time!'

'How long since you have been in London?' sighed Tally. 'The cost of even a humble sandwich, the crowds, and the miserable climate–'

'Don't be so *Australian*,' he chided. 'We might have the weather, the food and the lifestyle, but England has history.'

'It also has lots of stolen art and cultural items, which, if you remember, is why we are here.'

'Oh, come on, we're in London! Let me enjoy this moment before we launch our counter attack on the British establishment.' Sven continued to gaze out of the cab window, dreaming of the 1980s when young Lady Di and the Sloane Rangers ruled Knightsbridge in their Harris tweeds and pretty Laura Ashley frocks.

Dragan's phone rang and he screeched to a halt somewhere in Fitzrovia. After a rapid-fire conversation he ordered the pair out of the car.

'But we need to get to Smythe's house in Belgravia!' said Tally. 'And I am wearing heels.'

'Is a big problem, I must fix,' said Dragan. 'I will come soon.'

He left them outside the rather glorious multi-hued wedding cake of a building that was London's Natural History Museum.

Tally checked her phone again for Smyth's address. 'My contact says the arms dealer is really only interested in the case the heart sits in – a fine example of a starburst reliquary. It's covered in gold, ivory, gems and enamel.'

Although Kensington was as flat as the Netherlands, her inappropriate shoes with killer heels, while giving her long and slender legs an enviable shapely appearance in her tight, bondage skirt, made walking for endless blocks uncomfortable. She wobbled and cursed. Sven enjoyed the view.

'Tally, you should have worn something more appropriate for art theft,' said Sven. 'Not that you don't look amazing, but just saying.'

'I wasn't planning on *walking* there,' Tally replied. 'Let's call a proper cab.' She was pleased Sven noticed her outfit – and her body. But she agreed it was a foolish choice of attire. Partially because her decision had been dictated by her desire to make Smythe suffer on as many levels as possible. She wanted to look good, especially considering at the age of 45, she didn't have access to the fountain of youth that kept her old lover young.

As she looked around for a cab, Tally had the strangest feeling that someone was watching her. Of course she was being watched. Men looked at her all the time – she was as familiar with the male gaze as animals in the zoo were by the attentions of excitable children. Still, it did seem odd that the man, or men, watching her kept appearing and disappearing in the crowd.

After hobbling to the end of the block, Tally had enough. 'Let's sit down,' she said, easing onto a wooden seat against the railings outside the museum.

Sven was only too happy to join her, remarking that it was a pity they didn't have time to go inside to see the dinosaur exhibit. 'Still, the wildlife garden is amazing, isn't it? They even have a large pond and ducks – right in the heart of London!'

'Talitha Nakos?' The accent was smooth, clipped, and very British. Without waiting for a reply, Tally was hauled up roughly by the elbow, and pushed against the railings.

Sven started to protest and raised his voice, 'I'll call the police!' he thrust his phone into the air, pressing camera and clicking off incriminating photos. The other man grabbed it from Sven, and threw it over the iron railing fence, into the pond.

'That's an iPhone 6!' Sven gasped. 'It's not waterproof!' The man laughed and Sven demanded to see a lawyer.

'I don't think so, Dr Mortensen. We have the ability to hold you and Ms Nakos for 24 hours on suspicion of art theft,' said the man with a thick Scottish accent.

'Art Theft? Ridiculous!' yelled Tally. 'Check my handbag – it's Prada – hardly a tampon fits in there, it's so small and expensive!'

The Scot had grabbed Sven's forearm and by now was pushing him into the waiting black car, while Tally was bundled into the back seat by the larger man, who said nothing. The questions started immediately.

'Who is your contact?'

'Where is the backpack?'

'I don't know what you are talking about,' protested Tally convincingly. 'I am simply a Greek-Australian journalist here in London to write a piece about Amal Clooney's push for the Greek Government to take Britain to the International Court of Justice over the Parthenon Sculptures.'

'You mean the *Elgin* Marbles,' said the Scot. 'Acquired by Lord Elgin from the Ottoman Empire 200 years ago.'

'No. I mean the *Parthenon Marbles* which were stolen from Greece!' Tally glowered as her handbag was thoroughly searched, and hissed as the Scot yanked the SIM card out of her mobile phone.

'Why did you do that?'

'Save you on international roaming charges.'

'It was a Lebara card picked up at St Pancras to use in Europe!'

'Well, we'll look with interest at the calls you have made – and received.'

Sven was preoccupied by the sensation of sitting so close to Tally and feeling her body against his. He began to shuffle a little closer, to enhance the experience. Which worked until the silent man slammed a hand down on his thigh to stop him wriggling.

'Not planning on going anywhere, are you?' he asked. Surprisingly, he had an Irish accent.

Sven gulped and looked down at the hand and noticed something he'd been too preoccupied to see before. The man had a tattoo between his thumb and finger, a perfect circle with a thunderbolt searing through the middle. It was the same tattoo that the man yelling at Tally also sported. *A thunderbolt!* Sven's body suddenly went rigid, fists clenched, eyes closed, with his head thrashing from side to side.

Tally screamed. 'Stop the car! Stop the car! He's having one of his seizures!'

The men looked at their captive in alarm. Sven's body jerked. He groaned and mumbled incoherently.

'We have to get him flat on the ground or he will choke!' screamed Tally. 'Please – call an ambulance – pull over!'

The car veered through the heavy traffic and hit the kerb. The men carried Sven to the pavement and stood over him. Tally bent down and put her face to Sven's to check his breathing.

'Are you faking this?' she whispered.

Sven nodded, and continued to thrash around on the asphalt. Tally could hear a police siren in the distance. She glanced around, unsure of what to do. They needed to continue the charade at least until the real police arrived.

'We need a doctor!' she screamed.

As luck would have it, a teacher crossing the road with a group of primary school children broke through the crowd and rushed over.

"I'm trained in first aid" she called out.

Tally and Sven's abductors tried to block her, but as the police siren grew louder, they suddenly fled the scene. Sven sat up just as the teacher was about to start CPR.

'Thank goodness, it's a false alarm,' said Tally. 'This sometimes happens when his blood sugar drops.'

'You should watch your health, young man,' the teacher warned him, before she returned to her students.

'We've got to get away,' hissed Sven. 'Those men weren't the police or Interpol.'

'Who were our abductors then?' asked Tally.

'The tattoo between the thumb and finger – shape of a circle with a thunderbolt plunged down the middle.' He said. 'The mark of the Society of the Dilettanti.'

'You mean SOD?'

Sven nodded.

'And the tattoo?'

Sven was in his element – the Society was a particular interest for him. He continued, 'It was an obscure neo-classical reference, possibly referring to the more secret breakaway group instigated by Payne Knight.'

They walked slowly down Brompton Road, while Tally cursed her high heels. It had been Sven's idea to stash the relics in a locker at Knightsbridge station. He'd jumped out of the cab while Dragan yelled that it was a waste of time.

Sven, however, was frankly glad to get rid the piece of mummified flesh, which was disturbingly growing pinker and warmer each hour. He didn't like to point this out to Tally – but it was almost as if Saint Aspasia's body parts were *alive.*

'Unless I am mistaken, the oath taken by the Dilettanti was to *protect* artworks,' said Tally.

'Indeed, that was Joshua Reynolds' intent. But things got a little more, shall we say, murky with the more, shall we say, risqué Diletanti Payne Knight. He was renowned for his interest in phallic imagery. You know, etchings of huge cocks with women riding them like horses, that sort of thing.'

'Oh, please. No wonder this is a special interest of yours. The guy sounds like he had an adolescent sense of aesthetics.'

'On the contrary, as a member of the SOD, Knight was considered to be an arbiter of taste.'

Tally screwed up her nose. 'I am sure generations of schoolboys drawing dicks as sad graffiti would applaud him. But the question remains – how *did* the Society know we were after Saint Aspasia's body parts?'

The two friends pondered the thought for a moment. As they came within sight of the station, however, they realised something was very wrong.

Very, very wrong.

Two blocks out, roads were cordoned off, and police were holding the line. TV stations had sent vans and trucks with their antennas now winced to the skies and ambulance vans were hovering at an anxious distance.

Tally tapped a woman who'd stopped while walking her terrier. 'Excuse me, what's happening?' she asked.

'Something caught fire in the station, apparently, they sent robots in. It could be a biological weapon.'

Sven went pale. He grabbed Tally's hand. 'It's the relics! They have caught alight or something. I told you it wasn't safe. The tongue and toe have self combusted!'

'Stop getting hysterical. No one will suspect us – or the mummified flesh. This is London. What are the authorities more likely to believe: that the object is a biological weapon planted as part of a deadly terrorist attack; or that it's the stolen mummified toe and tongue of a long dead Saint caught fire after it was stashed in a locker by two Australian art thieves?'

'You do have a point,' conceded Sven. 'However, it's not theft if we are returning it to its rightful burial place.'

'Well thank you for clarifying that, Mr Egalitarian, but we are in London, home of the stolen *Parthenon* Sculptures. The police won't take kindly to us if we admit we plan to take the body parts back to Greece.'

'So we let them close down the entire London train network even though we know it's not a terrorist attack?'

Tally nodded. 'That's exactly what we do. Shut down British Rail. It will at least create traffic chaos and a diversion as we make off with the heart.'

Sven sighed and looked towards Knightsbridge station. Fire trucks were spraying the building with water. The toe and tongue had the potential to create another Great Fire of London. Saint Aspasia was every bit as fierce as the stories that preceded her. 'You're right, we need to forget about the relics that are on fire and get to Smythe, and take the heart.'

They managed to hail a cab to Cadogan Square, Belgravia. Sven went pale as he watched how much the short trip cost.

'We won't be eating dinner.'

'I'm wearing heels,' Tally pointed out. 'It was bad enough standing around watching the tube station on fire. My feet are killing me.'

They were expected.

Of course they were, thought Sven. Tally had seen to it. He watched as the front curtain twitched when they arrived at their destination. Sven sighed at the impressive white stucco terrace, with views of the acres of private communal gardens across the road. This was Georgian splendour. This was opulence. It was a side effect of his visual training that Sven looked at all nuances of architectural detail but usually forgot people's names and faces.

Tally on the other hand couldn't tell Ionic from Doric but could place everyone, instantly. Sven often thought together they made one complete person. Alone, they floundered, each overburdened with a brilliance of one sort but not another. He knew he was a better man with her. He also knew that she could find a better man than him.

'No wonder Smythe could afford to steal the reliquary from Thessaloniki,' said Sven. 'I am just surprised he didn't get the whole city transplanted while he was at it, take everything he wanted. He could probably afford to wipe out the Greek debt with his shoe money.'

The door opened. There in front of them stood the richest man Sven had probably ever met close up. And he didn't look a day older than 25. Was this professor Smythe's son? Or grandson?

'My darling,' he said, reaching for Tally's hand. 'How delightful to see you again. I have just been following the Twitter feed – there's been a suspected terrorist attack on one on the tube stations.'

'I think you'll find that's a little exaggerated,' Tally replied.

They were invited into the front sitting room, furnished with crystal chandeliers, carved ceiling trims and oak paneling. Sven noted an artwork by Damien Hirst above the fireplace. Professor Smythe sat uncomfortably close to Tally and grilled Sven.

'Tell me, what do you hope to achieve with your third doctorate? What for instance, couldn't you discover in the first two?'

But Sven was used to such bait. Every doctorate provided a layer of thicker skin over his soul. 'Each doctorate, no matter who undertakes it, hopes to extend the sum of human knowledge by a small fraction,' he replied.

'I did mine some time ago, when they meant something,' said Smythe. 'At Imperial College.'

Sven nodded. 'Along with fiction writer H.G Wells, Darwinian biologist Thomas Henry Huxley and rock star Brian May, of Queen, and, of course, Holocaust denier David Irving, an impressive and rather eclectic Alumni.'

Smythe laughed and patted Tally on the thigh proprietorially. 'One day you have to tell me exactly what you see in this man,' he said.

'Isn't it obvious?' replied Tally. 'I enjoy the company of smart men with appalling behaviour.'

'Touche,' he said. 'I'll drink to that.' They downed their drinks, the champagne hitting the pleasure sensors of the brain as it fizzled its way into their blood stream. Tally smiled and then looked at her watch. 'Any time now,' she said.

'Any time for what?' asked Smythe, running his hand up her arm. Suddenly, he dropped his crystal champagne flute and flopped to the floor, hitting his head on the glass table as he fell. It made a terrible crack and blood started to ooze from the deep cut in his head.

'This is the reason you should never have a white cotton couch,' said Tally, stepping over him. 'Come on, the relic is in the bedroom on the third floor. Dragan will be here shortly,'

'But he just passed out!' yelled Sven. 'And he might bleed to death.'

Tally walked up the stairs and gestured for Sven to follow. 'I drugged him, and if he bleeds to death, no one will care. The man is an arms dealer, for heaven's sake. We are probably saving the lives of entire third world villages by rendering him momentarily unconscious. Come on.'

Sven knew Tally had said 'bedroom' and as she made her way there with all the accuracy of a heat seeking missile, he felt sick. It got worse as they entered the room, and he saw the massive four-poster bed. As Tally wrenched open the Cabinet of Curiosity and grabbed the starburst reliquary from its carved niche, Sven sat on the bed, his stomach in knots. He could almost feel Tally lying there, naked, with Smythe pawing her.

Dragan came through the door.

'He's not breathing. How much of the hebenon did you give him?'

'Twice what you suggested. The man is used to strong chemicals, I had to be sure.'

Sven sat upright and looked at Dragan and Tally in amazement. 'You gave him *hebenon?* It doesn't even exist outside Shakespeare.'

'Tell that to my grandmother,' said Dragan. 'She said anything that killed Hamlet's father is okay in her books for dealing with the enemy.'

'She knows *Hamlet* is a work of fiction, right?'

Tally held the reliquary aloft. 'Behold – Saint Aspasia's heart!' She pushed the reliquary towards Sven. 'Hold this while I use the bathroom.'

'You're kidding, right?' said Sven. He took the reliquary, inside which a bright, fleshy heart stood suspended in what looked like aspic, with a spear plunged through the centre. It looked liked a clenched, angry fist.

'The police could be here any second, we have a man lying unconscious and perhaps dead in the front room, we are about to steal a stolen relic, and you need to go to the *bathroom?*'

Tally held up her hand to Sven's face. 'Hey, women's problems, okay?' and slammed the ensuite door behind her.

'Women,' muttered Sven.

'For a doctor, you are an idiot.'

'Because I don't understand women?'

Dragan kicked the nearest chair. 'Moron! This woman she loves you for some reason. You aren't good enough for her. I am glad she makes the arms dealer so sick he won't remember his name for three years. I put extra Versed in the hebenon for good measure. Now, he have a little problem with his memory. Forever.'

'You gave him *dementia?'*

'A little trick where I come from, to deal with traitors. He makes people's lives a misery.'

'My life isn't so great,' Sven hated Dragan. 'I don't have tenure.'

'Tenure? Most of Europe can't get jobs to feed their families and you complain about tenure?'

'Well, my pain happens to be located higher up on Maslow's hierarchy of needs,' Sven retorted. 'You wouldn't understand.'

Dragan laughed. 'You sit on plane for 27 hours, ticket paid for by arms dealer you don't even know who only wanted Tally to come here so he could get her into bed again. But she double crossed him and drugged him to get the relic but I gave her corrupt medicine and actually poisoned him to revenge the deaths he caused in my village. *Understand?'*

Sven clutched the relic, which was making him perspire. 'I am doing my third doctorate in art history, not Shakespearean plot machinations. I don't follow at all. *You wanted Smythe dead?'*

'Dead is too difficult. Just, confused. Forever.'

'I get it, a living death. Clever,' Sven looked at the closed ensuite door. 'What's taking her so long? We need to get out of here before it's too late.'

Dragan sucked on his electronic cigarette. 'What would you know about too late? You don't look in front of your face to see the woman who dragged you on this adventure just so you might wake up before its too late.'

'Too late for what?' Sven watched Dragan as he sucked deeply on his electronic cigarette.

'When is it too late for love?'

'For love?' What was he saying? That Tally... *loved him?*

Dragan shrugged. 'We are all stupid in love. You are doctor-doctor and still keep studying and Tally – beautiful, strong woman – still thinks you worth loving.'

'She told you she loved me?'

'See it on her face. Look her in the eye. You love her?'

Sven looked to the ensuite door, as if he could see Tally with x-ray vision. 'Yes,' he nodded. 'I love her.'

'Then go fucking tell her, idiot!'

Emboldened by the dare, Sven strode out purposefully and knocked on the door. When she opened it, Sven realised she'd been crying. He pushed the door open and took her in his arms and pulled her to his chest, and gently kissed the tears away. Saint Aspasia's heart throbbed between them.

'What's the matter? We found all the relics. Okay, some set alight, that was strange, but we have the heart, and we will return the reliquaries tomorrow when we get to Thessaloniki and then take Saint Aspasia back to her church. It's all worked out perfectly. And who knows – by the miracle of Saint Aspasia, the Greek Debt crisis may be over.'

Just as Tally was about to answer, they heard police sirens, louder and more insistent by the second.

'Now we run,' said Dragan.

THESSALONIKI: RETURNING THE RELIC

The Aegean sea glinted and shimmered in the bluest of azure hazes, merging seamlessly into the cloud-free sky. A bowl of steaming octopus tentacles sat in front of Sven and as he sipped his large glass of ice cold lemony *Oenoforos*

Asprolithi, and stared out at Mount Olympus on the horizon, he thanked Saint Aspasia. Last night, after attempting to return the relic of her heart, but finding the church closed, he and Tally had ventured back to their room at the Elektra Palace Hotel and there, with the starburst reliquary on the bedside table, made love passionately. Now, sitting in the outdoor café, enjoying the view and the food, he cheerfully waited for Tally to finish shopping.

'You want more bread?' asked Dragan, sitting opposite him. Between them, wedged firmly at their feet, was the new backpack Dragan had bought for Saint Aspasia's heart, which they had carefully wrapped in toilet paper, as it had started oozing blood. Soon, the adventure would be over, and a new one would begin. Whatever happened to the Greek debt crisis, Sven knew one thing – after last night, there was no longer any Tally crisis. She was his, he was hers, and together, they would make their long overdue love affair work. That much he knew.

Dragan had dispensed with the electronic cigarettes in a city where smoking seemed as natural as the chips stuffed into souvlaki and instant coffee frappes. A plume of smoke hung over the table. Sven wondered if their unshakeable 'companion' might even return with them to Melbourne where apparently he had relatives in St Albans. As it was, Dragan had decided to flee London with them, and disappear into Greece's second largest city, blending into the strangely Ottoman and Byzantine town. With his many languages, he could pass for any number of nationalities.

A hopeful stray dog lay on the sidewalk, at once scrawny and proud. Sven marvelled at the way the Greeks respectfully fed and treated the stray dogs with kindness. In Melbourne someone would have called the lost dogs home, or kicked one out of boredom, but not in Greece. Sven tossed the piece of bread to the dog, in a magnanimous gesture of inter-species friendship. The large black dog on Aristoteles Square was one of several sunning itself, and lazily grabbed the bread as it landed nearby.

'You should not feed them,' said Dragan. 'It is bad luck.'

Sure enough, the dog and several others moved closer to their table. Sven happily tossed another piece of bread over to the pack.

'Stop that!' warned Dragan. 'You have bedroom brain, huh? All that sex went to your head?'

'What do you know?'

'I heard both of you last night – all night,' said Dragan. 'At least you are man enough to please her.'

Sven was about to reply when one of the dogs moved in and instead of begging for another piece of bread, ran under the table.

'Hey!' yelled Sven. He jumped up, upending his white wine, the glass smashing to the ground as the dog growled and grabbed the backpack with his teeth. Sven went to wrench the bag from the canine when Dragan hissed 'rabies!' Sven froze in terror. The dog ran off with Saint Aspasia's heart. He could probably smell it. It was rather ripe.

'Stop that dog!' screamed Sven.

The dog swerved and weaved through the people strolling in the park, and as Sven – tall, blonde and out of breathe – chased after it, short elderly Greek men cheered the dog on, urging the stray to escape to freedom.

At that instant, Tally ran to Sven's side, throwing her shopping bags on the boardwalk. 'Where is the backpack?'

'The dog grabbed it!'

'How?' Tally pushed Sven hard in frustration. 'HOW did you let a dog get hold of it?'

'It wasn't my fault – I was hungry. We came here for lunch and Dragan asked me if I wanted bread and I tossed some to the dog and–'

'You FED the stray dog?'

'I just put the backpack down for a second and the dog came running up out of nowhere.'

Tally grabbed Sven's arm. 'Come on – we need to run after it.'

She dragged him onto the waterfront, where they raced down the boardwalk, dodging skateboarders and rollerskaters and cyclists and mothers pushing prams, as they pursued the surprisingly fast and strong canine thief.

'Stop the dog!' screamed Tally, unable to remember how to say it in Greek.

Finally, as the White Tower loomed ever closer, the dog veered left and into the greenery, disappearing from view. Sven bent over double and panted. It was amazing what energy a stray dog made of skin and bone could have.

'If we don't get the backpack away from that dog, then I will have nothing to write about; no journal article, no book deal – no tenure,' wailed Sven.

He and Tally slumped to the cobblestone step at the foot of one of the fountains dotted around the gardens. In front of them was the ruined church and foundations of a Roman bath that had been uncovered 25 years beforehand when plans for a supermarket were afoot. Now, the labyrinth was a haven for all manner of pick ups. At night, stray cats and dogs copulated with as much earnest frenzy as the humans amongst the piles of stone and barely discernible buildings.

'Why did it take the heart?' asked Tally.

'Food, probably,' said Sven. 'The poor thing was starving.'

'What do you think will happen if the dog eats the relic?'

'Well, according to the legend, the restorative powers go to the rightful clan of the person who unites the body parts,' said Sven. 'I suppose that applies equally to humans and animals.'

He turned to Tally and laughed: a great, roaring, belly thumping laugh.

'Oh Tally – don't you see? It's just like Marx said; 'outside of a dog, a book is man's best friend, and inside of a dog, it's too dark to see!' '

Tally frowned. 'Karl Marx said that?'

'No, Groucho Marx.'

'So what do we do now? Greece's future is undecided. This week, the Greeks vote on a referendum on continued austerity. Without Saint Aspasia's relics returned to the church, I don't think we are going to be able to turn the country's fortunes around.'

Sven nodded. 'On the other hand, the stray dogs may collectively rise up to rule Greece.'

They watched as, in the distance, the ownerless dogs from around the city gathered near the waterfront. Soon, there were hundreds.

'I suppose a pack couldn't do a worse job of managing Greek's financial situation than the politicians,' said Tally. 'And we do still have the starburst heart reliquary, empty though it is, in the hotel room safe. I suppose I can still write a literary piece about the adventure.'

'And I'll curate an exhibition on reliquaries and public and private forms of relic veneration,' said Sven. He took Tally's hand in his. 'We might not have got what we wanted, but I have what I need.' He pulled Tally to his chest and held her tight. 'I love you.'

'I love you too,' said Tally. They smelled smoke nearby and turned to see Dragan puffing away nearby.

'Bravo!' he shouted. 'I shall dance at your wedding.'

'He's not coming back with us,' said Sven.

'I can't afford to pay him anymore and he put his last employer in a nursing home so I said we'd sponsor him to come to Australia.'

'As what?' asked Sven. 'Does he have any qualifications beyond driving?'

Tally shrugged. 'Well, he does have a doctorate in Slavic Literature.'

'Great,' said Sven. 'Just what Melbourne needs, another over-qualified barista.'

PETER M. BALL

Deadbeats

She's seated in Tennyson's Grindhouse when the first message comes through: briefing at 15:00. Cody Jones stares at it a couple of seconds, puts the phone away. Figures, what the hell, and orders another drink. Downs a glass of the cheap rocket-fuel that masquerades as booze, brewed in canisters in the basement of the Grindhouse. Tastes like shit, but it's potent, and potent matters more in this stretch of Downside, pressed up against the grimy shore of the river, all the squats and gangs and homeless communes living on the scraps that Cityside throws out.

Cody Jones stares at the drink, thinks about the debt. Thinks about the job and the hangover waiting for her when she's on the right side of sober, and the fact she still can't sleep right.

She drinks.

It doesn't help.

So she orders another.

Cody figures it for 13:00, given the crowd packed onto the Boundary Road. She's tired and hungover and heading home, trying to blend in with the crowd: worn jeans and a black t-shirt, sunglasses over bloodshot eyes, her stomach still burning through the last of Tennyson's liquor. A foul breeze rifles through the stunted buildings, brings with it the petrochemical stink of the river. Cody slinks down the Boundary, takes a left at the wreckage of the first Valhalla Bar. Weaves through the street-markets, dodging elbows and shouting vendors, Cityside Tourists looking for bargains and taking in the local colour. There's a rat-boy working a grill at the base of the squat, young kid still on his first run of gene-morphs, stubby tail hanging through a hole in his jeans and fuzzy grey down on his face. The smell of the mystery meat sets her stomach roiling, reminds her how long it's been since she ate.

She crouches, points. 'What?'

The rat-boy shrugs, holds up two fingers, doesn't bother identifying the source of his protein. Cody weighs up the odds, hands over her money. Walks away with two bamboo skewers in hand, the grey meat pasted with a chilli-flecked sauce that glistens in the afternoon light. She wolfs the first stick down, lets the gamey meat wage war with the sick feeling in her guts. When it stays down, she takes her time with the second, rips free small mouthfuls as she climbs the stairs and heads towards home.

Sweat clings to her forehead by the time she hits the top floor, thumbs her code into the keypad with a grease-slick thumb. The lock is Wanton's work, just like the steel bars across the door. The tech a gift from the company, although she expects they're paying for it, another budget line added to their debt, another pittance attached to the monumental sums they pay back by working in the heart of Downside's feral squalor. Wanton's waiting for her when the door slides open. Wanton in his camouflage gear, provided by the company at a generous discount. Wanton with his crew-cut and his broad, grinning face. Wanton with his fists, designed for blunt-force trauma. Wanton with his chest like an adult silverback, wide and thick with muscle. Cody figures they grafted a little gorilla DNA there, inserted it into the embryo just to get the soldier they wanted. Wanton glares at her, thick arms folded over that chest. 'You're cutting it close,' he says.

Cody nods, heading for the bathroom. Wanton trails behind her. 'Job comes from Bellamy. Figured you'd want some warning'

'Ugh,' she says, and it's enough. She doesn't have more, right now.

'The briefing may require actual words, yeah?' Wanton follows her to the bathroom, stands outside the door. The floorboards creak beneath him as he waits, patiently, for her to splash cold water over her face and swallow a fistful of painkillers. One pill for the nausea, another for the headache. A third, laced with nanobots that mimic liver function, speeding her through the left-over booze that's burning a hole in her gullet. She sips water from the tap, figures the artificial bacteria the company injects every six weeks will take care of most infections. Then she hauls the bathroom door open, fixes Wanton with her sweetest smile. 'Better?'

'Better would be a partner who follows protocol and orders.'

'Orders are for soldiers.' Cody heads to her bunk, selects another shirt from the neatly folded pile. 'Soldiers work for the people. We do this for the money.'

Wanton glares. He doesn't like that. Doesn't like hearing anything about the debt, all the shit they owe the company for the cost of defrost and decanting.

'What?' Cody says.

'I'm not a mercenary.'

'No,' she says. 'Of course not.'

Wanton turns away, lets her get dressed in peace. She grins at his retreating back, shucks herself free of the sweat-stained clothing. Shimmies into the fresh shirt. Fresh pants. Heavy boots, and an armoured vest. Corp supplied, all of it, hard enough to turn aside most knives. Good enough for field work, this side of the river. Wanton nods when she emerges, checks his watch and nods again. 'Minute and a half to spare,' he says. 'Bellamy will be pleased.'

'I couldn't give a shit what pleases Bellamy.'

'And yet you're here, waiting for his call.'

'You trying to be an asshole?'

For a moment she thinks he's going to yell, going to vent his frustrations for that crack about the merc. Instead, he grins at her. 'Should have brought me breakfast. Whatever shit they spiked on those skewers smelled pretty good, you know?'

He punches her shoulder, all friendly and shit, but it's still hard enough to register. A spike of pain flares through the peaceful sheath of the meds, reminds her there's still a few parts of a hangover that modern medicine can hide without completely fixing.

Cody hates it when Wanton tries to force camaraderie, make her feel like a friend instead of a partner. He's not bothered by the world outside their front door, full of Rat Boys and Crow Boys and the hulking brutes who join up with the Rampage; the zealous motherfuckers from the Evangelical White and the well-dressed, sack-masked kids who make up the Scarecrow Dandies. All those gangs fighting for territory, going to war over the scraps Cityside throws over to their side of the river. Ever since they cracked Wanton out of stasis, he's been all kinds of loyal the company doesn't deserve.

Downside doesn't bother him. He doesn't know much else.

Cody, she knows better and it makes her hate everything. She hates the gangs and the squat and being on call. Hates the fact she can't go home, back to Cityside. That she's stuck here, in Downside, until Bellamy says otherwise and tells her those three, sweet words she never expects to hear.

The call comes through at 15:00, right on goddamn schedule. Lucas Bellamy's face fills the screen, lean and quietly handsome, dark hair slicked back away from his forehead; his suit costing more than Cody's yearly retainer.

He smiles, leans closer to the camera. 'Good to see you're both ready. It's going to be a day,' he says. 'We got reports one of the local gangs has uncovered some Sleeping Beauties. We'd like you to track 'em down, give coordinates to a recovery team.'

Wanton's breath catches and his fingers tighten against the arm-rests of his chair. Cody just nods, remembers to be professional. 'How much?'

He gives her a number. It's higher than expected.

'Alright,' she says. 'We're on it. Send through what you've got.'

They both hate the mission, but this is the job. Bellamy handles defrost and decant, finds the Company its workforce. It costs a lot, to wake a sleeper. A hell of a lot, for the older jobs, back before cryo was common. Plenty of those decanted end up on the same track, trawling Downside for other sleepers, paying down their debt; trying not to think about what happens once the job is done, or what happens to the decanted who don't have the skills for mercenary work. They just do the job, watch the debt go down. Dream about the day they're finally cut loose.

They let Bellamy talk through all the stuff the Company wants 'em to know, pretend like its useful intel. Truth is, Bellamy can't offer them shit. He's tucked away, safe and sound, in a com-ops room on Cityside, far from the sweaty heat and the streets full of gene-freak weirdos. He's reading back notes fed into his computer, adding details from satellite imaging and data scraped off the net. Treating it like it's military, like they're a couple of soldiers.

Truth is, that shit ain't useful, not for the job they've been given.

They gear up, once the call ends. Go in search of intelligence that won't get them killed, working their way through the brokers and dealers who know what's really going on.

Mackie Pelican, down near the tunnel, gives them the beginning of a story: turf wars between the Rampage and some rogue Evangelical-Whites, shit moved out of a warehouse under the cover of darkness. No guarantee it's sleepers, but the odds are better than most. The Ev-White like their cryo victims, like to indoctrinate while the newly wakened are groggy, slip 'em a few hits of Rapture to make sure the conversion sticks.

After that, they hit the second Valhalla Bar, check in with this skinny runt of a Corvidae by the name of Odin8. He tells them about a fight where the Rampage got stomped, six of the big boys ripped apart by three dozen Ev-White with swords. Way he hears it, Odin8's putting money on the Rampage getting payback, storming into the Ev-White territory and going at it, full-Kaiju, until there's nothing left but rubble.

From there, they hit the Floating Market, let Wanton talk to his own. Cody rides shotgun, ignores the discordant buzz of voices and the unsteady lurch of the boats beneath them. Wanton walks through the flotilla like he's born to it, even if this version of the market built up a good decade after he was first preserved in cryo. He smiles a little easier, out on the floating market. Learns more, too. Finds this little punk named Jun who tells 'em one of the Ev-White Pious is putting the call out for her paladins, gathering all swords to the Church of Razors deep in the heart of Ev-White turf. Consolidating the churches, building a small army. Bad news for everyone, Cody figures – specially the Rampage.

No-one likes the Evangelical Whites. Not the Rampage, not the Rat-Boys, not the Scarecrow Dandies. Not even the Corvidae, who chew avian-sequenced gene-morphs like they're some kind of goddamn candy and welcome the dangerously psychotic into their fucked-up family. These days the Ev-White are everywhere; white robes, white hair, white skin; a mad hate for the genetically-modified and a prayer on their lips. Crosses tattooed into their skulls and big, fuck-off swords held in a bloody grip.

The Evangelical White don't believe in a higher power; they take so much Rapture they're *sure* which gods exist, and they ain't afraid to tell you it's time to take their words as gospel.

Cody figures they can use that, once they've got confirmation the Beauties are in the Ev-White's possession. All they gotta do is talk to a primary source; separate the rumour from the real. She says as much to Wanton, and he scowls at her.

'We ain't going to The Slaughterhouse. Tell me you ain't that stupid.'

'When ain't we that stupid,' Cody says. 'Less you want to go fuck with the White, when we don't really have to.'

He screws up his face, thinking that over. Knows that he's already lost this fight, and the night is going to get nasty.

She leads Wanton down to the river, takes point as they thread through the rusting husks of old cars left to decay on the shore. The river stinks, this time of the afternoon; the dark sludge of sewerage and chemical run-off baked into a fugue by 12 hours of daylight. Cody listens to the scuff of Wanton's boots, keeps her breathing shallow; swings underneath the old bridge, through the slices of sunlight filtering through the gaps where the roadway should have been; hears gunfire in the distance, over on the far shore – the staccato song of Cityside, discouraging any attempt to cross the river. She ignores it. Heads for Slaughterhouse Bar. Knocks three times on the old iron door set into the redbrick wall.

The hinges protest when Naga finally answers, one hand held up to fend off the orange light. He's old, for a Rampage. Near blind in daylight, even if his night-vision is good. Still big, still dangerous, with shoulders that brush against the doorway and steel teeth like the fangs of a snake. Grafted scales cover his face and his nostrils flare as he sniffs, scenting the air like a half-mad dog, eager to pick a fight. Wanton reaches for his pistol, but Cody grabs his arm.

'Nag,' she says. 'Been a while, eh?'

He eases, a little, at the sound of her voice. Lays one hand against the door to keep himself steady, reaches out with the other to touch Cody's face. Wanton growls a little, but Cody shushes him; keeps her focus on the half-blind giant trying to feel the contours of her cheek. 'Jones?' he says. 'Shit, babe. You can't be here.'

She takes hold of his blunt fingers, pushes them away. 'Wish we had a choice in that. Unfortunately, we don't.'

He blinks into the sunset. 'Always got a choice, babe.'

'Not today,' she says. 'Today we got a job. Heard some rumours about the Rampage, figured we might have a chat to the Kong, yeah? See if he knows what's what?'

Naga sucks on his fangs a moment. 'You got that big fucker with ya?'

'Yeah, I got him.'

'You know what it'll take, getting the Kong onside?'

She looks back at Wanton. 'Yeah, we know.'

Naga lets out a short, barking laugh. Shuffles back into the darkness. 'Best you come in then,' he says. 'We'll see what can be done.'

Cody steps over the threshold, feels the temperature drop. The inside of the Slaughterhouse lives up to the name: wrecked tables, wrecked chairs, wrecked walls. Steel hooks dangle from the ceiling, where the Rampage hang the losers after a brawl. Bloodstains on the concrete, benches and tables made of stone. Hard enough to survive a fight between men who jack up on rhino DNA after they hit the limits of traditional steroid enhancement.

The sour stink of old sweat and blood wages war with the river. Naga limps over to the bar, grabs a bottle of piss-yellow booze from the shelf and pours a trio of drinks. He knocks one back, pushes the second Cody's way.

Wanton ignores the third, focused on the hallway leading into the freezers. Naga scowls, drinks it for him, his eyes a little better away from the daylight. 'Well,' he says, 'why d'ya need the Kong?'

Cody toys with her shot-glass. 'We got some questions about salvage his boys found.'

'Boys find a lot of salvage.' Naga says.

'This happened a few days back.'

'Not sure he'll remember.'

'He'll remember,' Wanton says. He stands away from the bar, makes sure he's got room to move. Probably a smart call, given the way their last visit played out.

Naga doesn't say anything.

Wanton doesn't say shit, either.

'Christ, Nag, just get him,' Cody says, 'or it's me who'll kick your ass.'

Naga blinks, a little amused by that. He may be old, but he's still hard. Hard enough that the Rampage don't kick him out, when they live to break the weak. He reaches for the intercom, holds his thumb against it. 'Visitors,' he says, when someone finally answers. 'Two of em, corporate. Let him know they'd like to talk.'

The Kong's entrance doesn't shake the room, but he's big enough that it should. Three more Rampage trail along behind him, a good head shorter than their boss's massive bulk. The Kong is all muscle and scales, ridges of bone grafted to his skull. An ugly lump of rage with some extra rage heaped on. He lugs a haunch of meat, lips stained with the juice. The fingers wrapped round the bone are steel chords, his teeth like the blades of a thresher. Bare chest covered in scar tissue that score his dark flesh like a hashtag. One of those scars is Cody's work. Another – the biggest of them – he got from his last clash with Wanton.

The Kong glares, attention focused on her partner. He points his haunch of meat. Says, 'Well, well. The big man.'

Wanton drops a hand to the knife sheathed at his belt. 'Kong,' he says. 'You're upright.'

'I heal fast, big man. Learn from my mistakes.' The Kong slaps his chest three times, each one loud as a gunshot. 'You ready for a rematch, Wanton? Want to show me how strong you are?'

Wanton shrugs. 'Business first. Fun later.'

The Kong leans forward, heavy knuckles ground the granite bar.

'Business,' he says. 'Alright. Let's pretend we got business, then, before I rip off your arm.'

'Take the left arm,' Cody says. 'He shoots right-handed.'

The ponderous head swings towards her. 'Ain't concerned with his shooting anyone, girl.'

'You're not, I am.' Cody puts herself between The Kong and her partner, meets the slitted yellow eyes inherited from some serpent. 'We ain't here to rumble, Kong. Just looking for information.'

The Kong shows his teeth, all shards of gleaming steel. 'Ain't got nothing for you, Miss Jones.'

'Really? That's surprising. We heard you lost some boys to the Ev-White last night. Heard they came after you, on your own turf, so they could make off with some shit you found.'

The Kong's eyes narrow. He turns and glares at Naga. 'You hear a lot.'

'I have good ears. It comes from avoiding the kinds of body-mods that'll turn me into a lizard.'

'Ears can be ripped off.' The Kong says it cold and angry, but she knows that's just a front. Naga is still in the room, watching the exchange. Naga who used to be Kong, way back, before he stepped aside to let a stronger man rule. Weakness can be fatal, when your crew worship strength.

Cody lets the Kong straighten up, lets him come round the table and loom a little. Lets him have his moment, before he looks down at the pistol she's pointing at his knee.

'You can take out an ear,' she says, 'but I can blow out your knee. Nothing glamorous 'bout hobbling round with a slug in your leg, Kong. Sure as hell not going to help you when Wanton starts getting nasty.'

She holds his stare, smiles at him. 'We choose not to do that, 'cause it would be impolite, but the option is always there. It's good to have options, yeah?'

The Kong snarls, but he backs off. 'Like the big man better,' he says. 'He don't fight dirty, Jones.'

'I'm at peace with being the lesser option.' She shrugs, raises the gun. 'So, we going to be reasonable 'bout this?'

'Reasonable ain't our way.'

'Adapt,' Cody says. 'You're missing boys?'

'I'm not–'

She puts a bullet into the floor, right by his feet. The Kong doesn't flinch, neither does Naga. Both of them, hard as concrete.

'Alright,' The Kong says. 'My missing boys got worked over by the Ev-White. Three of my best, all dead now.'

'And what were your best doing, when they got cut apart?'

'Like I know,' The Kong says. 'Ain't like we're Ratboys, living in each other's pockets.'

Wanton's boots scuff the concrete. He advances, gets in The Kong's face. 'You're full of shit,' he says. 'You may be a pack of Mastodons, but you're still a damn pack. Ain't none of your boys doing shit worth getting killed for, not without you knowing.'

The Kong rips a hunk of meet off the bone, glares at Wanton while he chews.

'Mastodons,' he says, 'I like that.'

And Cody sees the twitch at the corner of his mouth, recognises the intent in his tone. The cold invitation to brawl, one on one, with the only other male big enough to make a fight of it. The Kong rises and discards the meat, wipes his ham-hock fingers against his bare chest. The greasy smear highlights the scars. It ain't like The Kong is a pushover. He's tough as boiled leather and built like a tank, keeps coming regardless of the injury. Makes it easy to forget that he's smart, underneath the attitude and testosterone.

He goes nose-to-nose with Wanton. Smirks as the two of them stare at each other. 'You wanna know 'bout my boys,' he says, 'you gotta fight me for it. Draw blood, I answer your questions.'

'An if you bleed me?' Wanton says.

The Kong jerks his head at Cody. 'We move on to the bonus round, and I try to take an ear,' he says. 'Owe both of you scars, one way or another. Mean to–'

Wanton snaps his forehead into The Kong's nose. Bunches a giant fist and smashes it into a scale-covered throat, leaves The Kong gasping and struggling for air. Neat work against a normal man, designed to incapacitate, but the Rampage are built tough.

The Kong wraps his arms round Wanton, drives his back into the stone edge of a bar. Naga shuffles forward, ready to help out. Cody intercepts him, holds an arm against his chest. 'Leave it,' she says, and Naga nods.

That's good. It means she doesn't have to shoot him.

The two behemoths stay locked together, struggling for leverage. Wanton gets it first, puts The Kong down. Punches him in the face until he sees blood. Holds the bloodied fist in The Kong's eye line. 'We done?'

The Kong glares. Spits blood. 'Done,' he rasps, his throat raw. 'Get off me.'

Wanton sits back, wipes sweat off his face. Tries to hide the fact that his hand is hurting. Trying not to show weakness, not while Naga and the other Rampage are watching.

Cody takes his place, crouches down beside The Kong. 'So,' she says, 'your boys?'

The Kong pushes her away, struggles back to his feet. 'Follow Nag, he'll show ya.'

It's still cold down in the bunker. White tiles streaked with rime, a thick sheet of mist clinging to the ground. Cody hugs herself to keep warm, follows Wanton in. Blue lights on the ceiling keep everything just this side of visible, hurts her eyes. There's blood splatter on the walls, obvious signs of a fight. Three corpses in the centre of the room, all of them big and dead.

The walls hum, the ancient tubing that kept the cryonics active struggle to keep working now the glass coffins have been opened. Eight cryo-tubes are pressed up against the wall. Seven of them are empty now, their doors open and coughing out plumes of cryoprotectants.

Naga lingers by the door, refusing to come in. Leaves Cody and Wanton to poke through, piecing together what happened. They're two storeys down, underneath an old church on the fringe of Rampage turf. Cody figures it for a black-market facility, from the days before preservation became commonplace.

She eyes the open doorways, does the math. Seven sleepers are worth good money, if you can get 'em across the river. They're citizens of another time, desperate people who trusted technology to catch up with 'em one day. Figured they'd hit the future and someone would thaw 'em out, reverse the effects of cryogenesis without damaging the grey matter.

In truth, they got it half right. The Company loves the sleepers, for all sorts of reasons. Some get used as human subjects, when there's no official records to make it complicated. Some get decanted and put to work, paying off the debt incurred by the process. The rest? She tries not to think about it. That's how she sleeps at night.

Wanton examines the tech. 'Vintage stuff,' he says. 'Very old-school. Poor bastards are lucky the generators lasted.'

Naga coughs, from his place by the door. 'Not so lucky if the Ev-White got 'em.'

'No,' Wanton says. He gives Cody a look. She ignores him, heads for the eighth tube. It's an archaic design, steel and thick glass, red light blinking at the bottom of the casing. She rubs her sleeve against the glass. The cold bites into her arm like it's a savage, desperate animal.

The girl inside is withered, mummified by the cold, lips thin and blue. Killed when the sealant on her tube deteriorated, letting the body freeze instead of keeping it preserved, ice crystals forming and destroying the cells.

'You sure all the others were alive?'

Naga grins. 'Would you two be here, if they weren't?'

She lets that go. Steps aside to give Wanton access to the corpse. He knows more 'bout Cryo than she ever will, learned all the details before his own trip through ice. Part of his training, way back when. Nothing like her own experience.

She's asked him about it in the past. Wanton didn't say much, just told her he's thankful he didn't end up a husk. That he came out with a chance to do right by the Company.

Almost made it sound sincere, which is why they like him better.

He gets quiet, as he looks over the dead girl. Cody knows just how he feels, wheels around to glare at Naga. 'You should have called us,' she says, 'the moment your boys found this place.'

Naga's eyes narrow. 'You ain't the only popsicles working this patch of turf.'

'Ain't talking about the company,' she says. 'You should have called us.'

Naga tilts his head, lips hooked into a crude smile. 'The Kong made a call. Figured he'd get more, letting people bid.'

She nudges one of the dead Rampage with the toe of her boot. 'How's that working out for ya?'

Naga doesn't answer. She doesn't really blame him. If they're looking for confirmation, the three corpses do the job. Swords leave distinctive wounds, specially when there's lots of 'em, and in Downside it's the Ev-White who have a monopoly on that kind of violence. She crouches, takes a closer look at the stab wounds on a corpse.

The Ev-White work ugly, hacking at their victim, but they get all kinds of delicate once they've put a man down. Little cruciforms carved into their victims, to aid passage to the afterlife. A good wound could tell her which sect took the bodies, narrow down which Pious they've got to hassle on the Street of Churches. This one is messy work, 'cause the Rampage are hard to carve. Too much thick skin and muscle. Too many scales to work around.

'Would have thought you boys were too careful to let the Ev-White know 'bout this,' she says. 'Had to know they'd come recruiting, if they heard tell of the sleepers.'

'The Kong got careless.'

'He put guards here.'

'Three guards ain't a lot,' Naga says.

'Can't think of anyone that'll tangle with three Rampage willingly.'

'Except the Evangelical White.' Naga shakes his thick head. 'Mongo,' he points to the closest dead Rampage, 'he was going to be Kong, one day. Smart kid. Strong. Stupid, him going down like this.'

'Not many smart ways to die, mate.' Wanton looks up from the dead girl. 'We got what we need?'

Cody nods. 'You healthy enough for a run at the White? The Kong put a beating on ya.'

Wanton shrugs. 'I'll manage.'

'We can head back to the base, give you a few hours to heal up, you know?'

Wanton thumbs his tablet, shows her a page of data. 'Computers are old enough that the encryption ain't shit,' he says. 'Skimmed all data. According to what we got here, the Ev-White prepped 'em for defrost.'

Cody looks around, takes in the ancient tech. 'These guys?'

Wanton nods.

'How in hell they manage that?'

'Poorly, is my guess,' Wanton says. 'Figure we've got an hour, maybe a little longer, before there's no chance of decanting 'em safe.'

He puts the tablet away. Pulls out a stopwatch and sets it.

'Shit,' Cody says.

'Yeah.' Wanton nods. 'That's about the size of it.'

They head home, gear up: shotguns, spare ammo, and body-armour. Part of the gig, this side of the river, is avoiding a show of force. Letting the fragile ecosystem of thugs and gangs do its thing, maintain the status quo. Let everyone think they're corporate mercs, not soldiers on a payroll.

But screw that, when you're heading into Ev-White turf, home of sword-wielding maniacs with the power of faith behind 'em. Home to churches devoted to mixing up Rapture, each hit designed to let you see God, or Gods, or Goddesses. Eliminate any doubt, until faith becomes certain knowledge.

The Evangelical White took over the cliffs by the river, built the Street of Churches looking towards the far bank and the city. Bonfires in the evenings, letting Cityside know they're there. Loud, moaning group prayers as the faithful maintain their vigil. And everywhere, Paladins, the most faithful of the faithful. Men and women in pristine robes, sodium-white hair left to grow long and wild. Yellow cruciforms tattooed onto their foreheads, daubed with neon face-paint that lights up like rays of the sun.

Cody takes point as they walk along the river bank and turn left onto the Street of Churches. Everyone looks the same on the street: same hair, same robes, the same wild-eyed beatitude that comes from too many drugs. So the

Ev-White look, as she strolls down the Street with Wanton, everyone aware there's outsiders in their midst. Wanton unholsters his shotgun, keeps it handy to discourage the onlookers from making an unwanted conversation.

They pass the Church of Razors, daubed with blood and viscera. The Paladin's out front sneering at them with red-stained lips as Cody and Wanton walk past.

They pass Last Pure Church and the two men standing guard have skin the same shade as their hair. They eye Wanton, eye the shotgun. Whisper among themselves, looking for a fight.

They pass the Forgotten Church, little more than an empty lot amid the close-press of buildings, a place for new preachers to unleash fire-and-brimstone sermons among the poor and the forgotten that wash up on the street. The lot stinks of unwashed flesh and bleach, lines of newcomers crouched by plastic bowls, dying their hair to fit in. Up the back of the lot, perched on a stone, one of the Pious is working. He looks up when they walk past, turns his eye towards the heavens. 'Interlopers,' he says, 'unfaithful.'

'Like we fuckin care,' Cody says, moving on, ducking into the shadows.

They head to the First Great Church of the White, the sole building that started out as a place of worship. Wide expanses of marble, the building trimmed in gold. Dead fountains, in the courtyard, flanking a small angel statue. The place where the Paladin's gather, waiting for their orders.

The home of Pious Demeter, the source of all Rapture, who welcomed in the sick and the homeless, who gave them a place to exist. Demeter who preaches against the gene-grafts and body-mods that make the other gangs distinct, tells the faithful that they must stay pure if they want to get another hit.

Demeter, who made the Ev-White possible, who keeps them running through drugs and intimidation as much as her own damn cunning.

The courtyard is big, lots of stairs and marble. Thirty meters to the building, two short sets of stairs as you follow the rise of the hill. Paladins camped out, armed and half-mad with Rapture. Cody figures there's 20 of 'em, maybe 25. Another 30 Ev-White, no signs of a blade, but that doesn't mean much once a fight starts. A bell-tower in the church itself, the bell long-removed and replaced by spotlights. Two men in the tower, both armed with crossbows, keeping a look out. Archaic tech, but it'll do the job. The snipers are both trained, know how to shoot. The fence is steel bars, hard to climb, easy to see through. But getting in without being noticed takes time, planning, and they're running short on both.

The smart move would be letting it go, pretending the job ain't worth it. No chance they can do the smart thing either, so they're going to play this dumb.

The Honourable Hades sees them coming, separates himself from the pack. Old, for a paladin, his white thatch of hair receding, his face scored with creases worn into to the flesh. He knows them both, 'cause that's his job. Knows everyone in Downside who presents a danger to the White. His eyes are wild, pupils the size of pinpricks. He sways, blocking the gate, eyes shifting from Cody to Wanton. 'The Church is closed to visitors,' he says. 'Demeter cannot meet with you today.'

Most days, they'd try to talk their way in, play upon the fact that Hades doesn't really want a fight. He's nervous about the shotguns, nervous about Wanton's strength, nervous about the gear the Company's provided to make a team like Wanton and Cody more dangerous than any two men in his crew.

Most days they'd try to talk their way in, but Wanton's ten types of pissed right now; focused on the mission and the ticking clock. He looks to Cody, gives her a nod. Pulls the trigger on the shotgun. The sound of it spills across the empty courtyard, puts a slug deep into the meat of Honourable Hades' arm. Cody swears and throws smoke, yellow canisters tumbling across the courtyard and belching up their contents. Wanton doesn't hesitate, dives into the billowing cloud with the shotgun pressed tight to his shoulder. Cody gets her pistols out, follows close behind.

Honourable Hades' runs, screams orders as he retreats; his voice is drowned in the frightened shouts of half-blind, rapturous Paladins looking for a target.

Crossbows fire, up in the guard tower, bolts whistling through the air. The first instinct is to flinch, but Cody trusts the smoke to keep her safe. The bolts hit the concrete by the gate, well short of their position. Cody keeps moving, following the dark silhouette of Wanton's bulk. He moves fast, shotgun booming as he clears a path. She follows behind, her pistols the precision against the wide-scatter blast of Wanton's gun. She double-taps a Paladin who comes charging through the smoke. Double-taps another who stumbles close, sword raised and his eyes watering.

They hit the first stairs at a run, take them two at a time. The Paladins are everywhere, bellowing warnings, screams, and orders. The other Ev-White are no better, milling in a panic. One of them leaps at Wanton, trying to drag him down. Wanton swings the shotgun stock, connects with the right cheek. Bones break. Blood splatters the concrete. Creates an opening for a Paladin who lumbers in, swinging his sword. The metal bites a chunk out of Wanton's leg, blood soaking the marble. Wanton swears, plants a boot in the Paladin's guts, kicks him free to buy some space. Cody follows up, puts two into the Paladin's chest, forgets him as they move on.

Another set of stairs. Three meters to the front door. The Honourable Hades reaches it first, heads in and slams the doors behind him. Wanton moves like a wrecking ball, smashing through all opposition. He applies his shoulder to the seam between the doors, before they're properly shut. Cody drops another canister, leaves the smoke to cover their entrance. Kicks the doors closed, once they're through, and slams a bar down to lock them.

The long hall stretches out in front of them, lined with ancient pews. Hades limps backwards, bleeding from his bullet wounds. He's got his sword drawn and ready, holds it like a barricade that will keep Wanton from coming.

It doesn't. Wanton advances on him, doesn't even bother using the shotgun as a threat. Now it's just size, the relentless rejection of pain. Hades swings and Wanton jerks sideways, comes back with a punch that sends Hades sprawling. The sword skitters away, disappearing under the pews.

'Sleepers,' he says. 'We know your crew took 'em.'

'Unbeliever,' Hades hisses. 'Foul beast of–'

Wanton jams his shotgun against Hades' spleen. 'Losing patience, man.'

The Paladin spits. Wanton doesn't like that. A big boot stomps The Honourable Hades' face, busts open that leathery skin. Rears back for another shot, but Cody grabs his arm, hauls him back, before he breaks Hades' skull, and leaves them with a whole church to go through and no real clues where to start.

Hades grins. Knows what he's doing. Paladins thump on the barricaded door. Feet hammer the marble down the sides of the church, his men scrambling for another way in. Kill enough time and they'll be outnumbered, trapped in the close confines of the Church, nowhere to run.

The bell-tower door swings open: the sniper from up top. He bursts into the room, like he's expecting an easy fight. Hesitates, when he sees there's no other Ev-White around.

Cody drops him. Two to the chest. She kneels beside Hades, holsters the gun. 'That shit you're on,' she says. 'I know what it does. No pain, no fear. I get that. Means my friend can beat on you and there's no reason to tell us nothing, so I ain't going to bother with hurting ya.'

'Bride of–'

'Yeah, I get it. Genetic abomination. Creature of the devils and the nine hells and all that.'

She produces a syringe, lets him have a good look at the stainless-steel tip. 'Thing is, I don't give a shit 'bout any of that, but your lot certainly do. And I figure that shit Demeter cooks up, it's gotta have one hell of a come-down, yeah?'

She jams the needle into his arm.

'Borrowed that from a friend of mine, one of the Corvidae. Enough gene-morphs to turn Wanton into a fucking crow-boy, let alone a scrawny runt like you. Won't hurt too much, but it won't be all that pleasant.'

Hades writhes, trying to break free. Fear in his eyes now, behind the chemically-induced bravado. Wanton plants a boot on Hades' chest, holds him in place. Cody brushes Hades' bloody forehead. She puts her thumb against the plunger. 'Shh,' she says. 'You know it won't hurt.'

He doesn't talk. He won't talk, even with that threat hanging over him. But his eyes flick towards the small door at the rear, tucked in behind the altar. She presses down, injects him. Waits the few seconds it takes for the needle to do its work.

Wanton takes his foot off the body. Raises his shaggy eyebrows. 'Never seen a mutagen that knocks a guy out.'

'Morphine,' she says.

Wanton shakes his head.

'Gene-morphs are stupid expensive,' she says. 'And we owe enough already.'

The door leads down, into the basement level. Overhead lights powered by solar batteries, a little gasp of cold air that causes their skin to dimple. Cody thumbs her headset, puts a call through to the company.

They answer and Fredrick Bellamy's voice oozes into her ear. 'Miss Jones, good to hear from you. I take it you have something for me?'

'Sure,' she lies. 'Send in an extraction team. Centre on our coordinates.'

'Excellent,' Bellamy says. 'Team will be there in five.'

Wanton is resting his bulk against the pew, keeping his weight off the leg. 'Calling in the cavalry?' he says. 'That'll get expensive, if we've got this wrong'

'We still got five minutes,' she says. 'Figure that's enough to search this shit-hole, even with your leg to slow us down.'

The underground level is where the Rapture happens, little black-market labs where Demeter mixes up her drug. They find a handful of white-robed assistants, clear them out without much effort. Find Demeter herself, way up the back, hiding among the glass-fronted coffins stolen from the bunker. Coffins sweating moisture as they warm, dark puddles on the concrete. Demeter half-crouched, too tall for the low bench to provide any cover.

Wanton flies across the room, pins her against the wall with his shotgun barrel. Demeter throws useless punches at Wanton's face, trying to break free. It's annoying, instead of effective. Wanton snarls and slams his forehead into Demeter's face, stuns her long enough to get her on the ground. He uses his weight to keep her there, knee in the centre of her back. Produces a zip-tie and secures her arms, then covers the entrance with his shotgun.

'We good?'

Cody crouches beside the first coffin, plugs in her tablet. Checks the readings: dropping temperature; blood filtration; a lot of familiar drugs. Some of them pharmaceutical, to keep the sleeper calm. Some of them nanotechnology, repairing any long-term damage caused by the decades sleeping. It's slick, professional work. Expensive as hell, just for one person, half the reason she and Wanton owe the company so damn much.

And Demeter's got seven popsicles, thawing out in her lab. 'Selling god to junkies pays better than I thought,' she says. 'Jesus, Dem'. Where in hell'd you get all this?'

Demeter gurgles a response that could be laughter. Wanton raises his knee, glances in Cody's direction. 'All what?' he says.

'She's got a full thaw happening. Everything that's needed, right here on the premises.'

'The fuck?' Wanton reaches down, grabs Demeter by the throat. Drags her over with one hand, so he can take a closer look. Demeter's laughing for real, now that she can breathe.

'The Gods work in mysterious ways,' she says.

'Not that goddamn mysterious.' Wanton drops her, trusts Cody to keep her out of trouble. Picks up the tablet and scans the details, brow creased, fingers scrolling from screen to screen. He grunts, once he's done with it all. Unplugs the tablet and moves to the next goddamn coffin. 'This ain't right,' he says. 'No way the Ev-White can pull this off.'

'We do this for holy glory,' Demeter says. 'We do this here, where we can be seen, so that all shall know–'

Cody slaps her. 'Shut up,' she says. 'If the next words out of your mouth aren't "this is how we did this", he's going to get angry.'

'Does the how of it really matter? It's done. That's what's important.'

'No,' Wanton says. 'Cody, if these readings–'

'That isn't the job,' Cody says, and she hates herself for saying it.

'Screw the job,' Wanton says. 'If they can wake up out here, without the Company's help–'

'They're already on their way. No way can we smuggle seven coffins out on the sly, not before Bellamy gets his crew in here.'

Wanton closes his eyes a moment, takes a long breath through his nose. He lumbers over on his bad leg, hauls Pious Demeter upright. 'Answers,' he says. 'How?'

'A gift.' Demeter's grin is crimson and she's forced to spit blood. 'Even a gene-beast may learn the error of his ways, and do his best to secure the help of an angel.'

'The fuck?' Wanton turns to Cody, ready to plead. Ready to ask her if she'd please just screw the debt, do this one thing and help him get the coffins out. Help him make sense of the shit Demeter's talking, if it's even possible to make sense out of all that.

But there's a commotion down the hall, up the stairs, up on the surface. The groan of the drop-ship coming down. Gas canisters, gunfire, *go-go-go*. The symphony of the retrieval team securing the landing zone, coming through the building. Fredrick Bellamy and a team of loyal company soldiers already here to take out the cargo and deliver them to the corporate office for processing.

The drop-ship lifts off, tubes safely stowed. Three members of the extraction team bleeding, waiting for the medic to finish checking the Beauties vital signs. Bellamy sits in the seat by the door, shit-eating grin in place. He beams at her, beams at Wanton, keeps telling 'em they did good.

Cody doesn't feel it. No adrenaline, for starters, which means the aches are starting. The dull burn along her arm where a blade got too close, the bruises and scrapes that didn't register as they got the job done. Wanton looks worse, all beat-to-hell and bleeding, unwilling to accept treatment from the medic before he knows how the defrost is going.

Cody figures what she really wants is series of cold drinks, followed by hangover pain that's well and truly all her fault. It's better that way, she thinks, having someone to blame. Makes her think, one day, she can change all this. Leave the pain behind.

'Listen,' Bellamy says, and his smile disappears. So she listens. Focuses her scowl on him, makes it clear she doesn't want to be doing this. Wanton is still distracted, looking over his shoulder at the Sleeper's pods. Still dripping blood onto the metal floor, the cloth pressed against the wound in his thigh doing fuck-all to stop the bleeding.

'Listen,' Bellamy says, 'we can't take you back over the river. You both know that, right? You've got facilities, in the safe-house; take care of all this?'

He nods at Wanton, like he actually gives a damn. Cody feels ready to crack up and laugh, but she holds it together. Nods.

'Yeah,' she says, 'we got this. Get us clear and drop us by the river, we can make our way back from there.'

'Great.' The smile is back again. White teeth. Thin, bloodless lips. 'Great to have you on board, both of you. Great job down there, on the ground. You've got a bonus coming. I'll put in the paperwork, once we get back. Just–'

'Bellamy?'

His perfectly manicured eyebrows rise, and she wonders how long it's been since someone interrupted him. Cody shakes her head, appalled. Doesn't bother hiding it.

'Shut up,' she says. 'We don't actually give a damn.'

'But the money,' he says. 'Buying out of your contract?'

'We both know that's never happening.' She nods her head at Wanton, still watching the medic work. 'We're out here for the long haul, me and him both. Don't try and shit us, and we'll do the damn job.'

Bellamy's eyes narrow, like he's trying to figure that out. 'Okay,' he says, 'no shit.'

'That's all I ask,' Cody says. She thumps Wanton in the shoulder. 'You good to go, big guy?'

He grunts, and she takes it as yes. It's more than he's said since take-off.

The drop-ship angles left, swings towards the bridge.

'By the way,' Bellamy says, 'I've got another gig for you. Quick one, but solid money. Enough to drop a few days off your debt.'

He reaches under his chair, produces a black case. Pushes it into Cody's hands and nods at her, encouragingly. 'Drop that off at the Slaughterhouse, for your friend Kong. It's the money corporate owes him, for the finder's fee.'

Cody scowls at the money. 'You dealt with The Kong directly?'

'Nah, one of his flunkies called us. Old bloke. Spoke on The Kong's behalf.'

Right, Cody thinks. She holds the case in a tight, white-knuckle grip. 'Alright,' she says. 'Delivery.'

The Slaughterhouse is empty. No meat, no bar, just hooks, concrete, and steel. The coppery stink of drying blood, an old smell that's never coming out.

Wanton follows her in, pulls one of the hooks from the ceiling. Tests it with the flesh of his thumb. 'You reckon they all cleared outta here?'

'I reckon there's been a coup.' Cody heads for the meat lockers, pistol already drawn. She holds it low, keeps the case in her other hand. Moves slow and quiet as she approaches the steel doors. She can hear someone groaning, deep in the darkness. Wanton produces a flashlight, shines it over her shoulder. They go three doors down, slide the locker open.

The Kong, lying on the floor. Blood seeping through the wound in his stomach, intestines exposed to the world. Already so far gone he's ready for the water, just another ex-resident of Downside getting dumped into the river.

'Damn,' Cody says. 'Kong, man, what the hell.'

'Jones.' He peers up at her, eyes little more than slits. His voice rasping out in a weak, trembling whisper. 'Big man, owe you some scars eh?'

Wanton steps into the narrow locker, crouches down beside the dying man. 'Good thing you heal fast, man. That one looks nasty.'

'Ain't nothing.' The Kong's voice is little more than a whisper. 'Kick your ass, when I'm healed.'

Cody bites her lower lip. It's not just the gut-wounds, although that's bad enough. It's the bruises, the signs of a beating. Lots of punches delivered by big men with a grudge, determined to do some damage.

She considers the case hanging from her left hand. 'Thought this was for you,' she says, 'but I'm guessing you ain't The Kong anymore.'

'Always said you were smart.'

She turns, and Naga is standing in the doorway, big shoulders blocking the morning light. He isn't quite so hunched anymore, stands like a man who isn't in any pain. He watches her, no trouble seeing at night. Points to the case. 'Pretty sure that's mine.'

Cody raises the .45, holds it steady and trained on Naga's chest. 'Not the orders we were given,' she says. 'Don't get paid 'less it goes to the right man.'

'Jones, please.' A low smirk hooks the edge of Naga's mouth, made horrible by the teeth and the scales. 'You and your friend, you're good at what you do, but you've never been known for stupidity. You've already fought one war, you don't need another.'

He steps aside, lets her see through the door. All the Rampage are gathered, lined up on the street outside. Watching, waiting, to see how this goes down. To see how the new Kong handles things.

'This isn't personal, it's politics,' he says. 'The Kong was weak. We needed someone strong.'

'And you figured that was you?'

Again, the smirk. 'I was qualified for the job. Stronger, smarter, more experience. Richer, too, once that case gets handed over.'

'And if we don't?'

'Then I finish what the Ev-White started, grind your bones to dust.' Naga shrugs, studies the steel talons attached to his fingers. 'Not the option I'd prefer, given all you've done for me, but I'll take it. I need a show of strength. You can back down now, and give it to me, or I can make with the grinding. Either way, I get the victory.'

Wanton snarls and launches himself across the room, steel hook in hand. He whips it through the air, steel point whistling, but Naga ducks back, gives ground, stays safe. He waits for an opening, drives his foot into the wounded leg with all the force his frame can manage. Wanton stumbles, teeth clenched in pain, and strong hands wrap around his wrist. Bones creak as Naga twists, forcing the hook from his hand.

Naga looks up, meets Cody's stare. 'Can't help but notice you didn't shoot me.'

'Didn't want to hit my partner.'

Naga grins and pushes Wanton over, plants a kick in the big man's ribs. 'No chance of that now,' he says, spreading his big arms wide. 'I'll make it real easy for ya, Jones, but you know what it means when you leave.'

'Yeah,' she says, 'I know.' She puts the case on the floor, takes three steps away from it. Wanton stares at her, his face a bloody mess. Stares like he can't believe what she's doing.

Naga steps over him, heads for the case. Gets within three steps before Cody raises the pistol.

'You set this up,' she says. 'That's why you left the others out there. Don't want them to know that you were paid to make it all possible. You told Demeter where to find the Sleepers. You fronted the cash she needed for seven defrosts, so hitting the bunker seemed like a good deal.'

Naga doesn't raise his hands. Can't, when there's other Rampage watching. But he nods his head, just slightly. 'You're a smart woman, Jones. Always liked that about you.'

'Called in the tip to Bellamy 'cause you knew we'd come looking. Knew Wanton would beat down The Kong–'

'Ex-Kong,' Naga says.

'Whatever. It doesn't matter. You played us, Nag'. That was smart. Right up until this point.'

'Because your wrath will be swift and terrible?'

'Cause it cost you a bundle to fund a full-thaw, and now you need that cash. And now you've got two witnesses who know exactly how all this went down, which means you have to kill us or find a way to keep us quiet.'

'Killing you was always my preference.'

'Harder than it looks,' she says. 'Paying us would be cheaper.'

Naga glances back at Wanton. 'You think I can't take that lump of meat?'

Cody holsters the gun. Shrugs off her jacket. 'Wasn't thinking about him,' she says. 'You ever been beat by a woman, Nag? Can't imagine how that will go down with the boys.'

Naga looks her over. 'Ain't afraid to kill a woman, Jones.'

'You seen the world out there, moron? Outside your little coven of overly mucho gene-twists, people ain't been afraid of killing women for a couple of hundred years.'

Naga snarls, charges. Swipes at her with a giant paw. She grabs it, twists, uses his momentum to send him across the room. Up into the corner, away from the door. Far away from prying eyes.

He spins, ready for another charge. She doesn't give him a chance, gets up close with a combat knife and puts it in his stomach. 'People think Ton's the dangerous one,' she says. 'Truth is, he's just the nice one. He'll let you walk away from a fight. I'll force you to fucking crawl.'

Naga snarls, but he buys it. Backs away a little, one hand over his gut.

'You really want to do this, Nag? Ain't going to go well for you.'

Naga breathes heavy. Bunches his shoulders. She reverses her grip on the knife, drops down and waits for him to come closer.

He takes a step, winces at the pain in his guts. Looks at the shiny point of her blade. 'Alright,' he says. 'The contents of the case?'

'That'll do for starters.'

'Jones.' Wanton stands, unsteady on his feet. 'Jones, what–'

'Shut it,' she says. 'I said it'll do for starters. We take the money and we keep our mouths shut. Let everyone outside think you beat the Company. But you owe us, and not just money. For starters, we want a name.'

The snake-faced moron blinks. 'A name?'

'A name. Your contact who put it together, all the tech required for the defrost.'

'But that's–'

'I can talk real loud,' Cody says. 'I can make a challenge every asshole out there will hear.'

Naga nods. 'Alright, the name; the name and the money. Deal?'

'For now,' Cody says. 'Wanton, get out of sight. Load the case with all the cash, then you and I are out of here.'

'Cody–'

'Not a conversation. This is how it is.'

She stares at him and he stares back, but she's not the one who looks away. Naga kneels down, collects the case. Takes it to the granite bar where his boys can't see, unloads the contents in neat, pretty stacks. Steps away so she can collect it, makes sure he stays out of arms reach.

Cody smacks herself in the face hard enough to break the skin. Grins through the bloody mess and points towards the door. 'Over there. Look scary,' she says. 'Keep the case in hand.'

Naga's jaw is tight as hell, but he does it without question. Stands over Wanton, case in both hands, ready to bludgeon him. Wanton rolls over, his face a bloody mess. 'I give,' he says, just loud enough for someone outside to hear.

For a moment, Naga teeters, ready to go through with it. Cody almost wonders if she'll have to kill the bastard.

Then he takes it. Lowers the case. Helps Wanton to his feet. Claps the big man on the shoulder, like it's just another victory. Keeps all the focus right on him while she collects the money.

She gets Wanton over one shoulder, steadies himself beneath his weight. Gets them out of there, while Naga's still celebrating. Gets some distance between them and the Slaughterhouse.

Wanton groans as she gets him staggering, steering him back towards home. 'Money ain't going to be nothing,' he says. 'Ain't going to buy down the debt that much.'

'Ain't for the debt,' she says.

'Yeah?'

'Give it a week,' she says. 'Maybe longer, if he broke something. Enough to get you back on your feet, ready to handle things. That happens, we head back over there. Remind Nag of his obligations.'

Wanton coughs, spits blood into the gutter. 'Can't say I won't look forward to that.'

They walk another block before she asks: 'Do you remember?'

Wanton lifts his head. 'Remember what?'

'The sleep,' she says. 'The passage of years. For real, this time, don't fuck with me.'

He can't walk, while he thinks on it. Just becomes a dead weight on her shoulder. She lowers him to the ground, up against a low wall. Sits down beside him and takes a breather.

'You know,' Wanton says, 'I don't really remember shit. I just remember coming out, the bright lights and the sure-as-shit confusion. The shit that went down after, once they explained how things would be.'

'Yeah,' Cody says. 'Yeah. That sounds familiar.'

Wanton shifts his leg, winces a little. 'We really going to lean on Nag?'

She nods. 'Man owes us,' she says. 'An someone out there can do what we can't. Figure we should talk to him, now we know what he charges. Ain't going to do us any good, but, well, you know...'

For a moment Wanton just wheezes through the bloody wreck of his nose. Then it clicks into place, and the big man is smiling through the carnage that used to be his face.

She stands, gets him up again. Helps him get moving.

Wanton keeps smiling the whole damn way home.

NARRELLE M. HARRIS

Virgin Soil

A MORAN & CATO ADVENTURE

It was the classic bump-and-lift pickpocketing technique, with a follow-up second-man runner, only it wasn't a fob watch or a billfold they were snitching, it was a baby.

Fellow one, a wiry cove, collided with the weary missus and her bub trying to get out of the godawful Melbourne rain, and while he apologised and fussed with getting her set to rights – and her protesting all the while – fellow two, short but broad of shoulder and younger, scooped the babe out of the perambulator and into his arms and legged it down Bourverie Street towards the town proper.

Fellow one ran like the clappers in the opposite direction, several gentlemen in pursuit. They bally-hooed for assistance as they all rounded into Queensbury Street, but the wily beggar disappeared into the Queensbury Hotel and all the looking in the world didn't find him out. He was well and truly gone, like a rat up a drainpipe.

In the meantime, the stocky youth held the squawling child close to his chest and ran like he had all of hell's demons on his tail, which was as darned near the truth as Melbourne's outraged folk could oblige him with. The child's mother was somewhere in the middle of the pack, shrieking curses and entreaties for the safety of her babe. Honestly, the child-snatcher was quite impressed with her stamina as he hurtled across Victoria Street between carriages and horses.

Just when all looked like reaching a violent conclusion in short order, the man with the baby hurtled down an alley off Therry Street, through a tin door held on with wire and hope. He kicked the door closed again and paused in the squalid bolt hole, jogging the kid in his arms. 'Hush, little thing,' he said to it in an accent from East London, 'Not long now.'

The infant, no more than a year old, was in no mood to be hushed, naturally, and the fellow was mightily relieved a moment later to foist his caterwauling load into his partner's arms, him having shown up out of nowhere.

'Hurry!' he urged, pressing his ear to the thin door and fetching a pocket knife and a jar from his trousers.

The wiry one fetched from his own pocket a tiny stone vial with a cork in it. He pulled the cork out with his teeth and took his turn at jogging the baby, with just as much influence on the howling urchin. 'Ready?'

'Yup. Hold him still.' And while one held the squirming kid tightly, the other seized a little hand, forced it to splay open with a thumb dug into the palm, and he jabbed the nib of the blade into the tender flesh.

As soon as blood was drawn, he dropped the knife and held the jar over the little pink mouth that opened in outrage and fear and pain.

The child screamed, right into the jar over its mouth. At the same time, the wiry one dextrously pushed the stone vial against the spill of blood and caught up a few drops.

The jar was filled with screaming and then with three or four heartbroken sobs, before the container was lifted away and a lid clapped over the top of it. Another stone vial was produced, from the fellow's other pocket, and some of the fat, frightened, frightful tears were gathered as well.

Blood and tears and cries all bottled – the last looked like faint, fractured ribbons inside the jar – and tucked into pockets, the pair of baby thieves tried to make amends. The one who'd stabbed, so sudden and shallow, that little hand dabbed the blood away with a kerchief that was quite clean, and offered the child a boiled sweetie.

The child threw the raspberry drop back in his face and scratched him on the nose with tiny but sharp nails.

The other braved those wee fists and stuck his face right close to the boy's ear. He whispered something sing-song, a kind and lovely lullaby in some antique language, and then there were three warm and muted bodies simply breathing in the little room.

'I will set the cherub down where the posse can find him, Lucius,' said the wiry one, 'We shall meet again by the wharf.'

Lucius nodded and waited for his partner to leave. He counted to 50 and then slipped away. He caught a distant glimpse of the mother pouncing in delirious joy on her babe, and the mob looking about for the one who'd deposited the child on the hotel stoop, but of course he'd disappeared.

Rain had made a mud creek of Queen Street, and the blighted stuff stuck like tar to boots of toff and toiler alike. All these thousands milling off the ships at the wharf were no ruddy help either. Sooner the fools were all off to Ballarat for the diggings, the better; or it would be, if there weren't thousands more on their way, just as foolhardy.

Lucius wove in and out of the crowd, as mud-footed as the rest and more threadbare than most. He darted between the shifting bodies, dodging low to look under elbows and past waists, or stood on tiptoe trying to see over shoulders, and much luck to him, little titch that he was. Finally, he caught sight of his quarry. He shouldered between a burly blacksmith with his knapsack and a Chinaman late arrived from California's Gold Mountain in pursuit.

'Oi, Cato,' said Lucius, coming up shoulder-to-shoulder with his wiry mate, 'Put it away, eh?'

The accosted Cato, as grubby and as threadbare as his friend, raised an eyebrow at him, his clear blue eyes all bemused, until Lucius jerked his head at Cato's rear endage, and at the long, slender, and slightly scaly tail that hung down low enough to be seen under Cato's weathered Dutch pea jacket.

'Oh, go to,' Cato cheerily scolded his tail. He wriggled and the tail disappeared, not only from under the jacket but back into his actual flesh, 'Alas, I forget to reel the whole in, sometimes.'

'Well, it is a handsome tail,' Lucius observed. His eyes were also blue, and sometimes he and Cato were mistaken for brothers, though there was no blood and 260 years between them. Yet they were brothers enough.

Cato plucked at Lucius's sleeve. 'There's the fellow.' He nodded at a strapping young lad of 19 or so standing with his whiskered father, directing the unloading of goods from *The Lady Jane*, new arrived from the old country, that had something more useful than gold-diggers on board.

'Aye,' breathed Lucius, head close to Cato's, 'That's our virgin lad. It's a shame. He seems a good chap.'

Fourteen people nearly trod them into the mud for standing still, so they lifted their heels and went with the stream a little way, till they could draw aside into the relative stillness of a cart awaiting a load. One of the horses blew a raspberry with its big hairy lips and gave Cato an affronted look, but horses never paid him much mind. Dogs were another matter.

'If he is a good fellow,' said Cato, his lips pursed in a way that made his whole face sharp, 'Then he would not begrudge his sacrifice for the greater good.'

Lucius scowled, unimpressed with the argument. 'And would you go whistling to your doom for such nobility?'

Cato, who had tried to do so once or twice, pushed his cheek against Lucius's shoulder and rubbed. 'There, there, my Luke. The deed must be done.'

'I know. Don't have to like it, though.'

'No, cousin, you do not,' Cato agreed. 'Come. Let us do that for which we came.'

They darted through the thinning crowd, the planks alongside the ships giving them brief respite from the treacherous, muddy ground. They approached warily, sideways on, all watchful, until some jack tar was careless with the crates and the whiskery old man strode towards his cargo, issuing shouts and instruction. That's when Cato dashed to one side of their fresh-faced virgin lad, and Lucius the other, both dragging off their caps and bowing.

'Begging your pardon, young sir,' said Lucius, proper and polite, 'But I have a message for you from a lady, sir.'

The lad, who had been watching and learning from his father, started at the voice so near him, and flinched a little at Lucius, though well-bred fellow that he was, he did try *not* to flinch.

'What lady?' he asked, 'I don't know any lady.' He clearly meant, *not the kind of lady you would know*.

Cato bowed lower and smiled, bright and friendly, at the tall young man. 'We beg your forbearance sir, but the lady knows you right well. She bid us say, 'You will find Joshua Cole, the bonniest lad in the colony, working by the wharf with his father. Pray tell him from me that Nettie Wilkins is free this evening to see the young man, when the circus revels are done', and so we have come, sir, to pass on what the lady says.'

'Just as she charged us to,' added Lucius earnestly.

The bonnie Joshua Cole grinned, happy and shy and pleased as Punch. 'Nettie sent you? Are you certain?'

'As certain as the sun does rise and set,' said Cato, when Lucius was disinclined to embellish.

Joshua beamed like sunshine on a field of flowers. 'Isn't she the most lovely creature?' he asked, 'And she says she will meet with me?'

'Aye, sir. Tonight,' said Lucius. He pressed a folded piece of paper into the lad's hand. The young man opened it eagerly, read it with shining eyes, and then refolded the parchment and tucked it down his shirt.

Joshua's beatific smile seemed to hurt Lucius somehow. Cato edged back from Joshua's side and sideways so that he could reach out and pet Lucius's back, unseen.

Joshua reached into his pocket for a coin and pressed it into Lucius's hand. 'Tell her I'll come at the appointed hour,' he said, low and conspiratorial, as though he could be heard by anyone but the three of them in this cacophonous dock.

Cato tugged on the hem of Lucius's coat. Lucius nodded a friendly farewell, and he and Cato dissolved into the crowd again.

Cato pressed close to Lucius's side as they took rapid strides eastwards to the new bridge that spanned the muddy river. Lucius's hands were jammed deep in his pockets and he stared at his feet, squelching in the mud as they walked.

'We must go to the hospital,' said Cato gently.

'I know.'

'And thence to our lodgings, and thereafter the circus, and–'

'Out to the diggings. *I know.*'

'We do only what we must, cousin,' said Cato. He plucked at the edge of Lucius's coat again. He felt sorry for his Luke, just a lad himself, younger even than Cole in years, though much older in experience.

Lucius sighed. 'I know.' He drew his hands from his pockets and patted Cato's hand; took and squeezed his fingers and then squeezed them again. 'We have to, and we'll do it right.' He lifted his chin, and turned north, along Swanston.

The colony's Melbourne Hospital was a grand thing, what with all the new works done in the previous year. Its block on Lonsdale Street boasted healthful gardens for the recovering ill without, and within, new equipment and more beds for their patients. Well, perhaps not so grand after all, given that no sooner had the work been commissioned and funded than gold had been discovered, rendering materials expensive and workmen scarce, for most had scarpered off to dig for better fortunes. The insult added to this expensive injury was that, once more, the hospital was too small for the population it serviced.

However, some men still forsook soiled hands and the promise of wealth for other kinds of treasures. Depending, of course, on how a body defined a *treasure*.

Doctor Henry Sawyer, for example, treasured knowledge and its classification and, like colleagues in London, he collected samples for his own studies and the erudition of fellow scholars. He had many treasures preserved in jars on his shelves, including two interesting cancers taken from a sailor who drowned before the disease could kill him; a hanged murderer's tattooed lip; the skull of a native child; and the preserved fingers of a pianist (cruelly separated from his digits by an ill-tempered crocodile that appreciated neither the narrow cage in which the carnival roustabout had confined it, nor the prodding fingers of the general public trying to make it move).

Lucius, who had his ears out for this sort of thing, had learned about the Doctor's latest serendipitous acquisition. Some poor new wife had miscarried a tragic miscreation last night, it was said. Doctor Sawyer had assisted the mother, who lived, and taken away the freakish babe, which did not.

Lucius and Cato sauntered through the paths of sapling trees and ornamental shrubs before finding older growth. Then they crept through that sparse concealment around to the back of the hospital, where old bandages, wound-packings gruesome with blood and infection, unidentifiable pounds of flesh, broken syringes and other hospital refuse were sealed in old airtight, watertight, tarred barrels, awaiting removal to a place where burning them wouldn't affect the patients with their diseased miasma.

Their prize was not in one of those barrels, however.

Lucius leaned against an outside wall and eyed the grounds around him watchfully. The air beside him was now vacant of Cato, and a large Norway rat scurried to the doorway leading to this gruesome medical midden. The door opened, although nobody on either side had turned the handle and Cato, as Rat, darted inside.

At first Lucius spent the waiting time considering the old question – where did Cato's clothes go when he thus transformed into a rat? Come to that, where did the rest of Cato go, given the relative sizes of rat and man? When he had asked that question all the way from infancy to boyhood to manhood, his father and never-aging Cato had grinned at him and told him nonsense answers. Perhaps now he was better at commanding his own simple magic he should ask again, and seek for a better answer than, 'Why, Lucius, I keep it all in a rubber balloon!'

Someone walked by, and Lucius conjured a cloak about himself. Only a weak one, but few people actually wanted to contemplate what was in this yard, and it was easy to project *I am wall I am air I am silence I am nothing* until they went away. Perception magic was easy, in the scheme of things. Flesh magic – the thing Cato did – was the hard stuff.

When the stranger had passed, Lucius regarded the midden instead. He contemplated what might be contained in the barrels that would be useful for another day, and then decided not to look today. The yard would be here later, after all, its detritus of human suffering (and, for some, relief) stored for any who might find use for such grisly things.

He hoped Cato wouldn't take long.

Cato-as-Rat hugged close to the skirting boards. No scent yet led him on; he relied instead on the map they'd acquired from a labourer who'd worked on the hospital's expansion. Cato's hybrid brain was good with translating the grubby sketch into real world pathways.

Then the smell of preservative chemicals stung the back of his throat, and he followed this even more reliable map to Doctor Sawyer's preparation room.

Another door opened with no hand to supply the necessary force – Cato's nose twitched with the effort though, his sharp centre teeth bared in a manner most ferocious to any who didn't know the true cause of the grimace. Once egress was possible, Cato slunk inside the room and scurried under a workbench.

Doctor Sawyer was absent, and wasn't that a keen blessing on this difficult day? Cato slunk out from his shelter and commenced the search, his grey-brown-furred head lifting as he scented the air. Too many stinks mingled all at once to easily identify what he wanted, so he reached outside himself for other senses, whiskers quivering, and that led him to the preparation table.

And there it was. They were. Lying in the pan, waiting to be lowered into the jar with its pungent solution. The poor, monstrous little thing, under-formed and malformed, soft and pink like a wee foetal mouse, only with its two heads and three arms. Cato wondered if the doctor had hidden it from the bereft mother's sight and knowledge, and knew that Lucius would hope so. Cato hoped so too, he found. Perhaps Lucius's tender heart for ordinary mortals was a catching thing.

The easiest option would have been to seize the specimen in his teeth and drag it back the way he had come, but apart from being conspicuous, it struck Cato as disrespectful. It might also damage the potency of the offering, for this was tricky magic they were working. The fault lay not in this poor double-child. Any miscarried babe would have done, of course (though not aborted, wrong kind of sorrow for this kind of spell) but these conjoined siblings weighed twice the lost potential.

Let their loss contribute to a greater cause, Cato thought, *and their lost potential help avert a greater horror.*

Instead, Cato darted to the stand where the conscientious doctor had hung coat, hat and scarf. Nice hat, too, rabbit felt, silk-lined. A warm and cradling coffin. Cato climbed the coat, took the hat in his teeth and returned to the floor, across the room and clambered up chair and cupboard to the bench.

Being a larger rat than even most Norways, Cato's paws were likewise large and more dextrous. He took the double-child – so tiny and weighing so little – in his soft paws and conveyed it into the hat. He bruxed at them, the soothing *chitter-chitter-chitter* of incisors, a Morse code to the spirits of the dead to fear him not, nor his deeds, nor what would follow. Dark magic was not necessarily *wicked* magic, after all.

Getting the laden hat from bench to floor took a little longer, but Cato was careful with the burden, pushing it ahead of him or dragging it behind in fits and bursts to the still-ajar door.

Cato sniffed the air, but his head was still full of sharp chemicals, so he thought his way was clear when he dragged his treasure into the hall.

'Dear God!'

Ah. Fie. He should have known that coat, hat and scarf still indoors meant that the good doctor was not himself outdoors.

Cato bit the edge of the hat and ran, lolloping sideways, squealing alarm as he went. Doctor Sawyer and several of his staff pursued, one with a broom, which was unpleasant but less unpleasant than a fox terrier.

He ran fast – much faster than a normal rat, which is fast indeed – even with his burden, and yet the disgusted and outraged medical fraternity were on his tail before the door to the yard was flung open from without. Lucius filled the space, his short and stocky frame tense and coiled. He flung his hand towards the pursuers and a haze of darkness and cold and shrill sound filled the hall behind Cato.

While the mob were engaged in crying out their terror and confusion, Lucius bent and scooped up Cato and the coffin-hat. Holding both close to his chest, he took to his heels.

Once far enough away, and taking refuge in a quiet spot near the Catholic churchyard, Lucius set Cato down. In a moment, there stood the man instead of the rat. He was grinning.

'That adventure was a near thing, Master Moran,' he said, panting.

'You stole a man's London hat worth a good six schillings, Cato Sminth,' responded Lucius, grinning too, panting with exertion and the thrill of escape.

'Good now, at least eight schillings in this market, I would think,' Cato corrected him. He took it from Lucius's hands and checked the contents. 'I thought the poor creature deserved a soft place,' he added.

'Aye,' agreed Lucius. He took off his neck kerchief, folded it and laid it over the top of the little body. 'And all ceremony we can give it. Shame we can't bury the poor thing proper.'

'Thou art soft-hearted.' But Cato's accusation was gentle.

'One day I'll be laid to rest or used as you see fit,' said Lucius, 'I find it makes me have a care.'

Cato didn't like to think about what would happen when Lucius was old and Cato was still just as he was today. No guarantee that would happen of course, but for 260 years it had proven so. Each generation's Moran was born, grew up, grew old (if lucky) and died and left Cato ageless and history-less to make his home with the next Moran. He had loved them all, and mourned them all, and would not think of each one's passing until that reality had to be faced.

'Come on,' Lucius interrupted his friend's melancholy train of thought, rubbing his hand along Cato's arm, 'Let's take our foragings and prepare for tonight.'

Their lodgings were in a grubby back room of a grubby building. They paid slightly above the odds for it, but it had a door they could close rather than merely a cloth partition. It didn't halt the sound of the dollymop next door going about her business, all times of the day and night. Once they'd heard Annie's minder come to get most of the cut for it, and they knew for a fact she'd earned more than she told him, but they kept that counsel to themselves. Her minder, Silas, was a bastard and Annie worked hard for her push.

Lucius had even sent a flicker of perception magic through the wall, and Silas never even suspected the extra coin Annie hid in a stocking inside the thin mattress.

'You should call on Annie's favours when we are done,' Cato told Lucius, laying out the hat on the narrow bed they shared.

Lucius, who had kept chaste for the month in preparation for the work, shrugged. 'Maybe. She's a laugh, I'll grant you. I like her.' He lay out the other materials on the bed, too: the two stone vials, and the jar with its fractured ribbons of sound curling and spinning like shining worms within the magic-sealed glass. He laid a square of soft leather too, marked all over with sigils in old blood. Lucius's great-great-grandfather's blood, Cato said.

Cato also said the soft vellum was tanned from the skin of a stillborn goat, and not a girl-child at all, despite rumours, and he ought to know because he'd been there and contributed his own piss to the preparation of it, along with the lime, and that's what made it so enduring.

With great reverence, Lucius took away his kerchief from the soft felt hat and Cato lifted the double-child from the well of it and onto the vellum. With gentleness as though the babe had ever taken breath and breathed still, he folded the ends over it, and made words and sounds beyond Lucius's hearing. The vellum sealed over the little body, and within, the flesh no longer decayed.

'Put the little thing back,' suggested Lucius.

Cato took the bundle up in his hands and gently laid it back into the hat. Then hat, jar and vials all were placed into a satchel by the bed, wherein lay two more corked vials for the evening's work. The vessels were packed round with clean hay stuffed into old stockings. Lucius dropped the flap over the satchel and patted the bag.

'Here, good fellow,' said Cato, 'Rest your eyes. I'll wake you for the Circus.'

Lucius did as he was bid and lay on the hard mattress, the thin blanket pulled over his shoulders. Cato took the time to disrobe, taking off each old garment and folding it.

'Cato,' said Lucius, 'Will you tell me where your clothes go, and the rest of you, when you change yourself into a rat?'

''Tis as well to ask where I find my excess flesh when I turn into a man,' said Cato.

'Da said you always joked that you may have been a rat before you were a man.'

''Tis no jest, my Luke. Yet it troubles me, for I do not remember,' said Cato, not looking at his friend, 'The decades have been long and I perceive dimly that there was an accident. Sometimes I dream I am a boy, and glad that Queen Bess won't burn any more Catholics; and sometimes I dream of a nest in a burrow, sleeping tight-close with my brothers and sisters, all furred and tailed like me.' He shrugged. 'The longer I live, the less it is of any matter.'

'But where does it go, really, or come from? I won't ever get the hang of flesh magic till I understand.'

Cato patted Lucius's head. 'Flesh magic is not a skill for all, Lucius. The magic you have is strong and fit and need not be more than it is.'

'But truly, where? It's not really a balloon, like you say.'

''Tis so, in its way, and also not.' Naked, now, Cato sat on the edge of the bed. 'Our magic makes bubbles in the earth and air, though yet with thin skins and fine tethers. When I shift my form, I place all the parts that I do not currently require – my clothes and all this excess body – and transform it into…' He searched for a useful analogy. 'Light. This light I hold inside a bubble, if you will, of the finest, most delicate skin – like a soap bubble, or rubber stretched so thin the sunlight filters through. For this, I make an anchor in my belly, right close to my heart, and what is left of myself, I alter. Thus, I run on my four rodent feet, this balloon of buzzing light trailing me, and it squeezes into all the little spaces into which I fit, until I am done. Thereafter, I work my magic to transform the light back into *things*.'

He grinned at Lucius's dubious expression. 'Aye, tis not a tale well told. Magic is and is not like anything in the mortal world, yet I know no way else to say it. Mayhap I knew better words, before the accident which I believe befell me. Mayhap magic is a thing you do and feel but cannot describe.' He shrugged.

'Why do you undress for sleep, then, if you can make your clothes into light?'

'Why, Master Moran, tis less effort, and why make work for myself when I seek my rest, for I am a lazy blackguard given my chance.' Cato's eyes sparkled in good humour, and Lucius laughed at him.

'Are thee well, then, my Luke?'

'Yeah, Cato, I'm good. We best rest up now, ready for tonight, and for tomorrow.'

Cato's body shrank down – he putting the bulk of himself away into that ill-described invisible balloon – and as a large grey-brown Norway rat, he scurried into Lucius's arms. He twitched his nose against Lucius's chin, then tucked his furry face and body up close. His teeth ground together, the *chitter chitter chitter* of soothing contentment; helping tender-hearted Lucius to sleep, as he'd done ever since his Luke had been a dark-haired babe in swaddling, back home in England.

Lucius cuddled Cato, nose burrowed in the rat's soft fur, Cato's tail looped around his wrist, and they slept the afternoon hours through, like little brothers, a litter of two.

Mr Noble's Olympic Circus performed every day excepting Sunday, whatever the weather. Melbourne's sporadic drizzle made no real difference today to amusements up on the hill at Spring Street. Some folks stayed away; some more came into the tents to escape the rain, it being no worse, and less cold, than some days in the United Kingdom left so far behind. Today was the usual run of pantomime, and the trampoline act, the acrobats leaping through hoops of fire and the very fine equestrian acts performed by Mr Henry Ashton and the other trick riders.

Lucius felt a kinship with the fellows tumbling through the burning hoops. Cato was partial to the nimble antics of the trick riders. But that's not why they were at the Circus.

Lucius spent a small coin for the cheap standing-room area. Cato became his rat-self and watched too for a time, before scampering off to loiter among the horses, keeping his large ears out for the participants in their next drama.

And there among the horses, after the show, was Nettie Wilkins, the ingénue actress from the pantomime, exchanging soft words with a slightly older young woman in a tight bodice and full skirts who had shown such balletic poise and deft timing atop a cantering filly in the hippodrome.

Surrounded by show folk grooming and feeding their star animals, the two women who shared a billet spoke with their heads bent conspiratorially together. Cato came up close to them to watch and listen. They whispered and laughed and giggled a while, until Nettie sobered.

'I have to go meet someone, Polly. A patron of the arts. He may have a place for me in a local theatre, so we don't have to move on to Sydney when Mr Noble takes the circus north. I may be back after dark. Don't wait up for me.'

'Of course I'll wait up, Nettie,' Polly told her, contriving to catch the girl's fingers in her own and to kiss her pretty cheek, 'You watch he doesn't get too handsy, my darling girl, and I'll keep the bed warm.'

Nettie's smile was, Cato thought, not as sunny as she pretended, though she was a very good actress. Then she was gone.

Cato waited, then, whiskers trembling, while Polly gave her horse a good brush down, and water and feed, among all the other riders doing the same. She took longer than the others, lingering perhaps for her friend's return. When that hope was disappointed, the young woman stifled a sigh and went away, no doubt to wash and eat and prepare for sleep.

Cato wasn't sure how long he waited – he perceived time differently in his rat body than his human one; and the human one, being so long-lived, perceived it differently to anyone else anyway. But the sun was long gone and the moon hanging heavy among the remaining clouds when Nettie returned to the stable, the boy Joshua Cole escorting her with laughter and teasing.

'Just a little kiss, Nettie, won't you say yes? We've had such a lovely supper, haven't we? Don't I deserve a kiss?'

'Perhaps you do,' Nettie agreed with a giggle, and she pecked him on the cheek like he was a favoured brother.

'Oh, a little more than that,' prompted Joshua. 'You can kiss better than that on the stage, Nettie.'

'That's only pretend kissing,' Nettie laughed, 'That's not a real kiss at all.'

'Give me a real kiss, then,' Joshua urged her.

'I bet the girls all kiss you all the time, Joshua Cole,' she said, dancing away briefly from his arms that tried to snag her and bring her close, but at the same time bumping her hip against the front of his trousers.

'I swear to you, no,' he protested, capturing her at last and reeling her in, 'Their fathers won't leave me alone with 'em.' He laughed, to show he was joking.

Nettie laughed too, coquettishly, like she did on the stage, and not at all open and uncontrived, like she did when she laughed with Polly Clewes.

'I don't have a father,' she said, tilting her head so that he could kiss her cheek and then her long, pale throat. 'There's only me and my friend Polly.' She petted his shoulders and chest, her fingers testing the shape of his body underneath.

'And me, now,' murmured Joshua, one hand on her left breast, 'Do say you'll let me show how fond I am of you.'

And so their teasing conversation continued, his hand now on her calf and her thigh as he rucked up her skirts, and she protesting without any real protest, laughing brittle-bright as though on the stage, yet willing enough.

Young Master Cole had lifted his giggling Nettie onto a hay stack when Cato detected Lucius's arrival, and the woman Lucius had brought with him on the pretext that Nettie needed to see her. Polly Clewes's expression was fierce and determined, and she gripped a hoof pick in one hand – taking no chances with the stranger leading her to the stables, clearly. She was a wiry, slender thing, but her spirit was mighty, which Cato liked, but it also made him sigh. The mighty ones fell hard.

As Polly fell now, seeing her dear friend with her skirts up around her hips and this unknown lad standing between Nettie's pale thighs, trousers agape and arse half-bared as his hips jerked, the erratic rhythm of him punctuated with his cries. 'Nettie, oh, god, yes, yes, unh, unfh...'

Nettie held on to Joshua's arms, her face turned from him, and Cato had to wonder at her obvious unhappiness, since she had so clearly acquiesced to the boy's impertinent imprecations for more. Her eyes were closed and her grimace demoralising to see.

Nettie had no idea that Polly saw all; Polly, who stared wide and liquid-eyed, a fist stuffed into her mouth to keep herself from crying out. She turned away and ran, Lucius at her heels, leaving Cato alone with the lovers and the horses.

The lad finished, gasping as though surprised, and perhaps he was. Climax wrought in the circle of his own hand was a fine pleasure, but the first time embraced inside a woman could be a bit surprising, in its softness and strength.

Not just the first time either. Cato didn't know if his remembered first time was really the first – the time before the imperfectly-recalled accident continued to be a secret history – but he remembered the first time after becoming who he was now, Cato Sminth. A lovely lass, she was, as fond of Will Shakespeare's theatre as he himself. Sweet Mary Sutton, died of ague in his arms. He'd have married her if she'd lived, though she would have died all the same, one day. The curse of the long-lived was to bury one's heart time and time again. At least with the Morans, a little of his heart was seeded in the next generation, growing to flower and to seed again. He felt less lonely, tending that family garden.

But Cato now caught the cadence of the couple's speech, and it was unhappy indeed. Joshua, buttoning up his breeches, was on the verge of tears. 'How can you? That's not... But you said you *cared* for me.'

Nettie's neck and face were flushed scarlet and her eyes were flashing ire, but shame too. 'You're a nice enough fellow,' she said harshly. 'But a girl must live, and she can't do it on pennies.' She tugged her skirts down, her knees squeezed tight together, and she looked away from the hurt and horror on his face. 'I thought you understood the... the terms.'

'Terms,' he snarled, like a wounded animal, 'I'll give you *terms*.'

'I'd rather you give me a sovereign.'

'You think you're *worth* a sovereign?'

'You said tonight I was worth silk and rubies.'

'That's before I knew you were a *whore*.'

Her lip curled in response. 'If you thought so highly of me, you would not have insisted on showing me how *fond* you are. You would have treated me like a lady.'

As they fought, the boy sounded more and more like a broken-hearted schoolboy, and she more and more like a mistress betrayed, and their mutual misery compounded in curses and volume until the lad threw at her a handful of coins – including, indeed, a sovereign – and he ran away.

Nettie, given now to sobbing, collected up each coin which had cost her so much. Then she stood tall, dried her eyes and sluiced her hands, face and crotch with water from the nearest trough.

There was more crying ahead of her, Cato knew, but that was not his concern, though he felt sorry for it. Poor, foolish child, thinking she was solving problems by heaping up new ones on top.

Once she had gone, Cato regained his human shape. He first stooped for the stone vial Lucius had dropped by the place he had waited with Polly. Vessels with magic properties were best not stored in the bubble-place, to avoid disruption to the spell.

He then went to the hay bale on which Joshua Cole had given his virginity to the actress, and plucked up straws stained with the boy's first given pleasure. The loss of innocence was twice-over, the betrayal hard on the heels of the lust. The actress's own betrayal – of her self and her Sapphic lover – made it a four-sided forswearing.

Task done, Cato tucked the vial into his pocket and went looking for Lucius.

Lucius should by now have employed a stiffish bit of perception magic to collect Polly's own tearful badge of betrayal. At a pinch, the clean kerchief he carried with him would serve the purpose.

Instead, Cato found Lucius awkwardly patting Polly's grief-shuddering shoulder.

'Nettie and I are friends, aren't we?' she was sobbing, 'More like sisters. Closer than sisters. I'd have done anything for her, and she for me, she said. She *loved* me, she said, and I love her, and what has she done? Why?'

'Here now, Polly, don't fuss. I'm sorry for it, but it had to be done.'

And there was Lucius's tender heart steering them straight into the cesspit.

The mighty Polly's sobbing stopped mid-breath and she gave young Lucius a look like she was a basilisk and he a mouse. 'What do you mean, *it had to be done?*'

Lucius blinked his bright blue eyes and went pale as a ghost and not a peep came out of his throat.

Polly's glare intensified. 'What did you do to my girl? She *loved* me. How did you make her betray me?'

'We didn't, I swear it,' Lucius protested, waving his two hands in the air to ward off a blow that wasn't let loose yet, but oh, it was coming. He held the corked stone vial in one hand, so Cato took comfort in the fact it had been filled, at least. But then Lucius, damn the blessed boy, kept on talking.

'We watched you all and saw the way the wind blew, with him pining after her, and you and her and the money problem, and we needed all of you. We needed for them to do it and for you to see it. We didn't *make* it happen, but we didn't stop it. I'm sorry. I'm sorry. But we *need* it.'

Polly's insipient blow remained a curled fist, pressed hard against her thigh. 'What for?'

'There's a monster growing in Ballarat and we need to put it down.'

'A monster?' Her glittering eye was equal parts rage and puzzlement.

Cato thought it best that Lucius stop talking now, but dear Lucius apparently found it impossible to do so, under the onslaught of that gimlet eye.

'It's… it's like this. All these people, coming here, thousands of 'em,' said Lucius, the words tumbling out and out and out of him, 'All going up there and digging up the land looking for a future, and they're pouring their *souls* into it. I mean that literally, Polly. Their *souls*, and sweat and blood and tears, too, filling up the dirt with *hope* and heaping muck on top.'

'Isn't hope a good thing?' Polly's tone was sharp still, and a bit wondering, and she should have been backing away and wasn't. Cato really did like her a lot.

Cato stepped out from the shadows, startling her and Lucius both. He took the vial from Lucius's hand and put it away in his pocket.

'Aye, Miss Clewes, the hope of man can be good. Much of it is so. Hope is the flame that makes a soul strive through mud and blood and loneliness and lifetimes without end.'

Cato swallowed hard, and ploughed on. 'But not all hope is a lantern to guide our way from darkness. Some hope is a will-o-the-wisp, lighting only a path to destruction. Hope can be selfish and desperate and cruel and greedy. Some hope, aye, is the hope your neighbour will discover at last his fortune, yet perish before he has told any soul but you, thus allowing you to grow fat on his fortune without the sweat of the gaining.

'Some hope is the hope you'll commit bloody murder yet 'scape the hangman, and so take what will not come by happy accident. Some hope steals joy from a goodly present and a future not rich but wholesome, and thence the future of your children, and sells it all for the vainer, greedier hope of velvet days, when cotton days are plenty and do not cost the life and health and soul of those you love. Such brutal hope eats and eats and eats everything good around it, perforce consuming all else's hope into the bargain.'

Cato reached out to take her hand and unfurl it from its unused fist.

'And some hope,' he said, 'is the wish and the thought: I will dig my future out of the dirt, not by nurturing growing things nor using my two hands to build, but by stealing from the earth and putting nothing back but curses and rage.'

'Oh,' said Polly, stunned to quiet. And then: 'And the monster?'

'Ah, me,' said Cato, 'such blind and selfish hope poured into the earth and, as my Luke has said, heaping greedy, cruel muck upon the whole, it plants a terrible seed. In such a bloody garden, a creature might grow from soil so infected. At Ballarat many thousands, and thousands more each day, all wishing harsh and desperate with their whole soul and heart, all at once, it is too much. It soaks into the earth like a flood, but the earth knows not that something is warped in all that power pouring in. The land is bigger and older and broader than all of us, and its concerns are not ours. This flood pouring into it, waterlogging its particles with poison, marries with the ground and grows tangible. And thence it grows into a creature that knows no better than to want everything, with a ferocious, greedy hope that it will get what it wants, and keep it, too. Forever, as the earth is wont to want things.'

'I don't understand.' Polly's lack of comprehension was accompanied by a teeth-gritting determination to wrest understanding out of it if it killed her.

Lucius tried to explain. 'It's like, all that energy, directed by all those thousands of minds and wishes, is making a kind of homunculus. A physical form made out of dark ideas. And it's not the soil's fault the wishing made it a monster. It doesn't have a mind except the one it's given. And it's forming now, from selfish hope and cruel wishes and blood and sweat and despair, and soon it'll hatch or be born or rise up like a tree, all made of poison and greed. Because it don't know the whole story. It don't understand yet that it don't have the right to just take what it wants. That there are other kinds of hope that ain't cruel, and there's sorrow in it too, and in the loss of it, not just rage. It's soil that don't know better, virgin soil, like. So Cato and me've got to teach it the whole story. Softer kinds of hope, and the sorrows of the human heart that hurts, and hopes anyway.'

'How do you do that?'

Lucius belatedly thought it unwise to reveal their full natures to her, but Polly was an entertainer, a traveller on the road, a horsewoman and an individual of both imagination and experience. She glowered at their silence.

'Show me then,' she challenged them. 'What kind of magic? Surely agents of the Devil aren't too shy to show what they can do.'

Lucius bristled. 'We ain't no devils.'

'Nor angels, either,' Cato felt honour-bound to confess.

'What then?'

'Say then that we are agents of balance, rather than chaos,' Cato said.

'Ain't no God or Satan in it,' said Lucius, 'Leastways, not with *us*.'

'Do you only talk incessantly?' Polly demanded to know, 'Or do you pull rabbits from your arse as well?'

Oh, Cato really did like her. She would be an excellent mother for the next generation of Morans, should it please her.

He didn't change his shape for her though – mighty as she was, that wizardry would likely be too much. He flickered his fingers instead, and from them crackled blue flames.

'Magneto the Miraculous does that on his sideshow,' she said, unimpressed.

Cato shaped the flame into a horse, which cantered from his hand into the air, did three laps of Polly's head (only mildly singeing her hair) before the blue-orange-golden phantasm cantered thence to Lucius's hand. There, it reared and shook its head, little sparks flying from its burning mane. Lucius waved a hand over the conjured creature and the flame turned to ice. He placed the cold figurine in Polly's hand.

'That's elemental magic,' he said, preening a little. 'It's harder than perception magic, but nothing like as difficult as fle… as other kinds of magic.'

Polly turned the figurine over and over in her hands, the ice horse's delicate ears and mane and tail already melting between her fingers. 'Right. So.' She drew a sharp breath in through her nose. 'This is pretty, but it doesn't seem strong enough to undo a *homunculus.*'

'It isn't, on its own,' said Lucius, 'We'll have to combine all kinds of magic. That's why we needed all these things we got today. A child's first betrayal – we got his blood and tears and screams for that. We got a wee unborn babe's lost potential. Two, actually. Two lives that should have been and aren't now, and all the hope their mother had for them, and all the sorrow of that hope lost. And now we have a virgin heart broken, and seed from virginity lost.'

'*Virgin sacrifices*, were we?' Polly's lip curled and her eyes gleamed cold.

'Yeah,' Lucius conceded unhappily.

'People misapprehend that meaning,' said Cato, 'Believing a knife's blade and blood pouring from a girl unpenetrated by a man is the most powerful magic. It has some potency, as does all blood, but not so great, and for certain, it will not meet this need. Virginity of the maidenhead is not more potent than other blood or other virginity. Lost innocence is more potent yet.'

'So you sacrificed my *innocence.*'

Lucius regarded his feet guiltily, but when he looked up his eyes were harder. Tender-hearted he was, but he knew the right of what they did. 'Yes. I'm sorry. We took a lot of innocence today, but we don't want to let that gold-fever monster get out of the mud. It'll get bigger and bigger. Kill hundreds, maybe thousands if it can. It could eat the world, given time, trying to eat enough to satisfy the starving hope in it. We have to put it down before it rises up.'

'And you'll do that by – what? By giving it my happiness?'

'All the hopes of the human heart that break a heart,' concurred Cato. 'Yet it is not a brutal thing we wish to feed to the monster to make it sleep. The baby this morning harmed for the first time has returned to the loving arms of his mother, and is protected once more. The miscarried babe will never know its brothers and sisters in this life, whose siblings will have their mother's more tender care in memory of the one she lost. You and Nettie and

Joshua Cole will love again, more cautiously mayhap, and more wisely, but the hurt now does not foretell future bitterness, nor forestall future tenderness. You will love again.'

'And why *you*? Why are *you* the ones to do this thing?'

'Ain't no-one else,' said Lucius, 'And some that has the power to do it, won't. This is difficult magic, and it's not *nice*.'

'No. It isn't,' she agreed coldly.

'Mark you, lady, we did not *make* your Nettie break your heart,' said Cato. 'That path chosen, she chose herself while we, charged with our mission, did but *use* her choosing. Human nature wrought all the rest, and we will use good nature's proceeds for our purpose.'

Polly's grim expression settled into her face, giving her skin the first of the marks of life that would travel with her forever. 'Then I'm coming with you. I want to see what use my broken heart is to you.'

The set of her jaw showed that she expected protest, but Lucius and Cato were wiser in the ways of the world, and had better uses for their energies, than to police other people's unwise choices. All Lucius said was, 'It'll be hard going. And dangerous. Make sure you keep up.'

Polly sneered. 'I'm a horsewoman born and bred in the colony, and I'm a woman who works in a travelling circus. I do hard every day.'

Polly took her own mount from the circus, while Cato and Lucius fetched the horses they had paid overmuch to an ostler to stable, for they knew it would be impossible to purchase mounts again later. The mad rush to Ballarat meant that beasts and carts sold at twice and thrice the cost again each week to those who would rather ride than walk.

Polly Clewes was as hardened as her good word. Dressed in breeches, her hair knotted up and hidden beneath a broad-brimmed hat, she was easily mistaken for a youth riding with her youthful kin. Lucius was in serious want of a beard himself, though scruffy Cato was whiskered enough for the three of them by the end of the fourth day. Lucius conjured perception magic to conceal them from bushrangers, who were running nigh unchecked since fully half the police force had thrown down their badges and taken up shovels and pans in the goldfields.

Much of the seven days' riding was done in strained quiet, Polly holding fast to her pain and anger. Lucius and Cato, more used to chatter as they rode, or the companionable silence of long and fond acquaintance, were subdued. Polly's glowering presence made the going uneasy. The prickliness of it was not eased by Cato's unpolitic and unsubtle suggestions to Lucius.

'Go ride with her, Lucius, make pretty talk with her.'

'She don't want to talk with me,' Lucius grumped back. 'Not if she can't stick me in the eye with a hairpin first.'

'She bears less ill will than you think,' Cato said, 'and will think better of you by and by if you but make the attempt.'

'Why would I want that anyway? She wanted to come, she's come. She wants to see what it's about, let her see and much good it'll do her. If she don't piss herself in terror or faint dead away from it, assuming we can put it down at all, she'll move along, one town or another, and that's an end. Whether she likes me or not don't figure much into it.'

'Surely she's to your liking.'

'Not really. I'm sorry for what we had to do to her, but she's too old for me.'

'Fie, cousin, she has only a handspan of years on you.'

'Cato, are you trying to play matchmaker with me and Polly?'

'She is a spirited woman. I like her strength. She would make a good partner for you, and a fine mother to the next generation of Morans. The next Moran needs to come from somewhere.'

Lucius's sideways look conveyed scepticism, irritation and compassion all. As Cato was his family's long companion, so his sorrows were known, father to son, father to son, for 260 years. As the family Moran held to their strange uncle and to their work like heirlooms both, so Cato clung to them for purpose. For each generation, Cato must have his Moran, so he could bear to go on in an otherwise friendless world.

'I'm young, yet,' Lucius said, 'And you forgot, Polly Clewes doesn't love men.'

Cato sighed. 'Perhaps not. Perhaps she loved but one woman. Perhaps her love is not defined by pistol nor purse–'

'Perhaps you're a meddlesome rat,' muttered Lucius, 'And will leave her and me alone, now that you know I've no more interest in her than she in me. I'm 17, Cato. I'll find me a proper mother for Moran babes some other where and when than now.' Lucius's expression softened at Cato's unhappy drawing off. 'Though I'll grant you, she's brave and feisty enough to bear a brat by the name of Moran.'

Cato, mollified, sighed and admitted defeat to himself. Lucius was right, and though not much point in allowing her to travel with them remained, he let it be. They could hardly drive her off now, when they'd let her come so far with them.

The perception and elemental magic worked well enough to disguise them from most fellow travellers, or from those lying in wait to molest them, but Lucius and Cato had learned early in their journeys in this far land that the dark-skinned people who lived here first could not be distracted by a twist of perception. Lucius's skin prickled with the knowledge they were watched despite his best efforts, though not followed. Curiosity rather than malice was in those looks.

The one time one of these fellows confronted them, two days out from Ballarat, the hunter barred their horses' way by standing in their path. Cato, who did not speak the language but knew spells, dismounted and met him with open palms.

Cato communed with him a moment. The hunter frowned and walked in a circle around Cato, pausing to prod at his backside, before completing his circumnavigation of the wizard. He spoke rapidly, gesturing in sharp, aggravated movements in the direction of the diggings. Cato replied, and the hunter laughed, squinted at Cato, laughed even harder and walked away, still laughing.

'What was that about?' demanded Polly.

Cato, amused and thoughtful, pulled on his lower lip. 'He says that the land is in upheaval with a whitefella curse that the blackfellas will have to mend or be blamed for. I told him we were on our way for the mending.'

'He seemed to find that funny,' Polly observed sourly, no doubt taking it for a bad omen.

'His humour was otherwise tickled,' Cato shook his head, 'He said I brought to mind an ancestor named Bogoon – a water rat that took a duck for a bride, and so made the platypus.'

That satisfied Polly for the time being, but when mounted again, Cato rode close by Lucius and leaned in his saddle to say for his ears only, 'The son of this land wishes us luck with our whitefella monster, and says it will probably eat us. That was the jest he found so mirthful.'

'Could be right,' Lucius said, 'But I bet it won't be funny.'

And then, a day out from their destination, the stories began to filter in. Wreathed in magic obfuscation, Cato would steal away from their nightly camp on four feet, large ears flickering and tail flicking, and listen to the talk from those making their way back to Melbourne. Mine collapses and floods. Bitter fights among old friends and brutal ones among enemies, both ending up in blood and sometimes corpses. Sickness and acrimony and death in waves up and down the goldfields, coming all of a sudden on one another, and so widespread, that a less that natural explanation seemed to Cato to be more likely than coincidence.

He crept back to the camp, he put back on his human body and lay close to Lucius. 'It's waking,' he whispered. 'We must make the most of our too short time.'

The sun dipped below the horizon that night, washing the rough road, the tangled bushland and the three riders in ink-black, and they didn't stop. The horses picked their way slowly, but their way was aided by a pool of perception washed around the beasts' eyes, so they saw as though it were daylight and moved on. Polly kept pace behind them, her determination undimmed, her anger keeping her warm in the depth of her weariness, aching body and aching heart all one to her.

The sun had not yet risen on the other side of the earth when the travellers reached the Yarrowee River. Cato sniffed the air, dismounted and knelt by the edge of the water.

'The restless thing lies upriver from this place,' he said. 'Traces of it are washed towards the city and the sea. I will call it to us, when preparations are complete. Lucius?'

Lucius had already dismounted and Polly followed suit. She guided her horse to the fast-flowing yet muddy river, filled with detritus from the diggings. She meant to let her mount drink, and was annoyed when Lucius stayed her with a hand on the animal's reins.

'Don't let it drink from that muck,' he said, matching her glare with a stubborn one of his own. 'That dirt flowing downstream's as good as the piss piddled out of that golem we told you about. Won't do our horses any good. There's rainwater in a hollow over there, for now. They can drink from the river later, if we manage to clear it up.'

'*If?*'

'Well, if we don't, we'll probably be too dead to be over-bothered by the failure.'

'You didn't say anything about it *killing* us.'

'Don't do to be pessimistic.' Lucius bared a hard grin at her, 'And we said it was dangerous. Ain't our lookout if you wanted to come anyway.'

The hardness in him softened a touch. 'You don't have to stay, Polly. Only you said you wanted to see what use we made of your hurt, and that seemed fair.'

Polly nodded, and led her horse, and theirs, to a hollow bounded by roots and stones and filled with rainwater. Mindful of this new notion – *too dead to be bothered* – she didn't unsaddle any of them, instead taking the time to check cinches and saddle blankets. She fed them a small handful of feed from the last of their provisions. When she was done, she stood in the midst of the horses, comforted by their solid, warm presence, as though they offered protection.

Lucius and Cato were kneeling by the river. Cato had shoved his hands in to the soft earth in the bank and was fashioning the thick, cloying mud into a bowl. Lucius, meantime, stoked up a small fire and built an A-frame over the top of it from narrow, green sapling branches that smoked slightly but didn't burn. Cato set the mud bowl on top of the frame and the flame below began to heat and dry the odd vessel.

From his satchel, Lucius withdrew four stone vials, a jar of spangling light, and a roll of soft, tan leather covered in rust-red markings. It appeared to contain something precious, from the way he handled it so reverently.

Using a tin mug, Cato scooped a little of the mucky river water up and dribbled it into the mud bowl.

'Thing of ravenous hope, I call thee,' he said.

'Thing of relentless expectation, we give you these gifts,' said Lucius. He uncorked one of the vials and upended it into the murky water. 'I give you these tears of a babe's first deliberate hurt.' A glow like phosphorus flashed around his hands as he poured, and was gone.

'Blood of his first deliberate wound, I give thee,' said Cato, a similar light playing off his long, elegant fingers as he opened and poured the second vial.

'We give you the cries of his first rage.' Lucius held the jar over the bowl and twisted the lid. A sharp crack was audible over the sound of flames and running water, and then a wailing, outraged scream that slipped from one magic state to another. The liquid in the bowl shimmered.

'Here we gift thee virgin seed spilled by a virgin heart so soon betrayed by she who did not love him.'

Cato shook out the semen-smeared straws. 'Mingled with the sacrifice of her body, given for she whom she betrayed out of love.'

Polly frowned at this, but did not speak, as Lucius, hands aglow, emptied the last vial.

'We give you the gift of a broken heart, her future lost, the happiness in bloom wizened on the vine when trust was sundered.'

Tears burned in Polly's eyes at the truth of it, but she held her silence still. Finally, Cato lifted the tiny vellum-wrapped package. He pressed his finger in a line down the leather and it unsealed down a seam previously invisible. From within, he carefully drew a tiny, misshapen body with too many limbs and heads. He lowered it with the gentlest care into the swirling water, bubbling against all reason in a bowl that should not have held integrity for more than a child's playtime.

'Thing of boundless, hungry confidence, we give thee this child, these siblings, forever linked. The hope that grew with them, all potential, all things they may have been, lost now. Their future, unspent, we offer thee.'

Both men then pressed their hands to the bowl and squeezed on its lip, moulding it closed.

'Learn thee of sorrow,' said Cato. 'Learn thee of tears. Learn thee that not all hope is fulfilled. Learn thee that with life comes hurt.'

'Learn that because you hope, it don't mean you can have. Wanting don't mean getting. Getting don't mean keeping. Other things have hope in 'em too, you thing of endless need.'

'Learn thee compassion, learn thee kindness.'

'Learn mourning, learn grief.'

Together they closed the top of the bowl at last, leaving a muddy ball baked over the low fire.

Then Cato went to the river and buried his fingers in the mud and he crooned a summons in words alien to this land and this time. Cato sent his flesh magic into the ground and called to the hope-monster upriver.

And sure enough, the call was answered, and while Polly watched in horror, the river bank *stood up*.

The monster made of unchecked hope rose, a clump of dirt with arms and legs and a mouth wide open, trying to eat the air, soft jaw opening and closing like the maw of a slow-moving predator of the sea. It shambled towards Cato and Lucius, trying to act on the impulses that gave it form and life. All of that desperate, determined focus, every conflicting hope of all those thousands who *wanted* so hard it made them throw all else aside but that desire, that bright and dangerous hope that this time *me*, this time *rich*, this time *safe*, this time my troubles *vanquished, this time, this time*.

The horses screamed and galloped into the bush.

Cato scrambled backwards, his heels slipping in mud, as the thing came for him. Its huge paw swiped at him, catching his ankle, and Cato kicked to free himself while Lucius approached cautiously on its blind side, the horrible gift in his hands.

But a thing without eyes has no blind side, and another paw, solid as the mountain that its mud had once been, crashed into Lucius's chest and knocked him over. He clutched the mud ball instinctively to himself, to protect their hard work, but that gave the creature time to abandon Cato and open its jaws above Lucius's head.

Cato staggered up and hit the thing with a stone. It absorbed the stone and spat it hard out again, dashing it onto Cato's forehead and drawing blood. Cato shook his head and threw fists instead, to make it leave off from Lucius. The creature pushed him aside and grasped again at Lucius, who was shoving at the ground with his feet, scooting backwards, the mud ball cradled against his middle.

Polly, her terror as large as her rage now, was yet calm. She perched by one foot on the rump of a cantering horse, the other extended in balletic grace, for a living. She leapt on and off and between great beasts every day, and fended off the men who thought such strength and courage made her unwomanly, and therefore in need of a lesson they would teach her. Polly Clewes was never bowed by something so common as mere *fear*.

She seized upon a broken, dried branch, leaves and twigs and all still attached, and darted towards the monster. She stabbed it with her unwieldy weapon and yelled at it:

'Leave off him, you bastard! You're the reason they broke my heart, and I'm damned if I won't let 'em give it to you like they planned.'

The thing lumbered towards her, maw agape, and she stabbed at him again with her useless branch.

'Nettie and me were going to go off together,' she shouted at it, her face red, hair wild, tears of grief or despair striping her grimy cheeks. 'We were going to start our own act, our own travelling show for a while, maybe. We were going to save for a little place to live, our own patch, and we'd have a garden and a cow and horses, and I'd teach riding and she'd teach dancing and singing, and maybe it was silly. Maybe it was never, ever going to happen, but we wanted to be happy and be together and it's all ashes now, and you're going to swallow all of it.'

Lucius had clambered to his feet while the thing bore down on Polly, and Cato was beside him, helping him up. Then both men were behind the creature, with that gift of grief in their hands, bracing to *push*.

Polly kept yelling and stabbing, backing away until there was nowhere left to go. 'You're getting a baby learning that the world can hurt, even though you've done nothing wrong; and there's a babe that was maybe one baby trying to become two, or twins trying to be together as one, but that was still two hopes, even so little, and who knew what they might have been? There's a boy's shame in there, like he wanted to be a noble lover or something, and he was just a stupid boy, and my Nettie doing something wrong and shameful too. You get it all.'

Its grip settled on her wrist and it began to swallow her up, and behind, Cato and Lucius pushed, shoving the mud ball into the mud man, through its back and into its stomach, until the ball sat in its belly like a womb.

Polly, too frightened and spent to scream, looked at her arm buried in the clay arm of the creature – and watched as the clinging mud of the thing drew back from her skin, like a sucking swamp reversing its grip.

The creature sat down heavily on the bank of the river, its gross arms folded across its belly, swollen with the baked ball, and opened its maw and keened – soft, high, grieving in its new knowledge of sorrow. The thing learned from its gift, not only of the rage and despair of disappointed hope, but the sorrow and human sadness of it. Its greedy, blind heart – innocent in its way, for being so ill-informed – broke and fell to pieces. All of it fell to pieces, melting back into the ground, dissipating to nothing but a swathe of sticky, putrid mud beside the river.

The three of them stood around the slime. Lucius pushed at it with the toe of his shoe.

Cato kneeled and rested his hand on top of it. 'Tis gone, dust to dust, as the priests say. The land will remember our gift to it, and not allow the foolishness of humanity to rebirth this thing. What humans will do to one another will be a sufficient monster for the future. Now,' he rose and peered into the landscape, 'we should recover our horses.'

He left Polly and Lucius to such a recovery while he washed his hands. When they returned, their horses jittery but unharmed, Cato grinned at them.

'The water is not clear, yet tis not infected with abomination as before. Let them drink and we shall rest awhile before moving on. And see, Polly, the land has given a gift in return for relieving it of its madness.'

He held out his palm. In it lay a gleaming lump of gold, as big as an apple.

Polly flinched from the treasure. 'Congratulations. I wish you well of it.'

She led the horses past Cato and to the water, where she let them drink as she unsaddled them one by one and ran her hands over flanks, legs and hooves, testing for cuts and swelling and heat that would foretell a strain. After, she retrieved a soft brush from her saddlebag and brushed each mount down in a ritual she found as soothing as did the beasts.

Cato and Lucius spoke quietly together, leaving Polly to her industrious solitude. Lucius built a fire, a little way downstream, and Cato hunted for birds eggs. He bagged a possum as well. By the time Polly was ready to face them again, food had been cooked. Cato chattered of this and that to his companions, who hadn't much to say.

Then they doused the fire, re-saddled the horses and rode back to the path teeming with hopeful prospectors. Polly sneered at them, at what their unthinking need had cost her.

'We'll see you back to Melbourne,' Lucius offered.

'Don't bother,' said Polly.

They rode with her anyway, although she refused to speak to them. Eventually, they joined up with two carriages on their way back to the city. Polly, taken still for a boy, was invited to ride with them, on the theory that there was strength in numbers. Cato and Lucius stopped the night with them, but had decided to travel on to Adelaide. Melbourne, they thought, might not wish them well after their efforts of the previous week, especially if Polly was anyone to go by.

Before they parted in the morning, however, Lucius went to Polly.

'I know you got no time for us, Polly, and I ain't blaming you, but let me say my piece and I'll leave.'

Polly folded her arms and glared and waited.

'Go back to your Nettie,' Lucius told her. 'She did the wrong thing, but she thought it was for a good reason.'

Polly's lips pressed together in a hard line and it was likely in a moment she would spit.

But Lucius knew more of the story than he'd already told. 'She was getting desperate to get out of there. Her brother who works taking the money for the sideshows, he was setting to marry her off 'cause he didn't like how friendly the two of you were. She was just trying to make the money so you could run off together. Stupid of her, I know, but maybe what the two of you have is worth saving.'

Then he held out his hand, shielding the gesture from the other travellers so they couldn't see. In his palm was the nugget.

'You should take this. Whether you use it for both of you, or just yourself, it don't matter. But you paid for what we had to do, and you kept it listening so we could finish the job, and Cato and me agree – this belongs to you.'

Polly stared at the nugget and didn't take it. 'I thought you gave all my heart and hope to the monster.'

'Nah,' said Lucius, 'Only the old ones. Hope and hearts grow back. Forgiveness is something humans do and that monsters never learn.'

'Do you think my heart can grow back?'

'Thing about people is, we're like a tree. Parts can break off, bits of us can die, but they can grow back. Hope and love can always grow back, if we're willing to let it. That's the fundamental nature of hope, isn't it? Trying again?'

'It won't be the same.'

'New growth ain't ever exactly the same,' Lucius said, 'but it's usually stronger.'

Polly huffed a sudden laugh at that, and with it sprang tears. She took the lump of gold from his hand and closed her fist over it. 'I still love her,' she said, by way of explanation.

'Then go back, try to forgive and see if you can't hope up a new dream together.'

When the carriages left, Polly went with them, the nugget tucked safely in her corset, an uncomfortable yet comforting lump trapped against her skin.

Cato led his horse to where Lucius waited, and mounted.

'I wove a little perception magic into the carriages and her saddlery,' Cato said. 'They won't be bothered by bushrangers.'

'Thanks, Cato.'

Cato shrugged and then smiled crookedly. 'I like her. She has a mighty soul.'

'Don't you worry none,' Lucius told him. 'One day I'll meet a woman strong as my mother and we'll have a dozen sons and daughters, and you'll sleep curled up in their cribs with 'em, like you did me, and like you'll do one day with my great, great grandchildren. There'll always be Morans to look after you, and you, them. We won't ever let you be lonely, Cato.'

Cato, not knowing what to say, said nothing. But from under his pea jacket a slender, scaly tail curled out and brushed across the back of Lucius's hand.

Then they set off toward Ballarat, to branch off for the way to Adelaide. For who knew what the world was getting up to, that needed Moran and Cato to do the ugly things that needed to be done, in order to keep the balance?

Tipuna Tapu

'Storm's coming in,' Maddy said, ramming down the gas pedal in a burst of rancid bioethanol smoke.

'I see it.' Ihaka didn't need to be told. He tugged his goggles down and grabbed the nailgun trigger grips, checking that the air pressure was solid and the ammunition belt was running free. It didn't pay to get caught out in a storm without plenty of firepower. He braced his feet in the metal stirrups at the back of the jeep, swivelling the gun on its gimbal. Quickly, he touched fingers to the pounamu at his throat in silent benediction to unseen ancestors, then gripped the twin triggers again and scanned the sky. A glimpse of a shape, all wing and spiral, twisted through the boiling clouds. 'How far to the caves, *e hoa*?'

'Too far!' Madeline shouted back, her hair whipping about her face as she slammed through another gear, jerking the steering wheel to avoid a skein of fallen fence-posts.

'Thanks,' Ihaka yelled back. 'That's really helpful.'

'Not exactly Highway 66 out here,' she snapped in her thick English accent, wrestling the wheel as the front tyre slid in a slurry of mud. The jeep slewed, gripped, hurtled forward. The engine snarled as she revved it hard, a plume of smoke spilling from the tailpipe. Ihaka tried to hold the gun steady, sighting down the barrel for something –anything – he could draw a bead on. The storm writhed closer, rushing across the darkening sky with all hell's fury. But the way the jeep was jinking and jiving across the tumble-down paddocks strewn with rusted farming equipment and collapsed fencing, he could barely keep a bead on the horizon, much less anything darting through the clouds above.

Lightning flared, followed by rolling cracks of thunder. Something swooped across the clouds, banking and descending. Ihaka swung the nailgun, lining it up, judging speeds, distances, range. Black wings, folded into razor sickles, carved a line across the grey before the creature twisted off and vanished back inside the cloudbank. White light burst sudden, brilliant, as it swept away. The heavens shook.

'Tell me it's not right on top of us already!' Madeline yelled.

'OK,' Ihaka shouted, rain streaking his goggles. 'It's not on top of us already.'

'Don't lie to me, Ihaka!'

'Wouldn't dare.'

Maddy threw the jeep into a hard right, then a left, and Ihaka glimpsed the skeleton of a tractor whip by them, almost obscured by the tall grass. 'You just keep your eyes on the road. Leave the *taniwha* to me.'

'Road?' Madeline yelled. 'What road?'

Movement then, a shadow against the black, a glimmer of fire within, spiralling towards them, twin scythes sweeping toward the kill. Ihaka wove the cannon, matching the beast's descent, counting off the distance between them as it closed. He could make out the open jaws, the spark within, the bright glints of its onyx eyes. A lesser man would've emptied the ammo belt at the mere sight of it, but Ihaka had lived through such nightmares more than once, and he had done so through a combination of a steady hand, iron nerves, and a skilled and cocky driver at his back. He let the monster close in. Most folk wouldn't believe it if you said you have to wait until you see the white of their eyes before you shoot. Most had never been that close, close enough to see the white pinpricks at the centre of those pools of black.

Ihaka had. Lonely stars in an empty night sky, those eyes. His fingers settled on the triggers. 'Steady if you can,' he said, his voice firm but suddenly calm. '*Taniwha* incoming. One click.'

'Six hundred metres to the caves, the last 200 uphill,' Maddy replied, her own demeanour also level as they both found their calm at the eye of the storm, with danger drawing close much too fast and safety still too far away.

'Steady,' Ihaka crooned as wings and claws swelled in the gun's sights. Cold rain slapped his face, hard and sharp as needles, but he didn't waver. Didn't lose the target. 'Steady.'

The jeep jerked sideways. Ihaka swore as he instinctively gripped the triggers. A handful of shots spat wide in a burst of hard air.

'Sorry, ditch,' Madeline grunted, hauling the jeep back into line.

Ihaka grated his teeth and glanced sideways, the overgrown furrow in the ground almost invisible in the rain. He brought the gun to bear again, hunting, hunting.

The nightmare sliced through the rain: mouth, teeth, wings, eyes. White spots, tiny and hot as distant stars. He squeezed the triggers in two short bursts. With a thumping hiss of compressed air, a dozen nails sped from the cannon barrels, shrieking through the rain and rising wind. Cold iron peppered the descending beast and it screeched, arcing away, and for a moment there was nothing but cloud.

Then the lightning struck.

A tree barely 50 metres to their right burst into incandescence, sparks erupting from its boughs as a thread of jagged energy hooked it to the raging clouds.

The jeep bounced and tilted as they hit the slope. 'So it's close then?' Maddy quipped as she dropped a gear. The wheels slicked sideways.

Ihaka scanned the sky, wiping rain from his goggles. 'Close enough.'

The jeep jounced over rocks, and Madeline turned hard, gunning the engine again as the cave entrance appeared.

Wings broke the clouds, and the *taniwha* dropped towards them. Ihaka held it in the sights, stomach churning. It rushed closer, mouth opening, its gullet a glow of white fire against the black of the storm.

Closer, closer...

The beast roared, rain exploding off its wings in great ghostly plumes as it thundered towards the jeep. Ihaka fired, two hard bursts of air-powered steel, right into the beast's approaching maw. Lightning blazed as the beast howled, and the jeep became airborne. The engine shrieked in protest as the wheels spun free, then they crashed down, bounced, and were swallowed by darkness.

Ihaka breathed a heavy sigh as the storm and her winged kin was obscured by solid rock and earth. Maddy braked hard, the jeep skittering and grinding over rock and moss as it slid to a halt. Ihaka kept the nailgun trained on the cave entrance, and focussed on his breathing.

Maddy killed the engine. 'Guess it can't come in then,' she grinned, like she hadn't been on the run from a creature of myth and nightmare intent on shredding them limb from limb and devouring their mortal souls. 'That's good. Means it must be *tapu* in here, right?'

Winding up the clunky dynamo-lantern fixed to her helmet, she powered down the jeep's headlamps. 'Come on,' she said, opening the long metal toolbox behind the driver's seat, a battered rifle chest Ihaka had brought back from the ruins of Europe. She shouldered a leather backpack, and strapped on a utility belt tucked snug with an assortment of tools. 'Leave your dragon in peace.'

'*Taniwha*,' Ihaka said, still watching the fractured triangle of grey light beyond the cave mouth.

'Dragon, taniwha, whatever. We've got bones to find.'

'They're not dragons,' Ihaka protested, but he eased off the triggers and let the nailgun droop on its gimbal. 'They're older than dragons. Nastier.' Which was somewhat true, and somewhat not. Plenty of *taniwha* were placid, or guardians, or otherwise not a danger. It was the ones that scoured sea or sky looking to feed their hungers on human suffering that worried Ihaka most.

'Dunno.' Madeline shrugged, pulling a hank of climbing rope from the toolbox. 'Met some pretty old, nasty dragons in my time.'

Ihaka sighed. After the Awakening, as some folk so delicately termed that terrible day in 1945, Madeline Sweet had made a name for herself hunting down monsters from Istanbul to Tokyo. She'd collected what she'd learned into a chapbook, a primer if you like, which she'd had printed in Shanghai and made a fortune selling from the back of a truck. She knew a lot about monsters, it was true. But there was a hell of a lot she didn't know. A hell of a lot she chose *not* to learn. Not because knowledge was dangerous, no; quite the opposite: knowledge was wealth. Rather, there were things she chose not to learn because when you walk with monsters, knowledge is fear, and fear is paralysis. A hunter cannot fear. Instead, she let Ihaka carry all that dangerous knowledge. Let him carry the fear.

They'd met in Auckland, near the docks, not long after the troop ship had deposited him in the city along with thousands of other veterans, returned to a world as changed by the war as by what came after. With her skills and his local knowledge, it had made sense for them to move into the business of unearthing sacred relics, which seemed to be the only thing that kept the *taniwha* at bay. Even New Zealand had not been spared the scourge of the Awakening, its landscape rife with spirits and monsters of legend now brought to life. So they hunted the *tapu* places up and down the length of *Aotearoa* searching for lost bones, the more obscure the better, apparently. And there was nowhere with more obscure relics than New Zealand.

Thunder boomed beyond the cave, distant. The *taniwha* was moving off. Ihaka unhooked his feet from the cannon stirrups and climbed from the jeep. 'Come on then,' he muttered, grabbing his own backpack and another rope. He jammed on the dented helmet he only wore on a dig, or when he thought he might get shot at. It still smelled like sweat and mud and cordite. He switched on the headlamp. Rough flickering electric light ghosted over the cavern walls as the pair descended into a narrow cleft and regarded a sheer bluff rising up one side. There was no sign of light from above, but shadowy patches suggested a cave entrance. Water spilled down the outer cave wall, but not the inner.

'Doesn't look like much here,' Maddy noted, scanning the cliff face for a good point to start climbing.

'Never does,' Ihaka grunted. But they both knew that. In this part of the world there were no convenient temple ruins or ancient maps scribed in human blood to lead them to lost relics. No catacombs shrouded in jungle growth and peppered with complex engineered traps like he'd seen as a *tama* at the cinema house with its big silver screen. Only secret, sacred places where the most precious artefacts lay hidden under centuries of dirt and leaf litter and dust. Ihaka gripped the wall, and began his ascent.

'Whose land is this again, anyway?' Maddy asked, pulling a belaying pin from her belt and looping a hammer over her wrist before following him, taking her time, checking each foothold, each handhold.

Ihaka gained a shelf on the cave wall, cast his light about, and asked himself where, if he was a Māori warrior of a thousand years ago, would he have carried a *kete* full of a dead man's bones?

'Ngai Tekawhiti,' he reminded her. Bitter words. But Maddy needn't know that. She made a conscious effort not to let tribal squabbles colour her business decisions. She found it easier to go into a dig without the background noise of ancient feuds cluttering up her perceptions. For Ihaka, forewarned was forearmed. What Maddy called *tribal squabbles* were, to Ihaka, the shape and weave of his heritage.

'Sounds familiar,' she said. Ihaka shook his head. She may have crossed a continent battling the mythological beasts unleashed in the Awakening, but in many ways she was still a tourist. She got results, for sure, but she often reminded Ihaka of a sledgehammer knocking in a thumbtack when he watched her work.

'This place hasn't changed in hundreds of years,' he said, holding on with one hand and unshouldering his pack, testing its weight. It felt about right as a substitute for mortal remains. Replacing the pack on his back, he gripped another outcrop and continued climbing. He had the advantage of longer arms and legs, stronger hands, and he made the most of it, leaving Maddy behind.

'You know, it's still a 50-50 split even if you do all the work.'

'Shit Maddy, that's not like you, only thinking about the money.' He stretched across the gap, found a handhold, swung over.

'Money?' she retorted, as if the comment could actually offend her British sense of decency. 'I'm not here for the money. We're helping save lives, protect people.'

'Of course we are,' he said dryly, feeling the stone under his fingers, solid, dependable. Unlike people. More to the point, it felt like it wasn't prone to rubbing away, or suddenly cracking and collapsing. The lack of rockfall in the cavern was testament to this. The cave was probably very much as it had been a thousand years ago when the bones they sought were laid to rest.

He felt his way along, holdfast to toe grip. Was this the same path by which the ancestor of some ancient rival of his own *iwi* had come, long ago, looking for a sanctuary?

'Why don't we just belay to the top and rappel down, moving side to side?' Maddy called, her voice tight with impatience. 'Be faster than free-climbing.'

'This land was bush for thousands of years, and farmland for less than a hundred,' Ihaka argued, even though she was right. 'The ones who came before us didn't have ropes and climbing gear. There's only one path, that's why the bones are here.'

There was something about bringing the bones to light by locating the original path that had been taken to lay the remains to rest that sat well with Ihaka, even if the bones were Ngai Tekawhiti. If any *iwi* deserved, in his eye, an ignominious tearing from the darkness of legend to the cruel craven light of the 20th century, with its wars and its holocausts and its genocides and its swarms of monsters, it was Ngai Tekawhiti. But respect for the bones was, ironically, tantamount to centuries-old tribal feuds.

'You're so old-school,' she accused him.

'Have I let you down before?'

'Not really.'

Ihaka sputtered, nearly lost his grip. '*Not really?* The hell's that supposed to mean?'

'Well,' Maddy said, 'there was that little slip-up in the Bay of Islands with the sea serpent.'

'Little slip? I harpooned that *taniwha* and it dragged us for three nautical miles before the line snapped.'

'Yeah, but it got away, so we didn't get paid.'

'Whose fault was that, *e hoa*?' Ihaka spat, grappling with a slick ledge and dragging himself towards the darker opening.

'Well, yours, of course. You were meant to hold it.'

'You had *three miles* to cut off one scale. *One scale.*'

'It was moving.'

'It was 400 feet long and all muscle, in the sea, *where it lives*. With a goddamn harpoon in its back. You'd be moving too.' His foot found purchase, and he hauled himself towards the shaft opening.

'Don't try to lay it on me. You had one job.'

'So did you. No idea why you're moaning anyway,' Ihaka jibed her. 'You got your 50 percent.'

'Huh? 50 percent of *nothing*.'

'Exactly.'

Ihaka pointed the weak beam of his torch into the low space before him. Shadows leaped and danced, shapes of black against black. He looked around the cliff face again, but could see nowhere else to go. If he was that long-dead warrior, this is where he would've chosen. Unhitching his backpack and tossing it in before him, he hefted his bulk into the cavern.

'Hey,' Maddy's voice echoed up to him. 'Where'd you go?'

Ihaka grinned. It wasn't professional, but he'd enjoy letting her sweat for a bit. Reaching around his neck, he pulled the sliver of pounamu and hung it from his finger. If Maddy didn't want to learn all his secrets, then there were things she didn't need to know.

Taking a long deep breath, he tried to clear his mind of all thought. Tried to forget the guilt of pillaging sacred *urupa.* Tried to forget the sheer trembling terror of facing down mythical beasts as they rose from the sea and earth and sky to burn the world.

Tried to forget the way Maddy's face looked when she laughed in the light of a campfire, and how she didn't ever look back at him the way he sometimes secretly looked at her. Because they were too far apart, too different, too impossible to contemplate. Fair-skinned, blonde-haired Madeline Sweet, and a rough Maori lad from the back-blocks like Ihaka Kahu. Never going to happen. The world could disgorge an endless swarm of nightmare, but a good English girl would never make eyes at his kind. They could work together, but nothing more.

All *that* he tried to forget.

One image arose. Old bones.

He lay silent and soaked up the taste of cold earth, the solid patience of stone. Long moments drew out, then the pounamu twitched – once.

Ihaka slung it back over his head and crawled in the direction it had tugged.

'Ihaka?' Maddy called, closer now.

There in the corner sat a tumbled pile of stones, and a darker space behind them. He wormed forward, came up to his knees.

'Found them,' Ihaka yelled, fear and excitement in his voice. The bones sat stacked on an elevated rock, dark with stain and leach, the skull in the centre of the pile and the rest of the skeleton layered carefully to fit the now long-rotted flaxen *kete* that had been their final resting place until now. A layer of grime and dust covered the bones, but apart from that, they appeared untouched for hundreds of years.

It didn't take Maddy long to find him, and together they set to the task of cleaning the bones and laying them out on a clean canvas roll. The drum of distant rain faded into the background as they focused on the meticulous detail of the work. Carefully they folded the canvas over the bones, trussed it tight, and looped leather lashes around the whole affair. After easing the package out of the narrow cave and lowering it to the wet rocky floor below, Ihaka and Madeline scrambled down the cliff face with the speed and grace of monkeys at play.

'Good tip-off, then,' Maddy said, as Ihaka hefted the canvas roll-bag and started back up the incline towards the jeep. Water sloshed and gurgled around their boots.

'Only the best,' Ihaka said, not wanting to be drawn on the topic. It might've been Maddy's money and business sense that allowed them to carry on in this trade, but it was his local knowledge that kept them solvent. Ihaka knew the land, the people, who to talk to, how to sift truth from legend, and to recognise legitimate leads from outright deception. Books were next to useless in that regard. The information came from people, and people alone. Moving the merchandise? *That* was Maddy's specialty.

When they reached the jeep, Maddy crouched in the rainwater sluicing through the cave entrance and opened the side-locker, arranging the sackcloths to lay the canvas in.

Ihaka paused, sniffed the air. 'Smell that?' he asked.

'What?' Maddy gave him an arch look. 'Did you wet yourself? Big boy like you–'

But Maddy didn't get to finish her quip as Ihaka launched himself forward, lobbing the precious cargo into the front seat of the jeep and wrapping an arm under Maddy's armpit before leaping from the ground. How he found the strength to jump, plant his feet on the tyre of the jeep and grip the roll cage with his free hand, while lifting Maddy's weight, he'd never know. But even as he teetered, the lightning flash exploded by the cave entrance, the detonation of thunder shaking the cavern. The water running through the cave sparked and cracked with the massive discharge, and then the hot reek of ozone and crisp, burned air wafted over them.

Gradually, Ihaka realised Maddy was looking at him. Their bodies were locked together, her back pressed hard against the roll cage, her chest crushed against his. They were close enough to breathe each other's air. Close enough to kiss.

'Ah, so your dragon's still out there,' Maddy whispered, her voice hoarse.

Ihaka held the awkward embrace for a fraction longer than was comfortable, before easing himself over the back of the jeep into the gunner's seat.

After a breathless moment, Maddy recovered the canvas bag and stowed it in the side-locker, snapping the padlocks closed, then slid into the driver's seat. Before she started the engine, she turned back to Ihaka. 'What did you smell? Before the lightning?'

Ihaka looked over his shoulder at her. 'Taniwha piss.' He resisted the urge to say all the sour things he wanted to say, like, *'You're welcome.'* He pulled his goggles down.

Maddy turned the key, dropped into reverse and let out the clutch, and the jeep skidded backwards towards the cave mouth and the storm beyond.

Ihaka swivelled, searching for the taniwha. As the jeep burst out into milky daylight, Maddy spun the wheel and cranked the handbrake, spinning the vehicle around in a full sweeping arc before slamming it into gear and accelerating down the hillside in a spray of mud. Ihaka lined up the nailgun, sighting dead centre on the taniwha perched on the hillside directly above the cave mouth. It had to be 20 metres, both nose to tail and wingtip to wingtip, if he was any judge. Not huge, but big enough. His fingers teased the triggers, waiting for the thing to lunge.

It didn't, and as they streaked away, it diminished, its dark eyes smouldering after them. 'Ihaka?' Maddy yelled in a singsong voice that belied the gravity of the moment, 'What's it doing?'

'Watching us.'

'Why's it watching us?'

Ihaka chewed his lip. 'I don't know.'

'But that's good, right? That it doesn't want to kill us, or it's given up trying to kill us, or something.'

'Well, we just desecrated a sacred burial site, making it no longer *tapu,* even though we now have the *taonga*. So it tried to stop us leaving, but now we've got the bones with us...'

'So maybe the jeep is *tapu*? So it can't attack us? That'd be shit hot.'

'Maybe.' Ihaka doubted it. It hadn't happened like that in the past. He'd never seen a *taniwha* let grave robbers like them drive off with the *taonga*; they always put up a fight.

'Maybe it's his first day,' Maddy called. 'Hasn't learned the rules yet.'

'Or it tried to stop us taking them, and failed, but now we've got them...'

'They're ours for the keeping?' Maddy offered helpfully.

'Not what I was going to say. More like, they're *our* problem now.'

'Ooh, dramatic,' Maddy mocked. 'Just be glad we're not walking home.'

'I'm glad we can still walk at all.'

Harrison's Bay, or Kokoruroa as local Mâori called it, had always been a special place. In years long past, a great battle had been fought on this very ground between warriors of Ngai Tekawhiti and Ngati Horua, for the love of Hokaka, the beautiful daughter of the Tekawhiti chieftain. Many men had wet the earth with their blood that day, rendering the site *tapu*. With time, this memory had receded, and the *pâkehâ* had come, and streets were built, pipes laid and power-lines erected, houses and shops sprang up, new memories layered over the old.

But when the Awakening had changed the world, old memories became valuable once more, and tales of the love two men had for one woman, and the lives they were willing to sacrifice to keep her, suddenly bore new significance, the stories finding new listeners.

And a town like Kokoruroa, built on all the blood and tears of that fateful day, became a haven, because the *taniwha* could not pass over land that was *tapu*.

Maddy drove slowly through the crowded streets, eyes alert for trouble. In the back, Ihaka sat at ease, scanning the press of humanity forced to make their lives within these few hundred square meters of *tapu* land. Every building now sported tumorous growths as hovels appeared on rooftops, in alleys, along decks and balconies; anywhere there was space to make a home, however meagre.

People watched them, suspicious, envious, murderous. Ihaka had long since stowed the firepower and locked the *taonga* in the side-locker, and now they tried to maintain their facade of itinerant workers, simply moving from place to place, labouring and doing odd jobs for a meal or a coin. But there were always some who could tell, those who knew them from a distance. Other relic hunters. Ihaka looked for faces he recognised, but the only familiar thing staring back at him was the cold, the hunger, the desperation. Inside his coat, his fingers gripped his pounamu *mere*, a traditional Mâori fighting club of polished greenstone. If anyone should make a move against them, whether to steal their jeep, or their hidden *taonga*, or even the pretty girl in the driver's seat, he'd be ready.

Far off, a storm rumbled. Flickering lightning scored the horizon, and a dark shape moved within its depths. Even though the *taniwha* couldn't touch this *tapu* earth, there was still plenty for Ihaka to worry about. Not the least of which was why the *taniwha* on the hill hadn't pursued them. He'd wracked his brain as they'd crossed the muddy kilometres from there to here, but still had no answer. *Taniwha* didn't just let *taonga* go free. It was against their nature.

One possible answer was this: the bones weren't blessed, and if they weren't, that must mean they were cursed. Not buried with honour, but in disgrace. That could be bad news for whoever possessed them.

He scanned the crowd again, but there were no pale, hollow faces; no *kehua* to be seen. The ghosts of the shamed dead sometimes came forth to claim such cursed relics, and they had no care for sacred earth. The sooner Maddy could move these bones, the better.

'Crap,' he said aloud, as a few unsettling shards of information crystallised in his mind, painting a very disturbing scenario. 'Crap,' he said again.

'What?' Maddy asked.

'Nothing.'

'It's never nothing.'

Great, trust my instincts now. 'I thought I saw Tiaka's truck down there, that's all. This is his home territory, remember.'

'Well?'

'Well what?'

'Did you?'

'Did I what?'

'Did you see it? Tiaka's truck?' If she could've reached him, she probably would've punched him.

'Dunno,' he shrugged. 'All those Bedfords look the same.'

'We'll keep on our toes then.'

'Park somewhere up here. That's the Regent over there.'

The shuffling masses, moving between stalls of produce and chickens and knitted goods, grudgingly parted to allow Maddy to pull over and squeeze the jeep in among the mud-crusted assortment of trucks and utes parked along the street, mostly farm vehicles or ex-military hardware that had been modified to run on crude home-brewed biodiesel or bioethanol. The sight of so many vehicles, all drab-coloured and caked in mud and dirt, reminded him of operations in the Med, first in Crete and then Italy, as the Mâori Battalion had done their bit to drive back the fascists. War had been so much simpler than this. In war, you always knew where you stood, who your enemy was. Not anymore.

As he clambered out of the jeep and double-checked the padlocks on the side-locker, Maddy cranked on the handbrake. His key hung on a string against his chest, beside his pounamu. No deal got done without both of them buying into it. Maddy kept her key just as close, nestled between her–

Ihaka bit his tongue to push the thought away. No time for distractions.

'Right, let's go find this Mercer chap, shall we?' Maddy said, dropping from the jeep into the muddy street. 'See if he's good for it.'

'Better be,' Ihaka grumbled.

Together, they pushed into the pub. The noise and the stink swelled around them: sweat, dung, mud, piss and stale home-brew. It was a long time since there'd been any beer come out of a real brewery, so every huddled enclave brewed their own. Some places had the knack of it. Others, like Kokoruroa, didn't. The stench of sour yeast sat above it all like scum on a lagoon. Ihaka looked over the hunched sea of dour, sullen faces. Pubs used to be places of both sorrow and joy. Now they were just pits of despair. Men and women of all colours crowded bar stools and leaners, glowering together and muttering in low voices, occasionally glared across the room at some disturbance or other. Ihaka could feel it. Kokoruroa was a town on a knife-edge, ready to tip at the slightest provocation. All they needed was an excuse; a target. Even more reason to make the sale and move on in a hurry. He'd seen towns like this fall over that precipice, into riot and madness, when there was nothing left to rage against except each other.

Mercer was sitting in a corner booth, a gaunt balding *pâkehâ* with two lanky helpers to either side; bodyguards by any other lexicon. He was obvious, not because he was any fatter or better-dressed than the rest of the human flotsam in the Regent—he'd thought far enough ahead to at least dress to blend in—but by the way he held himself, the set of his shoulders, the way his eyes darted about with a blatant lack of subtlety. He appeared positively eager, expectant. The locals of Kokoruroa didn't have that hopeful look about them, like the next stranger walking into town might be bringing good news. They'd probably just shoot the messenger and eat him anyway.

Maddy made a circuitous line for the booth, checking out the dark corners of the pub for any more of Mercer's helpers. It wouldn't be the first time a relic hunter had walked into an ambush. That was another good reason for operating as a duo, so someone always had your back.

Finally, they rounded on the booth and Maddy slipped in at the edge of the seat, while Ihaka turned to watch the room, the crowd, one eye on the bodyguards and Mercer, *mere* gripped loosely inside his jacket. In a hushed whisper which was not so low that Ihaka couldn't identify his thick British accent, the buyer ran through all the usual questions which could be summed up as: Would the bones really make his property safe from *taniwha* attack?

Was he a veteran as well, moved over here after the war to escape the wyverns and ogres that ran rampant across the British countryside? Only to arrive and find the skies and hillsides and forests swarming with *taniwha*.

Maddy fed him all the replies he wanted to hear, carefully driving up the price and cementing the deal while omitting the fact that while the bones would, indeed, keep *taniwha* at bay, the same could not be said of other, more ruthless hunters. To those people, his illusion of safety would make him *more* of a target, not less. But that would be Mercer's problem, not hers.

Yet even though the deal was going as well as could be hoped, Ihaka's skin crawled. Something wasn't right. Was it possible Mercer seemed *too much* of a fool? For some obscure reason, he wanted to break and run back to the jeep, but he couldn't leave Maddy there, unprotected. Still, he itched to get outside. Something was happening. Something bad.

Then there was movement in the booth. Maddy had struck her deal. She was pocketing a wedge of bills – the security – and they were heading out to inspect the merchandise. Ihaka took point, moving through the bar, eyes everywhere. This was the critical moment, when people got scared or greedy or just downright bloody. When it came time for money to change hands, some people—stupid people, mainly—thought that maybe they wanted the goods but didn't want to part with their hard-earned cash. Ihaka thought he'd seen every trick, every deception, every bungled attempt to scarper with the relics without paying for them. But when he stepped out of the Regent onto the street, he realised he hadn't seen it all, until now. There was their jeep, swinging through the air on the end of a sling connected to a hydraulic hoist, operated off the back of a flatdeck Bedford truck.

Ihaka shot forward, a shout on his lips. 'Oi!'

The man operating the hoist controls looked up in surprise, but the driver showed no such hesitation. With a roar, the Bedford cranked forward, crashing gears as it swung into the street, people scattering out of its path, the jeep swinging wildly.

Bringing out his *mere*, Ihaka leaped at the hoist operator, an unshaven half-caste with arms like tree trunks. Ihaka struck, but his opponent was faster. Ducking and swinging hard, he collected Ihaka in the chest and pounded him to the ground. Ihaka's breath exploded in a rush and lights danced before his eyes. He rolled clear before the goon could follow through with a rib-cracking kick.

The sound of compressed air biting at metal, sinking into flesh, accompanied a sudden grunt of pain. As Ihaka staggered to his feet, the hoist operator dropped to his knees, blood blossoming around a trio of nails embedded in his chest and throat.

'Come on, I'm not paying you to have a bloody lie-down,' Maddy shouted as she ran past him, nailgun in hand. Ihaka sucked in a painful breath, stuffed his *mere* inside his jacket and ran after her. The truck was halfway down the street now, people scattering in its wake, the jeep rocking wildly on the canvas strops. Ignoring the pain in his chest and the colours swirling before his eyes, Ihaka sprinted. Legs pumping, he passed Maddy, hope surging as the truck braked, turned hard.

Headed for the edge of town, Ihaka thought. *The open road.* If they made it, Ihaka and Maddy were sunk. Not only would the merchandise be lost, but without the jeep, their days of hunting relics were over.

The truck slewed on the wet tarmac, its unsecured load nearly tipping it off balance, its right wheels coming dangerously close to leaving the road, but then the jeep swung back, returning the Bedford from the brink of overturning. *Dammit*. But taking the corner had slowed it enough.

Ihaka burst across the cracked concrete and leaped for the back of the truck. By some miracle, his fingers slid along the rear of the deck and found purchase. His boots scraped over the tarmac as the truck gained speed again, and his arms burned with the effort of clinging on. Ihaka grunted, dragged himself in, while the jeep swayed and spun over his head. He hoped like hell the strops were strong enough. The truck jerked suddenly in a hiss of air. Swerving, the Bedford slowed, and Ihaka was able to haul himself onto the flatdeck. To his right, he heard the sputter and flap of a disintegrating tyre. One glance back confirmed his suspicions: Maddy was at the corner, receding, nailgun raised. Damn, she was a fine shot.

Ihaka crawled commando-style across the pitching deck, a tonne of deadly metal twirling above his head. Through the back window, he could see the driver fighting the wheel, the punctured rear tyre – which wouldn't normally have been a major problem –causing him grief as the shifting weight of the jeep kept rolling the truck hard over the soft rubber. Not Tiaka, but definitely one of his boys. Ihaka gained the back of the cab, and hauled the passenger door open.

Maddy strode across the broken asphalt towards the truck where it lay on its side in the ditch. Steam poured from the grill, obscuring the cab as the wind took it and kicked it about. There was no sign of Ihaka. 'You better not've damaged my jeep,' she shouted. Despite the sweat staining her back from running after the Bedford, a chill ran through her, and she gripped the nailgun tighter. Ihaka was one damned tough grunt, but the truck had gone off the road hard. He'd be lucky to walk away from it.

'*Our* jeep,' came the reply from inside the cab, and Ihaka emerged, bloody and bruised, almost grinning. As close to grinning as the surly bastard ever came, anyway, except for those rare moments when he dropped his hundred-mile stare and let his mask slip.

Maddy dropped the heavy handgun and its canister of compressed air into the holster on her belt, and put her hands on her hips. 'I believe you'll find that the jeep is *my* investment and *my* property.'

'Maybe,' Ihaka said, hauling himself out of the cab through the window, sliding down the door and crossing to where the jeep lay, still half-way suspended by the hoist, two wheels resting on the ground in a furrow of dirt beside the truck. He jumped onto the side-locker, using this purchase to clamber up to the roll cage, and drew his bowie knife. He sawed through the strop, causing the jeep to drop onto its wheels with a creak of springs and metal. 'But this is stolen property, and I'm claiming salvage rights.'

Maddy opened her mouth, closed it again. Damn it all, but he had the right of it. 'You can't,' she said, her skin flushing. 'It's *my jeep*, Ihaka.'

'If not for me, it'd be Tiaka's jeep right now.'

'If I hadn't shot the tyre out, it'd be his anyway. So it was teamwork.'

'Tell you what,' he said, sheathing the knife, 'I'll go you halves. Equal shares. Because we're partners, right?'

And there it was, the grin. That slice of ivory in his brown skin, the shine in his eyes. One of those moments when he forgot, for a second, that he was *Tangata Whenua*, and she was a colonial, and that never the twain shall meet. One tiny splintered fragment of time when the world was not a hellhole ravaged by monsters, a pit of vipers, thieves and traitors. When they could just be two people, standing under the sky, looking at each other without watching each other's backs at the same time.

'What happened to Mercer?' Ihaka asked, hopping down off the jeep.

The moment was gone. Maddy slipped her own mask back into place. Distant, unattainable. Resolute. 'He's behind me,' she said, turning.

The road lay empty.

'I don't like this, Maddy,' Ihaka growled, working to unhitch the strop from around the jeep's chassis.

'What?' Maddy replied sharply, swallowing her own disquiet. 'That we outran a couple of townies?'

'Feels like a set-up.'

'Go on.' She turned slowly, watching the road, the bush-thick hills, the sky. Danger everywhere. And no one had a better sense for danger than Ihaka.

'This is Ngai Tekawhiti land, Tiaka is Ngai Tekawhiti, the bones are Ngai Tekawhiti. Kokoruroa, Ngai Tekawhiti.'

'I think I see the pattern, but tell me something new, Sarge.' She grinned sourly. He hated it when she called him that.

'I'm Ngati Horua.'

Whatever he expected her to infer from that statement, she didn't. These Māori names all sounded the same to her. She shrugged, drawing her nailgun, just in case. Her hindbrain was shrieking, but what it was trying to tell her, she wasn't sure.

He rolled his eyes. 'We try to hide who we are when we're hunting leads, but it's a small country. We can only pass incognito for so long before we get recognised.'

'And?' she said, walking backwards as rain spattered in fat wet sheets across the overgrown paddocks. Rain was bad. She had yet to decide if it was the rain that brought the dragons or the other way around, but it was never good being out in the open when they were on the hunt and the rains came.

'Do you ever listen to anything I say?' He finished carving through one strop, and started on the next.

She blew him a kiss, which he swiped away before it could hit him. He knew she listened. She just had an odd, British way of showing it. With sarcasm, usually. As the last strop fell, he checked the jeep over for damage. Maddy resumed her survey of the hillside and pondered where Mercer might've got to. He had been *just* behind her as she ran from Harrison's Bay.

'We need to know more about the bones. If they have anything to do with the battle that made this place *tapu*–'

'Ihaka, maybe this isn't the best time, or place.'

He looked up from his inspection of the steering column, following her eyeline into the storm-dark sky, where sudden bursts of crisp white light silhouetted a vast winged shape through the clouds. Thunder rolled, tainting the air with ozone. 'Right,' he said. 'Let's just see if the old girl still starts, eh?'

'Best idea you've had all day,' Maddy agreed. This was why Mercer hadn't left the safety of Harrison's Bay and its sacred earth. He'd seen the storm gathering on the horizon, or he was too damned scared to step outside what he thought was safe. Coward could choke on that plum in his mouth.

The jeep coughed, turned over, ground, coughed again. Ihaka pumped the gas pedal and turned the key and, in a cloud of sickly-sweet bioethanol smoke, it growled to life. Maddy swung into the driver's seat, handing off her hand-cannon to Ihaka as he slid out of her way. Ihaka snarled himself into the back as Maddy threw the jeep into gear and sped across the paddock in a flurry of sodden clods.

'Times like this,' Ihaka grumbled, bracing his elbows as best he could with the smaller gun in hand, 'I really wish gunpowder was a bit easier to come by.'

Maddy turned a wide arc through the mud, and headed towards town. Which was worse – the monsters within, or the monsters without? Tough choice. But in a pinch, she'd take humans over *taniwha* any day. Especially since no-one was paying her to kill *taniwha*. If that sort of silliness started, the relic business would go belly-up faster than she could make a pot of tea. Who'd need *tapu* relics for protection from monsters if someone started killing off all the monsters?

Given the choice, Ihaka would likely take the monsters over people. But he'd probably seen worse of people than she had ever seen of monsters. 'So, what makes you think this was a setup?'

'Bunch of reasons,' Ihaka said. 'Mainly, it was too easy.'

'The bones?'

'Finding out about the bones, but not knowing whose they are. Usually you find the name of the dead along with where they were placed. This was just too...convenient.'

'You reckon Tiaka got someone to drop you the information because you're his old ancestral enemy, part of that tribe, what's it called?'

'Ngati Horua.' A sigh.

'Yeah, that. You reckon they decided to lead you to a fake treasure, something like that?'

'Something like it. The bones are real, but they feel wrong. That *taniwha* let us go. I don't know why. But if Tiaka knew it would, and knew we'd come to Kokoruroa, then he'd have a chance to steal the bones from us without having to risk facing the *taniwha* himself, and into the bargain he could shred our business by stealing the jeep. But mainly, he wanted us to get the bones, because he couldn't.'

'Because of the *taniwha*?'

'No. That'd just be cowardice, and Tiaka's no coward. He's Ngai Tekawhiti, and so are the bones. If any of his *iwi* disturb them, they're *tapu*, but not good *tapu*, like the land. Bad *tapu*. Cursed.'

'Hang on.' Maddy was confused. '*Tapu* means blessed or sacred, but also cursed?'

'It's *tapu*, it is what it is. You can't translate it into meaning good or bad.

Don't go imposing your diametric Judaeo-Christian concepts on my culture, lady.'

'Wouldn't dream of it. Your language is confusing, that's all.'

'And yours isn't?'

Maddy shut up for a few heartbeats. English wasn't confusing, was it? Couldn't be. She'd spoken it all her life and never been confused by it. 'So, they wanted the bones, and stealing the jeep was just a bonus to stitch us up? So whose bones are they?'

Ihaka didn't answer. The hiss of the nailgun, a rushing wind, and the blast and crack of electrical discharge told her he was otherwise occupied. The *taniwha* snaked by them, claws gouging earth and sky to either side as Maddy twisted the wheel hard right, swinging out of its path. Over the roar of the engine, barking back and forth through gears, the whispering of the nailgun, the screech of the *taniwha* as it was lashed with cold iron, and the hammering of rain on the bonnet, Maddy let out a wild yell, something deep and primal and lustful, a defiance of the madness the world had become. Running with the dragons again. It was exhilarating to be alive.

The jeep slewed past the ruined remains of the old town and skidded into Kokoruroa's circle of *tapu* earth. Ihaka fired at the *taniwha* one last time as it wheeled away. Maddy slowed, weaving onto a lane between two leaning buildings which might've once been school classrooms, and which now had at least two extra stories tacked precariously onto their roofs. Rainwater cascaded off crooked downpipes. Ihaka tugged his weathered army jacket tighter about him. This was no time to relax. Too many desperate rogues in this town willing to kill you for your boots.

'So, what now?' he said. 'Find Mercer, shift the merchandise?'

'If you're right, and Mercer was part of the set-up, he'll lead Tiaka straight to us. If Tiaka wants the bones, he won't give up just because we left his truck in a ditch and two of his chaps dead.'

'So we cut our losses, dump the bones.'

'Woah! Hold up there, cowboy. I know you're no accountant, but we need that money'

'You got the security.'

'And no doubt Mercer's going to come looking for that too.'

'So we need to get out of town. Hightail it, find a new buyer, someone genuinely wanting the protection.'

That's what he told himself anyway, how he justified it. Yes, they raided the resting places of the dead, but they did it so people could be *safe*. Same reason he went to Europe and fought the Hun, so people could be *safe*. And then those damned Americans had dropped that bomb, and the world had gone all to hell. The Yanks had thought it would be a masterstroke to end the war, unleashing their atomic *coup de grâce* on Japan. But world war had been nothing compared to what they lived through now.

'Maybe we let Mercer find us.'

Ihaka slid over the back of the seat into the cab. 'Say again.'

'If Mercer's involved, he might be able to tell us what Tiaka's getting out of it.'

'You mean, besides stealing our merchandise and burying us? Taking out the competition?'

Maddy shrugged. 'Whatever Tiaka's paying him, we pay him more to lead us to Tiaka.'

'OK, now I'm really not following. I came back from one war, I'm sure as hell not starting another.'

'We can't just run away, not with people tracking us and trying to kill us. Instead of looking for new relics, we'll be looking over our shoulders all the time.'

Ihaka scanned the road. 'I've done my time hunting people,' he said coldly.

Maddy shot him a sharp glance. 'It's us or them, hun.' The silhouette of the Regent loomed against the sky. 'We need to look at these bones.'

It took a decent chunk of the cash she'd taken from Mercer, but Maddy didn't mind paying for the room for an hour, despite the lecherous looks she'd got from the barkeep when she'd enquired. 'Cup of tea?'

Ihaka grunted as he laid the canvas bag on the bed and began to unfurl it. Maddy stirred the coals in the pot belly and stoked a few dry sticks in the flames, dropping the black-bottomed kettle over the heat and looking for mugs. By the time she'd found the teapot, dug her precious supply of tea leaves out of her backpack, and had the brew steeping, Ihaka had arranged the skeleton on the bed in some semblance of its original form. He stood back from the bed, regarding it critically. Maddy studied the remains. She wasn't used to seeing them like this. Usually they gathered them up, a stack of dry old bones brittle as sticks, wrapped them in canvas and didn't look at them again. It came as something of a shock to see the bones laid out, almost in repose; reminding her that they had once formed a human being. Her throat choked a little.

'It's a woman,' Ihaka said reverently. 'Look at the hips.'

Maddy picked up the skull and jawbone, turning them over and studying the teeth. 'Young, too. Not worn out like an old person's.'

'Oh shit,' Ihaka staggered back, sinking into a threadbare armchair.

'What?' Maddy set the bones down and returned to the sideboard to pour the tea.

'I know what he's doing.'

'Tiaka?'

'We have to get back there.'

'Where? What's going on?' She fought to keep the tremble from her fingers as she set the teapot down and took him a steaming mug. She'd never seen him this rattled.

'We've got it all wrong.'

'As far as I knew, we were in the dark anyway, so being wrong is an improvement. Drink tea. Explain.'

'It's all been a distraction, Mercer, the truck, all of it. We should go now.'

Maddy fought the sudden urge to straddle his legs, hold him down, and push him against the chair with both hands. That could only turn out badly. 'I've just made tea. Do you know how hard it is to get tea around here? You're not going anywhere until it's drunk. So explain.'

Ihaka took a deep breath and a slug of his tea. 'This place, it's *tapu* because there was a vicious battle between Ngai Tekawhiti and Ngati Horua here, and many warriors died, right?'

'We know that, Sarge.'

Ihaka scoured her with a look, drank more tea. 'There was a Tekawhiti *rangatira*, Arohura. He led a raiding party across the lake, and while the *kâinga* was undefended, a warrior named Korangi led a *taua* of warriors into the village and abducted many Tekawhiti women, including Arohura's own daughter, Hokaka. Long story short, Arohura went after Korangi, raided his *pâ* and took his daughter back.

'But Hokaka was in love with Korangi, and had been for a long time. She ran away to Korangi's *pâ*. Korangi anticipated that Arohura would come for her, so he led his war party straight down here. That was the battle when so many died, including both Korangi and Hokaka, because she refused to wait behind in the *pâ* while Korangi went out to fight for her. Our women were warriors, too. Arohura was angry, viciously so. It is custom to return the bones of the fallen to their *hapû*.

'Hokaka's remains were buried in secret, and whether out of spite for Ngati Horua or because Arohura was killed before he could reveal where they had been laid, my ancestors never saw Korangi's bones. Both were buried in shame, but before now no-one knew where, except for the three living descendants of Tekawhiti that this information is traditionally passed down to.'

Maddy waited patiently for the revelation. Ihaka had a way of drawing a story out when he was deep in oratory. That, and forgetting her grasp of

Mâori extended to 'have a *kai*', 'that's *kapai*', and '*taniwha*'. 'So,' she said, as Ihaka sipped more of his tea and swallowed like it hurt, 'what's the kicker?'

'Korangi was Ngati Horua. My *tipuna*. My ancestor.' They locked eyes for a long moment, before they both turned to the bones, as if expecting them to sit up and speak. 'Tiaka must've been handed down the information. He's used it to draw us into something.'

A chill shivered Maddy's spine. 'These are Hokaka's bones, aren't they?'

'I think so. Tiaka couldn't touch them, because they're Tekawhiti, so he'd be making himself *tapu* – bad *tapu* – if he tried. Until they were gone, he couldn't even go into their cave without tainting himself.'

'And Hokaka and Korangi were buried in the same cave?' Maddy said, putting the pieces together.

Ihaka thumped his cup down and came to his feet, eyes flaring with the light of a soldier back from war, generations of warriors burning in his blood. 'He needed us to take the bones away, knowing we wouldn't damage them because we're professionals, and then he needed to distract us long enough to get to the other bones: Korangi's. My ancestor's.'

'Ihaka,' Maddy said, 'what happens if Tiaka lays his hands on your ancestor's bones?'

Ihaka's jaw set in a grim line. 'Can't let it happen.'

Maddy bundled the bones, and within a few minutes they were back in the jeep, hurtling out of Harrison's Bay and across the pitted fields. Ihaka braced himself in the rear, mounting the cannon on its gimbal, while Maddy's stomach churned. She shouldn't be so upset. It wasn't *her* ancestor's ghosts being disturbed. This was a dangerous business, dealing with monsters and spirits and the men who played them like a game, for fun and profit. Why should it feel any different, knowing that if not for her, Tiaka might never have cast his vengeful eye on Ihaka, drawing an ancient feud back into the present? It wasn't her fault, not at all. This was business, and in business there was always risk. But how much was too much to risk? Her own life? Ihaka's?

They crossed hills and thundered across paddocks. Up ahead, the hillside loomed, growing darker. The omnipresent rainclouds swirled and thickened overhead, condensing into a sickening spiral. Lightning danced nearby. Maddy grappled the wheel as the jeep bucked over boulders hidden in the long grass. On the hillside, something moved, vast and serpentine.

'So have you figured out why the dragon didn't chase us?'

'The *taniwha* left us alone because of the other bones. Hokaka's remains were cursed by Arohura because she betrayed him, daughter to father. Korangi was a warrior, defeated in battle. Even though Arohura shamed him by killing him and placing his bones where his *iwi* couldn't find them, he still wasn't cursed like Hokaka. The *taniwha* knew it was Hokaka's bones we were taking, and was glad to be rid of them. Cursed bones bring bad luck, even to a *taniwha*.'

Maddy thought about that; about losing the jeep, and their buyer absconding. Maybe he was right. Maybe they were carrying that curse. 'Well, I don't think it plans to leave us alone this time.' Great wings spread wide and dark against the sky as the beast thrust heavenward. They sure didn't need any more bad luck today. 'Nearly there!'

With a loud pop and a flapping of rubber, the jeep skewed sideways. 'Flat!' Maddy screamed, wrenching the wheel. The rim caught a rock, shredding the blown tyre in a shower of sparks, and the jeep tipped precariously.

Ihaka swung around, bringing the nailgun to bear on the ascending taniwha, diminishing as it strove for altitude.

The jeep slewed back into line, but struggled forward awkwardly. Damn the bones and their bad luck! She hit the brakes, and the jeep skidded to a lopsided halt, burying its grill in the wet earth. 'Leave it!' she yelled, snatching up her pack and nailgun and vaulting out into the mud. Ihaka looked ready to protest, then screwed up his face and leapt from the crippled vehicle, pack on his shoulder and nail-rifle in hand. They knelt by the jeep, withdrew their keys and unlocked the side-locker. With a wary eye on the sky, Maddy hauled the canvas roll onto her shoulders. 'The ditch!'

Ihaka nodded, and they set off at a dead run across the paddock.

Wind wailed, and they ducked into the shadows of a rusting tractor as the *taniwha* swept over them, the draught of its passage flattening the grass to either side. As soon as it passed, Maddy and Ihaka sprinted in its wake, weapons raised.

Like storming the beaches in Greece, only with less shrapnel, and more claws. 'There!' Ihaka grunted, spotting the collapsed fence hanging together with rusted wire and long grass, which marked the line of the ditch they had almost driven into the last time they came this way.

Maddy slid into the depression first, Ihaka close behind. A shadow swept over them, and the rain pelted down. Ihaka dropped, working his way forward on his belly in the mud; yet another reminder of Europe, inching across a continent ravaged by war. *Just like the old days.* He could almost hear the shriek of shells, the rattle of machine-gun fire, the screams of falling men; things he had left behind, and didn't need to bring home with him.

After what felt like far too long sloughing through the mud, the ditch came to an end where the hillside sloped up from the paddock. Ihaka and

Maddy crouched in the long grass, scanning the sky for the *taniwha*, and the cave mouth for Tiaka and his soldiers. Another fence, fallen to ruin, lay in the grass; they must have driven right over it the first time.

'Ihaka,' Maddy whispered, fingering the trigger of her nailgun, 'whatever happens in there...'

'Don't get all weepy on me now.' Ihaka threw her a look which she caught and threw back.

'I was going to say whatever happens, we still split the profits 50-50.'

'You take the big ones, I'll take the little ones,' he grinned. 'Let's move.'

Heaving himself from the ditch – *the trench* – he ran up the hill at a crouch, ready to duck, to dodge, to shoot back. Maddy sprinted at his back.

Wings scythed the sky. Lightning flashed.

The cave beckoned, swallowed them.

The smell hit Maddy first. Pressing herself against the cold rock face inside the cave, she watched as Ihaka slipped across the space, each of them edging down the cavern with an eye on the opposite side. It was the hot faecal reek of an outhouse, laced with the darkly familiar smell of blood.

Ihaka wrinkled his nose. She gestured vaguely, in a signal which was meant to convey the question: *Hey, you smell that?* They must've been working together too long, because he nodded. It was the smell of dead bodies. Sure as hell hadn't been any bodies when they were last here. Not fresh ones, anyway.

Sneaking from shadow to outcrop, they reached the cleft they'd climbed earlier in the day. Ihaka pointed. Three motorbikes, US Army surplus, rested against the walls or on their kickstands. They'd been modified with saddlebags and mini air compressors for charging nailguns. Beyond the bikes lay two bodies, spread-eagled, necks and limbs twisted at odd angles. Blood spattered the jagged stones and collected in dark pools beneath them.

Maddy glanced up to the slit in the rock where Ihaka had found Hokaka. She imagined the bodies falling, pinwheeling, arms flailing, spines and skulls cracking as they hit the earth. Did they slip, or...?

She glanced at Ihaka, who returned her look, his eyes narrow. Three bikes, but only two bodies. Someone was in the inner cave. Tiaka was up there, looking for Korangi's bones.

Outside, a long rumble of thunder pealed, fading away only slowly, echoing strangely in the cavern. He crossed to the bodies, while Maddy covered him with the nailgun, watching the cleft above for movement.

Ihaka nudged the corpses with his toe, turning one of them over. He crouched, pulled the sleeves back from their limp arms to study the tattoos on their biceps and forearms. He pointed overhead. *Tiaka*, he mouthed, and began to ascend the wall.

Maddy holstered her weapon and darted across the cave, just a few metres behind him. 'Ihaka!' she hissed, but he didn't stop, didn't even glance back. She'd seen that look in his eye; the walls of iron slamming down, the warrior from a broken war reborn, emerging to do battle once more. She'd seen it when all that had been at stake was money. Now, it was more than that, more than she could fathom. But she knew she'd better not fall behind.

Pain, where he had scraped his fingers raw on the rocks, where his knees barked against remorseless stone. The pounding in his head.

He killed them.

Tiaka must've pushed them, his own men, let them fall and die and for what? Because they weren't Ngai Tekawhiti. This was a glory he wanted to savour for himself, this shaming of Ngati Horua. That, and the money he could make by selling the bones would go further if he didn't have to split it three ways. Oh yeah, it was all working out *kapai* for Tiaka, wasn't it? Or it would, if Ihaka didn't do something about it. Like break the bastard's neck. Hell if he was going to let that Ngai Tekawhiti scum piss all over his *mana*, the *mana* of his *iwi*, his ancestors. Not without a fight.

Ihaka gripped the lip and hauled himself into the cave, scanning the shadows. From deep within there came sounds of scraping, and a ghosting of light. Ihaka crawled forward, choking back the war-cry on his lips; past the pile of rocks that had hidden long-dead Hokaka, and into the darkest gullet of the cave, where they hadn't ventured, hadn't thought they'd needed to. Into those deeper shadows where, long ago, some ancient enemy had hidden away the mortal remains of his *tipuna-tane*. And now, a living and supremely dangerous enemy was unearthing those bones, breaking the *tapu*, disturbing the sleeping spirits.

The cavern roof dropped so low that if Ihaka hadn't seen the lights and heard the sounds beyond, he wouldn't have guessed the cavern extended so far under the hill. On one side, some rocks had collapsed, partly obscuring the hole. Ihaka squeezed into the space, his belt catching and dragging. He stifled his grunts. Water trickled somewhere nearby.

The space beyond opened up, a grotto where a man could stand at his full height. Ihaka paused, bunching to spring.

Then he saw the bones.

And then he saw the light.

Maddy scrambled towards the gap Ihaka had disappeared into. Damn, but he moved fast. Must be all that scrambling around under machine-gun fire.

But for a few seconds there, she was alone in the pitch black, his body in the opening, masking what little light was spilling from the other side; a pale, sallow light hinting at rot and corruption. She should've put her torch on her helmet before diving into the dark. That'd teach her for rushing. She wormed forward, muscles aching.

'Ihaka!' she hissed again, contorting to twist through the gap, working by feel. She slipped, colliding with Ihaka's boots, and looked up at the soft, eerie grey light that bathed the far side of the grotto she found herself in. Ihaka was transfixed, rigid, poised halfway up as if ready to leap at the man who stood in the middle of the cave over a pile of dark bones.

Maybe Tiaka hadn't seen them, or maybe he was too lost in whatever mad pit he had fallen into to realise they were there. Clutched at his belly was a skull. He was facing them but his head was down, staring intently into the hollow eye-sockets, which stared back at him. It seemed the light came from within, casting Tiaka's face in soft, sickly shadows. His torch lay extinguished in a puddle. The only light came from the skull, and ... from behind Tiaka. Maddy gulped hard, as an amorphous pale glow drifted up from the water, took on form, substance. A feminine shape, slender and smooth, like the lines of a *mere*, gentle to the touch but deadly when wielded with intent.

Maddy rose to a crouch, but Ihaka laid a hand on her arm. Silently, they waited. The figure behind Tiaka moved closer, indistinct arms that may just as well have been tentacles wrapping around the relic hunter, fingers closing around his hands. If the apparition had a body, it could've been mistaken for a lover, embracing her dearest from behind, one last time. Then Tiaka threw his head back, a strangled choking sound bubbling in his throat. Muscles and veins bulged on his neck, picked out in sharp relief by the sickly light as the *kehua* squeezed. Blood trickled from his nose, frothed at the corner of his mouth. His knees gave way and he sank, like a falling tree, the skull rolling from his hands and staring, now, at Ihaka and Maddy.

Tiaka twitched once, twice, and was still. The *kehua* turned towards them.

'Hokaka?' Maddy managed to breathe, then Ihaka was wrestling the canvas roll bag from her shoulder. She let him take it, open it out, and spread the bones on the ground before the ghost. From the second skull fell a pallid light, and from beneath the scattered pile of flat stones—beneath which lay, she suspected, what remained of the fallen warrior Korangi—another soft glow arose. It took on shape, a lithe figure of taut muscle, with a warrior's bearing.

Ihaka scooped up a skull in each hand and dropped to his knees, head bowed, proffering the age-dark orbs towards the two shining figures.

Maddy watched, horror-struck, as the two spectres drifted toward each other. Each lifted a hand toward their lover's skull. As their spectral hands met the light flared, and Maddy looked away, dazzled. When she turned back, the cave was velvet black; silent but for the dripping of water, Ihaka's laboured breaths, and the roar of her heart in her ears.

'What just happened?' she whispered.

'I'm not sure. But whatever Tiaka thought he was doing, he did it wrong.'

She dug her torch out of her utility belt and wound the tiny dynamo, the light waxing brighter and the gears churning softly as it ran. While part of her was freaking the hell out over what she'd seen, another part of her was seeing something else entirely: two sets of bones. Twice the profit.

'Wakey wakey,' she said, her voice suddenly loud in the tense silence. 'Work to do.'

Ihaka turned very slowly to look at her. What she saw burning in his eyes chilled her. To the bone.

Ihaka stooped, setting first one skull, then the other, back into the canvas roll. 'We're taking them,' he said, finding his own torch, fixing it on his helmet, and winding the crank.

'Course we are,' Maddy quipped, an edge in her voice. 'Cost us a lot, this little escapade. We almost need two sets just to pay for repairs on the jeep.'

Ihaka shifted aside more rocks, groping in the spaces between them for the bones. They hadn't been buried with so much as a shred of dignity, not preserved like Hokaka's had been. Just scattered in this deep, dark hole to rot. Here where the damp had rendered them soft and fragile.

'Why here, why now?' Ihaka asked aloud as he worked.

'Why what?' Maddy replied, as she took the bones he handed her and delicately laid them on the roll-bag for cleaning.

'We've been in any number of *urupa*, but we've never seen *kehua*, not like this.'

'Love is a strange and powerful thing.'

Ihaka paused in his work, taking a second to digest this. Arohura had broken with tradition, a father with a broken heart and a *patu* to grind. Maybe that was why the *kehua* had remained here, waiting. And Tiaka – Tiaka was Arohura's blood. Had they waited all this time, Hokaka and Korangi, for him? A shred of a man long gone to his own resting cave, carrying his griefs and his guilt? 'We're not selling them.'

'But Mercer–'

'Not to anyone.'

'Ihaka, we need the–'

'These are my *tipuna*!' he growled, swivelling to face her. His fists clenched and unclenched, blood hot in his veins. He took a deep breath of the cold, fetid air in an effort to calm the rage that wanted to surface, wanted to take him over. 'My ancestors. I will bury them well. Like they deserve.'

Maddy opened her mouth to protest, then appeared to think better of it. 'Sure,' she said slowly, in the tone of voice one settles on to soothe a wild animal. 'Let's pack up and get out of here.'

'We take them home. We bury them, the proper way, with dignity.' Ihaka could see her thinking, already planning how she might later change the game and make her precious profit, but she didn't argue. For a time they worked in silence but for the scraping of rocks and tools, and the sighing of bones.

Maddy tightened the straps on the bag slung on Ihaka's shoulders before swinging her legs over the cave lip and free-climbing down the cavern wall. As she hit the ground, she spun around and found herself staring into the hand-filed muzzle of a nail-pistol, so close she could see the needle vibrating on the air-gauge. Shifting her focus, she looked past the gun to the man holding it. One of Mercer's cronies from the Regent, a nervous grin on his face and a finger to his lips, with a twitch of the gun in her face to emphasise the point. She could smell the iron, and as she weighed her chances of dropping the man without taking a nail through the skull, she saw two more figures: Mercer, standing near the motorcycles, and his other bodyguard, who was aiming an air-powered rifle over her head – at Ihaka.

Damn it all! Whether Mercer had plotted this whole thing, or simply taken advantage of the opportunity when it presented itself, he was going to walk away with the goods and probably leave them for dead, along with Tiaka and his soldiers. Maddy had been in some tight places before, and come out of them with some scrapes and bruises, but this one topped them all; pinned down by two guns while her partner climbed blindly down the wall behind her.

She raised her hands, palms out. Ihaka's boots crunched on loose stones. 'Come on,' he said, turning. Then, 'What? *Aue!*'

'So nice to see you both again!' Mercer drawled, walking forward. 'We seem to have some unfinished business to attend to. Here's what we're going to do.' He paused a safe distance from the relic hunters, interlacing his fingers in front of him. The guard with the gun trained on Maddy backed up a step. She could feel Ihaka tensing beside her, seething.

'You're going to hand over the bones, and I'm going to leave, and if you disagree, I'm going to nail you both to the floor. Understand?'

Maddy shot Ihaka a glance, but he wasn't looking at her. His eyes blazed, locked on Mercer. Through gritted teeth, Ihaka spoke. 'You don't want these bones. They're cursed.'

'I'll be the judge of that.'

'If you take them, a monster will hunt you down, and rip you apart.'

'Oh really?' Mercer said, pacing a little, his Cockney accent twanging in the echoing cave. 'And I suppose that monster will be you?'

Maddy swallowed hard. Ihaka shivered with barely contained rage. There were still two guns levelled at them, and that was two more than she was happy with if it came to a fight, especially now the first bodyguard had moved out of kicking range. Outside, lightning blazed, died.

Maddy saw the shift in Ihaka's eyes and gave him the slightest nod. He knew how to judge the odds as well as she did, and this was a gamble they couldn't win. With pronounced reluctance, Ihaka unshouldered his load, and laid it on the ground before Mercer.

'See, there's a good native,' Mercer beamed, an ugly smile in an ugly face. He knelt and lifted the bag. 'Heavier than I expected.' Mercer grimaced, but backed away quickly. His bodyguards joined his retreat towards the dim grey light spilling through the cave entrance.

Maddy and Ihaka followed carefully, arms still raised, passing the abandoned motorcycles.

As they ascended the rise, Maddy's breath caught. On the paddock beyond sat a light aircraft, a Piper Pacer maybe, painted in olive drab and with rugged wheels for landing in hostile terrain. If Mercer could afford the fuel to operate an actual aeroplane, when the price of gasoline had soared ever higher since the tankers had stopped coming in, he must be wealthy and well-connected indeed. Which meant she had underestimated him. They would pay for that mistake.

'I'll have no more part in this,' Mercer said, waving a vaguely dismissive hand at the two captives. 'Broyles, Higgins, dispose of them once I'm in the air. I'd rather not be a party to any more of this unpleasantness.'

The bodyguards exchanged a puzzled look, nervously scanning the sky. 'Mr Mercer sir, you can't leave us out here. The dragon–'

'Take the motorcycles,' Mercer said, striding away. 'You're big boys. Now, tidy up those loose ends and I'll meet you back in Wharitangi.'

Maddy glanced at Ihaka. His shoulders were slumped, but not in defeat. He was breathing, low and deep, easing the tension in his muscles. The warrior readying to strike.

Warily, the two guards raised their guns again.

Mercer swung the plane's door open, throwing the bag ungently into the back before hauling himself into the pilot's seat.

'You know, boys,' Maddy said, as the Piper's engine sputtered and then roared to life, 'when you take people prisoner, it usually pays to take their weapons away.' She didn't give them time for a witty comeback. As Ihaka dropped and threw himself forward, she twisted and rolled to the side, coming up with her nailgun raised, primed, barking. The second guard went down as Ihaka's shoulder ploughed into his solar plexus, both tumbling to the ground in a rain of the first guard's blood.

The aircraft rumbled around in a lazy half-circle, lining up for take-off on the lumpy paddock.

Maddy jammed her gun back in its sheath and dived for the rifle the dying bodyguard had dropped, slipping in the slick mud and loose stones at the cave entrance. Behind her, she heard the grunts and cries and wet sounds of fists connecting with skin, bone. She scooped up the rifle, rose to a crouch, and sighted down the barrel.

The plane roared as the throttle opened up wide, bounding and jostling across the paddock on its fat ungainly tyres, gathering speed. Maddy breathed slowly, closed an eye, let out her breath, and squeezed the trigger.

Something slammed her hard in the side, throwing her to the ground and knocking her shot wide, the gun skittering out of her grasp. She went down, winded, rolling into a ball and coming up with fists clenched, the world spinning, anticipating a blow from the wounded bodyguard.

Both men lay unmoving. Ihaka was nowhere to be seen.

The airplane roared away.

Maddy looked up. Into eyes, teeth, talons. The *taniwha*'s tail swung past her, tentative, like the claw of a cat toying with a trapped mouse. Its jaw parted, revealing the flicker of deadly fire within. Her legs were frozen. She'd been close to monsters many times, but never flat-footed, empty handed. Always as hunter, never as prey.

The motorbike howled as it tore up the cave entrance and Maddy threw herself forward in an utter leap of faith, grabbing onto Ihaka's shoulders as he slowed for her, then he gunned the throttle and they hurtled away from the cave. Wrapping an arm around his waist, she yelled in his ear: 'You took your time!'

Ihaka leaned into the wind, as the *taniwha* screamed and took to the sky behind them. The bike pelted over the paddock, following the deep furrows the Piper had left in the mud. Ahead, the plane lifted its nose, ascending. Ihaka dropped a gear, racing after it, shifting up again.

Maddy drew her handcannon as the distance between motorbike and airplane closed. It would only be moments before Mercer streaked into the sky. As best she could on the bouncing ride, she sighted the plane and unleashed a string of concussive shots. Metal scraped against metal, the plane wavered, righted itself, kept climbing.

'Can't you get any closer?' she yelled, but knew it was useless. They could never outrun an airplane on a motorbike.

A dark streak, black sickles against the grey sky, swooped across the plane's trajectory, and it dropped, tilted, veered off, righted itself. Ihaka gunned the engine, the bike leaving the ground as he crested a dirt mound, spraying mud as they hit the earth on the other side.

Clutching him tight, Maddy lined up the plane, weaving drunkenly left to right, and fired again. The plane resumed its climb, gaining altitude, leaving the bike behind.

'Shit!' Maddy yelled. It was a long way to Wharitangi, especially with a hungry *taniwha* on their tail.

The plane drew higher, its shape blurring among the low clouds, its engine fading to a muffled roar.

Ihaka rolled the bike to a stop, breathing hard. Maddy could feel the tension in his muscles, where she held him so close. He was shaking. She wanted to say something, to promise him they'd get the bones back, whatever the cost. But hell, she hated committing to things when the bottom line was a row of zeroes.

Still, it was Ihaka. And wouldn't that make him smile that glorious, secret smile?

'Ihaka–' she began, when a hint of movement overhead caught her eye. A wing, maybe, or a tail. They both looked up. The flicker of lightning lit up two silhouettes in the cloudbank: one, a small plane; the other, a hulking monster of myth and fury.

In the wake of the resounding thunderclap, they heard the engine cough.

'He's hit,' Ihaka said, a grim smile crossing his lips. 'Hold on.'

Maddy gripped his waist with both arms as the bike leaped forward in pursuit.

Ihaka spotted the plane when it dipped below the clouds. The motor was hunting, missing, and a trail of smoke marked its passage through the clouds. Not surprisingly, Mercer had turned and was making for Kokoruroa, the nearest *tapu* ground. Ihaka lost sight of the Piper behind the hill, but the smoke trail led him on. For nail-biting minutes they sped uphill, through the bush. As they crested the rise, Kokoruroa lay below them like a cancerous boil on the green landscape. Buried up to its nose in a long furrow of dirt, the plane lay smoking in the paddock outside town, not far from where Ihaka had run Tiaka's truck off the road. Between Maddy's shots and the *taniwha*'s lightning, enough of the plane's workings must've been fried to negate any chance of a smooth landing.

The bike skidded and slid down the hillside as Ihaka slalomed around rocks and manuka scrub, glad for the thick rubber tyres and small, powerful engine, even if it did reek of sugar and alcohol.

'He'll be in town already,' Maddy yelled.

'We check the plane.'

'He wouldn't have left the bones behind.'

'Unless he wants us to think that.'

'You're driving.' He felt her shrug, in that cold exasperated way she had when he'd made his mind up about something and she knew she couldn't talk him out of it. *Aue*, but she was the most infuriating woman.

'There he is.' She pointed past Ihaka, to a tiny figure stumbling across the paddock towards town. 'Run him down, then we can come back and check the plane!'

Briefly, Ihaka considered complying. Then the smoking fuselage crackled into flame. He revved the engine hard and charged for the plane.

Skidding to a stop in a spray of wet earth, Ihaka launched himself off the bike and ran through the haze of caustic smoke.

'Ihaka!' Maddy yelled. 'It's not worth it! It could go up any second!'

Ihaka ducked under one tilted wing and peered into the cockpit. Nothing. Cursing, Ihaka dived under the wing and sprinted for Maddy. She'd taken his place on the motorcycle's front seat. He got on the back and held tight as she accelerated away from the wreck.

With a *whoomp*, the fuel erupted, and a concussive wave of heat swept over their backs, a fireball bright as noon boiling into the sky. Ihaka grabbed Maddy's gun from her hip and drew a bead on Mercer.

Maddy slapped his wrist down. 'Don't be an idiot! You'll hit the bones!'

Ihaka lowered the gun. 'It's not the bones you're worried about.'

Maddy shrugged. 'He's rich. Stupid rich. Play this right, we might never need to hunt relics again.'

It wasn't a bad thought, Ihaka supposed. 'But then, what would you hunt instead?'

Maddy didn't look back, but he heard her smile. 'There's always something to hunt.'

As if hearing her, a shadow sliced across the paddock, ragged wings passing overhead. Ihaka brought one leg up onto the bike's back seat, as Maddy slewed around to cross behind Mercer. He leapt, *mere* in one hand, and a cry of war on his lips.

Maddy dropped the bike and ran to where Ihaka and Mercer rolled on the ground, his *mere* rising and falling like a diesel piston. The Englishman writhed beneath him, trying to cover his face as the blows rained down. She drew her gun and approached at a jog.

'Ihaka!' she called out. 'Stand down, soldier!'

Delivering a final sucker-punch to the prone man's ribs which left him gagging, Ihaka rolled Mercer over and hauled the canvas roll off his shoulder. Mercer sprawled, face-down in the mud.

At the fringes of Harrison's Bay, curious townsfolk had gathered to watch the spectacle. Yet none were so bold as to leave the safety of the town. Not with a dragon prowling the sky.

Ihaka shouldered the bag and turned to Maddy. There was a look in his eye she didn't like, because she'd not seen it before. She'd survived this long by learning to understand her monsters before she tried to defeat them, and the same was true of her allies. This was a look she wasn't prepared for. Something final, determined.

'I'm ending this,' he said, and swivelled away, striding towards the conflagration.

'Wait, what? Ihaka, where are you going?'

'I'm tired of it. Time to do something about it.'

Maddy watched Mercer, still rolling weakly on the ground, not wanting to let him escape but also not wanting Ihaka to wander off with the bones without her. 'Like what? What are you sick of?'

Ihaka stopped, turned, veins throbbing in his neck. 'This. All of it. The running, the fighting, the hiding. Always being afraid of...of *taniwha*, of *kehua*, of people. I fought a war which was all sorts of horror, but if I'd known coming home would mean living every day afraid of whether I'd be alive the next morning, I would've rather died there. So no more. I'm done.'

He spun away and stormed toward the burning plane.

'How, exactly?' Maddy called, gaping, but he didn't reply. She wasn't sure she'd ever heard him speak so many words at once, if he wasn't recounting histories. 'Dammit, Ihaka!' she growled, then dropped to her knees in the mud beside Mercer. She'd lost the jeep. She had a sinking feeling she was going to lose the bones. Hell if she was going to lose Mercer as well. Snapping a length of stiff twine from a belt pouch, she hogtied him and in a trice was up and running after Ihaka. He was already at the plane, unslinging the roll bag.

'What are you doing with my bones, you crazy bastard?' she grunted under her breath, and sprinted towards him.

Ihaka hefted the roll bag, with its weight of human remains; of love and tragedy, betrayal and murder; of all the seasons etched into those bones by years falling away to dust and grit and empty echoes. For too long these *taonga* had lain under the earth, protecting those hallowed places, so neither man nor *taniwha* dared tread there. But the world had changed. Now, the *taniwha* were among them. The legends, the symbols of what mattered, what was *tapu*, what was cursed, all *meant* something dreadfully real. And, in the way of men – like those he had gone to war against, and those he had fought for – everyone wanted something for themselves. Everyone wanted to keep the treasure.

These were his *tipuna*. Korangi, by the long slow passing down of bloodline to bloodline, and Hokaka, by a whispered promise, long ago, one heart bonded to another. What they had shared had made Kokoruroa a sacred place, yet it was a dark, brooding blessing, bought with blood and pain and loss. Now that they were together again, flying to distant Reinga where they would at last be at peace, their memory might offer something to a world blighted by war and fear.

Dimly, he heard Maddy screaming as he flexed his shoulders. She'd be pissed, but she'd get over it. There was always something else to hunt. He swung, released. The bag spun twice before thumping down on the burning plane in a spray of cinders.

He saw the *taniwha* descending, its razor talons stretched wide. It knew, too. Knew the truth Ihaka had finally come to realise. It knew this was no longer a game, and the humans were no longer mice to be toyed with. It knew Ihaka had reached his epiphany, and in this moment the reign of the *taniwha* had faltered. He held his *mere* to the sky, fluttered a hand across his chest in the ancient *wero* of *toa* long gone to their graves, stamped a foot and thrust out his tongue, staring down the onrushing juggernaut of winged tooth. Daring it to challenge him.

The hiss of the nailgun behind him was a distant sound over the roar in his ears, the rush of battle and bloodlust and the sudden shriek of the beast as it tasted cold iron and passed through the acrid smoke.

The *taniwha* howled, banking away.

Ihaka relaxed. The bag was burning well, black smoke coiling away from it like ghosts escaping the flames.

'Just...' Maddy stammered, faltered. 'Why?'

Ihaka took a long breath, calming his racing heart. Hundreds of years of tradition made him a monster; worse than just stealing bones and desecrating sacred earth, he had thrown those bones to the flames, let them burn. But it was the right thing to do. It *had* to be.

'Come on,' Maddy said, no doubt taking his silence as the only answer she was likely to get. 'That thing'll be back soon.'

'No,' Ihaka said. 'It won't.'

'Really? Scare it off with your little song and dance, did you? Why didn't we think of that sooner?' Her sarcasm was hot as acid.

'You asked me why. You really want to know?' He met her eye, and she bit back whatever smart remark had first sprung to her lips.

'Yes. Yes I do.'

'The ashes. The ashes are the bones. The fire will lift them, carry them on the wind, carry them far.' *Distant battlefields, miles and miles of fire and falling ash.* 'Everywhere the ash lands becomes *tapu*.'

Maddy frowned. 'So, the *taniwha*...?'

'Will be driven out. And when they go, they'll take their fear with them.'

'But the ash will wash away–'

'And become part of the *whenua*, the land. Part of everything.'

The heat of the fire rolled over them, smoke and cinders and ash spiralling into the sky and fanning out on the breeze.

For a long while they were both silent, watching the ashes spread high and far and wide. Finally, Maddy spoke. 'You do realise you've just put us out of business?'

Ihaka grinned, that sliver of something glorious shining out from under his bleak armour. 'Maybe.'

She sidled nearer, and gripped his hand in hers. 'But we're still in it together right? 50-50?'

'There might be room to negotiate,' he shrugged, but that grin didn't fall away. His touch was warmer than she had expected.

'I'm sure there will be. Always room to negotiate.' She smiled – because nothing tasted quite as sweet as the promise of victory at the end of the hunt.

In The Company of Rogues

Randall the Rogue sat in the waiting chamber of Pidderill's one and only apothecary office with an incessant itching in his groin.

'It won't stop,' he said, turning to his familiar, Dennis the Budgerigar of Doom.

'Of course it won't, if you don't stop scratching it,' said Dennis in a strong antipodean accent while pecking at the tatty velvet chair. A bored apothecarial assistant cleaned her nails with a quill behind the reception desk layered with unfiled medical scrolls.

'What? A man's allowed to scratch his sword,' said Randall, taking his hands off his codpiece. He looked at the public service scroll on the wall:

Sheath your sword in a scabbard during convivial relations.

Dennis preened his feathers. 'It's probably got to do with all that wenching.'

'I'm a rogue. Wenching goes with the territory. I enjoy women of all forms,' said Randall.

'Well, you've got one of their forms right now,' Dennis squawked with laughter.

Randall sighed, slumping in the chair. 'Me! Fought the dragons of the seven kingdoms. Stole the flying carpet of the Sultanate. Made love to a thousand women. Brought low by this.'

Dennis shook his head while Randall continued. 'Of all the women I've loved, or at least loved loosely for a couple of hours on a wet and windy night. Who gave it to me? The blonde at Foul Ferril's House of Fungus? Or the brunette?'

They were interrupted by a thin-lipped man dressed in black. 'Gentlemen, this way.'

The apothecary motioned to his examination chamber. Randall and Dennis strutted in, sitting down between a severed unicorn head broiled in a vat of green goop and a rack of discounted +10 health potions.

'What can I do for you today?' said the apothecary, taking out a scroll and quill to record notes.

'Well, um,' said Randall. 'I've got an itching.'

'Where is the source of this itching?' asked the apothecary.

'If I knew that I wouldn't have slept with her.'

The apothecary pursed his lips, hovering the quill over the paper. 'I mean the location on your body.'

Randall looked at his codpiece.

'Ahhh.' The apothecary leaned over the edge of his desk to look. 'You'll need to remove your pants so I can inspect the infection.'

Randall wore the garb typical of his guild: leather and lots of it. He styled a brown jacket with puffy sleeves, an un-ironed shirt once white, now discoloured, and a *large* codpiece, which one might say was too large. Randall dropped his pants.

The apothecary donned a pair of tight fitting leather gloves and examined Randall's appendage.

'And?' said Randall.

'You have a carnally transmitted illness. Have you been frequenting brothels or ladies of the night in recent times?'

'With this face and this charm, why would I need to pay for sex?'

Dennis perched on the edge of the Apothecary's desk and shook his head. 'I keep telling him to settle down, find a nice girl, and be a career rogue. But does he listen to his familiar? No, it's always "Dennis use your magical powers to get us out of here. Take a message to my mum telling her I won't be home for Yule *again*, because I'm too busy drinking and wenching." I'm not a carrier pigeon.'

'You can't be a rogue with a wife,' said Randall, his pants still on the floor.

'What about your brother, Rick the Rapscallion? He's got five kids.'

'Five hungry, screaming little brats to feed.' Randall pulled on his pants and turned to the apothecary. 'How do I fix this?'

The apothecary tapped his fingers together. 'First of all, I would recommend avoiding convivial relations until the problem is remedied. I have most of the ingredients for a salve, but unfortunately there's a kingdom-wide lack of Whisper of the Valley.'

'So where do I get this Whisper of the Valley?' asked Randall, as the apothecary began mixing the salve on his potion table.

'Unfortunately, Whisper of the Valley is only found in the skeleton-infested Valley of the Deadish. Hence the kingdom-wide lack,' said the Apothecary.

Randall huffed. 'Do you mean to say we'll need to go on a quest? I told you we should've consulted a witch. Would've been out in five minutes. I could've dealt with a curse. Now I have to go on a quest. And a quest without wenching is no quest at all. I'm not doing it.'

'If you don't,' said the apothecary, 'Your *sword* will, how shall I put this... wear down to the hilt?'

Alarmed, Randall jumped into action. 'Right. Dennis, you hear that? We're going on a quest. Ready the steed. Pack the satchels. Steal some gold from a chest.' The apothecary looked up from his table and handed Randall a metal jar.

'Don't forget the salve. When you find the Whisper of the Valley, add it and apply it to the infected area straight away.'

Randall grabbed the salve and flicked the apothecary a silver krud.

The town of Pidderill had one distinguished claim to fame, having made the Isolated Worlde list of the Kingdom's Worst 10 Backwaters for seven years running. It usually ranked first, except for the year when Yer-Bogswill's dubious plumbing system was broken by an unusually large turd.

In the street, the scent of the late morning sewage ran through the gutters like a bad perfume. Randall and Dennis narrowly dodged a washerwoman throwing a slop bucket out a window. They strode past Ye Coffee, a closed Kebabopolis – 'What! Kebabopolis is closed! Where am I going to get breakfast?' said Randall – and Fashione ByGone, where young maidens sought the latest in corsetry. Randall tried to peek inside, but a sales assistant closed the blinds on him.

Dennis hopped up and down with excitement. 'We're going on a quest! Want to do some research first? I hear Pidderill has some great libraries.'

'Research smesearch,' said Randall. 'You always bang on about researching and we never do it.'

'Which is why we usually run into trouble. You never bother to bring a street directory!' said Dennis.

'First things first,' said Randall. 'We'll assemble a team of brave adventurers to fight the skeletons in the Valley of Whispers.'

'We're getting Whisper of the Valley. Not going to the Valley of Whispers. That place gives me a headache,' said Dennis.

Randall, unfazed by his familiar, continued, 'I want a crack team of all blonde female half-elf rangers, in skimpy chain mail.'

The budgerigar banged his tiny head on Randall's shoulder, over and over again. 'Why, in the wisdom of all the Gods of Sidarth, did they have to link me with you? I must have been a vulture in a past life. All I came here for was a birdpacking holiday, to see a few sights along the way. If I wasn't forced to connect with you in a secret magical ceremony, I would have retired to a palm tree off the south coast with a rosella by now. How many times have I told you? No self-respecting female adventurer would wander into the wastes wearing only a chain-mail bikini and high-heeled sandals, leaving the rest of their body subject to stabbing, maiming, death or heaven forbid, the athlete's foot that seems to be present in every inn from here to Racksalon.'

'Yeah, but it's hot,' said Randall.

The bird contemplated flying away into the sun, but he knew the magical bond between him and Randall wouldn't let him get much past Ye Coffee. Instead, he offered his sage advice in the hope that one day, Randall might listen. They'd only been bonded for 10 years. 'Get yourself a nice, sensible adventure team. You never bring a healer along,' said Dennis.

Randall shuddered. 'They always wear such frumpy robes.'

'What about a barbarian?'

'Usually a bloke,' said Randall, distracted by a passing gaggle of maidens, who promptly turned up their noses at him. Dennis nipped him on the ear, and asked, 'How about a dark-elf wizard?'

'Have you seen their faces? If they're so skilled in magic, why can't they look better?'

'Fine. A dwarf.'

'Nope. Never. Nup. Not getting a dwarf. They're the most obnoxious, self-important species on the planet.'

'Aside from you, that is.'

They entered the town square, where a large bulletin board advertised local notices: see the Joglamash dump, visit the Kingdom's least funded library, buy one onion get half free.

'Let's post a recruitment ad,' said Dennis. Randall pulled out a parchment and quill from his bag and began writing, 'Sexy rogue seeks adventurous maidens for quest. Preference blonde.'

The bird hid his face under his wing, in a move known by familiars of the avian variety as wingpalming. 'This is a job ad, not a personal,' said Dennis. 'I'll dictate. Team of adventurers needed for exciting quest to fight skeletal forces in pursuit of loot. Apply in person at the Socks and Sandals Inn, 6pm. Please supply your own weaponry and two references.'

'Preference blondes,' added Randall.

Seventeen beers and two bottles of oldy-wine later, Randall and Dennis were drunk. Dennis rolled his blue feathered head and bobbed on the table, sipping up spilt beer with his beak. Randall lounged in regulation rogue posture: legs crossed on the table, one arm around the chair back, other hand stroking his stubble, eyebrow raised with confident swagger, which would make most ladies swoon if they didn't get wind of his smell first.

'You know, I wasn't always this good looking,' slurred Randall. 'Kids teased me at school.'

The Aussie birdpacker looked up from his drunken puddle. 'What did they call you again? Fatty fat fart from farty fat.'

'Stop it!' he said, staring into the empty pint mug. 'It took me a long time to lose the weight.' Randall scratched his groin as a small, cloaked shadow moved towards the table.

'Are you the ones recruiting for adventurers?' The mysterious voice with mysterious arms threw back the cloak and sat down at the table. Randall struggled to focus; all he saw was a blob of green with a beard.

'There's one of you, right? You're not very tall for a blonde half-elf,' said Randall.

'You got the blonde bit right. I'm a Dwarven rogue. I have my own bow and arrows, and here is a list of references from successful jaunts to the Kraven Underworld and the Bestial Archipelago.' The dwarf laid out two scrolls, each marked with a golden seal of the completed quest.

'Ooh, the Kraven Underworld,' said Dennis. 'That's quite impressive.'

'The bird is drunk. As am I.' Randall tried to focus on the dwarf through the powerful lenses of beer goggles. His long beard was plaited into two braids with pink bows. Somewhat curvaceous yet stocky body. Were his eyes blue? And was he a Cyclops? Nope, the second eye appeared.

'But I don't hire dwarves. Besides which, aren't you meant to all have axes or something. Doesn't it come with the territory? Have axe, will mine for gold?'

The dwarf groaned. 'Cultural stereotyping is so last century. So you're not going to hire me?'

'No, of course I'm not going to hire you.' Randall picked up his beer stein, went to drink it and realised it was empty. The dwarf crossed his eight arms. Or was it six?

'That's discrimination. I have as much right to join your questing party as that half-elf at the bar.' Randall got distracted by the sexy half-elf at the bar, but the dwarf slammed a dagger into the wooden table. Randall turned back quickly.

'It's not because you're a dwarf. You're a rogue. I'm a rogue. What's the number one rule of rogues? Never quest with another rogue, they'll steal your heart then steal your clothes.'

'Fat chance of that happening,' said the dwarf. And he was right. There was no chance of romantic hijinks for Randall with a dwarf. Romantic hijinks had hijacked his jinx.

'True. But my familiar says I need *complementary* skills.' Randall gestured to Dennis, who was relaxing in a pint of beer as one does with a hot spa.

'How is lockpicking not a complementary skill to theft?' said the dwarf. Randall didn't want to admit that the dwarf had a point.

'It's because I'm a woman, isn't it?' said the dwarf.

Randall reexamined the green and blonde blob before him. Where was the cleavage? The buxom bottom? And most of all, why was there facial hair?

'You're a woman? You've got a beard.'

'Some men find it quite attractive,' said the lady dwarf. Randall hazily read through her resume for any indicators that this he was a she.

'Look,' interrupted the dwarf. 'My name is Bernice the Breaker and if you don't give me this job, I'm reporting you to the Anti-Discrimination Commission for the Equality of Non-Human Peoples.'

'Ooh, not the ACENHP,' said Randall.

'That and I've got your wallet.' She held up his leather coin purse. The lack of Randall's coin posed a problem, especially since he wanted another drink.

'One moment.' Randall held up a finger and turned to his familiar. 'Let's face it, we haven't been inundated with applicants.' They looked around the almost empty Socks and Sandals Inn. The half-elf at the bar had left. The only other patron was a drooling octogenarian in a tin helmet. Randall turned back to the entirely unattractive dwarf known as Bernice the Breaker.

'You're hired. But don't expect me to treat you differently because you're a woman or a dwarf. Wouldn't want to get reported to the Anti-Discrimination Commission.'

She grinned and threw his coin purse back at him.

Randall woke up in an unhygienic bed and proceeded directly to the less hygienic bathroom. His bowel movements splashed through the hole in the window into the street far below. He stumbled back to bed and slept for another hour, until he was woken by a rapping at the door. To his hungover head it sounded as if a baby stone golem was smacking rocks for breakfast.

'Get that will you Dennis?' said Randall.

Dennis rolled over in his birdy-bed, shielding his eyes from the shards of light coming through the moth-holed curtains. 'I'm a bird, I've got no opposable digits to open the door with.'

The rapping at the door got louder. Randall's headache got worse.

'Coming!' he moaned, rolling out of bed wearing nothing but a sheet wrapped around his torso. He opened the door.

The pert, wide-eyed Bernice the Breaker stood four foot at the lintel holding two flagons of Ye Coffee. She eyed Randall's shirtless chest. At least Randall had some reason for women wanting to sleep with him besides his charm and personality; the taut six-pack hinted at what lay behind the grimy veil.

'What time is it?' he asked. Any sexiness begotten by his entrance was dispelled by his need to scratch his balls. He took a swig from the flagon of coffee and sprawled back on the bed, his sheet precariously balanced over his manhood. The scent of his unwashed body was so thick, it could have become an embodied cloud. Bernice studied the knots in the wooden wall.

'It's nine,' said Bernice. 'I've been up for hours.'

'I bet you have, spending all that time thinking of me.'

Bernice, so enthused that she had joined the questing party of Sidarth's number-one bachelor, (if you discounted all the people who bathed, held regular jobs and practiced safe-sex) said, 'Hardly. I've been researching.'

Dennis flitted on a wonky flight path to Randall and stuck his head into the lukewarm coffee. 'I feel dead. Am I dead? This is the worst hangover since the night out with the goose that lays the golden eggs. He was a real alkie.'

Randall nursed his pounding head. 'What did you find out in your research, pray tell?'

'That you haven't told me where we're going.'

'Dennis, where are we going?' asked Randall.

'The Valley of the Deadish. Although at the moment, I feel pretty deadish,' said Dennis. Randall got up, dropped the sheet and began to relieve himself again, while continuing to talk.

'So how are we going to get to the Valley of the Deadish if we don't know where it is?'

'Like I said, we go to the library,' said Dennis.

'If there's one thing I hate more than dwarves, it's the library. So many librarians and learned tomes.' said Randall.

'I dislike your dwarvist tone,' said Bernice, determined not to look at the now naked Randall.

'Get used to it. I hate everyone. Elves. Dwarves. Humans. Budgies. There's not a people group who haven't ripped me off at some point. And what've I done? Stole right back from them. Rogueing is my form of vengeance.'

'Rant over?' said Bernice. Randall nodded.

Randall pulled on the same clothes as he was wearing the day before, and the day before that. He stopped to examine a new, nondescript yellow stain on his shirt and tried to establish which sort of bodily fluid had formed it. Settling on a combination of liquor and piss, he flicked up the collar of his jacket and ran his hand through his greasy black hair.

'To the library!' said Dennis, flapping off the dresser into a spiral on the floor.

Three streets over and 15 minutes later, they entered the not-so-silent atrium of the library, where a band was rockin' some tunes with a lute, a horn, a harp and an overturned barrel. Libraryfest 1450 was in full swing with librarians hanging loose. And by hanging loose, they'd unbuttoned one button of their shirts and creased a few book pages. Wild.

'This isn't as bad as I thought a library would be,' said Randall, distracted by a lusty librarian fluttering her pages at him. 'Love, do you know where the maps are?'

She immediately switched into professional mode. 'Maps are in the back stacks, right at the end. Be careful, I just saw Bruce of the Backwash go down there. He gets *nasty* at Libraryfest.'

They moved cautiously through the partygoers into the main hall. Their footsteps echoed in the large space. The shelves crossed two levels, with precarious ladders leading to the uppermost books underneath the vaulted ceiling. In the cooking section, leather-bound tomes oozed smells both pleasant and rank. A green slime dripped over the spines of the books. At the end of the slime trail, they discovered Bruce of the Backwash, a flabby, naked man running around decorating the books with fungus spells. The shroom fumes were getting to Bruce's head.

Bruce of the Backwash ran towards them with his magic wand which emanated a foul green smoke. The questing party took a strategic step back, just as Bruce landed a spell at their feet.

Dennis muttered an anti-fungal spell under his birdy breath. The column of books filled with the scent of lavender. A purple bubble burst over Bruce, showering him in a rain of flower petals.

'Why can't you cast that on Randall?' said Bernice.

'I've tried. He's spell resistant,' said Dennis.

No longer able to spread fungus everywhere, Bruce of the Backwash slumped his shoulders and scuttled off to the biographies.

'Maps, maps, maps.' Randall ran finger across the spines of the books. 'Where are the maps?'

'The maps are in the books,' said Bernice. 'Leave it to me.' She scanned the shelves. *A broken geographie of Sidarth. An incomplete mappe of the Sweatlands. The Isolated Worlde Guide to Pidderill.*

'Here we go,' she said, pulling a thin tome from the shelf. She blew a layer of dust off the cover. Embossed into the leather were three skulls in a circular formation, and the title *Places of the Dead*. She scanned for Valley of the Deadish in the index and flicked to the correct page.

To get to the Valley of the Deadish, take the 415 Horseway towards Yer-Bogswill. Exit the horseway and follow the trail north until you see a skull etched into a terrifying rock face. With two associates, put your fingers in the eyes, nose and mouth and push hard. Follow the valley through the canyon and you'll find loads of skeletons and not much loot. Not really worth a visit unless you're after a certain something something, as this writer was at one point after a...

Bernice snapped the book shut. 'So why exactly are we going to the Valley of the Deadish?'

'Whisper of the Valley is in high demand due to a nationwide shortage. I have been informed by an associate that it can fetch a hefty price. More than saffron and rubies. Or saffron coated rubies.'

'What does it do?' asked Bernice.

'What does it do?' gulped Randall. 'What doesn't it do? It's a potent healing herb which cures a wide range of illnesses.'

'Such as?' Bernice stuck her hands on her hips and tapped her foot on the floor. If this was what all dwarven women were like, no wonder they lived underground. When Randall didn't say anything, she turned to the bird. 'Dennis?'

'Carnal infections,' confessed Dennis.

Bernice threw up her hands into the air. 'Is that why you've been scratching your balls non-stop since I met you?'

Randall stopped scratching his balls for a moment, then continued. 'I have merely been alleviating the symptoms which have plagued my genitals since last Wednesday morning.'

She rolled her eyes and stormed off through the stacks. Dennis looked at

Randall with wide bird eyes, 'She's leaving! Your infested manhood has scared her away. Go after her!'

'Why? We can do this quest by ourselves.'

'No we can't. The book said you need *two* associates. Go after her!'

Randall sighed and dumped the atlas in the wrong section of the shelves, where some pissed librarian would curse his name for not using the returns system. Dennis clung to the leather epaulettes on Randall's jacket, as he strode at a cracking pace between the shelves. He found her stuck in the Libraryfest crowd, being accosted by a drunk researcher. 'You're gorrrrrgeous,' he slurred. 'Fancy a shag in the shelves?'

'Rack off,' she said, kicking him in the nuts. Randall grimaced for the man and stepped over the body now curled in foetal position. 'You certainly have a way with men. Are you currently single?' said Randall.

She turned to throw a left hook in his face and stopped. 'Oh, it's you again. I don't want your clammy clampidoa or whatever you have.'

'Look, I need your help. I promise you can take a 10% share of whatever I make selling the Whisper of the Valley. In return, I swear upon the gods of my ancestors I won't give you whatever is in my pants.'

Bernice's eyes went wide. 'The gods of your ancestors are Rapatoosh and Scoundrel, Keymaster and Thief. No true rogue would swear on their souls, for they are the guardians of the underworld.'

'I swear on their souls, I will not give you what is in my pants.'

'I want 50%,' she said.

'Of what's in my pants? It's an all or nothing type of thing,' said Randall, gesturing to his leather codpiece.

'The money, buffoon.'

'You can have 20%. Dennis needs some for his hedge witch fund.' Dennis nodded his birdy head.

Bernice crossed her arms. 'Make it 30% plus any additional loot, and you've got a deal.'

Randall and Bernice shook hands. She then wiped her hand on her pants.

In the dark of night, the three adventurers stole across the empty horseway. They snuck up to the fenced paddock, where the locked stables sat adjacent to the blacksmith's house.

Bernice took out her lock-picking tools. 'Light please, Dennis.'

The budgerigar breathed fire from his puny beak. It was just enough to see the padlock, a solid, wrought-iron goblin lock. Only a master locksmith could get into the duel-barrel broken-pin system. The faint sound of whinnying horses came from behind the wooden door. Bernice jiggled her picking tools with both hands, stuck them into the padlock, pausing as she found the balance. The lock snapped open.

Randall stood back, nodding in reluctant admiration. The way she'd slid it out silently, cradling the delicate metal in her hands, deftly moving it between her fingers, manipulating the barrels...

Randall shook his head: *No, no, no, no. Absolutely not. No way. Not at all. She's dwarven. And a rogue. That's a bad combination in itself. Nope, nopeity nope.*

But she's blonde. And she can pick a lock like Grandma Quilty the Quickfingered.

Shut up brain.

Man, dwarf and bird sidled into the stables. Randall headed straight for an enormous black stallion, calming its nose as he approached. 'Here you go boy, that's right. Strong horse you are.' The rogue took the horse by the reins and guided him out of the stables.

Bernice opened a second gate, where a tawny mare with a white forehead nuzzled into her beard. Bernice whispered to it as she buckled the saddle and adjusted the stirrups to her height. Randall stared at Bernice, her beard illuminated by the dull glow of the budgerigar's magic.

His mind roiled with thoughts of lock picks and sliding barrels, although his lock pick was temporarily snapped. When he noticed Bernice staring back, he quickly busied himself with the last of the tack and led the horse out. Bernice followed, Dennis perched on her head.

They mounted the horses and kicked them forward into a canter. Randall looked behind for any sign of alarm, but only the faint sound of snoring echoed in the night. The hooves clipped on the cobblestones.

After riding down the road for a few minutes, Randall said, 'By the way, nice work back there with the lock. Not many people learn the Klavieri technique these days.'

Bernice looked at him in disbelief. 'Randall the Rogue, are you trying to give me a compliment?'

'Don't let it get to your beard.'

They raced through the night, using the cover of darkness to put distance between them and their illicit deeds. Dawn rose over the horseway, an insipid sunrise promising overcast clouds and mild to moderately cool weather. Dennis snored in Bernice's hair.

Up ahead, a long stone bridge crossed the Joglamash River and marked the road towards Yer-Bogswill. The horseway patrol checked registration papers next to a metal sign: *Don't Drink and Ride.* The adventurers clopped into the queue, behind a banked-up trail of wagons entering Yer-Bogswill for the morning market.

As they got closer, the horses whickered to each other. Bernice patted the tawny mare. 'What are we going to do when they ask for our papers?'

Randall grinned. 'Don't worry about that, I'll talk our way through the gates.'

They were nearly at the front of the horseway queue. Dennis cleared his beak. 'Whatever your plan is, you better be ready...'

A horseway patrolman inspected their horses. He wore the traditional uniform of a green doublet with the insignia of a pony emblazoned in black and silver, riding helmet and dark sun spectacles.

'Registration papers?' asked the guard.

Randall looked around nervously. 'Funny you should mention that. There was a guy...'

Bernice gripped the reigns tightly. Dennis dug his claws into her shoulder guard.

'A guy?' said the horse guard, lowering his sun spectacles.

'A guy, yes. He stole my horse registration papers. Back at the *Socks and Sandals Inn.*'

'If he stole your registration papers, why didn't he steal your horse?'

'Insurance scam. Happens all the time. Don't know what the world is coming to.'

The horseway guard motioned to his superior officer, a tall expanse of a man wearing plate mail. 'Says someone *stole* his registration papers.'

The superior looked over the black stallion, the dwarf on a horse and the blue budgerigar on her shoulder. Bernice smiled at him. He smiled back, a straight kind of smile that only authority figures know, keeping the ends of his mouth turned up while the rest of the lips formed a straight line, which is not really a smile at all. More of a grimace. 'These horses match the description of two stolen from Pidderill last night.'

Randall pulled the reigns tight and broke into a gallop, dodging the log obstacles on the bridge to Yer Bogswill. Bernice followed behind, jumping the barricade. Three horse guards leapt into their saddles, to give chase.

Randall leaned close to his horse, urging it faster across the bridge. Bernice side-swiped a guard who stumbled backwards over the bridge's low barriers into the churning Joglamash below. She fletched an arrow, turned backwards and sent it flying to the hooves of the horse behind her. It reared up, causing the second guard to fall off onto hard stone.

Up ahead, they rode into the inevitable traffic that jammed at the Yer-Bogswill exit, the last horse guard in rapid pursuit. Randall narrowly missed an oblivious manure cart driver by seconds. He flicked the cart's securing rope with his sword as Bernice passed him, the cart leaving a pile of steaming poop on the bridge. The guard dodged the dung, but it slowed him down enough for them to get further through the crowded exit.

'The trail to Des Pair must be around here somewhere,' shouted Bernice, dodging between a slow lane cart and a family of four in a caravan. Dennis flew up above the traffic. 'Over there,' he chirped, directing them with his wing. He flew towards the barrier on the left of the bridge. The wall dropped steeply towards the river, where a wooded trail inched towards the mountains.

'It's time to get off this horseway! The traffic's terrible anyway,' shouted Randall. They dismounted the horses. Randall jumped the barrier and clambered down the rocky escarpment. Bernice followed behind, scrabbling through the scree to join him at the base of the bridge's supports. Guards shouted down at them from the bridge. Bernice pulled a small leather ball with a fuse from her utility belt and held it up to Dennis. 'Do the honours?' said Bernice.

Dennis blew a bright flame from his beak, lighting the fuse. Bernice threw the grenade straight at the guards. They ducked as smoke exploded over the bridge.

'Come on,' she said. 'Before it dissipates.'

They ran north into the forest, finding a single worn trail meandering along the riverside. Twisted oak trees pushed their roots into the path, flush with the broken sticks and leaves of autumn. Birds cawed in trees in the desolate environment. They slowed down and settled into a quiet, rhythmic march.

The biggest problem with questing was not the deadly hordes of skeletons, nor the egotistical mages, not even the occasional nesting cephalopod in large bodies of water.

It was the hiking.

In the legends of Sidarth, nobody ever mentioned how much bloody hiking they did to cross the continent. The bards had a lot to answer for. Questing, when it came down to it, was boring.

And Randall the Rogue was not a man with a long attention span, unless there was a blonde half-elf involved.

'So, what are we going to talk about, Bernice? Benefits of leather armour versus steel? Price of sardines in coastal regions?' he said, dawdling through the forest.

'I prefer to walk in silence, thank you,' she said.

'I'm up for a chat,' said Dennis, flitting onto Randall's shoulder.

'I don't want to talk to you. You can't talk about armour or sardines.'

'Yes I can! You prefer leather for its supple lightness and superior flexibility. And sardines cost much less in the southern isles.'

Randall ignored Dennis and picked up a long stick. Over the next three hours, he proceeded to whack grass and trees, hum tunes from the Battle of the Bards and flick his fingernails until Bernice punched him in the arm.

'You are driving me insane,' she said.

'Questing is boring,' he said. 'We've been walking along this track for hours, without a sign of a deadly ambush. If I wanted to go hiking, I could have done that at home.'

'Where's home?'

'My family's all from the capital, Racksalon. Born and bred. But at heart I'm a wanderer, a dark horse, a lone soul on this narrow road, not tied down to anything, free as a bird.'

Dennis squawked in indignation. 'I'm not free. If I was free, I wouldn't be here.'

'You don't want to settle down, have a family?' she said.

'Become a career rogue? Never.' Randall recoiled at the thought.

'Don't you get lonely being on the road all the time?' she asked. 'Never having a place to call home?'

Randall looked out towards the river, where two cranes scooted across the breaking water. 'Nah. I've got Dennis for company.'

'He just hasn't found the right bird yet,' said Dennis, nudging Bernice.

Randall ignored his familiar's sad attempt at fixing him a date. 'Which mountain are you from?'

'Actually, my family are woodland dwarves. Much different to our mountainous cousins. We've got better eyesight.'

The trees beside them rustled ominously. The long awaited deadly ambush! Randall pulled his sword from its sheath; Bernice notched an arrow. A six-foot blonde half-elf emerged from the woodland, wearing a chain mail bikini and gold high-heeled sandals. Randall fully appreciated the half-elf's sylvan form.

Bernice glared.

'Are you Randall the Rogue?' asked the elf.

'Yeeeees?' said Randall. 'And who might you be?'

'I am Sel'am'a'rafi'aa D'argent'inium'm'm.'

'That's a lot of apostrophes for one name. How do you like Rafi?'

Bernice eyeballed the apostrophic woman. 'Can we talk?' she said to Randall. Bernice turned her back to the elf and pulled Randall down to her ear level. He could feel her breath on his skin, the faint scent of pine trees from her hair. He felt a rush through his body. He couldn't be attracted to the bearded dwarf, when a half-elf was standing right there. Never.

'I don't trust her,' said the dwarf.

'Why not? She's beautiful. And we all know, beautiful people are trustworthy people.'

'You have a weakness for blondes,' said Bernice.

'You're blonde and I'm not even mildly attracted to you.'

'Don't tell me you haven't thought about it.'

'Never. Not one tiny iota of thought about what it would be like to kiss a woman with a beard. Let alone what it would be like to, you know, with a dwarf.'

Bernice raised an eyebrow. 'Not one tiny iota of a thought? It doesn't matter anyway; you'd need 15 baths before I'd even think about touching you.'

'Only 15? Well I'd better get to an inn.'

The blonde half-elf stood watching their exchange. 'I am waiting,' she said, tapping a sandalled foot.

The half-elf sidled up to Randall as Bernice gave her a death stare. Randall flicked his best eyebrow up and said, 'Weren't you the half-elf at the Socks and Sandals Inn yesterday?'

Rafi took Randall's arm firmly and whispered in his ear. 'I need to speak with you *privately*.' A lot of women wanted to talk to him today. He'd found that when women wanted to talk, it usually had very good or very bad consequences. Never a middling thing, women wanting to *talk*. He gulped. 'Must go, she wants a private audience. Toodleoo.'

Randall walked deeper into the forest with the blinging half-elf, leaving Dennis and Bernice on the trail. The elf stopped in a grove of shedding pine trees, which would have been romantic, had the season not decimated the branches of the trees, leaving the grove with an altogether creepy feel. A lone picnic table sat next to a disused fire-pit.

'Just so you know,' said Randall, 'I'm inconvenienced by a slight illness and I've been advised to avoid convivial relations.'

Rafi turned and looked at him quizzically. 'I'm not here for – what is it you humans call it? Convivial relations? I have tracked the dwarf for days. There is a bounty on her head for stealing the entire loot from a quest to the Kraven Underworld.'

'Really?' he said, not paying attention to anything the woman said but rather the cut of her chain mail bikini.

'Are you listening to me? I am retrieving the criminal known as Bernice the Breaker. She's dangerous.'

'You're dangerous.' He wiggled his eyebrows at her.

Rafi sighed, in the way only the elvish can make sighing seem like the winds of the forest. She turned to leave the grove but Bernice blocked the way with her bow, ready to shoot. Rafi pushed past Randall, pulling a golden sword from her sheath.

'We were having a private conversation. It doesn't include you, woodland scum,' said Rafi.

'There's no privacy in the forest, honey,' said Bernice. 'You elves have gotten lazy with your carved homes, magic leaf juice and gourmet fairy bread. Try living in the actual wilderness for a day, then you'd know the true heirs of the forest.'

Randall weighed up his options. Two women fighting in the forest, one in a chain mail bikini. It might get bloody. He stepped behind Rafi before making his next point.

'Umm, Bernice,' said Randall. 'Rafi thinks there might be a problem with your last quest. Something about making off with all the loot?'

'And? We're rogues.'

He thought about this for a moment. It was a fair point, that stealing other people's post-quest loot was perfectly acceptable in the rules of rogues, and quite frankly, the questing party should have been aware of Clause Seventeen of the Rogues Code. Randall turned back to Rafi. 'She's got a point. I'd probably do the same thing. So I'm not judging anyone, otherwise it's a bit of pot calling kettle black.'

The women glared at each other and circled around the grove, weapons ready. Randall and Dennis cozied up on a rock to watch the unfurling battle.

Bernice released the arrow, narrowly missing the half-elf, who commando rolled as it whistled past her ear. The dwarf jumped on the tabletop in one swift move, loading another arrow. Rafi swiped at her feet, but Bernice jumped the slicing blade.

'Go Dwarves!' cheered Randall from the sidelines.

'A little help, Randall?' shouted Bernice, narrowly ducking another slice from the golden blade.

'I'm a pacifist when it comes to women-on-women fighting. It wouldn't be fair if I joined the battle now, would it?' He sat there and scratched his balls.

'I'll help you!' shouted Dennis, and flew into the fray. The Budgerigar of Doom swooped Rafi, breathing fire from his beak, like a flying fluid lighter. Rafi swatted Dennis to the ground. The distraction gave Bernice enough time to swap weapons and pull the dagger from her belt.

She passed the blade from hand to hand, following the movements of the half-elf. When Rafi lunged with her golden sword, Bernice jumped forwards off the table, grabbing Rafi's head in a lock and slamming her back to the ground. In one movement, she thrust the dagger between Rafi's protruding breasts.

Bernice stood, body drenched in the green blood of the half-elf. Rafi's body splayed next to the picnic table, dead.

'And that's why you don't wear a chain mail bikini on a quest,' said Bernice, wiping the green blood from her beard with her sleeve. Randall stared at the dead half-elf.

'She's got really nice armour. Seems a pity to leave it here.'

'I'm not wearing that,' said Bernice, still dripping with blood.

'Don't you ever need a change of clothes?'

'Look Randall, I've just killed a half-elf, I'm covered in her blood and I haven't eaten all day. Do you really, really want to push me right now?' She pointed her dagger towards Randall.

He raised his hand to speak, then thought better of it. Bernice stalked off towards the river, her eyes bright and fuming.

Dennis swooped onto Randall's shoulder. 'She's in a foul mood and no wonder. Look at you sitting around scratching your balls while she does all the dirty work of getting rid of that rude half-elf. Mate, I know you've got family expectations to live up to, but there's a fine line between charming rogue and douchebag, and you just crossed it.'

But Randall wasn't listening to his familiar. He watched Bernice clean her dagger on the edge of her green cloak, her face sprayed with elvish blood. She looked up at him, with a furious gaze that made him want to be a better rogue.

'She's glorious,' he whispered.

Late in the afternoon, they turned inland along the trail, walking through a gorge towards a series of high hills. Bernice stalked ahead, blatantly ignoring any attempts Randall made to chat about the weather, non-combative uses of ice arrows and the price of eggs in Racksalon.

As the trail opened up, they stood in front of a cliff carved with a thousand dancing skeletons, twisting their bones in shapes which could have been torture or a chiropractic appointment. At the centre was the largest skull, etched deep into the wall, a thin groove around its edges. Randall stared in wonder at the secrets hidden deep in the wilds of Sidarth.

Bernice glared at Randall, who sheepishly returned her gaze. He tried to say sorry with his eyes, but a non-verbal apology can often be confused with constipation.

Dennis, designated peacemaker, said, 'I don't reckon we should hit up the Valley of the Deadish at night. What say we camp here?'

Bernice swung her rucksack onto the ground and laid her blanket on a clear spot. Dennis found an abandoned nest in a tree fork and curled up for the night, his tiny snores soon echoing off the skeletal wall. In awkward silence, Bernice and Randall collected wood for a fire, crunching through the undergrowth until sunset. He made a base out of brush then piled sticks into a pyramid on top.

'Let me,' said Bernice, pulling a flint from her bag. She struck a spark into the brush. Within minutes, the fire burned orange and they warmed themselves in the cool evening air.

Randall wrung his hands. 'Look, about before. I was a jerk. I should've helped you fight. We're part of a team. I'm used to being a lone operator, just me and the bird. It's different having someone along who understands what it's like being a rogue.'

Bernice pursed her lips and nodded, taking in his little speech without saying a thing. Randall continued. 'I know you're still angry with me about the half-elf thing. So I'm going to make it up to you. Dinner's on me.' He held up a bag of freeze-dried brown cubes. 'Guaranteed questing quality stew cubes. Beef, vegie, rat, seaweed, leaf and my favourite, undisclosed meat flavour.' He took out a cooking pot from his satchel, collected water from the gorge and began boiling up undisclosed meat stew. When it was ready, he dished it out into two wooden bowls.

After a few bites, Bernice began to speak.

'Look, I'm not angry any more. Being a woodland dwarf, I really hate those half-elves.'

'So I'm not the only one with a racial bias?' said Randall.

'No, my bias is based in fact, whereas your hatred against dwarves stems from ignorance.'

He looked into the depths of his stew, wondering what sort of meat it was that tasted so good. He tried to resist scratching his sword and spoiling the mood. Nothing says romance like a dirty rogue with a carnally transmitted infection.

'I don't hate dwarves anymore,' said Randall.

She smiled at him, and it was the most incredible thing he'd ever seen, a great beaming smile across the fire. 'Really? You're not just making fun?'

'No. Turns out there's a lot of things I don't know about dwarves. You still like gold right?'

'Do dwarves like gold? Gold is our god, Randall. Gold is everything.'

'That one's true. But I've been doing a lot of cross-cultural communication in the last few days and I feel that I may have been slightly prejudiced against your kind based on appearance. So, I'm wondering... have you learned anything about me? Interesting facts? Things you'd like to clarify? Questions about my hygiene? Scratch that. Or don't scratch that, no questions about hygiene at this present time.'

She laughed. 'You're not what I expected from the stories they tell about you.'

'What kind of things do they say about me? And should I kill them?'

'No, not at all. You've got a reputation for taking rogueing seriously. People know you're aiming for legendary status. Word gets about. Your mum's very proud.'

'Dennis, did you hear that? Mum's proud of me!' he shouted. The bird snorted in his sleep. 'But still, if she's been talking, I'll need to kill her at some point.'

'I just didn't expect you to be so... *funny*!'

He cursed himself. *Funny! Is that what she thinks of me? I'm just some funny guy? I'll show her how a true rogue rogues when we hit those skeletons.*

Soon after, they both curled to separate sides of the fire, his thoughts running to bearded women and how the itching in his groin had forced him to get to know a woman for the first time in his life.

He wished she'd taken that chain mail bikini... Oh no. He didn't want to go there.

The next morning, Randall spent an hour excommunicating the remains of his dubious dinner. After his bowels had completely emptied, he wiped his bottom on a leaf and rejoined the party.

They packed up camp and walked to the skull rock. The empty granite eyes leered at them, almost challenging the adventurers to come into the valley.

Dennis flitted up to the wall, pecking it with his beak. 'What did the guidebook say? Put your fingers in the eyes, nose and mouth and press hard.'

'I'll take the eyes,' said Randall. 'You get the mouth, Bernice.'

'And the nose?' asked Dennis. 'Yep, leave the snotty job to the familiar.' He flew into the nasal cavity. 'Ek, there's rock slime in here.'

'On three, we push hard. One, two, three.' They pushed. Nothing happened. Dennis emerged from the nose, covered in rock slime. 'I'm just not big enough,' said Dennis, panting through his beak. 'You'll have to stick your feet up there.'

'If we do one foot each,' said Bernice, 'That should be enough to open the door.'

Randall reluctantly slid his foot into the left nasal cavity, while Bernice stuck her right foot into the other side of the nose.

'One, two, three!' shouted Randall.

The door rolled back on metal rods into the rock face. Bernice and Randall's feet stuck in the nose holes and they fell onto their backs beside each other. Randall could smell the pine scent in her beard. It must have been dwarvish shampoo. He made a mental note to ask her where she bought it. Then he erased the note from his mental notebook. She was making him want to bathe! What sort of woman inspires a rogue to bathe?

He wasn't sure if the warmth in his chest was a result of his carnal illness or something else. Was he falling in love with a dwarf? He cursed her, then regretted it because she smelled so... he couldn't think it. Dwarves were the ones at school who bullied him. Who called him fatty fat fart from farty fat. They were not for falling in love with.

Randall jumped up. It was time to impress Bernice. 'Unsheath your swords my friends, for we are entering the Valley of the Deadish.' He pulled his sword from his sheath (not the itchy one) and sallied forth into the valley. Dennis flew high, monitoring for any skeletal activity.

They dodged a pit trap which had been disarmed and replaced with spinning circular ornaments covered in mirrors. As they passed a large cave, Randall brushed a flag that read 'Partay this way' hanging off a former trip wire. 'Why are all these traps disarmed?' asked Randall.

'Could be a trick to lure us in?' said Dennis. 'Be on your guard.'

But all they could hear was the faint hum of music echoing on the vertical rock walls. Their weapons and conviction hovered between alert and not-so-dangerous-but-could-be-a-trick. The music, now audible as doof-doof dance music, bashed out a thumping beat.

Armed and ready for battle, they entered a narrow canyon. The end of the passage opened into a large grotto, where numerous animated skeletons congregated in floral shirts and board shorts. Some of them were possibly dancing, although equally it could have been a necromantic ritual to summon hordes of the undead. When the DJ looked up from spinning rough tunes on two stone wheels, he saw them and stopped the music. 'Humans!' he shouted 'Get that smell out of here. I can't work in these conditions.'

Despite the unfamiliarity of their reaction (skeletons were meant to run blindly towards you with disregard for their death, right? That's what it said in Steve the Stealthy's *Guide to Rogueing: the definitive edition*), Randall held his sword aloft and shouted, 'We have come for the Whisper of the Valley! Are you ready to fight?' Bernice pulled the string tight on her bow. Dennis tried to look menacing and puffed out a little breath of fire.

A nearby skeleton turned to Randall, holding an empty glass with a parasol in it.

'Urgh, no, why would we fight you? We're trying to change the image of Deadish tourism. Less skeleton slaying, more relaxed atmosphere. You can get Whisper of the Valley at the bar.' She flicked her skeletal hand to shoo them away.

'You don't even want to skirmish a little?' said Randall, slightly disappointed. The skeleton pushed the sword point away from her body, as if it were a dirty tissue.

'Um totes no. Think of what that sword would do to my skeleton. Piercings are so out right now.'

Randall, frustrated, looked for something to stab. Bernice wouldn't think of him as more than a *funny* guy if he didn't show off his prowess with his sword. And he was so good with a sword.

'I just want to fight some bloody skeletons. It's not going to be a good story if we don't fight some skeletons,' he said. The relaxed skeleton scratched her skull with a bony finger.

'How about you say you fought us when you get back home? That's no skin off our backs.' The other skeletons chortled.

Bernice and Randall sheathed their weapons in disappointment. He liked it better when the skeletons weren't co-owners of a skele-trash resort.

'Fine. We'll be at the bar then,' said Randall.

'Amazeballs. Just don't stink out the place with your life scent, okay?'

Bernice hopped up on the barstool. Dennis rolled on the cold stone bar, pretending to be dead. Randall collapsed on the chair, too tired to take up regulation rogue drinking posture, and called over the waiter. 'We need as much Whisper of the Valley as you have.'

The bartender handed over three leaves of a grey, waxy plant.

'Three leaves. Three stinking leaves. How much?' he asked the waiter.

'They're ten kruds each sir.' Randall parted with three silver kruds and slipped the leaves into his bag.

Bernice laid her forehead on the bar. 'I give up. There was no point to this quest, except 30 kruds worth of stinking leaves. No loot. No rewards. Nada.'

'I did say you could have the chain mail bikini, but you didn't want it. All in all, I think this has been a positive experience.'

'Of course,' she said, looking up from her bar pillow. 'You get what you want out of it. I get nothing.'

'Didn't we agree that you could have 30%? So technically you're entitled to one of these leaves,' he said, handing her a leaf. 'Anyway, don't you have loot left from that quest to the Kraven Underworld?'

'That's not the point. The point is, I want more loot, and I want the loot I was promised.'

'How about I buy you a drink and this'll all be better.' Randall raised his hand at the bartender wearing an apron over his skeletal remains. 'Do you have any beverages of the alcoholic variety?'

The skeleton placed two bottles of red wine on the counter. 'That'll be 50 kruds.'

Randall opened his now empty wallet. Bernice rolled her eyes. 'I thought you were going to buy me a drink?'

'I have put my own personal payment on hold so that you could share in this loot.'

She reached into her coinpurse and exchanged a gold krud for the wine.

'Do you know if there's a place we can rest up?' said Bernice.

'Nuh-uh, no can do. We can't have human scent on all the rock furnishings, can we? I'll tell you what. There's a nice cave near the valley entrance. Feel free to stay there. We get a lot of adventurers this way, looking for Whisper of the Valley. What do you use it for?'

'Secret human business that skeletons wouldn't understand,' said Randall, taking the other bottle of wine. They left the way they came in, just as the DJ launched into an epic mix of *I Met My Girl in Racksalon City,* and backtracked to the cave, shoulders and feathers drooping.

'I've got to do something,' said Randall, taking the Whisper of the Valley into the ferns. Dennis hopped on his shoulder. 'Want to come and watch?' said Randall.

'I've seen worse. No, I wanted to have a word.' He waited until they were nestled in the ferns next to a small creek. Randall took out the apothecary's salve and mixed in one of the leaves. It dissolved, turning green and sparkly.

'I have to talk to you about Bernice. She's nice, Randall. Why don't you ask her on a date when this is all done? She's the sort of rogue your mother would love,' said Dennis.

Randall turned to his familiar. 'She's got a beard.'

'I'll guarantee she doesn't have a carnally transmitted infection. I've seen the way you look at her.'

'Me? Look at her? Never.'

'Mate, it's obvious. You've never had a woman that could keep up with you, and now you've found one. Sure she's got a beard. Sure she's a dwarf. But if I found the love of my life and she was an albatross, would I let it stop me from experiencing true happiness? No. Go ask her out.'

'Maybe I will,' he nodded. 'You don't think people would think that's weird, you know, a human and a dwarf, together?'

'Love is an unstoppable force, my friend.'

'So's a carnal infection. Speaking of infections, can you please give me a modicum of privacy while I, you know?'

'Oh, sorry.' Dennis flew further up the valley.

Ten minutes later, an itch-free Randall the Rogue decided to tell Bernice how he felt.

They sat on the cave rocks with a bottle of wine each, amid the ferns and the faint sound of dance music, and clinked the bottles together. 'Here's to a successful adventure.' Randall smiled at Bernice. The grey palette of the morning valley made her blue eyes sparkle.

She chugged the wine and wiped her mouth on her sleeve. Randall sipped silently, thinking about how he would tell her. What would he tell her? He had feelings for her. Deep, mysterious feelings of a kind he'd never felt before. And it wasn't the carnally transmitted illness speaking.

After three quarters of a bottle, Randall felt sufficiently soused to start on his soliloquy. He took a deep breath.

And didn't say anything.

Bernice tipped her head to one side, examining Randall. 'You look like you want to say something. I bet the first thing you'll do now is start wenching again,' said Bernice, looking sadly at her empty bottle.

'Well,' said Randall, 'I'm thinking about giving it all up. Settle down and become a career rogue.'

Bernice's eyes grew wide. 'You can't do that!'

'Why not? I'm not enjoying rogueing anymore. Once you've stolen from half the kings of Sidarth there's no challenge. Most of the women I've slept with don't care about me,' he slurred. 'All they want is a bit of this body, then off they go.' He pulled his shirt over his head, revealing his ripped chest. Bernice tried to look elsewhere, but he reclined in the cave, sculling the wine.

She sighed and smiled. 'The fact is, I wanted to come on this quest because of you. You're legendary. Everyone talks about you at College. I've wanted to meet you since I heard about your exploits with the Golem of Ganadia.'

'Ah, the Golem of Ganadia. Those were good times. I really wish you'd been there.'

He took another swig from the bottle. Upon realising it was empty, he threw it down to the cave entrance. This was his chance. Shirtless, smelly and drunk, he prepared to declare his love.

'I used to hate dwarves,' he said. A good start.

'Not that again! I've heard enough of your dwarf-bashing for one quest,' said Bernice.

'I hated dwarves because they bullied me in school. Do you know what they called me?'

She shook her head.

'They called me fatty fat fart from farty fat. All the time. And I was fat. But they didn't have to say that,' he drawled. 'And then you came along, with your bow and arrow, and you got me right here.' He tried to point to his heart, but his drunk hand pointed off to his left shoulder.

She looked up at him, eyes wide. 'What?'

'I've never met a woman like you. You steal horses. You fight half-elves.

You get along with Dennis, and I think most of all, my mum would really like you which is saying something because she's never liked any of my girlfriends.'

'So,' said Bernice the Breaker, shuffling closer towards him, her dwarven armour making it awkward to move in any seductive direction.

'So,' said Randall the Rogue.

He reached out and stroked her plaited beard. It was unexpectedly soft. He smiled a sheepish grin and took her by the hand, so small in his long fingers.

'Now that I'm cured and all, do you think, would you? I mean, could we?'

She grabbed his face and pulled him into her embrace.

After a day and night of passionate convivial relations, in which he came to understand why Bernice was called the Breaker, Randall the Rogue woke to find his clothes missing, the remaining Whisper of the Valley stolen and Dennis tied up with wool in a nearby bush. Dennis squawked as he came free. 'What did you say at the start of this bloody quest? Never quest with another rogue, they'll steal your heart then steal your clothes.'

But Randall stood up, buck naked in the Valley of the Deadish and proclaimed, 'I'm in love.'

Just then, his groin began to itch.

SOPHIE MASSON

The Romanov Opal

The world, my father used to say, is divided into three types of people: those who run and hide when fate comes knocking, those who slam the door in its face, and those who open the door wide and welcome it into their lives.

Dad was a man of strong opinions and easily-hurt feelings, a combustible combination. So I never had the heart to tell him there is another way to deal with fate's meddling: and that is to outwit it. To be always ready, to be one step ahead and trick fate out of coming to your door in the first place. It was how I'd lived my whole life. And it had worked for me. Outwitted, outgunned, outfoxed, fate had left me alone to live my life exactly as I wanted it, as I'd planned it to be ever since my chaotic childhood left in me the profound desire to be ordinary, unnoticed, and in control.

Long success at staying under the radar had perhaps made me complacent. Or perhaps it was a simple matter of being ambushed by memory. Whatever it was, the appearance of my twin sister Amy in my bookshop that bright

Sydney winter's morning caught me quite off-balance, so that for a moment I lost my advantage, and fate, that demon goddess, had her chance.

I hadn't seen Amy for years. Correction, I hadn't seen Amy *in the flesh* for years. But like hundreds of thousands of others, I saw her frequently in the pages of newspapers and magazines and heard her voice on radio programs. Her books recounting her thrilling adventures in remote and dangerous places were bestsellers, of course, but it wasn't just that. Beautiful, smart, and brash, with a string of love affairs behind her which, in their own way, were as spectacular as her close encounters with lions, bandits and mountain storms, Amy was a headline-writer's dream. She was as famous as any film star, only more beloved, and generally referred to by her first name, as if she were a part of every reader's family.

Her real family however, wasn't quite as close – but that's another story, for a little later. For the moment, here was Amy, coming into my shop, Fate in white Capri pants and turquoise twinset. She gave me a little wry smile. 'Good morning, Andy.'

I looked around for cameras, reporters, fans, the usual tralala that swept along in Amy's wake. Either they were very good at hiding, or there weren't any. 'I'm Drew now,' I pointed out, struggling to maintain my composure.

She raised an eyebrow. 'Yes. That's why it took me a while to find you.' Lightly, she traced the name on my door with pearl-painted fingernails. 'Drew Sandon, Bookseller. You're using Mum's surname,' she observed. There was a question in her voice which I chose not to answer, knowing from childhood experience just how she could tie me up in defensive knots. She was the elder of us two by only a few seconds but those few heartbeats of time meant everything as far as our relationship was concerned. And of course also in terms of the life of our mother, whom neither of us remembered meeting, for she'd died moments after I drew breath.

'I'm sure you could have found me any time you chose to,' I retorted. 'Why are you here, Amy?'

'To see you, of course.'

'There's no *of course* about it,' I shrugged.

'Aren't you the least bit glad to see me?' she said, her big green eyes misting over, on cue.

'I never said I wasn't,' I said tightly, 'but it's a surprise.'

'So is life,' she murmured.

'Not mine. And I prefer it that way. So, why are you really here?'

She smiled. 'To give you a job.'

'I have one. I'm a bookseller. As you see.'

'This?' A contemptuous gesture of her hand swept around the shop, taking in the tottering but neatly-arranged shelves, the dusty table of special editions, the cluttered front desk.

'You're a writer, I'm a bookseller,' I observed. 'Without bookshops, books can hardly get out into the world. Shouldn't you respect that?'

'No book here will get out into the world, ' she snapped. 'This is where old books come to die. Besides, this isn't a job, it's a mask. A disguise. '

Our eyes met. I shrugged and said, 'I have no idea what you mean.'

'Come on, Andy. This is me, remember?'

'Forgive me if I don't,' I shot back. 'We've hardly been in each other's pockets the last few years, after all.'

Mistake. I knew that as soon as the words left my lips. Amy's a word girl as much as she's Lady Action. She laughed. 'True enough, the pockets you've been in are not mine. '

'If you've got something to say,' I snapped, trying to ignore the thudding of my heart, 'then say it plainly and stop talking in riddles. Or else go back to your life and leave me to mine. '

'Very well. May I sit down?'

'Be my guest,' I said. As we faced each other across the desk, I was suddenly reminded of all those times when as primary school kids we had laboured over our homework at the single desk Dad had installed in the living-room. He was a keen one for homework, the old Dad. Keener even than our teacher, the fearsome and misnamed Miss Sweet. And that was saying something. A feeling came over me then that wasn't nostalgia, not exactly. But close enough that it made me say, in a softer tone, 'All right. I'm listening.'

She leaned forward and looked earnestly at me. 'We need your help to find something very important, which you—'

'Whoa, stop right there. Who's *we*? '

'Did I say we? Okay, so I did,' she corrected, hastily, seeing my expression. 'Slip of the tongue, I'm afraid. I need you to help me find something very imp—'

'Yes, yes, I remember the rest,' I said impatiently. 'I'm not going to listen to any more unless you tell me plainly what this so very important thing is.'

She gave me a strange look. 'You're not going to like it.'

'I'm sure I'm not, but I have to know anyway. Spit it out.'

'It's a jewel, ' she said. 'A very special jewel. The Romanov Opal.'

I stared at her. After a moment, I said, 'It's a legend. It doesn't exist.'

'It isn't. And it does. It's as real as this desk,' she said, rapping the wood. 'And more real than that sign on your door.'

The Romanov Opal! I'd heard the story, of course. It went something like this: Sometime in the final year or two of her imperial husband's reign, the last Tsarina of Russia, Alexandra, had been given a magnificent Fabergé pendant made from a single, huge, flawless black opal, one of the rarest gemstones on earth which is found only in Lightning Ridge, in the Australian outback.

The Romanov ladies were fond of opals but this one was particularly fine, exotic, and worth a king's ransom. But sometime during the period when the poor doomed Romanovs were sent to their exile and deaths in the faraway Urals, the opal had disappeared. It was not among the jewels looted by the Bolsheviks from the belongings of the murdered imperial family and their servants, and it was not to be found anywhere else at all. It had completely vanished from sight. If indeed it had ever existed.

'Well, I suppose in your line of work it's good policy to believe or pretend to believe in six impossible things before breakfast, ' I said, feigning indifference.

Amy didn't even take offence at that, which should have rung alarm bells in me. And indeed it did, but what is the good of alarm bells when the danger's already upon you?

'Just listen, Andy. You can make up your mind when you've heard it all. It was thought by all parties that the Romanov Opal was gone for good, lost somewhere in the maelstrom of the Bolshevik Revolution but very recently news reached us that it has resurfaced. And not in Russia, either, but right here in Australia.' She paused dramatically. 'I assume you've heard of the Petrov Affair. '

I raised an eyebrow. 'Don't tell me. Mrs Petrov had hidden the opal in her coat pocket. That's really why the Soviets wanted her back.'

The dramatic scenes at Darwin Airport, with Evdokia Petrova, the wife of the defecting Russian spy Vladimir Petrov, being the subject of a tug of war between KGB goons and ASIO goons, had been in every paper for days. And that was only two weeks ago. Since then, the Petrovs had vanished, spirited away no doubt into some remote hidey-hole out of sight of avenging Soviet hit squads.

'Don't be facetious, Andy. It doesn't suit you.'

'How do you know what suits me, Amy? You've never taken the trouble to–'

Oh dear! I could hear myself whining. 'Okay,' I growled, catching myself almost in time, 'so you're saying the Petrovs gave the low-down not just on a ring of spies in Australia but also on the whereabouts of a legendary jewel that may or not exist. A very likely story – for a pulp fiction thriller, that is. I didn't know you'd switched to writing them.'

'Who said anything about the Petrovs knowing anything about the opal?' Amy said, sounding genuinely startled.

'You said…' I began, then gave up. 'All right. Tell me. I can see I won't be left in peace until you tell it all.'

'I only mentioned the Petrov Affair because it's something everyone's heard about. It's big and splashy and noisy. But quieter things happen, quieter people disappear without fanfare. What if, in the middle of the uproar, when all the Soviet security people were looking the other way, someone else took the opportunity to slip out through the exit door? '

I smiled. 'You mean, another Russian defector. But a secret one.'

'Not exactly. Maybe something a little more complicated.'

'Can't see what's more complicated than a secret defector,' I muttered, before realising that wasn't the point at all and that my unease was due to more than her sudden re-appearance in my life. 'How on earth do you know all this, anyway?'

'I get around. I hear things,' she said, airily. She looked at me. 'A bit like you, in fact.'

Our eyes met. I could see she wasn't telling the whole truth, but I had my own reasons not to press the matter. 'All right,' I said. 'So let's say that in your getting around and hearing things, you have learned that this mysterious runaway Russian has something to do with the lost Romanov Opal.'

She nodded.

'He either has it on him or he's looking for it.'

'The latter.'

'And you want me to find it before he does.'

'I want you to help *me* find it,' she corrected.

'Why? Why do you want to find it? And why ask me?'

'In answer to your first question,' she said, calmly, 'the Romanov Opal needs to be restored to its rightful owner.'

'But the Tsarina's long dead, and all her family.' I saw her expression. 'Don't tell me. You're one of those believers in the Anastasia thing. You think she's still alive?'

'I never said that. In fact I am pretty much certain she did not survive. But there are other Romanovs, you know.' Another of those dramatic pauses. 'And one of them, in fact one of the closest living blood relatives of the Tsar, is living right here in Sydney and working as an aircraft mechanic. '

I laughed. 'Go on, pull the other one!'

'It's quite true,' she snapped.

'Okay. Let's say you want to restore the Romanov Opal – in a blaze of publicity no doubt – to this exiled Russian prince. I get that for you it would be a coup. But why don't you go about it in your usual way? I haven't heard any announcement of your latest quest in the papers.'

'For good reason. They don't know. And neither do I want them to know.'

'Ah. I see. All the better to spring the surprise at the end. Maximum effect.'

'You really don't think much of me, Andy, do you?' she said. For the first time there was a hint of sadness in her voice.

'It's not that. We haven't seen each other in years,' I mumbled. 'And then you come waltzing in and expect me to just...' I paused. 'Anyway, you still haven't told me why you've come to me.'

'Two reasons. One, you are good at what you do—'

'Selling books? I hardly think that's a qualification for—'

'Come on, Andy.' The hint of sadness had gone from her voice. 'Stop it. I *know.* And you know I know. So let's cut to the chase, shall we? You're good at what you do. And second, well, remember the Talbot Twins, Inc.?'

'How could I forget?' I said. When we were around ten or so, we'd started a detective club. We called it the Talbot Twins, naturally, after us. And naturally, Amy was its guiding light. I was the assistant. We drummed up – or rather, she drummed up – a few tame followers. But it didn't last. Amy was too bossy and I was too lazy and our followers melted away. I was soon the only foot-soldier left, loyal to the end. Silly me.

'I know we've drifted apart, Andy,' she went on, ' but in my mind, we've always been the Talbot Twins. You're my brother. You're the only person in this world who I can completely trust.' There was no softness in her voice this time, only a calm statement, but somehow I found it more affecting than her sad tones before.

After a moment, I managed to say, 'You must be in dire straits if that's really the case.'

She looked at me. She didn't answer but she didn't need to. I nodded, and plunged. 'All right. I'll help you.'

Her face lit up. 'Oh, Andy, you are a darling! I always knew I could—'

'But I want to make three things perfectly clear,' I hurried on. 'One – that you tell me everything there is to know about the opal; two – I *only* want to know about the opal, not anything else you're mixed up in; and three – you do not interfere with how I choose to go about this recovery operation. You can't boss me around like when we were kids. Is that all understood?'

'Perfectly,' she said, smiling. 'In return, there's something I need to make clear too.'

'Yes?'

'We start right now. '

'What? But I need to—'

'Time is of the essence. And besides, what do you need to do except pack a small bag?'

'A small bag?' I repeated, weakly.

'Yes. The plane's only little.'

This was going from worse to worse. I've never liked planes. Especially little ones. And most especially when...

'Are you piloting it?' I asked, remembering one of her recent exploits – a seaplane adventure around the islands of the Pacific. It had sounded like the worst possible combination to me – the unstable sea, the unstable flying contraption. And Amy at the controls!

'No. Not this time,' she answered, serenely unaware of my secret relief. 'Friend of mine will take us and pick us up again when we've got the opal.'

'Amy,' I said sternly, 'remember my first condition? I need to know everything there is to know. You haven't started well. Where are we going that needs a plane to get there?'

'Sorry, I thought I said,' she answered, blithely. 'The trail of the opal ends where it began – in Lightning Ridge. And we've got no time to get there by road. Now let's get a cab to the airfield and I'll give you all the background.'

Just as well the cab was one of those that give you privacy in the back, because the taxi driver's eyes would have popped out if he'd heard the story Amy told. 'It was found in 1913 in the Ridge,' she began, 'by a miner named Darko Koren, who sold it on to a visiting gemstone dealer, Thaddeus Miller, who then sold it on to a Sydney jeweller. This was a dodgy fellow named Nikolai Orloff, who–'

'Ah-ha,' I interrupted, 'now we come to the Russian connection!'

Amy gave me an impatient frown. 'Yes. Anyway, this Orloff fellow knew the Russian imperial consul in Sydney, Prince d'Abaza – I suspect Orloff was working as a part-time informer for him – and it was through the Prince that the opal was eventually sold to a wealthy St Petersburg merchant, who had it set as a pendant and presented as a gift to the Tsarina Alexandra in 1916. She wore it in public only once. The story goes that Rasputin told her it was cursed, so she didn't want to wear it anymore.'

'Good old Rasputin,' I observed. 'Oh, to have such power over women!'

Amy ignored this pathetic attempt at a joke. 'After the Bolshevik Revolution and the murder of the imperial family, the opal vanished. Until–' she paused dramatically.

'Until you found out where it was,' I obliged.

'Exactly! I was intrigued by the story, and managed to track down Nikolai Orloff, that Sydney jeweller. I just intended a feature story: but then he hinted that he'd found out the opal was back in Australia! He wouldn't say where – but I happened to see the corner of a map of Lightning Ridge under a pile of papers on his desk.'

'Of course you did,' I murmured.

She gave me a stern glance. 'I couldn't get anything more out of him that day but decided I'd try again. But before I could, on the very day that the Petrov scoop broke, Orloff was murdered – shot dead, apparently in a bungled robbery.'

'I don't suppose it was a bungled robbery,' I observed, and Amy gave me a wry glance. 'Well done, Sherlock. The KGB are masters at misdirection.'

'Are you telling me the Petrov story broke to cover up the Orloff murder?' I said.

'No, of course not! I'm just saying nobody took any notice of Orloff's murder, because of the Petrov thing. The murder was a KGB operation, I'm sure of it. But apparently Orloff had a lot of bruises on his body from a beating he'd had made just a few weeks earlier. So the police reckoned the two must be connected, to do with Orloff's underworld dealings. I didn't believe that at all.'

The least said about the flight to Lightning Ridge, the better. Amy's friend turned out to be an ex-RAAF aviator who after the war had turned to stunt flying, and though no doubt you'd call him a superb airman, he was also superbly uncaring of the stomachs of his passengers. Not that Amy appeared in the least bit troubled, in the stomach department or otherwise. She sat beside him gossiping unintelligibly – I could hear nothing above the alarmingly tinny roar of the single engine and the pounding of my own heart – and seemed to be having a grand old time. As for me, I was sure we wouldn't get to the Ridge in one piece.

Why on earth had I agreed to this mad escapade? Usually I was so cautious, when I started a new project. I planned for days, weeks, even. I was going against all my own rules, the ones that had kept me safely under the radar for so long. Never work with other people. Never make a spectacle of yourself. Never go for famous or very valuable targets. And always do your research. Thoroughly. But all I had was Amy's story. And the unsettling rumour of a runaway Russian, no defector, but a State assassin. Licensed to kill, as they say.

During the war I'd seen death up close and even afterwards, in my work occasionally you got the whiff of deadly danger. But I kept well away from that class of person, the killers for hire, the casual murderers, the panicky armed robbers. My safety depends on being quick, quiet and non-violent. Yet now I had to factor in the element of a killer on the loose, a trained one at that, and what was more, one whose description we did not have. He could be anyone, according to Amy. One thing she was sure of was that he wouldn't stick out like a sore thumb, in Lightning Ridge. The place was full of Eastern Europeans, and a thick Slavic accent wasn't going to be out of the ordinary. If, that was, Comrade Death, as I'd taken to calling him in my mind, had a thick Slavic accent in the first place.

No, I didn't like it. But I hadn't done too badly in the war. And I still had my service pistol. So that had gone in the bag along with a couple of changes of clothes and a few other things I thought I might need.

Now, as the pilot banked sharply down, preparing to land on the dirt airstrip, I felt that I had been railroaded into something that I was going to regret. If I live to regret it that is, I thought, as my teeth rattled in harmony with the jolt of our hard landing.

'Thanks, Sam! That was a wonderful flight! See you in three days then!' Amy was bright as a button, fresh as a flower in her fashionable casual gear, while I looked and no doubt smelled like yesterday's crumpled shirt. Scrambling out of the flying torture chamber, I took a moment or two to get my land legs, and my bearings.

Not that there was much to get bearings on. Level horizon, ground of flat pale brown dirt, strewn with stones, a few scrubby trees, and a little distance away, a tin shack from which emerged a character in floppy hat and ancient jacket and trousers. The walking-scarecrow effect was completed by a mass of unruly straw-coloured hair emerging from under the hat, but the blue eyes in the tanned face were friendly, and the cut-glass English accent a real surprise. I pegged him as in his late 30's maybe five or so years older than us.

He greeted Sam the pilot with easy familiarity then turned to my sister. 'Good afternoon, Miss Talbot, and welcome to Lightning Ridge, ' he said, with great formality, as though he were a local dignitary greeting visitors. Which in fact it turned out was in a way what he was – not a Mayor in robes and chains, but a semi-official representative of Lightning Ridge miners, a collection of motley waifs and strays from around the world whose one commonality was their thirst for opal. There were only a hundred or two at the most permanently living here though a few others floating in and out, depending on the time of year.

Amy introduced me – as Drew Sandon, I noticed, not as Andy Talbot, my birth name – and I duly shook hands with Richard, as he introduced himself.

'Just Richard, cobber,' he said in that posh voice that made the Australianism sound positively exotic, or perhaps ironic.

Amy had told me that people in Lightning Ridge prefer to be known as 'Just: *insert first name here*' and that surnames were really not a subject for polite conversation. Unless you happened to be blow-in strangers, like us, you were on first name terms from the start. Didn't mean you were bosom friends either, of course. I suppose it's the opal, does that to people. Everyone has their sights set on a shimmering dream. So you keep your cards very close to your chest in case someone decides to turn rat on you and comes in the dead of night to steal the little bit of colour you've managed to wrest from the hard ground.

I'm a city boy born and bred but I don't mind a small dose of the bush, in its place. But this wasn't the bush. Not the bush I knew, anyway. Not the Blue Mountains or Bathurst which was as far west as I'd ever been before. This was – desolate. A nowhere place.

The tin shack turned out, like the cut-glass accent of its owner, to be something of a surprise. It was neat, scrupulously clean, with the only decoration being a gun rack on which rested a couple of well-kept hunting rifles. And it also gave little clue to the past the man had left behind. No photographs, no mementoes, nothing that was personal. Not even any books, which was a pity, because in the absence of photographs, the books a person has on their shelf can provide valuable clues. Richard was clearly not a reader however. Another surprise. I'd have cast him as one of those gentleman tramp types who wander the roads in dusty shoes with a volume of the Classics in their pocket. An Oxford graduate gone to seed. Something like that. I was keeping an eye out for anomaly, of course. For the hint that would tell me we were face to face with Comrade Death. This could be such an anomaly. Or it could be entirely innocent.

Amy had introduced me as her research assistant. Ha! Fair enough I suppose but as I sat and drank the cup of strong tea Richard gave us and listened to him telling Amy he absolutely insisted on driving us around in his rattle-trap old truck (a dismal object parked just behind the tin shack), I could tell I was to be cast as the spare wheel. Which, come to think of it, I hope he had in that old banger of his. I was thrown, in truth. The feeling I was not in control, that I could not see the whole picture, that Amy had not told me the whole truth, was getting to me. She was using me, just as she was using poor Richard, who believed that we were here to scout out the location for her next adventure story. 'The romance of opal mining', as she called it. Well! I suppose in a way she wasn't lying.

She managed to bring the conversation around to a discussion of the 'famous opals I have known' variety, and on this Richard proved quite garrulous though not altogether helpful as far as our particular concern was related. He did however mention the Romanov Opal, but only offhand, and appeared to think that the opal's association with Lightning Ridge had ended when the miner Darko Koren had sold it to the visiting dealer Thaddeus Miller. That, or he knew more and was a very good actor. I was glad though that Amy did not press him on the matter but changed the subject, asking Richard about his hunting rifles, and game to be bagged around here, and such things, very dull conversation to listen to but necessary to divert any suspicion. Better not to show untoward interest right from the start.

Presently, Richard gave us a bone-jolting ride to our accommodation in the local pub. True to my forebodings, this proved to be a flimsy and ramshackle affair, and the rooms we were proudly ushered into by the 'relieving' publican Joe – as he told us, he was looking after the pub for his mate who was away for a few weeks – were not much bigger than broom cupboards, with a spider or two being their only decoration of note. Still, I consoled myself, we'd only be here three days; Sam the Stunt Pilot being due to pick us up then.

Amy insisted we have a drink in the crowded bar. She caused quite a stir – it was likely the first time a woman other than a barmaid had braved that particular locality, and certainly a woman dressed in fashionable city clothes. But her fame had gone before her and the stir was not hostile. She's always had a head for liquor, our Amy, and she knocked back the whiskies – the only drink aside from beer that the bar seemed to boast – with aplomb, earning even more approbation from the rough and ready customers, and a wry glance from the scrawny bleached-blonde barmaid who went by the name of Pearl. As for me, I sipped on my beer and let Amy take all the attention while I sat back and observed the merrymakers.

It was like a United Nations in that bar, men from all corners of the world. They were all sizes, shapes, ages; some were silent, some talkative, like Joe and our mate Richard. Though it's true to say that even those word-lovers did not reveal much about themselves, despite their chatter. Some of the drinkers had the fever of hope in their eyes, others the grimly determined look of men who have set themselves the task of outwitting fate. Not all of them were miners; as well as the landlord there were a couple of shopkeepers amongst them and a travelling salesman named Karl. Silent, saturnine, with the eyes of a bird of prey, he might have fitted the bill of Comrade Death to a T only, as I soon understood, he had been visiting the hamlet for years, selling items such as hairclips, corsets and stockings to the ladies of the Ridge. Indeed, as far as I could ascertain, every man in that crowd was a local. Not one stranger, except for us two, of course. And Comrade Death had to be a stranger, a newcomer.

Amy didn't even have to use the same drill she had on Richard; he was thrilled to announce to the world, or such as was gathered in that flyblown place that night, of his great 'honour' at being our driver. He was getting a fair bit of ribbing too about his 'success' with the ladies; some young woman in the general store having given him the 'glad eye' according to his mates. Maybe it was to fend off such heavy-handed joshing that he led the conversation to 'famous opals I have known' and that brought out a flood of boasts from the talkers about the times they'd 'nearly got the big one' or been 'cheated' out of the prize catch; and then that led on to the fabulous stones that had brought bad luck to their finders. I think such stories are designed to make the unlucky – as in the majority who never find anything worth more than a few pounds – feel good imagining that those who make it big are really courting trouble and will come to a bad end.

But they didn't mention the Romanov opal in connection to any bad-luck stories. Nobody had apparently heard of the Orloff murder, and as to the murders of the Tsar and his family, that had happened too long ago. And Darko Koren, as far as we knew, hadn't come to a sticky end. Besides he had been and gone from the Ridge these many decades, and nobody here had known him.

Despite the lack of information on our matter of concern, tongues were well and truly loosened now, and we heard any amount of stories, getting more grotesque and ghoulish as the night advanced. Ghosts and mysterious disappearances; strange lights in the desert and Aboriginal curses; tales of murder and desperation and hatred; it was as though all the strangeness in the world, all the dark passions of human nature were all gathered in this place. Or as though, I thought sourly, the Ridge men were trying to give nightmares to the city slickers.

It wasn't those stories, however, but the disgusting plate of tinned bully beef and tinned peas that passed for dinner and the beer churning around in my stomach that gave me uneasy dreams and woke me with the sour smell of frustrated sleep in the late reaches of the night.

I tossed and turned for a little while before giving up the unequal struggle, and got up. I've often gone for night walks when I'm not feeling altogether right, it helps to clear my head. And there was a half-moon still in the sky, giving a faint light that would be enough to see by. I've always had the blessing of excellent eyesight, and over the years had trained myself to see almost as well at night as during the day. Nobody stirred as I slipped out of the pub, not even the three or four drinkers who had passed out on the floor of the bar.

In the grey half-light the huddle of shacks and tents that comprised the small settlement looked somehow different, the bleak landscape touched with something almost unearthly. I'm not usually fanciful, but it felt like a time when anything might happen, when those stories of ghosts seeking revenge that we'd heard in the bar would suddenly come true. I almost turned back; but the thought of the sweaty sheets awaiting me back in the pub was enough to spur me on. I'd walk for a while longer. The night air was doing me good.

I had walked a short distance from the hamlet when I saw it. A sudden small point of red light, some way ahead. It took me an instant to realise what it was. Someone had lit up a cigarette. Someone was standing there, half-hidden behind a scrubby tree, beside the bulk of a large car. I had spotted the car before. It had been parked in front of the pub. It was the travelling salesman's car.

If Karl was skulking out here at this time of night instead of being tucked up in his room, it had to be because he was waiting for someone. He hadn't seen me. In my grey coat and hat, I blended into the half-light, but I took the precaution anyway of ducking behind a bush. I didn't have to wait long. Presently, a figure on a bicycle came barrelling up the road and as they passed by, I saw that it was Pearl, the barmaid.

Ha, I thought, disappointed, it's just a banal assignation. I hadn't noticed anything between them yesterday; indeed, I'd rather thought that Pearl and Joe the landlord had a thing going. But that could be the case anyway. She wouldn't be the first or last to have two men at the same time. And in this place, with the ratio of women to men being something like one to five, the ladies could have their pick, and change their minds as they wished.

But I couldn't leave my hiding-place now, not if I wanted to avoid the embarrassment of being cast as a Peeping Tom. So I stayed where I was and watched as she reached the car and stood there talking to Karl. I was too far away to hear what she said but there was something about the way she stood that made me rethink my original idea of a lovers' meeting. There was a stiffness to her that suggested some other emotion. Then I saw him hand her something, and she did likewise. I was too far away to see what they were exchanging but by the rigidity of her posture, it wasn't a willing transaction. Almost at once after that, she got on her bike again and pedalled away, back towards the hamlet. He stood there for a moment longer, taking his time finishing his cigarette, then he got in his car, started the engine, and drove away, out of town, his tail-lights soon vanishing into the distance.

There was nothing to link what I'd seen to the Romanov opal, but my spine was tingling with a feeling that I've learned to trust. I had to know why she'd met him here in the dead of night, what they'd exchanged. And why she was frightened. Because that stiffness I'd seen in her movements, that was fear, I thought. Either fear of him, or of someone else. But who? And why? I had to get into Pearl's room. Search her belongings. But in order to do that I had to make sure she was distracted. And that meant I had to tell Amy what I'd seen.

I couldn't do anything about it right then of course. Using another route to avoid being seen, I headed back to the pub. I fell into a heavy sleep and woke to bright sunshine, loud banging on the door and my sister's voice calling, 'Get up! Something's happened!'

The pub was abuzz with the news. Joe the publican told me the story, over breakfast. A miner on his way into town had made a grisly discovery. 'At first he thought Karl must have crashed his car,' he said. 'It had run into a tree, and he was dead, slumped over the wheel of his car. But–' he paused dramatically – 'when he got right up close, he saw that Karl had been shot in the head! '

'Oh my God,' I said weakly, because Joe was looking expectantly at me.

'Yeah. See, the crash happened after Karl was shot, not before. The fellow reckoned he'd been dead about six hours.'

'How did he know that?' I asked.

Joe grinned. 'He was a medical student once, never made it to doc, but still knows a thing or two, he reckons.'

Six hours, I thought; would have been not long after I'd seen him. And Pearl. Someone had been lying in wait for him on the road out. Someone who knew he was meeting Pearl. I studied her covertly as she served up our plates of bacon and eggs. Unlike Joe and the other people who'd come into the bar for an early fortifying drink and a good gossip, including our mate Just Richard, who seemed terribly rattled, she appeared calm. Unnaturally so, I knew that. Her face was frozen into an impassive mask.

Listening to the others, it was clear that Karl hadn't been universally liked, in the usual way that men who hang around women too much aren't liked by other men. But it was more than that. There was a hint of something creepy; as someone put it, 'he wore soft shoes and you didn't hear him coming'. A portrait was building in my mind. A sneak. A snoop. Someone who listened at doors and heard things. A hoarder of secrets. Which gave him power.

I was not at all sure any more that my tingling feeling of last night was justified, despite the fact Karl had been shot in the head, like Orloff. Blackmailers – and I was beginning to suspect that's what Karl had been – play a dangerous game, one that often as not ends badly when someone they've pushed too far takes revenge. Whoever had shot Karl had known what he was about. The war had washed up all kinds of people here. More than one of them had pasts they might want to hide, and more than one of them would be handy around guns. Perhaps Pearl knew who it was. That mask of hers hid something. Glee, relief, or fear.

In all the agitation, I had not got around to telling Amy what I'd seen, and now I wasn't sure I should. But I didn't want her to think that Karl's murder

had anything to do with Comrade Death, so I had to tell her at least a version
of it. Drawing her aside in the corridor after breakfast, I told her, quickly;
only in this version I was much closer and had seen what he was handing her
– a packet of letters, done up in ribbon, while she'd handed him money. I
finished with, 'He was blackmailing her. Karl, I mean.'

'My God,' she said. She'd swallowed it hook line and sinker. 'Do you
think she killed him then?'

'No. I saw her go back on her bike. Whoever killed him was lying in wait
on the road out of town.'

'Then it could have been the Russian assassin!'

'I don't think so. I think it was another victim of Karl's.'

'We don't even know he was a blackmailer,' she said, quite reasonably.

'I saw them exchange the money and the letters. And you heard what the
others said.'

'They just didn't like him because he was a ladies' man. I thought he was
quite nice,' said my sister, with a glint in her eye that told me it would be
pointless to argue. 'Maybe they'd been having a secret affair and he'd ended
it and gave her back her letters like a gentleman, but she got furious and
killed him. Or maybe the assassin found out Karl had the opal only Karl
knew that too, hid it in the letters and passed it on to Pearl–'

'Oh for heaven's sake this isn't a penny dreadful! You can't just make
things up as you please,' I said, crossly.

'I think we have to prove it one way or the other then. We need to know
what's in those letters!'

I cursed myself. I really should have known better. Give Amy an inch and
she'll take a mile; or two. 'And how do you propose we do that?' I said, as if
it had only just struck me.

She looked at me as though I was mad. 'Break into her room of course.
I'll do it. You go back and chat her up. Keep her in the bar. Oh, and tell
Richard we'll be a little delayed. He was going to take us fossicking this
morning,' she explained. Seeing my blank look, she added, 'Don't you
remember?'

I hadn't. Richard had talked so much I'd taken very little in. Besides I
had been preoccupied by other things, principally, trying to identify Comrade
Death. I said, 'And why, pray, are we delayed?'

'Because I need to powder my nose. Or deal with women's issues.
Anything that will stop him asking questions,' she said, impatiently.

I did not like her tone. No, I did not like it at all, any more than I was fond
of the notion of her snooping around in Pearl's things and discovering I'd
lied about the letters. But as she was already heading off in the direction of
Pearl's quarters, there was nothing I could do, and so meekly I retraced my

footsteps back to the bar. There I found the crowd had much reduced, with only Richard and Pearl left, he gazing morosely into a half-empty glass, she polishing the bar top as if her life depended on it.

Yet I had the odd sensation that just instants earlier they had been doing something else. There was a tension in the air. I remembered the rifles on Richard's wall and the lack of any personal mementoes. And I wondered.

'Miss Talbot said to say she'll be a little delayed,' I said, settling myself at the bar beside Richard. 'Between you and me, she's a little shaken.'

'Understandable,' said Richard, absently, and took a swig of his drink.

'Beer?' said Pearl.

'Why not? Steady the nerves.' I was hoping to draw them out by this remark but neither took the bait, so I had to go in for the big guns. 'Did you know Karl well?'

I caught the look they gave each other then. It was Richard who said, 'He'd been coming here for years.' It wasn't any real answer, and he knew it, and didn't care.

'Where was he from?'

'No idea,' said Richard. Pearl stayed silent, still polishing the bar.

'I thought maybe he was German,' I persisted. 'Or Austrian.'

Richard shrugged. 'Maybe.' He was ill at ease, and I didn't think it was my clumsy questions, or he wouldn't have answered them. It was the fact there was something unfinished, between him and Pearl.

'You know, it's funny, but I think there was something familiar about him,' I lied, boldly. 'I think I saw him, years ago, in Vienna, in the offices of a gemstone trader.'

I'd only wanted to shock them out of whatever funk they were in, but it more than did the trick. Richard, who'd been lifting the glass to his lips, dropped it, spilling beer all over himself, while Pearl stared at me as though I was a ghost, or a poisonous snake rearing up.

It was at that moment that Amy made her reappearance. 'Andy, I'm so sorry.' Her voice was shaky. Her face was white.

'What's up with–' I began, then broke off, for I saw what was behind her. Or rather, who. Someone who held a very businesslike looking shotgun in his hands and had a look in his eye which said very plainly he'd not hesitate to use it. It was Joe.

'Don't even think about it, mate,' the 'relieving' publican said, as I made as though to move. 'One more step and I blow Miss Talbot's brains out.'

'Joe–' began Pearl.

'She was snooping in your room, see, love? But it'll be all right. You'll see. You go lock the door. That's right. Now go get some rope, Richard. Get a move on! ' he snapped when Richard scrambled clumsily down from his stool. 'What's up with you, mislaid your balls, mate?' He was smiling, seemingly at ease, but the predator's snarl was only just beneath the surface.

'Look,' I said, my eyes on Amy, willing her not to make a false move, 'just let Miss Talbot go. She's not done any harm, it was my fault that–'

'Shut up, dickhead,' he interrupted, unemotionally. 'I know who you are and what you're up to, so save your breath. All right, mate,' he said, when Richard came back with two coils of rope, 'tie him up first, then do her. We're going to take them for a little drive.'

I knew what that meant. I'd seen it in his eyes. And I'd heard the stories yesterday. Of remote mine workings and bodies thrown down them, never to be found again. Missing people who stayed missing. There'd be a hue and cry over Amy of course, if not over me. But who could search miles upon miles of this sort of thirsty country? These people were locals. They knew every inch of the land. Not like blow-in cops.

I had to do something. Me, it was one thing. But Amy was quite another. So it was her doing we were here but it was my doing she was in this pickle.

'You're making a mistake,' I said. 'Miss Talbot had no idea I was planning to steal the Romanov opal. She didn't–'

'Then why did she bring along a so-called master thief as her so-called research assistant? You think we're morons out here, mate? I've heard all about you: Shadow. That's what they call you, isn't it, master thief? They say you've never been caught. Till now, mate,' he said, smiling as Richard gingerly began to tie my legs together, not meeting my eyes. 'Till now.'

'You got the opal from someone here, didn't you?' I asked, trying to signal Amy with my eyes. He knew what I was, he just didn't know *who* I was. He didn't know I was Amy's brother, and I had to keep it that way. 'Come on, Joe,' I added, 'fair's fair. You guessed right. I am Shadow, right enough. And you've caught me, right enough. Nobody else has come within co-ee. You might as well enjoy the moment.'

'It was that old Nazi,' Joe said. 'Old Hans.'

Vaguely, I thought I remembered the name amongst the welter of stories yesterday. A German miner who had gone missing a few months before. It hadn't seemed relevant, for it was long before Orloff's murder. 'Bastard had stolen it anyway,' Joe went on. 'He was in Russia in the war, you know. Don't know where he found it, don't care. Thing is, he had it hidden in his place. He'd had it for years. Old miser. Didn't even try to sell it. Said it was bad luck. Can you credit it? Moron.'

'How'd you find out he had it?'

'Pearlie did, didn't you, love?'

She nodded, eyes wide, but didn't speak.

'Old bastard tried it on with her,' Joe went on. 'He was always trying that but this time he was well into his cups and he told her that he had something the whole world was looking for and if she went with him he'd show her.'

'So you did,' I said, looking at Pearl.

'My Pearlie's always been braver than anyone,' said Joe, proudly. 'She got that old Nazi to cough up. She got him to show her the opal. So we knew it was real. And Richard here, he knew a bit about it. See, his dad's a real toff, and used to hob-nob with Romanovs in exile.'

I looked at Richard who, finishing with me, was now tying up Amy. He looked miserable. Defeated. Ashamed. He didn't want this to be happening, I thought. Not that it helped us. The man was a coward.

'So Richard had heard stories. He knew what the opal looked like, what the setting was like,' Joe went on. He was enjoying himself. I'd met people like him before. Dangerous, vain, unpredictable. It wouldn't do to annoy him in any way. I looked over at Amy, and read the same thing in her eyes. She understood. About him; about what I was trying to do. She was with me. Really with me. My heart clenched. We were the Talbot twins again, each trying to strengthen the other; past hurts and coldness vanished as though they'd never been.

'That must have been useful,' she said, quietly, to Joe. He looked at her as though seeing her for the first time.

'It was, Miss Talbot, it was. But I'm careful. I always check things twice. So after we got rid of that old Hans, we took the stone to Orloff in Sydney. We thought he'd authenticate it cos he'd sold it in the first place, see?'

'But he switched stones,' I said, my mind working fast.

'Yeah. Didn't realise it at first. He was good, the bastard. But when we did find out–'

'You got it back,' I said, remembering what Any had said, about the bruises Orloff had sustained in the weeks before his death. 'After giving him a good beating. But it wasn't you who killed him.'

'Genius, ain't you?' he sneered. 'You're right, though. No need to kill him – fellow was a coward and gave up the information no problem. Suppose the Russkies did that, put a bullet in his brain.'

'Like you put one in Karl's,' I said.

'Karl deserved it. He found out Pearlie had been at Hans' before the old man went missing. Found her hairclip or something, one he'd sold to her a few weeks before. He was a snake. A rat. A snoop. Thought he'd make her pay. Money. And other things. Lecherous bastard. Dirty sod. Got what was coming to him, didn't he, love?'

Pearl nodded, giving a tremulous smile.

'So you arranged a meeting, then laid in wait for him and shot him,' I said to Joe.

'Right,' he grinned. 'Rumour was, the Russki who shot Orloff was heading this way. Crap, of course. But I thought it might look good. Left something there to link it to the other thing, a clipping about Orloff. The cops'll find it, put two and two together, and make twenty-two. Like Miss Talbot here. '

'I wouldn't discount the Russians if I was you,' said Amy, quietly. 'They don't give up. And they know Orloff had the stone. It's only a matter of time before they catch up with you.'

'Miss Talbot, I fought the Nazis, do you think I'm worried about some Commie bastard with a gun? Anyway I know every man jack in the place. No stranger's come here in months, apart from you two. '

'The cops will be here soon,' I pointed out. 'People will tell them we were here.'

'So what? I'll tell them you bought a car and a tent from me and that you've gone out to take photographs and look at mine workings, that you're planning to be gone a couple of days. Pearlie will back me up, and Richard. Besides, everyone knows me here. Everyone trusts me. I'm Jolly Joe. Joe the good bloke.' He grinned wolfishly.

'Sam will be back in three days to pick us up,' Amy said. Her voice had a calm to it that I knew masked fear. 'He'll raise the alarm.'

'No worries. I'll get on the blower to him,' said Joe. 'I'll tell him you've changed your mind. You're driving back to Sydney.'

My heart sank. It sounded all too plausible. 'You'll never be able to sell the opal,' I said.

'Bullshit. That will be easy. Already put out some feelers.'

'The Russians will know, once you try to sell it. They'll know for sure. '

'Who cares? By then we'll have long gone from this dump. We'll be living high on the hog, in London or New York or somewhere. They'll never find us. Face it, Shadow, your goose is well and truly cooked. Pity about Miss Talbot; but if she will keep such bad company, then she has to face the consequences, and–'

'I can pay you,' I said, desperately. 'Anything you want. Just let Am – Miss Talbot go free and I'll pay you whatever you want. I'll give you all the proceeds of my jobs, everything I've accumulated over the years. And you can do with me what you want then. But just let her go.'

'No way,' said Amy, fiercely. 'No way! I won't let you do that. Anyway, you know he wouldn't keep his word. He's scum.'

'How touching,' said Joe, but there was a nasty glitter in his eye. 'So the lady and the thief are dear friends, it would seem. Or is it more than that? Pity I don't have time to know more, but really there's been quite enough time spent on you. Come on, let's get them into the car,' he added, turning to his accomplices. 'Got to get the job done.'

'Joe, I really don't think this is necessary.' Richard said, unexpectedly making a last stand. Or first stand. 'I'm sure, if we swear them to secrecy.'

Joe laughed. 'You think they'll just meekly go away? Don't be so bloody naïve, mate. Now will you or won't you get on with it?'

'No,' said Richard. 'I can't.'

'Sure you bloody can.' In two strides he was on the other man, gun raised; but then Pearl stepped in front of him, crying, 'Joe, stop! Rich is our friend. You know that. Stop!'

'You're too soft for your own good, Pearlie,' said Joe, with a twisted grin. 'Or is it you're soft on him, maybe?'

'Joe! You know I'm not.' The fixed look was back on Pearl's face. Fear. That's what it was. Fear of the unpredictable, jealous, volatile cocktail that was her dangerous beau. She might have been flattered initially by his possessive passion; now it threatened her. She had gone along willingly enough with Old Hans' murder and Karl's too; but fear of Joe was part of it too. She might go along with our murders, too, for the same reason; but not Richard's. And that gave me an idea. I couldn't directly address the source of her fear; but I could channel it into something else. I said, 'Do you know what they say about the opal, Pearl? It's cursed. It brings people to a bad end.'

She stared at me. I thought I saw something flicker in her eyes. But all she said was, 'I don't feel well. I think I'm going to pass out. Joe, please–'

'Oh. For Christ's sake.' Joe lowered his weapon. 'I wasn't going to hurt that dingbat,' gesturing at Richard, 'just make him see some sense. Right, mate?'

Richard nodded, mutely, the small fight he'd had in him withered away. There'd be no more help from him.

I have been in tight spots more than once in my career around the world. But the boot of Joe's car was definitely in their top rank. And with Amy in there too it was as though we were back in the womb and pretty much as helpless. They'd gagged us. And it was dark.

But that connection that had clicked back between us was functioning strongly. We couldn't speak, we couldn't see, but we could still communicate. And both of us shared the same thought: we're getting out of this; and we're going to make them pay. Blow the opal. This is personal. They don't know who they've messed with. The Talbot Twins, on the warpath.

It sounds ridiculous, I know. But who cares? That was what it was like.

Richard was driving. As I'd noted yesterday, he wasn't a good driver at the best of times, and now nerves made him worse. Our bones really felt it as we juddered along the dirt tracks, and once or twice we went over bumps so big our heads banged against the metal lid. We were being taken into the wilderness. We'd end up joining Old Hans down the bottom of some deep hole. Poor old bugger. He'd trusted the wrong people. Just like us. Morons, Joe had called us. He wasn't far wrong. We'd been so concentrated on strangers and spies and all the folderol and we hadn't spotted the ordinary banal criminals right under our noses. Good old greed, that's what it had been about.

The car stopped. I could feel Amy's fear, and knew she must be feeling mine too. You can only be brave so long. All very well us being the Talbot twins again but we were also the trussed Talbots, the Talbots about to face a firing squad, the Talbots about to go to an unmarked grave, and that is not something you can take with a stiff upper lip. But hope dies hard as they say and deep inside me there was still a tiny flicker. My brain had been working overtime to try and find a way out and it had come up with nothing brilliant, nothing, that is, that might have a chance of working. But still there was that flicker of hope.

The light dazzled us as the boot was wrenched open and we were bundled out. As we lay in the grey dust, with Joe looking down on us, shotgun cocked and ready to go, Pearl and Richard hiding away in the car, no doubt covering their eyes and ears, I felt that last flicker of hope go out. This was it. We were gone.

'Please,' I began when suddenly there was the roar of an engine. Joe spun around, but not in time. The speeding motorbike was on him, bowling him over. The gun flew out of his hand. He screamed in pain.

The rider dismounted. He was slight, wiry, dressed in plain black: jumper, trousers, woollen beanie covering the hair. A young face – blue eyes, thin lips, high Slavic cheekbones. Quite good-looking, in an icy kind of way. Comrade Death, I thought, blankly, as he drew a pistol from his belt. Out from the frying pan, into the fire.

The assassin looked down at us, briefly, and I thought, this is it. But instead he turned away, and moved to Joe, shooting him once in the head. The screaming stopped. Joe lay still.

Then the motorbike rider started towards the car. I knew what he was about to do. And suddenly I didn't want him to. Struggling against my bonds, screaming against the gag, my face purple with the effort, I said, 'No, no, no, wait, the opal!'

He turned. Looked at me, then at the car where Richard and Pearl must be cowering inside. Seemed to be evaluating his options. Then he came back to us, taking something out of his pocket. A flick-knife. He bent down to us and cut our bonds. Ungagged us. Said, in fair English accented with Russian, 'What did you say?'

It wasn't a man's voice. It was a woman's. Comrade Death was a woman! 'Ah, ah,' I murmured, stunned. 'Um, you, ah, you want the opal, right?'

'Yes. It belong to Russian people.' The blue eyes were cold, direct.

'Of course it does,' I agreed, quickly. 'And those two in the car – they are the only ones who know where it is. You need them alive.'

She looked at me, thoughtfully, and nodded. Then she looked at Amy, who was getting up, gingerly. Her tone changed, softened. And she said something completely unexpected. 'Miss Talbot, I read your books. I like them. Most interesting.'

'Oh, thank you. That is very kind,' my sister gabbled, 'I, I am very glad.'

'I wish to read more. You write more, yes?' said the assassin. I saw Amy swallow. I knew she was trying to hold back hysterical laughter, because I was too. The situation was so surreal it was as though we were in the strangest of dreams. For God's sake, were we being spared because the assassin had a thing about Amy's books?

'Of course,' said my sister, and then, with a little gulp, she added, 'I do not think I will write about this, however. Or the opal.'

'No,' said Comrade Death, 'that would not be wise.' She added, with a little smile, 'And perhaps people would not believe, yes?'

Amy gave her a tentative smile back. 'Perhaps not. You are right.'

'Please,' I put in, 'may I ask how you knew we were here?'

'I know him,' she said, pointing to the car. To Richard. My mind whirled. Suddenly I remembered a conversation in the pub, last night. Joking references to Richard and the 'new girl' at the general store. I'd taken no notice, despite my interest in strangers. That a girl could be a trained KGB killer had never entered my mind, but of course I wasn't the only one. Joe had paid for that blindness with his life. 'I see him leave pub,' she went on, 'and go at great speed. I wonder. So I follow, at distance.'

'Oh,' I swallowed. 'I am glad you did. You saved our lives.'

Her eyes met mine, briefly, and I felt the strangest twinge then, of a feeling I couldn't put a name to. 'In my country, Mr Shadow, thief is social parasite. But this is different country. You are professional, like me. That is one thing. But I admire your sister Miss Talbot. What she does, it is good. And so, that is another thing. You see?'

'Yes,' I said, 'I do.' It did not surprise me that she knew all these things. What did surprise me was that I wished I could ask her name, though I knew I wouldn't. Shouldn't. For lord's sake, Andy, I told myself, the opal must have turned your brain too. She's from an enemy country. An alien state. A twisted philosophy that cares nothing for the person, only for the hive. Not to speak of her lethal profession. Yet still there was that ridiculous feeling of wanting a connection, where there could be none. Other than of course she had saved our lives. No small thing, mind. So I added, impulsively, 'We will always be in your debt.'

'Yes,' echoed Amy. 'Always. Thank you.'

The assassin shrugged. 'It is what it is. Now you must be on your way. Town is only two miles west from here.' She was heading back to the car, to Pearl and Richard, when Amy said, 'They love my books too. And they tried to save us before. Please, will you remember that?'

The assassin looked at her for a long moment. Then she nodded. 'Go. Now.'

We didn't wait to be told twice but hurried away as fast as our shaky legs would allow us. We did not look behind us, but heard the noise of a car engine, starting up. What would happen to Pearl and Richard now, we didn't know, but we had done all we could. We did not speak, at least not for quite a while, not till we had left that place far behind us, not till we were sure Comrade Death would not change her mind and come after us. It was only when the settlement was in view that Amy said, 'Well! So the pen is mightier than the sword after all.'

I looked at her. There was a gleam of mischief in her eyes, mixed with the shock of what had happened. 'Yes,' I said, with a gurgle of laughter. 'I bet you've never met a fan quite like that!

'You can say that again,' she said, with a small shiver, 'and I rather hope I never do so again.'

'Amen to that!' I said, fervently.

The disappearance of Joe the 'relieving' publican wasn't even a nine days' wonder. Apparently he'd been overheard saying he'd had enough of the pub game and was heading far away, maybe even New York, to make his fortune. He'd had enough of the Ridge, he'd told lots of people the morning of Karl's murder. He'd been rattled by that, everyone said. And then he'd found out, that very day, that Pearl and Richard had been having an affair behind his back. No wonder he'd taken off. There were some of course who said darkly that Pearl and Richard themselves had disposed of him; they'd been seen packing up Richard's old truck the day after and leaving the Ridge, never to return. As to the new girl from the general store, the fact she'd taken off too caused not the slightest bit of gossip. People came, people went. They often didn't stay long in the Ridge, and even those who did might take off unpredictably. It was that kind of place. And it didn't do to ask too many questions, anyway. Besides, the old publican had come back, he'd engaged a new barmaid, and life had gone on. As it always did.

But the sensational re-appearance of 'the People's Opal' as it was dubbed by the Russians (though still 'the Romanov Opal' everywhere else) was another matter, and it drew great crowds when it was displayed as the 'Last of the State Jewels', first at the History Museum in Moscow and then, by special permission, at a travelling exhibition in the British Museum. Where it had been in the decades since it had vanished, no-one knew, or at least no-one was telling, certainly not us. A grainy photograph in one of the Sydney papers was the closest Amy and I ever got to the real thing; and that was just how we wanted it. Never mind handing it back in a blaze of publicity to an exiled Romanov prince, as Amy had imagined; never mind having the secret pleasure of holding in your hand a legendary jewel, as I had dreamed. Those were childish notions. What was far better and more wonderful was that the opal which had brought bad luck to so many who had come close to it had brought us something much brighter. That connection we'd reforged had not gone away, and we'd got close again. And that had changed everything.

Shadow was not retired, not quite, not yet, for his skills were useful; but Drew Sandon the bookseller had taken down his shingle and vanished into the obscurity from which he came.

Miss Amy Talbot, famous adventurer and writer, had invested in a brand new enterprise: Two for Trouble, Inc, an investigative agency co-owned and run by her long-lost brother, Mr Andrew Talbot, returned, so the colourful rumour had it, from a foreign-based career of top-secret activities on behalf of important personages all over the world.

The Talbot twins were back in business.

TOR ROXBURGH

The Boudicca Society

A year after Connie Withers died there was a flurry of activity at her Albury address. Her niece Evelyn arrived with brooms and cleaning products and set to work on the kitchen. While Connie's neighbour took the lovely Chinoiserie sideboard and a great-nephew picked up the African masks, it was Evelyn and her teenage son Garth who got to run their proprietorial eyes over everything. Well, almost everything.

On Monday, Connie's great-nieces Mags and Brownie arrived on foot in the heat of the afternoon. They failed to recognise each other until they almost collided at the base of the stone steps to the house. It had been ten years since they'd met and even then they hadn't been friends. Mags had been a childish 11 to Brownie's 16. And now, in their 20s, they were different creatures: Mags in capri pants, sporting a pixie cut and false eyelashes; Brownie looking secretarial and clever in a pencil-skirted suit.

They shared a smile, commented on the circumstance of inheriting a shared dinner set, then made their way through the garden, past the wilting and sunburnt hydrangeas. Evelyn was a little rushed and a bit harried when she let them in, but she managed to usher them into the dining room with a semblance of good grace.

The missing sideboard had left a shadow on the wallpaper but the rest of the interior was intact: balloon-backed mahogany chairs and a polished dining table, upon which a magnificent dinner set was spread.

Evelyn realigned the handle of the coffee pot. 'I don't know why Connie was so insistent about giving this to you two. It's what you'd leave to people who entertained.'

There was a tiny tweak at the edge of Brownie's mouth. 'Not to spinsters?'

Evelyn looked uncomfortable. 'Well, I don't know that I'd put it like that, Brownie. After all, Mags, here, is only 21.' She glanced at the younger and more fashionable of the cousins before turning her attention back to the elder. 'And you're not too old. Not that I'd be letting the grass grow under my feet at 25. This might be 1963, but a woman's happiness has and always will be found in her family. Some things never change.'

'Has mum told you I'm leaving town to start a business?' the younger cousin asked her aunt.

'Dress alterations,' Evelyn sounded doubtful. 'In Melbourne?'

'A fashion label. I'm going to start one.'

Evelyn sniffed. 'Then half a dinner set is probably half a dinner set too many.'

Mags picked up one of the saucers. Her bangles slid down her tanned arm. The porcelain was so fine; the sunlight cast a pattern on her hand. She looked as though she was about to say something else about her new enterprise but it was Brownie who spoke.

'I might not, actually.'

The other two women frowned.

'Get married.'

Mags gave her older cousin an appreciative look then put the saucer she'd been holding back on the table. 'It's not really my bag either.'

Brownie didn't acknowledge the comment. Instead, she pulled out one of the balloon-backed dining chairs and sat. She reached for the stack of Albury Advertisers and commenced wrapping. Mags took the seat across from her cousin and began counting and separating plates.

Their aunt sighed and brushed a speck of dust from her twin set. 'You'll have to work out the split yourselves. There's only one soup terrine and the lid is stuck, although that might be a matter of giving it a good wash. And there are a few other one-offs. Oh, and I put those tea chests there for you.'

She waved at the small wooden boxes beside the table. 'One each. If you need help with carrying them, your cousin Garth can give you a hand. I've got him washing walls in the kitchen and he's itching to escape.'

Brownie and Mags seemed relieved when their aunt left and the conversation became easy as they packed up the set. Mags told Brownie about her plans to conquer Melbourne. She would find a job that gave her enough time to hawk her samples around the boutiques and the minute she got her first order she'd rent a studio in Flinders Lane. Brownie told Mags about her secretarial work: helping constituents who came into the electorate office and going to Melbourne with the Honourable Member when parliament was sitting. But for all their new-found familiarity, neither cousin told the other all that much that was real or true.

Mags omitted to mention the fact that she had pressing debts and had no idea how she was going to survive in Melbourne. Brownie was worse. She told Mags she was on leave until the next parliamentary sitting, which was an outright lie. She'd been fired, replaced by her boss's fiancée, who'd appeared out of nowhere. It was an appearance that put paid to Brownie's expectations of a proposal from the Honourable Member and cast a new light on the intimate moments they had shared on the shag pile rug in front of his desk.

When the serving dishes, the salt and pepper shakers, the jug and coffee pot had all been divided, wrapped and packed along with the plates, bowls, cups and saucers, Brownie held up the soup terrine and raised an eyebrow. In the distance, someone knocked at the front door. Outside, a mower started up with a roar. Brownie held the terrine to her ear and gave it a little shake.

'Something in here.'

'Ooh.' Mags grinned. 'Treasure.'

From the hallway, came the sound of rapid footsteps. Their cousin, Garth, slipped into the dining room, put his finger to his lips, then carefully closed the door.

'Brownie,' he acknowledged the elder of his two cousins, keeping his voice low. Then he turned to Mags. 'There's a bloke from the sheriff's office. Asking for you. By name. Says your mother told him you were here. Mum's put him in Great-auntie Connie's best room.'

Brownie raised an eyebrow and looked at Mags.

The younger cousin had paled and was already in motion, hurrying over to the open window.

'Magsy?' Garth whispered.

She gave him a less than reassuring smile. 'Stupid speeding fines but I'm damned if I'm going to let them seize my Beetle.' She turned away and swung her leg over the sill. 'Got to split. Pass me that tea chest, would you Brownie?' Then she dropped out of sight, her next words drifting up from the garden, 'Yours too if you want a lift.'

Everything about Brownie suggested she would say no: her stiff beehive, her sensible shoes, her expensive suit. Instead, an expression of longing flitted across her face. She didn't say anything, just picked up Mags's tea chest and shoved it into Garth's arms, pushing him towards the window. Then she grabbed the soup terrine and stuffed it into the remaining box and carried that over herself. After Garth had dealt with the first box, Brownie lowered the second into Mags's arms and lifted her leg over the sill. There was an awkward moment as her pencil skirt stretched tight and she teetered and almost lost her balance. Then, with a slight shudder, her seam split at the hem, giving her enough room to move.

The ladies lounge of the Globe was empty. Mags and Brownie paid for their drinks and carried them to a table in the corner, along with the soup terrine that Mags was still convinced held treasure. Evidently, they felt some awkwardness after the close drama of their getaway. At first they did nothing: didn't even look at each other; just sipped their G&Ts and swirled their ice with swizzle sticks. Mags's face was flushed and Brownie's beehive was flattened.

Brownie gave a little laugh as though she'd remembered something. 'She used to sunbake naked.'

Mags frowned.

'Great-auntie Connie. Mum and I went around there once. Front door open; back door open. We just walked right through. Anyone could have walked in. She was out the back – flaked out. On her stomach on a travel rug. Not a stitch.'

'Far out.'

'I know.' A smile crept onto Brownie's face. 'Mum was horrified.'

'Was she smashed?' Mags asked.

'Don't think so. She woke up; stood up. Nice as pie. Offered us a drink.' Brownie fiddled with her glass. 'I guess we should take a look at that terrine.'

Mags nodded and lifted the dish onto the table, pushing aside the newspaper it was wrapped in. Her hands were dirty and one long frosted pink nail was chipped. She tried the lid. 'Stuck.'

Brownie leaned forward and examined the slightly yellowed, plastic-looking line that joined the lid and the base. 'Super glue. Have you got any nail polish remover?'

Mags opened her Glomesh handbag and began pulling out cosmetics. She handed the remover to Brownie, who drizzled it around the lip of the terrine.

Then they waited.

Brownie opened a compact and re-applied her foundation. Mags sighed, reached for her cigarette case and began fitting a cocktail Sobranie into a long holder. She was about to light it when Brownie reminded her that nail polish remover was flammable. The younger cousin looked sheepish and put the cigarette back into the case. She folded her hands in her lap. 'How long?'

Brownie didn't answer, just reached over and gripped the lid, giving it a tug. There was a sucking sound and it came away, revealing a tissue-wrapped bundle.

'Outta sight!' Mags grinned, picking it up. 'I bet it's full of diamonds.' She tore at the paper and then her face fell as two old keys and a folded piece of notepaper dropped onto the table. Then her expression cleared. 'A safe. I bet they're for a safe.'

Brownie reached for the note and began reading:

> *Girls,*
> *I trust you will find, as did I, that fortune favours*
> *the active woman.*
>
> *To wit, two keys that will usher you into the source*
> *of my greatest joy.*
>
> *Connie.*

'It's signed, witnessed and dated,' Brownie looked up at Mags. 'Must be important.'

Mags picked up one of the keys. 'It says: *Chubb's Detector.*'

Brownie nodded and picked up the other. 'Key to a famous lock. First picked by Alfred Charles Hobbs at the London Great Exhibition of 1851.'

'Does it say that in the letter?'

Brownie tapped her head with her index finger. She looked down at the key in her hand and ran her finger over the engraving on the shaft. 'It says: *Boudicca.* That's curious.'

'Is that the model?'

'I don't think so. Boudicca was a Celtic warrior. A queen'

'Then it's some sort of Connie-style comment. Some sort of joke or a clue.'

'Let me think.' Brownie closed her eyes. A slight frown appeared on her freshly powdered face. The ladies lounge was quiet. The ice in the cousins' glasses made tiny cracking noises. Then she opened her eyes again. 'Okay. I think I've got it. It's not a key for a safe. You wouldn't use a pickable lock for a safe. But you might use it for a house because the type of burglar who breaks into a house isn't the sort that picks locks – except in the movies. In real life, burglars try the windows and look for keys under urns near front doors. So... Good enough for an ordinary home, but I suspect it's a key to a grander place, something unusual. I think it's a mansion called Boudicca!'

Mags looked impressed. 'Almost as good as diamonds.' Then she paused, looking worried. 'But how will we find it?'

'It will be in Melbourne.'

'How do you know?'

Brownie picked up the base of the soup terrine and turned it upside down, holding it out for Mags to see. There was a name, "Olive Billingham", and an inscription that read: "Women's Work 1907".

'We've been looking at this all afternoon,' Brownie said. There was a women's work exhibition in Melbourne in 1907. Connie wouldn't have put the keys in that particular dinner set for no reason.'

Mags whistled. 'Jeez Brownie, you're better than Barry Jones. You could go on *Pick a Box*. Okay my turn now.' She threw her head back, took a deep breath and closed her eyes. She was silent for a couple of seconds before opening them again and giving her head a rather theatrical little shake. 'My genius mind says Boudicca is an Art Nouveau mansion.'

Brownie looked impressed.

Mags smiled. 'The script's Art Nouveau. One of my favourite periods in fashion.'

'I think I'd better come with you to Melbourne.' Brownie looked thoughtful. 'If you don't mind. That way, we can find this place together. We can stay at the Windsor. I've got an account.'

'Really?' Mags looked impressed.

'Work has one,' as Brownie spoke, her eyes slid away from Mags's gaze, but Mags didn't seem to notice. Evidently the prospect of a stay at the Hotel Windsor was too absorbing. 'Far out!' Mags grinned. 'We're doing it and we're doing it in style!'

The cousins arrived in Melbourne the following afternoon. It took Brownie just three hours to get them from their starting point, which was the Exhibition Building's archive to their first real clue, which was an address on Olive Billingham's death certificate. The artist had died at number 57 George Street in East Melbourne. Mags was all for getting back in the bug and driving over to investigate but Brownie argued convincingly for a fresh start in the morning.

The cousins looked odd together as they walked into the lobby of the Hotel Windsor. Mags had a slightly battered suitcase in one hand and her portable record player in the other. She could have been a singer on her first ever tour: not yet a sophisticate; not quite all country. Brownie on the other hand suited the place. Unlike Mags she didn't bump hands with the valet when he took her cases. Brownie knew which smile was correct and where to step and how to ask for what was needed. She dealt with the hotel staff as one might deal with a taxi driver, a dry cleaner or any other person put on this earth to provide service: she was pleasant and assured and ladylike.

For all her poise, the previous day's adventure and the discovery of an address seemed to have loosened something in the older cousin because once they were safely within their room, she relaxed. She kicked off her shoes and bounced on the bed. On the other side of the room, Mags set up the record player. They played Mags's 45s with the volume turned up a little louder than it should have been. Brownie mixed them cocktails from the tiny bottles in the minibar and they danced – even Brownie danced – in the narrow spaces around the beds and told each other daring tales about their lives that weren't any the worse for not being terribly accurate.

It was almost eight when they finally dressed for dinner and went downstairs. The maître d' recognised Brownie and led them to a table in front of one of the big windows. They certainly didn't need more alcohol, but Brownie seemed to consider it gaucherie not to order claret with their meal.

By the time the waiter cleared the table, the cousins' stories had become a good deal more truthful and possibly overly revealing. Brownie told Mags about life in Melbourne, describing the time the Honourable Member broke his nose at the Fat Black Pussy Cat after buying cocaine from a mod in a dirty duffle coat.

'Fell over his feet when someone said the fuzz had arrived.'

Mags doubled over with laughter then smudged her makeup when she wiped away the tears. 'Far out! The family wouldn't be so keen on the idea of you marrying him if they knew.'

'I told you, I don't want to get married.' Brownie picked up her glass and drained it.

'So, is it always like that when parliament is sitting? Do they get high all the time?'

'God no.' Brownie shook her head. 'Drink, yeah, but not cocaine. Most of them are horribly square.' The older cousin lifted the bottle to refill her glass, then realised it was empty. She twisted around, looking for the waiter, then stiffened.

Mags followed Brownie's gaze. 'That's Henry Bolte,' she whispered. 'And... Ooh, Brownie! Guess who's with him? The Honourable Member! Let's go and say hello. Maybe we can join them.'

Brownie appeared to be having trouble breathing, but Mags didn't seem to notice.

Across the room, the maître d' ushered Bolte, the Health Minister Sir Ronald Mack and the Honourable Member to a table. The Premier sat with his back to the cousins. He lit a cigarette and said something that made the other two men laugh. The waiter delivered a round of whiskies without being asked. Then the Honourable Member caught sight of Brownie. The colour left his handsome, chiselled face and he missed Bolte's question.

Brownie turned back to Mags. She reached for the claret and then seemed to remember it was finished. Tears ran down her cheeks. She grabbed her linen napkin and wiped them away.

The smile on Mags's face faltered. 'What's wrong, Brownie? Did you two fall out?'

The older cousin took a deep breath as though she might answer, but didn't. Instead, she placed her napkin on the table and stood up. 'You're right. We should say hello. We mustn't be rude.'

'Brownie?'

But the older woman didn't appear to be listening and was already walking towards the politicians' table. Mags caught up with her as Brownie gave the Premier and the Health Minister a frosty greeting, then glared at the Honourable Member.

With an instinct for locating and diffusing trouble, the maître d' appeared at Brownie's elbow. He addressed the Honourable Member. 'Perhaps Sir could escort Miss Mason and her young friend to their room.'

'Yes,' Mags agreed, sounding far too cheerful. 'Groovy.'

The Honourable Member reached for his whiskey. 'Nothing to do with me. Former employee.'

Both Mags and the maître d' frowned. Then the maître d' leaned over and whispered something in Honourable Member's ear.

A ruddy colour suffused Brownie's lover's face. He probably should have whispered his response, but he didn't. He spoke quite loudly.

'She most definitely is not my guest; nor is her companion. If I were you, I'd be asking them some pointed questions about settling their account – or you could try calling the police. In fact–'

Bolte interrupted, his voice quiet but commanding, 'Out!'

The Honourable Member hesitated.

'You heard me. And take your *lady friends* with you. And don't even think about coming back. I'll see you in my office in the morning.'

The Honourable Member stood and turned away. As he came even with the cousins, he grabbed Brownie's elbow. She yelped but he ignored her and continued towards the exit, dragging her with him.

'Stop it,' Mags said.

The man didn't deviate. If anything he increased his pace so that Brownie looked as though she was skipping as she struggled to keep up.

Mags made her move: flew across the dining room and landed the solid square heel of her gold evening shoe on his left foot. He swore, let go of Brownie and slapped Mags.

In the background, the Premier and Mack stood and the maître d' signalled the waiter, who scurried off to the manager, who called the police. By the time they arrived, Bolte and Mack had left the building, the Honourable Member had been consoled with a whisky in the manager's office and Mags and Brownie were corralled in the parcel room, surrounded by their cases.

George Street was silent and dark and filled with expensive cars that were parked in front of terrace houses. Mags drove with the excessive caution of a woman who had drunk a little more than was prudent but was still confident in her capacity to pull things off. She passed a row of even-numbered houses and then did a u-turn.

'Are we trying to find it tonight?' Brownie asked, speaking for the first time since they'd left the Windsor.

'I don't know. I don't know what we should do.'

'Book into another hotel?'

Mags didn't answer immediately. She pulled over but left the car idling. 'Honestly, Brownie, I don't have the money. I was going to stay at the Y and they're not exactly going to welcome us at this time of night, are they?'

'I'm sorry,' Brownie spoke quietly.

'It's not your fault the Honourable Member isn't honourable.'

'True,' Brownie laughed, sounding a little more like herself.

'I guess we could always sleep in the car,' Mags suggested.

'Okay, but we're here so we may as well look for number 57.'

'It should be in the next block.' Mags eased the car back onto the empty roadway. They drove in silence, then she slowed down again, leaning over the steering wheel, searching for something. 'There,' she pointed, pulling over. 'Number 57, but that can't be our house. It's way too big.'

'That's part of the Epworth; got to be.'

The cousins stared at the shadowy, three story, red brick building with towers at either end. It was fronted by a well-lit, half-circle driveway and there was an ambulance parked beside the portico and behind it, a Jaguar and a Bentley.

'Private nursing home, maybe.' Brownie sounded tired and disappointed. 'Dead end.'

'Okay, but we have to try our keys, confirm it really is a dead end, then we can park somewhere and sleep. Figure out the rest in the morning. If it's a public building, no one's going to notice us at the front door.'

They took a minute to repair their hair and makeup, then walked up the driveway, both doing their best to look as though they belonged. Brownie's answer was to smooth her beehive with both hands. Mags's solution was to adjust the way the strap of her handbag rested on her shoulder. The gravel crunched under their shoes. The night was dark and silent beyond the driveway and the portico.

As they ascended the steps, Mags gave Brownie an encouraging smile, fished her key from her bag and walked to the door. A faint sound was audible from within the building: a shout and a sharp response; all meaning confounded by the thick wooden door.

Mags looked at Brownie, questioningly, the key still clasped in her hand. Brownie made a motion for the younger cousin to wait.

They stood, unmoving, but the voices had fallen silent. Instead, there was a faint noise of movement: thumps and scrapes.

'What's going on?' Mags whispered.

Brownie shook her head and shrugged.

As the cousins leaned in closer, the volume rose and muffled yells could be heard.

'I'm not going in,' Mags whispered.

'Okay, but put the key in the lock and see if it turns. Then we'll go back to the car and think what to do next. Maybe call the police.'

Mags looked doubtful about the suggestion of the police, but she followed Brownie's advice and inserted the key. She turned it, slowly, biting the corner of her lip with concentration. The lock responded. Inside, a woman screamed: a pitiful noise full of distress.

The effect on the cousins was electric. Mags swore, grabbed the door handle and pushed. At the very same moment, Brownie put her shoulder to the moulded oak. The door flew open and they fell forward into a large, tiled, brightly lit vestibule that was full of warring people. At the back of the room, two elderly women were involved in a loud tug of war with a couple of suited men over a wheelchair-bound woman with dishevelled and rather alarmingly blue-rinsed hair. Right in front of the cousins, two ambulance officers were attempting to pull an old woman towards the front door. She was tall and thin and wore some kind of turban and she had her arms wrapped around a carved stone column. She caught sight of Mags and Brownie and let out a laugh. Not the mad sort of laugh you'd expect of a woman being man-handled by ambulance officers; but a joyful laugh, full of relief and belly-deep amusement.

The laughter must have loosened her hold on the column. With a grunt of surprise, she landed on the tiled floor and, equally surprised, the men fell back.

Brownie and Mags ran to her side and helped her to her feet.

'I'm all right,' she managed to smile and groan at the same time, patting Mags's hand. 'Thank heavens you're here. Marvellous timing. Any more outside?'

Mags shook her head.

The woman's face fell. 'Still, two – that's almost enough.'

Mags glanced at Brownie, evidently wondering if the older cousin had made more sense of the comment than she had, but Brownie had already moved and was standing in front of the ambulance officers, demanding to see their identification. For their part, they were doing their best to escape, easing their way towards the open doorway.

'Leave them,' the turbaned woman said to Brownie. 'Go and help–'

The suggestion was interrupted by a thump and shouts from the other struggle.

'Quick girls. Over there. Get into it.'

The cousins didn't need any encouragement. They were already running into the fray.

The scene at the back of the hall would have been farcical if it wasn't so violent. The blue-haired woman was sprawled on the tiles and her wheelchair overturned. The other two women were being dragged, bodily, towards the front door. From outside, the ambulance could be heard, starting up and exiting the property at speed.

Brownie let out a furious yell as she closed in on the nearest man. She brought her hand down in a karate-style chop on his arm. He yelped and twisted, releasing the woman he was holding. As she fell, the woman grabbed his coat. The unexpected pull caused him to lose his footing and he tumbled forward, landing hard.

As Mags reached the second man, she slowed and spun and landed a colossal kick against his backside. He let go of his captive, who slid down to sit at his feet. Mags didn't wait for him to react, she spun a second time. This time, her kick hit him in the ribs and he staggered sideways, slamming into the panelled wall.

For a moment, there was even more noise and confusion as everyone began yelling. The two women who'd been released, struggled to their feet, angrily accusing the men of trespassing. The woman who'd been knocked out of her wheelchair had managed to sit up and threatened to sue the older man. The turbaned woman stood with her hands on her hips and then brought her fingers to her mouth and let loose a sharp, paddock-style whistle.

'New members,' she announced into the momentary silence.

One of the old women clapped and the blue-haired woman told the two men they could *put that in their pipes and smoke it*.

Then, without warning, the man Mags had kicked was moving, running at Mags. Brownie yelled and Mags turned and managed to jump out of the way as he took a swing at her.

'Stop that, Borthwick!' The other, older, man was back on his feet. He seemed unhurt and began brushing down his suit as he continued issuing instructions to the younger man, 'Use your head and start acting like a lawyer. Fetch those bloody papers and show these busybodies what's what. And call the coppers while you're at it. They can handle the old birds. Tried to do this nice and civil–'

'Civil?' Mags and Brownie spoke at once.

The turbaned woman hadn't moved. When she spoke, her words cut through the renewed crescendo, 'You hear that, Warwick?' She glared at the older man. 'New members.'

He snorted in disgust, 'Don't think you can fool me with a pair of bloody ring-ins, Doris. Who are they? Tarts? Scammers? Wherever the hell you found them, it's not going to do you a jot of good.'

Mags turned to Brownie. 'It's a club.' A look of delight suffused the younger cousin's face. 'We're members of some hoity-toity club and if it's Great-aunt Connie's club, it's bound to be a blast.'

Brownie didn't get a chance to answer because suddenly the whole room was talking on top of each other: Warwick insisting that the cousins weren't members; Borthwick removing papers from his briefcase and threatening to call the police; the women asking about Connie and wanting to see the cousins' keys.

This time it was Brownie's turn. She put her finger and thumb to her mouth and gave an ear-piercing whistle. Once again, the room fell silent.

It was the younger man, Borthwick, who was the first to speak. In a rather pompous voice, he announced that he was acting for Cait Calvert who wished to assert her right to repossess the assets of the Boudicca Society. He waved the papers about as though their presence alone had the power to persuade.

Brownie walked over, took them out of his hands and began reading.

The older man turned to the turbaned woman. 'Even if they are new members, it doesn't matter. Point is, Doris, even with two more, you only have six. You need seven for the AGM.'

Borthwick jumped in, speaking over the top of his client, 'And Mr Calvert does not concede that these violent intruders are members.'

'They've got keys.' Doris said, righting the wheelchair. 'They let themselves in. They're members all right. Connie's bequest.'

She waved to Mags to come and lend a hand and the two of them lifted the frail old lady back into her chair.

'Not good enough. Borthwick is right,' Calvert nodded at his lawyer, 'keys aren't proof as I'm sure the coppers will be able to tell you themselves.' He walked over to the sideboard and smirked as he picked up the telephone.

'I wouldn't do that if I were you,' Brownie spoke quietly, lifting her gaze from the paperwork. There was an iron edge to her words that saw him hesitate. 'You could find yourself on the receiving end of assault and trespass charges.' She folded the papers Borthwick had given her, retrieved her handbag, slipped the bundle inside and pulled out Connie's note. She walked over to the lawyer and held up the note for him to read, without letting him take it. When she spoke, she continued addressing the older man. 'Unlike Mags and I, who are members, you have no right to be here. Not unless, and until, the AGM fails to attract a quorum. And by your own acknowledgment, that meeting isn't scheduled until tomorrow afternoon.' She put Connie's note back in her handbag and closed it with a sharp click.

'Till tomorrow then, gentlemen,' Mags smiled and held out her arm, pointing to the front doorway.

'Yes,' Doris agreed, glaring at the two men, 'until four.'

Everything about the exterior and the vestibule of the Boudicca Society's mansion pointed to a club interior that would be staid: something furnished with winged-back armchairs and mahogany tables, something dotted with newspapers and ashtrays. But the clubroom wasn't remotely like that. While collectively the members were hundreds of years old, it was evident that they moved with the times. The sitting room was full of Featherstone and Fleur chairs and long sleek teak tables and its walls were decorated with bold and colourful geometric papers. The only concession to the past was the display cabinets: traditional and clubbish and full of curiosities.

Doris and the other elderly women ushered the cousins into the sitting room for restorative nightcaps, which everyone agreed would aid them in planning a strategy to save the Society.

Mags stood transfixed in the middle of the room, gazing at the décor. Brownie went straight to the nearest cabinet and read the plaque:

CHASTITY GWENDOLINE EVANS
BOUDICCA SOCIETY FOUNDER
1820 TO 1859

'Oh my,' she said. 'Mags, the cabinet is full of – of Eureka rebellion stuff. What is this club?'

'Chastity established it as a women's society in 1852,' Doris answered, 'after she struck gold and made her fortune. She worked her own claim. Great believer in encouraging enterprise in women. It was her idea that new members have to find their way to us. Bit of a problem, really, because we've run out of them.'

Brownie leaned closer to the glass and stared at the chopped remains of several dark-coloured, rough woollen dresses. 'And these? They were used to make–'

'The flag, yes,' Doris sounded impatient.

'This should be in a museum,' Brownie exclaimed.

'It is.' A frail-looking woman with dark, weather-worn skin handed Brownie a tumbler of whisky and hobbled back to the drinks trolley. 'It's in our museum.' She picked up another tumbler and hobbled over to Mags.

'The Boudicca Society is dedicated to action.' Doris swept her arms wide to indicate both the old-fashioned cabinets and the ageing members, seemingly oblivious to the irony. 'Workers' rights, Federation, our vote, sorting out that silly white army business, the wars. All that. And since 1939, our focus has been fascism. And now that you two have arrived, you can help frame something new–'

'Yes, yes, Doris,' the blue-haired woman agreed, accepting a whisky from her barely mobile friend, 'but not unless we have a quorum. So back to business. We've got less than 24 hours.'

Brownie, Mags and the old women sat down in a hastily arranged circle of colourful modernist chairs. Doris did the introductions. She began with herself, giving her name as Doris Austin and explaining that she was the Society's president. The blue-haired, wheel-chair bound woman was Helen Ledger, the Boudicca's business manager. The two other women who'd defended her were sisters Ethel and Zara Finch. The elder, Ethel, was responsible for signals, which had been a grand role during the war years but now seemed to involve answering the telephone. Zara, who'd served their drinks, was in charge of transport, which Doris told the cousins included having advanced skills in defensive and aggressive driving.

Mags stole a glance at Brownie, who looked as though she was about to start laughing at the incongruous image of the hobbling woman who'd served their drinks as a queen of the road. Brownie coughed to cover what appeared to be a giggle and took another sip of her drink.

The younger cousin began speaking, 'I'm Mags Agosti...' she hesitated. 'Fashion designer.'

The woman in her wheelchair looked delighted. 'We could do with someone like you. We recently lost our club artist–'

'Not now, Helen,' Zara, the speed queen, interrupted her. 'Introduce yourself, dear,' she turned to Brownie. 'Then we must get our skates on, so to speak, and start planning.' She took a sip of her whisky.

'Brownie Mason,' Brownie announced. 'Mags and I are cousins. We're Connie's great nieces. Oh, and I'm a secretary,' she blushed. 'Was a secretary.'

'She's brilliant,' Mags said, evidently aware of her cousin's discomfort. 'She knows all sort of stuff and she can find out anything.'

Doris took off her turban and scratched her bald head and then resettled it back in place. Her determined expression left little doubt about why the other women had chosen her as president and when she spoke, everyone listened. 'Good, because we need all the help we can get. We're between a rock and a hard place. No time left to track down the relatives of deceased members to see if anyone was left a key – and besides that's not the spirit of the thing.'

'What about that artist you mentioned?' Mags asked Helen. 'If she died recently, do you know what she did with her keys?'

Helen shook her head. 'Her papers disappeared, which was odd, but the short answer is no.'

'Other ideas? Anyone?' Doris asked.

'There are only two options,' Helen said. She rolled her wheelchair in a little closer, tightening the circle and then directed her next comment to the cousins, 'There are only two options because there are only two other members. Ruth Andrews and Cait Calvert. And it's Cait who has brought this calamity down on our heads.'

'That's Warwick's doing.' Zara corrected her and the other women nodded in agreement.

Helen sighed, 'Yes, but Cait has allowed him to.'

'What about Ruth, then?' Mags prompted.

'Unfortunately, Ruth is currently residing in Fairlea Women's Prison. And while our parole board contact, the estimable Mrs Phyllis Frost, is keen to see Ruth paroled to the Boudicca, Ruth has another four months before she becomes eligible.'

'Could we hold the AGM at Fairlea?' Brownie asked.

'Too late,' Ethel put her empty glass down on the table. 'Unfortunately, Cait, who is still officially our communications manager, put an advertisement in *The Age*, advertising the meeting at this address. No doubt it was Warwick's doing because Cait wouldn't remember to put her socks on unless she was reminded to and we haven't really heard from her for a couple of years, but… Well, AGMs are rather formal affairs and it's her notice that will count.'

Mags blew out long breath, 'Then how about getting Ruth out for the day?'

The elderly women shook their heads.

It was Brownie who spoke next, 'Then the only alternative is to convince Cait to come to the AGM.'

There was a pause as the elderly Boudicca members considered the matter. One by one, they conceded the point.

'A consensus then,' Doris stood up. 'Cait won't take our calls so there's nothing for it, we'll have to front up to the love pad in Hawthorn.'

'Love pad?' Mags asked. 'She's young, then?'

'Quite young,' Zara agreed. 'Only 73.'

Mags and Brownie looked at each other and, once again, appeared to struggle to avoid laughing.

'Brownie, Mags,' Doris pointed at the cousins, 'since Cait has stopped listening to all of us, you'll be doing the talking. I'll come and provide the introductions and Zara will drive.'

'Tonight?' Mags looked at her watch. 'It's past midnight.'

'Not tonight. Tomorrow when Warwick is at work. That's our only hope.'

The Boudicca members wished each other goodnight and Helen showed the cousins into the guest room, which was a good deal more luxurious than the twin room they'd had at the Windsor. The old woman was apologetic, telling them that their permanent rooms would be much more comfortable only none of the unoccupied members' quarters were made up and it was rather late in the evening to be rooting around in the linen cupboard.

After she'd left, the cousins climbed into their twin beds, almost too tired for sleep.

'I hope we can save the Boudicca Society,' Mags spoke into the darkness.

'So do I,' Brownie agreed.

Zara parked the Rolls around the corner from the Calverts' Hawthorn house and Mags, Brownie and Doris climbed out. The three of them stood on the pavement and ran through the story they'd rehearsed. When the housekeeper opened the front door, the cousins would ask to see Cait, claiming to be relatives visiting from the country. They'd changed into their most comfortable capris pants and espadrilles and all three were wearing sun hats and dark glasses, necessary not simply because the day was as hot as hades, but to disguise Doris. The Society's president was known at the Calverts' house and had been warned off after her last attempt to visit Cait.

Zara stayed in the car. She had wanted to keep the engine running until Doris reminded her that the Rolls had a tendency to overheat. Instead, she sat in the driver's seat with the window rolled down and her hand poised to reach for the ignition. She wished the others luck and adjusted the rear view mirror, her driving gloves disguising the mottled backs of her hands.

The women's pace was deceptively relaxed as they opened the black wrought iron gate and walked up the path to the Calverts' front door. Brownie broke off a hibiscus flower and slipped it into the band of her hat. Mags wore a pleasant and enquiring smile as though she was genuinely looking forward to reacquainting herself with a distant relative. Behind them, Doris appeared captivated by the gardens and never raised her eyes in case she met with an enquiring gaze from inside the house.

Mags was their spokeswoman when the housekeeper opened the door. Her persuasive powers were much stronger than Brownie's and her account of their sudden arrival on Cait's front doorstep was so convincing that the housekeeper looked genuinely regretful about having to turn them away. Apparently, Mrs Calvert hadn't been well and wasn't receiving visitors, not even family.

'I'll get Mr Calvert to call you when he gets home this evening. Just leave me your names and the details of where you're staying.'

'Darling Warwick,' Mags gushed. 'It would be marvellous to see him again. It's been such a long time.' She turned to Brownie, as though a thought had just struck her. 'Let's surprise him too. It'll be such fun.'

Brownie smiled, apparently enchanted with the thought. 'Oh, yes, let's. How clever.'

'Right then,' Mags turned her attention back to the housekeeper, 'No names or details. We'll just pop back on the weekend.'

While the housekeeper seemed significantly less enamoured by this idea than her own more conventional suggestion, she nominated Sunday afternoon as the preferred time. 'But I can't be certain. Are you sure you wouldn't like to leave your names?'

Mags thanked the woman but remained insistent on the idea of surprising Warwick. Then the three of them left, retracing their steps, Doris careful to keep her face turned away from the house even when they were back on the street.

They didn't speak until they were in the Rolls. Doris looked despondent but neither Mags nor Brownie were willing to give up.

'Let's storm the place,' Mags rested her chin on the back of the passenger seat.

Doris, who had turned about so she could face the cousins, shook her head, didn't even smile at the bold nature of the suggestion. 'No. That witch of a housekeeper was right about one thing, Cait isn't well. Never was very robust. Not really an ideal candidate for the Society but she's Chastity's great, great, granddaughter so her membership went without saying. No, if we stormed the place we wouldn't get any sense out of her.'

'What if we broke in?' Brownie sat forward. 'And did it quietly and carefully and didn't startle Cait?'

'What do you think?' Doris asked Zara. 'Might work.'

Zara didn't answer immediately. She used the rear view mirror to look at Mags and Brownie and seemed to be weighing things up. 'Yes, if it could be done. Perhaps not as good as being shown in by the housekeeper, but–'

'Even if we had been, it wouldn't have been straightforward,' Brownie pointed out. 'There was always a risk. Who knows what Cait would have said when the housekeeper showed us in?'

'But how do we break in?' Mags asked Brownie.

'Just look where we're parked.' Brownie pointed out the window and the others shifted in their seats to get a better view.

The Calverts' property was on a corner block and the Rolls was parked on the side street, right beside the wall of a garage that seemed to have been added to the building as an afterthought. It was a low, single story, rectangular structure that grew out from the corner of the grand terrace house. Its roof was almost flat and at its highest point, it was about three feet below the second-storey veranda.

It was Doris who got it first, but she wasn't impressed. 'The garage roof, yes, I see what you mean. But you can bet that Warwick will have locked all of those second-storey windows. He's that sort of man. And even if we could get one open, we'd have to get onto the garage roof first.'

Zara smiled. 'That bit I can help with. I'll park right beside the wall and you can climb onto the roof of the car.'

'And I bet Mags can remove one or two of the glass panes from that bathroom window.' Brownie pointed at the louvre window that was just visible under the second story verandah. 'That's the weakest point.'

Mags leaned across Brownie to get a better view. 'I'll need a screwdriver or a pen knife.'

'There's a picnic basket in the boot,' Zara said. 'Sterling silver cutlery.'

'Groovy,' Mags grinned. 'That will do the trick and if I'm caught I can argue that I'm returning some silver.'

'But it's not just you and Mags,' Zara interrupted. 'Doris has to be there too. Can you manage the climb?' she asked her friend.

'I'm tall,' the older woman sounded game. 'That should help. And I'm not dreadfully decrepit.'

Mags and Brownie frowned and even Zara looked doubtful.

'Don't look at me like that,' Doris complained. 'I'm young at heart and that's what counts.'

'You're still limping from yesterday,' Zara countered.

'That's as may be. We must do what we must do – for the Society and for Cait.'

'And getting back down?' Zara asked. 'You'll break your neck.'

Doris shook her head. 'We'll walk out the door with Cait, assuming these two have more luck with her than any of us have had. If not, we'll be thrown out. Either way, not a problem.'

Zara nodded, slowly. 'It's break and enter or give up on the Society's future.'

'Then it's definitely break and enter,' Mags said.

The four women were lucky that Hawthorn lacked the vivacity of Carlton or Richmond or any of the other less affluent and more heavily populated suburbs. It meant that there was no one about.

No one saw them getting out of the Rolls, discarding their sun-hats and glasses and rolling up their sleeves. No one watched as Zara repositioned the car beside the garage wall. No one noticed them as they scrambled up onto the car and then awkwardly and carefully climbed onto the garage roof: Mags first, then Doris, then Brownie.

They paused and waited, lay on their stomachs and caught their breath as Zara moved the car back onto the road. When the engine fell silent, Mags lifted her head and checked the street. It was empty, still. Even the overlooking windows from the property across the road seemed destitute of life.

Mags stood up and very delicately picked her way across the corrugated iron, stepping from nail head to nail head, like a dancer. The others followed.

At the far corner of the roof, Mags examined the yard below and then stepped across from the garage onto the outside edge of the veranda, hanging onto the balustrade for support. Then she climbed over the handrail. Behind her, Brownie and Doris hung back and crouched down, keeping their distance from both the street and the open backyard.

Mags pulled the silver bread and butter knife from her back pocket and walked over to the bathroom window. She began prising open the worn galvanised strip that held the lowest pane of glass.

Quietly, and with great care, she eased the pane out of its metal sides and laid it down on the wooden boards of the verandah. She turned back, reached inside the window and unlocked the louvers. The next pane was faster and the third faster still.

She crept back towards the garage roof and waved the others closer. Then she leant across the balustrade and whispered in Brownie's ear.

'I'm going inside. Don't try and climb over just yet. I'll see if I can open one of the sash windows. Then I'll come back and help you with Doris.'

Brownie nodded.

Below them, a door opened and the three women hurried out of sight as the housekeeper appeared. The woman walked across the backyard and out the back gate.

As soon as she was out of sight and with a flash of slender ankles, Mags climbed through the window and disappeared into the house, like a fish darting into a the dubious shelter of a rocky outcrop.

She reappeared a few minutes later, foot first then grinning face, after sliding open a large sash window. She hurried over to the balustrade and waved the others forward. Brownie gave Doris a leg up and Mags helped the elderly woman over the balustrade. Then Brownie scrambled across. Together, they entered the house.

They found themselves in a rear room that was quiet and still from disuse and held the baked smell of unused rooms. Doris took the lead. Her bald head looked naked without a hat or turban, but in the dappled light that nakedness seemed magnificent and almost beautiful.

They left the room in single file and took a half flight of stairs down to a landing and then another half flight back up again, to the front of the house. Everything in this part of the house was grand and the air smelt of polish.

They passed a bedroom and a study and a bathroom and the cousins waited in silence as Doris checked each one, only to return with a shake of her head. From the cousins' expression it was clear that they were growing increasingly anxious.

Then below stairs came the sound of a door opening and then the housekeeper's voice. She called out that she had returned and would be up with a cup of tea in ten minutes. From one of the front rooms a woman answered, her voice slightly slurred.

'Tea? Oh, yes, I suppose it is time. Perhaps I'll come down.' There was a pause and the sound of footsteps approaching and then she seemed to halt. 'No, perhaps not. Bring it up, if you wouldn't mind.'

The cousins had frozen, but Doris was smiling. Somehow it wasn't entirely reassuring. Magnificent she might be, but her smile made her look cadaverous. She waved for the cousins to follow her and walked confidently into the room from which the voice had emanated.

It was a library and Cait stood in the middle of it. She was a handsome woman with dyed blond hair that was set in a halo of curls. She was holding a book, a bemused expression on her face. When she looked up and saw Doris, she smiled as though her old friend was a regular visitor to the library, not someone she'd been estranged from for the past few years.

'Ah Doris, dear; did I… forget you were coming?' her voice was slow and filled with drifting pauses that spoke of alcohol and other sedatives. She frowned and peered at the book she was carrying. 'Where was I? Ah, yes, looking for something to read but now that you're here I'll ask Mrs Foster to use the larger pot.' She started towards the door, nodding pleasantly at Mags and Brownie, as though their presence was unremarkable. 'And more cups, I think.'

Doris put a hand on Cait's arm. 'No dear, no. We don't want tea. Best tell Mrs Foster not to bother for you either. Not just now.'

'Really?' Cait looked mildly surprised but called out to the housekeeper to leave the tea.

Then Doris introduced the cousins as new Boudicca Society members. That was when Brownie made a mistake. She told Cait they'd come to take her to the AGM. The expression on Cait's face changed, her inebriated confusion giving way to something sharper and more fearful.

'Oh no dear, I can't. Not possibly. Warwick is most insistent about that; most insistent. He's been very clear.' She turned to Doris. 'You really should leave Dee. He'll be furious if he finds you here. And then…' she frowned. 'And then…' She put her hand to her head. 'Well, military men are rather disciplinarian, aren't they? Must obey commands and all that.' Her eyes slipped to the drinks' cabinet, which was nestled between two tall shelves. 'A drink, perhaps?' She walked across the room, her gait wooden and studied. She poured herself a sherry and drained it, then poured another.

Mags held up her hand, indicating that Doris and Brownie should remain still. She walked over to the drinks cabinet and poured herself a sherry in a delicate glasses etched with grapes and vines. She lifted it but didn't sip it. Instead she looked around at the shelves. 'You like reading?' she said to Cait.

Cait looked up from her glass, a smile on her face. 'Love it. Can't imagine life without it.'

'I imagine you've got a few books back in your room at the Boudicca?' Mags's voice was gentle and unassuming.

Cait nodded. 'Plenty. Novels. Warwick doesn't approve of fiction so our library here has military history and biography. I read the biographies. Only two about women: Florence Nightingale and Lady Spencer-Churchill.'

She put down the book she was holding and walked over to a tall shelf and began scanning spines. 'The Nightingale biography is lovely. Where did it go?' She ran her fingers over several books. 'If I can find it, I'll show it to you. Can't lend it. Warwick is a bit fussy about his books.'

'And what about your books?' Mags asked. 'The ones back at the Boudicca? Do you miss them?'

Cait stood perfectly still, her back to the other women. She nodded. It was a tiny movement. 'Warwick says that once we have the Boudicca's paperwork straightened out, he can get inside my old room and he'll have all my novels packed up and sent over. He's going to turn the study into a ladies' library.' Cait turned around and gazed at Mags. There was an expression of longing on her face.

On the other side of the room, Doris appeared distressed and looked as though she was struggling not to cry. Beside her, Brownie was still. Only Mags looked relaxed. She sat on the arm of one of the worn leather couches and swung her feet, scuffing the Persian carpet. 'Such a pity that your friends will be turned out onto the street.'

Cait looked astounded. 'No, that's not right.' She shook her head. 'You're mistaken. They've all moved into a home. Warwick said they had to. Couldn't manage on their own. Too old. Sad, but the whole place is defunct. Kaput. Holding those bloody meetings just prolongs the pain,' although the last sentence was spoken by Cait, it could have been spoken by Warwick.

Mags didn't argue. Just nodded. 'Course, but that was before Brownie and I arrived.' She stood up and walked over to Cait, putting her hand on the old woman's arm. 'Everyone's back now, the whole crew, and we've got work to do. The Society's flourishing. Your room is ready for you – if you want it.'

A look of immense longing flitted across Cait's face. 'Oh... Oh, yes. That would be lovely.' Then her expression changed. 'But Warwick... He wouldn't allow it. I've made my bed, you see. One makes one's bed and one must lie in it.'

Mags smiled at Cait. 'That might be true for a lot of women, but it isn't true for you. You've got a room full of books and friends and a clubhouse.

And Brownie and I can handle Warwick. We're young. We can sort out his type. You wouldn't even have to speak to him if you didn't want to.'

Cait bit her lip, apparently uncertain whether the cousins' youth would be a foil against her husband. She glanced at the drinks cabinet and then looked back at Mags. 'It would be selfish of me. I couldn't let you risk it. He might do something to you–'

Mags waved away the thought. 'He wouldn't dare. Brownie knows Henry Bolte, personally. They were talking just last night.'

Mags turned to Brownie and winked and the older cousin managed to nod when Cait looked in her direction.

'Warwick admires Bolte,' Cait's voice was thoughtful. 'He says people need a strong leader to tell them what to do, just like a family needs a leader.'

'There you go then,' Mags turned back to Cait and offered the older woman her arm. 'Problem sorted.'

Cait looked at Mags's arm and hesitated. 'Now? You think we should leave now?'

It was Brownie who answered, 'Yes. Warwick won't bother you if we leave now. And if Bolte isn't enough, Mags has police connections and knows people in the sheriff's department.'

The cousins glanced at each other, their amused expressions almost a perfect match. Then Doris spoke up and told Cait it was time to come home.

The room was silent as Cait thought things through and then she nodded.

Together, the women crept downstairs, Brownie in front and Mags bringing up the rear, both ready to deal with opposition if they had to. Their luck held and with the smallest of clicks, as they turned the lock on the front door, they were out in the garden, down the path and through the front gate. By the time they reached the car, the Rolls was already purring.

The Boudicca Society's great hall was a relatively small affair, running the length of the western side of the building but it was ornamented with stained glass windows, depicting Boudicca and the queens who followed her. It was an apt setting given the nature of the witnesses Helen and Ethel had managed to assemble in the others' absence, most of whom had been beneficiaries of the present queen's honours. Clearly, Helen and Ethel had decided that their usual habit of using neighbouring housewives as witnesses wouldn't provide adequate ballast against any challenge by Warwick.

Mags, Brownie, Doris, Zara and Cait opened the double doors onto an extraordinary cast, including Mrs Phyllis Frost, Lady Violet Brooks, Dame Enid Lyons and Lady Jesse Street. There were no men present, of course, but the podium bristled with microphones and wires that led to an enormous and slightly antiquated reel-to-reel tape recorder. Evidently, Ethel, the Boudicca's ancient signals manager, was not taking any chances in terms of evidence.

Brownie and Mags walked on either side of Cait, ready to steady her if her nerves gave way. They needn't have worried. The woman seemed transformed. She exchanged a delighted wave with Enid Lyons and greeted Violet Brooks as an old friend. And while there was still a slightly wooden affect that spoke of medicinal sherry, there was no doubt she was of sound mind.

With the meeting called to order by Doris and the quorum named, the question of the Society's mission was tabled.

In the end, the fight against fascism was set aside, replaced by the pressing imperative of liberating women.

Emilie Collyer

The Panther's Paw

A Wild & Besen Adventure

It was too sunny for a funeral. Funeral days were supposed to be grey and cold, a bitter wind or drizzling rain. This day was picture perfect: blue skies, soft breeze, gentle sun, the kind of day people might fall in love, if you were into that kind of thing. Eliza Wild was not. She didn't want to be at the funeral. Too many people, forced politeness, boring conversations. But duty demanded her presence and she had felt genuine respect for Ariki Besen so she fronted up.

Besen's death had shocked not only the Grasslands Region. Ripples spread far and wide so guests were present from reps within all Grassland zones and many from neighbouring Regions.

Eliza kept her sunglasses on. It was easier to nod, smile and shake hands if she didn't have to expend the extra energy to make eye contact. Trailing behind work cohorts she approached the official mourning party knowing once this duty was performed she could leave.

'We mourn his passing, honour his life and seek to uphold his spirit,' the words spilled from her mouth, over and over. It was permitted to say anything of course, but Eliza found social talk hard at the best of times. If there was a standard phrase to use in any given situation she was happy for the reprieve.

Hand shake, sentence, move on. Hand shake, sentence, move on. Hand shake, sentence–

'My father spoke very highly of you.'

Eliza looked up from the hand gripping hers.

'Dash Besen,' said a young man, about her age, smiling.

'I know,' Eliza said, then realising it sounded too abrupt for such an occasion, 'um, I mean, your father spoke about you ... fondly. Also.'

Dash laughed. 'Nice of you,' he said.

Eliza could see something more complex in his gaze than she would have expected. Everyone knew Dash Besen's reputation as a party boy, so opposite from his father's serious scientific persona and career.

'Well,' she was surprised to find herself fumbling, actually wanting to try and find the right words to say, 'I'm very sorry for your loss. No matter what, it's, I mean, losing a parent, it's a big thing, right?'

'Right.'

Dash held her hand for just a split second longer than felt comfortable. His smooth brown skin was a taut contrast to the soft, golden hair that covered Eliza's body. It was almost invisible most of the time, but today it glinted in the full sunlight. She pulled her hand away and moved on. A few more greetings and she was done.

Eliza walked away from the courtyard, thronging with people. She passed a tall, slim figure dressed in the soft grey tunic trimmed with yellow sash that denoted Research. Eliza couldn't tell if the person was male, female, Dual, Non-Gen, Fluid or Al-Chem but whoever it was gave off a powerful charisma. The person bowed their head at Eliza as she passed and she caught something familiar in their eyes, wide set and pale blue. They must have met before, perhaps at a committee gathering. Eliza knew she was being rude to not stop and talk but she'd exhausted her threshold for social niceties. So she nodded in return and kept moving.

Not far away, paying their respects, the animals gathered.

Eliza crossed the wide gravel courtyard, slipped off her shoes and let the cool, soft grass brush against her bare feet. People were watching, some in admiration, others awe, a whole lot in snooty judgment: there goes the woman more comfortable with animals than humans.

Eliza didn't care. She pushed through the undergrowth, inhaled the scent of earth and the tang of blossom, and took her place quietly by the big cats. They acknowledged her presence just as she knew they would, with silent acceptance, no need for small talk or inanities. Here, she could just be, she could communicate as much or as little as she wanted, with no expectations or disapproving looks. She sat cross-legged and closed her eyes.

The sound of important speeches carried across the breeze. She didn't bother trying to make out the words, just enjoyed the warmth of the sun on her skin and the gentle rhythms of the big cats' breathing.

> *Besen's trailblazing work into new bio-communicative applications might be put on hold out of respect for his passing. Although surely it won't be long until other scientists, keen to carry on his outstanding work, take the baton and continue where Besen left off.*

'That's so incredible isn't it? I mean I've got no idea what the hell we'd ever learn from bacteria or microbes or whatever, but pretty amazing huh.'

Not for the first time Eliza remembered why she always got dressed and got out so fast after a Random Sex Swap. Physical attraction was one thing, great sex was integral to her life, but the small chat afterwards was nearly always dull or inane.

Most people took for granted the benefits of inter-species communication and had no idea of the vast, positive impact it had had on the human race, the state of the planet. In the past, Eliza had occasionally opened her mouth, started a conversation about what it meant but she'd learned not to. The less people knew about her own skills and what she did, the better. They either asked too many questions or demanded ridiculous requests like: Oh can you get me a ride on an eagle's back?

She wriggled into jeans, slipped her standard black t-shirt on, pulled on her new super light-weight windbreaker jacket and zipped up her boots.

'A lot of hype,' she said and flicked the screen off. At least there had been no mention of her so she could remain relatively anonymous, at least here. It was only a matter of time before the Council invited her for a formal briefing, to ascertain if she wanted to remain on the team and if so, was she ready for more responsibilities.

Eliza shuddered. More contact with people and less time out in the field. She couldn't think of anything worse.

'That was fun,' the woman said. What was her name? Kai? Or Cara? Shit, she couldn't remember. She had sweet lips that were now pressed gently against hers, teeth nipping playfully.

'You want to meet again?'

'Um sure; maybe,' Eliza said.

The woman laughed. 'No sweat either way. I can see you're someone who doesn't like to get tied down.'

Eliza softened, realising there was no need to load her uptight worries onto this welcome stranger.

'Tied up though,' she said winking, 'that I like.'

'Anyway, you can put a request through for me if you feel like it otherwise I guess we might end up together on another Random.'

They kissed again and the woman departed. Eliza did a quick check of the room. She'd left underwear, sunglasses, keys, phones, pretty much every possible small item behind in one Sex Swap or another over the last few years. One of the reasons she loved sex was that it made her feel relaxed and vague, the opposite to her usual state of being. Losing and leaving things was one of the unwanted side effects.

She splashed water on her face, tried without success to flatten her hair. Dyed electric blue at the moment, the colour seemed to have caused a startled texture to her hair making it stand up on end. She threw some water on it and that helped a bit, stood still for a moment, watching her own reflection. An ache of sadness surprised her, pulling a line through her shoulders, down into her chest. It was as unexpected as it was unwelcome. She hadn't been that close to Besen but he was a good man, in that kind of deeply good way that was rare.

'Loss hurts. You can't escape it, can't run from it, can't explain it away,' was what the female panther she'd sat beside while the ceremony took place had said. Not in so many words of course, but that was Eliza's interpretation and her big cat communication skills were – apparently – second to none. So, as much as she hadn't wanted to take any kind of grief on board, seeing it as a sign of weakness, she knew well enough to respect the words of the panther and accept that she'd feel a bit shit for a while and then, hopefully, it would pass.

Eliza's phone flashed with a message: *Incoming call from Dash Besen.*

The sad ache twisted into annoyance. Her shoulders tensed. What the hell did he want? She could ignore it. She owed him nothing. The panther's steady gaze came back, those eyes that always challenged her to be the best she could, not run from difficulty, face it head on.

'For fuck's sake,' she said under her breath, turned away from the scowling image in the mirror, reached for her phone and flicked to accept the call.

'I can see that you're very charming but you won't charm me.' Eliza sipped her coffee and trained her well developed don't-fuck-with-me stare at Dash.

'I wouldn't dream of trying,' he said.

'That right there! None of that semi-flirtatious, I'm used to getting my way, it's only a matter of time bullshit. I mean it.'

'Well Eliza, I can't promise to change my personality while in your presence, but I do accept your right to choose and not to warm to me in any way.'

A young, female Sustenant delivered a large glass of green juice to Dash. He smiled thanks and Eliza could see the girl's heart flutter. In fact the whole environment: the hydro paths, photo-synth walls, solar panels, other customers, hell even the chairs, tables and cutlery seemed to all swoon when Dash Besen smiled.

'So,' Eliza said sharply, 'obviously something is going on. I can't access his files either. He might have had an automatic lock-out system in place if he didn't personally log in for a number of days?'

Dash shook his head.

'I was in and out of Dad's stuff all the time. He wasn't secretive. He had terrible security on all his systems. I was forever telling him to at least put some kind of pass code in place. This is like a whole other entity has taken over.'

'What do you mean; like a virus?'

'I don't know, it's just, something seems really strange. Not just like we can't see the files or get to them, but like, they're actually hiding. Or – gone.'

'Maybe it's grieving.'

'What?'

'The comp system. Humans do it. Animals do it. Plants do it. Why not?'

Dash nodded slowly and took a long drink of the green goop. Eliza winced as she imagined the viscous liquid and slightly mouldy taste. She couldn't come at the latest craze in algae-pops and if she was honest, thought most people who jumped on every new health fad were both desperate and stupid. But that was why people adored Dash. He was into things. He was enthusiastic and optimistic. Not that he seemed into what she had just said, he seemed to be eyeing her the same way she'd seen the big cats approach a wounded cub. Nothing new there. She was used to people thinking of her as something to be wary of.

Eliza's co-worker, Van, who had known Dash his whole life, had sporadically suggested sexual, romantic or even platonic set ups. 'He is VERY nice.'

'Whereas I'm cynical, pessimistic and selfish,' Eliza had always said in response. 'Good thing too, the world would throw up on itself if everybody was sickly nice all the time.'

'I don't want you to be lonely,' Van would grab her in a tight, almost motherly hold and kiss her head.

'I'm not lonely! I love my life. Just because I don't like most people doesn't mean I can't be perfectly content.'

'Well there is that. You are kind of a genius. So maybe you have different needs from us mere mortals.'

'Shut up.'

On the whole people didn't know how to talk about Eliza's communication skills. There were others like her, of course there were, but it's not like they all belonged to some club or support group; the opposite if anything. While many humans could communicate across several species, each individual tended to align with a particular animal, which in turn made them both slightly protective and competitive.

There was no hard and fast evidence about where the skills had come from. Some people were just born with them. The most science could say was that it had become evolutionarily necessary for humans to learn how to communicate with animals and so the capacity had developed.

Eliza had always heard voices, nonsense and ramblings to begin with, from bugs, moths, local birds. The first time she'd heard clear and full expressions was on a school excursion to the grasslands where she'd come across a litter of baby tigers. The teacher had reported her to the local Council.

From there, tests, verification, special education, channelled into life as a Conduit. No choice really. Not that Eliza would have wanted another life. She was happy to spend as much time as possible with the animals and reluctantly report in to Council for scheduled meetings, query sessions, negotiations.

'Earth to Eliza. Come in Eliza.'

Dash, snapping his fingers, brought her back to the here and now. She blinked, took a gulp of water.

'You've got green stuff on your teeth,' she said.

Dash put his hand up to his mouth, a self-conscious gesture.

For the second time that day Eliza felt bad. One thing she was slowly learning from the cats was the impact her behaviour had on others, how to be a member of society, of groups, even if you didn't want it.

'Were you and your father blood related?' she asked, to be polite.

'Yes.'

She nodded. In some of the more remote Regions there were social divides between children brought up communally and then assigned a parent and those who had a life-long relationship with a blood parent. But not here, in the heat of C&R sector. Comms and Research residents were almost annoyingly tolerant and open-minded. Both ways of upbringing had benefits and challenges and both were treated as equally valid.

'Do you speak of your lineage?'

Dash upheld social norms and asked the standard question when the issue of family arose.

'My parents both died when I was young. Our lineage is fire forged.'

'Strong memories of conflict in your blood,' he murmured.

She didn't respond.

'Our heritage is water carried,' Dash said, then corrected himself, 'was – I guess.'

'It still is,' Eliza said, 'your father's death doesn't take that away.'

'Yeah I know. It's just weird, you know, saying I instead of we, was instead of is, it's… I'm not used to it yet. I kind of muck it up still.'

It was accepted that all people were products of their lineage no matter how far back they could or couldn't trace it or how much or little they wanted to identify. The choice was individual and all experiences valued. At times the extreme formality struck Eliza as disingenuous but she knew it was better than ignoring or assuming anything about anybody.

She nodded. Truth told she didn't have much fire in her blood that she could attribute to the way her parents had died, in a brutal, brief and unexpected regional conflict. She put it down to her animal communication skills – these had somehow filled the space where that pain may have otherwise lodged and grown.

'I miss him like crazy,' Dash said and his stupidly big brown eyes filled with tears.

Horrified, Eliza patted his arm again and pushed her glass of water towards him, anything to make the tears stop. She didn't do very well with human emotions. Dash sniffed, drank, smiled.

'So,' he said, eyes shining now in a kind of supermodel extreme handsome way, 'what are we going to do?'

'We?' Eliza screwed up her face and pushed back her chair, 'WE are not doing anything. I've got work to do. I guess, let me know if anything else weird happens.'

'Like the comp system getting over its grief and starting up again?'

'Yeah,' she said, a hot flush of embarrassment sweeping her face, but stubborn in her refusal to back down, 'like that.'

'Well I liked spending time with you Eliza Wild. I hope we can do it again.'

Dash stretched in his seat, clearly enjoying the alliteration of Eliza's name.

She stood to leave and caught a movement at the door, swish of grey material.

'Do you know that person? Grey robes, yellow sash, they were at your Dad's funeral as well.'

Dash craned forward in time to see the robes flicker away via the exit. He rolled his eyes.

'Febron. Odd one. Non-Gen. I mean nice enough, but I think kind of needy in that way super smart people can be, you know? Always hanging around Dad and now – I guess – me.' Dash looked sidelong at Eliza and raised an eyebrow, 'or maybe you. Next in line for greatness at the Council?'

Eliza shook her head. 'Next in line for some time off so I can get away from all that crap.'

The cool green was where Eliza felt most alive. Ever since the moment with the tiger cubs back when she was a kid, her body yearned to be in the grasslands. She would have shifted there, disappeared forever into the mint green of winter, the bright gold green of summer, the dripping emerald green of rain, but she'd been raised to be aware of her responsibilities. With a gift came a duty. It was her role to act as a Conduit, an interpreter as the world slowly and steadily righted past wrongs and kept on the path to equality and sustainability.

'There's so much talking, Van, I mean it just goes on and on and on and it takes forever for any decision to be made, any action to be taken.'

The first few years of work as a Conduit had been exhausting and Eliza had often debriefed with Van, the steady, solid and hard working support leader at Council.

'I know it's challenging but it's better than the alternative.'

'But it could be so quick!' Eliza would shake her head to try and get rid of the throb that came from hours and hours of concentrated interp and comms, 'it could just be one elected person, one elected animal, they talk, they decide the best course of action for the group, the herd, the area, whatever. Done.'

Van would raise an eyebrow.

'You really think that?'

Eliza would sigh.

'Of course not. I mean I get it. The emphasis is on slowness, patience, small steps, rather than huge leaps and damaging, radical change. It doesn't mean that I don't find all the negotiations and thinking time and silent discussions a giant pain in the arse.'

'You're helping make the world a better place, one word at a time.'

Eliza had repeated that lame line to the panther, once they'd developed a close relationship, stressing that she had no interest in any high flown ideas like that, just wanted to keep a low profile and get through life.

That is one way to view existence and it is perfectly fine. But some beings seek more. You may be surprised to find you are one of them.

No. Not me. No thanks.

The panther returned to licking her paw.

> I mean this is the life isn't it? Eat to survive, find other beings
> you want to hang out with, respect nature, relax in the sun.

The conversation with Dash had left Eliza uneasy, a restless pulse through her bones, under her skin. She went to the grasslands and found one of her hidden havens. When she was there it was clear to any of the animals nearby that she was resting, not working. They still sometimes came and joined her but only to sleep or tell simple stories about their day, never with a problem to present at Council or a dictum to translate for the humans.

She curled up against the warm granite, slipped her shoes off and dug her toes into the soft sand. The creek sang softly as it careened past and Eliza sighed, eager to let the water relax her mind and let some of the pent up tension from the last few days slip away.

She would remember this moment long after, how the world seemed to slow to a moment, the droplets of water hanging suspended from her fingers, shimmering blue and gold in the afternoon light. How unexpected and brutal the searing pain that ripped through her body, a line of fire up each arm, into her chest and right down into the depths of her gut. Worse than any of the pain she'd felt during her own teenage years, the time spent in the Blood Trials when she'd pushed hard against authority and had learned even harder lessons in her sessions with the antagonist animals. That pain had been tough, but fair, her scars earned and now treasured.

This was instant, immediate, gut wrenching violence that threatened to tear her body apart.

Eliza gasped and grabbed at the air around her, trying to clutch onto something, connect back to the earth. Lungs clenched, her breathing coming in short, painful bursts, Eliza called out to any animals in the area. News spread like wild fire in the animal community, faster than among humans, since the animals could communicate without words and via sensate pathways such as wind and water.

Shock. Fear. Anger. Disgust. But nothing clear coming through.

'What?' she cried out loud, a rare thing for her, animals did not respond well to harsh human vocal tones.

It was like her first experience, as a child, before the tiger cubs, a mess of noise and mixed messages. She could sense that real communication was happening, but somehow, for some reason, it was being blocked. Or, more specifically, some of it was being blocked from her.

Eliza pushed up from the warm sand, her body shaking and weak. She stumbled to the creek where a wave of nausea slammed through her and she vomited. She pushed out a few breaths, trying to steady herself, crouched down slowly. She'd learned a few breathing rhythms from the big cats over the years and put them into practice now, a way to centre the body and attune with the environment. After a moment she was calmer, still weak and feeling like the world was spinning unnecessarily fast, but able to stand without the vicious pain. She turned to see a brown snake coiled on the granite rock she'd just been leaning against. Eliza licked her lips, trying to draw some moisture.

Tell me.

She didn't get along that well with reptiles as a general rule but she knew one thing, they were incapable of lying.

The panther.

Dread, thick and cold, fell like a shroud. Eliza forced the word out, wanting to know the whole truth:

Dead?

The snake swayed side to side, head tilted, no doubt feeling vibrations in the ground for any further information.

Not yet.

Grasslands?

On the border of the city.

Eliza ran stumbling to find the path, get back to where she had left her cruiser. While all cruisers were made to fit seamlessly with the environment she still preferred not to bring it right into the heart of nature. The more spaces that were kept completely organic, especially around cities with higher human populations, the better the quality of air, water, energy, communications, everything was.

She found her rhythm and slipped into physical mode, focussing everything on her stride, the swing of her arms, her breathing. It was a skill she'd developed spending time with the big cats, to put her often over-active brain into rest mode and inhabit a more animal consciousness. The irony of using it now, for this purpose, didn't escape her, but she pushed the thought away. No point wasting energy on thinking, it would only slow her down.

To her surprise a small team of medics were already on the scene when she arrived. Generally speaking humans didn't interfere with animal injuries or sickness, the eco-system functioned best when natural cycles and predator relationships were left to take their course.

Eliza crouched next to the panther, and steadied her mind.

How did it happen?

A small human.

Eliza could see how much the animal loathed being at the mercy of the medical team. But laws stated that if animals were harmed by humans and could be saved, then all reasonable measures had to be taken. The team had set up one of their mobile medic clinics and had acted fast to initiate a blood transfusion. The dark seeping mass spread across the gravel told Eliza how much had already been lost.

An Al-Chem I think, but that is just my assumption.
She was riding a hawk, swooped down and sliced in one action.
Neat job, well executed, clearly trained.

Who saw it?
And how did the medics know to come?'

Eliza resisted touching the panther. She wanted to, for her own reassurance as much as anything but knew how sensitive the creature would be to unnecessary human touch right now.

Your friend.

The panther almost smiled. Then her eyes closed as the team moved in to administer a small amount of organic pain killer.

Eliza thanked the team, asked them to take special care and contact her with any updates, then stepped out of the cool blue clinic into the afternoon sun. Dash was about 20 metres away, chatting with a gathering of curious onlookers, journalists clearly among them. A swirl of relief and anger stirred in Eliza's gut.

She walked over to the group, pulled at Dash's arm, dragging him away.

'They can't be here,' she said, her voice hissing. 'The other cats won't come while they're around and she needs to be with her pride.'

Dash nodded, eased her hand off his arm, and approached the group.

'So as I said, thank you all so much for your concern. It seems like it was a training routine that went wrong and all parties are involved in positive communications to ratify and make amends.'

The group dispersed, a few audible grumbles from those who wanted more of a story, or a peek at the wounded panther but nobody protested or ignored Dash's directions to leave.

'What the hell?' Eliza spat the words at Dash as he farewelled the final stragglers.

'Is she all right?' he gestured to the domed shell of the clinic.

'I don't know. For now, she's alive. But it's, she–' Eliza stopped, not wanting to give voice to the brutality she'd seen.

'I mean it's very convenient that you happened to be so close. Is that just a coincidence?'

Even as she said the words Eliza could feel in her bones that there was nothing sinister about Dash. Her own instincts aside, the panther would have warned her, not called him her friend with that half smile.

Dash, eyebrows raised, as if to signal how far off the mark she was but that he'd let it slip given her obvious shock, guided her to a small patch of grass and pointed.

'Cloud watchers,' he said, 'they message each other all the time about stories they see, signs from the universe, you know how they are.'

This was a great area for cloud watching, raised slightly above the tree line, quiet enough to lie for hours undisturbed.

'Flakes,' Eliza muttered.

'Yeah, but well-meaning flakes, and in this case – life saving.'

Dash looked up at the sky, the display of cumulus nimbus currently on offer would have been a delight for the cloud watchers.

'They saw the hawk, nothing unusual in that, but drops of blood falling from the sky, that's something worth reporting.'

'And you're on their network?'

'I'm pretty tapped in, generally.'

'So you saw the message and called the medics.'

Dash nodded, squinted at Eliza. 'What did they do?' he asked with a quiet frown.

She gulped, then formed the words, slow and careful. 'Her front right paw, severed.'

'Shit.'

Eliza sipped at the water bottle the medic team had given her.

'Like a fight?' Dash asked.

'No. Deliberate attack. Out of the blue. Clearly pre-meditated.'

'And whoever it was took the paw as a trophy.'

Eliza glanced over at the clinic dome, she could sense that the panther had been sedated, and that members of the pride were gathering, keen to take her with them. She wanted to go and be with them, they'd accept her, she could probably help with any necessary comms between the animals and the medical team. But a fat drop of blood, still glistening on the sandy gravel just a few metres away caught her eye. Her own blood pulsed, and her body hair bristled. A hot spike of rage burst from her gut. She was up and on her feet, touching the cruiser to rev it into action.

'Where are you going?' Dash moved quickly, put a hand on her arm.

'To catch that little bitch.'

'That's not your jurisdiction.'

'You think I give a fuck? If we leave it to the official channels this will just get written off as an 'Unfortunate Human Animal Incident'. There'll be a round of education, some trade off between us and the cats, that will be it.'

'And what's your alternative?'

'Retribution. Fast. Effective.'

'Animal law,' Dash spoke quietly.

Eliza didn't respond, just pulled her arm from his touch.

'I'm going,' she said.

She straddled the cruiser. It throbbed into life.

Dash ran a hand through his dark curls and shot Eliza a darker look than she would have expected he was capable of. 'I'm coming with you.'

'The fuck you are.'

Heat was swelling up from the earth and with it the rich, tangy scent of the panther's blood. That one drop could give off such a pungent odour Eliza knew was partly her own sensitivity and relationship to the animal but it also smelled of something rotten, something other than a 'technical exercise gone wrong'. She could no more ignore it than she could deny her own need to breathe.

'You have two choices,' Dash spoke low and firm, 'either you let me come with you and I'll work out a story to feed back to the Earth Bred Consulate, or you go without me and I'll report you within seconds. They'll send a deterrent posse, you'll get about as far as,' he pointed to the flat topped mountain range skirting the edge of the Grasslands, 'Mount Oberon, if you're lucky, and then you'll have to face a tribunal. Who will help your panther then?'

Eliza suppressed the growl she wanted to hurl out at this arrogant and stupidly attractive man. To fight would only waste time. She flicked her head, shrugged and slid forward on the cruiser to make room for him.

'You can at least make yourself useful,' she said. 'Can your Cloud Watching flakes give us an update as to where the hawk went, which direction, how long ago?'

He pressed his body against her, it was annoyingly arousing. She pushed the physical desire down along with the anger. The price of having a body that relied on a high degree of sexual activity to stay in balance was that she had almost overwhelming urges at the most inappropriate moments. But not now. Not him.

Dash nudged her thigh and pointed north-west, away from the mountains, towards the ocean.

'That way,' he said.

The cruiser rose, Eliza gunned it, hoping the sudden acceleration would at least make his stomach curl.

'I don't do water,' Eliza said, her voice flat, face strained.

'What do you mean?'

'It's a bad mix. I freak out, panic, think I'm going to die.'

The cruiser buzzed, waiting for direction. Dash squinted into the sun. Their target had dipped beyond the crop of granite rocks and not reappeared. The only way was down. If they wanted to keep chasing, get the paw back, either Eliza would have to suck it up and get over her fear or he'd have to leave her here and go alone.

'It can't hurt you,' he said, voice rising, weaking in the statement.

'It can kill you. Not just drowning. My god, so many different ways. We are land creatures.'

'Well actually you know we're 70% water and we evolved from water, it's our natural state.'

'Spare me. Even you Water-Carried people are more comfortable when you're on land. It may be inside us but it's not where we are supposed to be.'

Dash flexed his hands to stop from scratching the skin at the nape of his neck, his default tic when situations started to slip out of his control.

'So what do we do?' he asked.

The cruiser shuddered. It would revert to sleep mode if they didn't move soon.

Eliza gulped, then put her hands on the controls and revved the cruiser.

'We go down,' she said.

'You sure?'

'Not at all, but there's no other choice. And you,' she spun around, eye-balled him, her green eyes piercing and fierce, 'your job is to be positive and – and vibrant and charming. Okay? I may hate all that bullshit in real life but down there,' her voice wavered, 'I'm going to need all your feel-good bullshit that I can get. Savvy?'

Dash dug his nails into his palms, then spread his mouth wide into one of his perfect smiles.

'Capiche.'

Eliza expelled short, sharp breaths as the cruiser morphed, flattening into its eel shape and swiftly sealed shut above their heads. She and Dash were prone, her body above his, separated by a buoyant but thin membrane. She didn't watch as the cruiser knit itself closed. She didn't close her eyes, but focused on a neutral spot, tried to see the amber membrane as safe, protective and reassuring, not – as would happen if she let her mind slip – a warm coffin about to carry her to certain death.

Dash hummed.

'What's that?' Eliza asked.

'Can't remember, it's from a TV show, old school, 20th century.'

Eliza rolled her eyes. It was the latest craze with the rich and restless, to dig back through time, before The Wailing, before the Re-Set that marked the end of the Roman Calendar era, and find quaint things to get obsessed with. The humming had a haunting tone, it sounded like the soundtrack to a dream, the shape of it was round, more like a whistle than a hum.

'I'll stop if it's annoying you,' Dash said.

'No.' She liked it. 'Keep going, It's like, I don't know, it's almost like a tunnel, like it's letting air in here or light. Something.'

She knew it sounded stupid but she was so relieved to not be dry retching with panic she didn't care what Dash thought.

Down.

Down through the blue. They couldn't see but both of them knew. Any ordinary ocean scan or adventure trip would have stopped by now, in among the bright colours, vibrant coral and iridescent creatures of the blue. They'd been down too long. Past the blue. Into the black.

Down.

> It's a pretty one, did you see?
> Oh yes a pretty one, a lovely one indeed.

'What?' The words floated in to Eliza's consciousness.

Dash was still humming though so it couldn't have been him. She brushed the cruiser's membrane so it went translucent for a moment and she saw they were being carefully watched by a myriad of sea creatures. Wide, flat rays, who were able to dip down and up, black to blue without too much trouble, pockets of gnarled fish with the bulging eyes they'd developed at this dark depth and an array of really bizarre looking things, more like science experiments gone wrong than any creature Eliza was used to looking at.

She pushed her revulsion down and muttered one of the mantras about difference and acceptance that Van had taught her. Then she focussed her mental clarity and sent out what she hoped was a message of:

> Help please. We come in peace. We seek something from the
> animal realm that has been stolen.

She heard a jumble of sounds, a cacophony of high pitched whistling, something bubbling and a few words not addressed to her but that she could just make out:

> *Not the one who speaks, the other one. The pretty one.*

An old, familiar resentment stirred deep inside. She'd never been 'the pretty one' and had never particularly wanted to be. But she remembered being disappointed once she learned the animal world, in fact all species as far as she could tell, were similar to humans in how they privileged things and creatures of beauty.

She sighed. Her communication skills opened up the conversation down here but it was Dash – *the pretty one* – that may actually get them through. Eliza wriggled, dug an elbow in to Dash, part thanks, part punishment.

Not long after that she could sense that the cruiser was receiving instructions about a safe place to dock.

> *The item you seek can be found in this human made dwelling.*
> *We neither support nor condemn their actions.*
> *We have no allegiance or quarrel with land creatures.*
> *We provide safe passage. We will provide nothing further.*

Eliza thanked the sea creatures and, as inter-species etiquette dictated, asked what favour she could provide in return.

> *The pretty one.*

Shit. Dash's warm body was relaxed beneath hers. He had no idea about the complex communications going on. He was just enjoying the adventure.

> What do you require of him?

> *To look, just to look. For the time you are here, visiting our*
> *realm. When you are ready to leave, he will also leave.*

'Are you fucking kidding me?' Eliza said this out loud, in her human-only voice; she hoped. Who the hell knew how much these strange animals understood; maybe everything? Maybe – like Ariki Besen had been close to proving – many answers to the mysteries of this world and beyond did indeed lie down here, in the depths of the ocean.

She gritted her teeth and acquiesced, what choice did she have? She'd explain it to Dash once they were docked and safely out of the cruiser. He wouldn't mind, surely, just like another day in his ordinary life, being gazed at and adored by a bunch of strangers.

'I'm not going to do anything stupid and I won't take long.'

Eliza spoke low and fast and tried to ignore the fire in Dash's eyes and the fact that he kept scratching the nape of his neck.

They were in a blue chamber, the walls similar in substance to the membrane of the cruiser. Eliza was quietly impressed with how this deep water bio-structure had been researched and adapted. Just like the cruiser that could move from air to water. She could see – and feel – that the membrane of this natural cave chamber was incredibly thick – to protect anyone inside from being crushed to death by the pressure down here. But it was also buoyant and flexible, more like a living organism than the kinds of caves she'd been in up on the surface of the earth, which always felt impermeable, fossilised into one set shape.

'Don't try and be some kind of hero,' Dash said, standing very close to Eliza. He was taller. That was annoying. And he had quite a presence when he put his mind to it. 'If it's just that Al-Chem playing a sick game, and you can get the paw back easily, then do it. But if it's anything else, like if you find some kind of storage facility for stolen animal parts, a bigger operation, we're going straight back up and we're going to report it. Understand?'

Eliza exhaled and her golden body hair bristled.

'You don't get to tell me what to do,' she said.

'Oh but you get to tell me? You just made a deal about me, about my body, with a bunch of deep sea creatures that I had no awareness of and made no consent about.'

Dash was breathing hard too and Eliza could see and smell a lot of anger and fear coming off him. Pissed off as she was at how he'd talked to her, instinct and years of animal familiarity kicked in and she knew the right thing to do was back off.

'I'm sorry,' she said, 'you're right. You're helping me and this was an unexpected twist. So yes, I agree with your observations about this situation. No risks. No heroics. I won't leave you here long, I promise.'

The conciliatory words had calmed her body. She put her hands out and Dash took them. They stood for a few seconds in the pose of reconciliation. His anger dissolved but she could still smell plenty of fear – a sour sweet combination, like high pitched citrus that she could identify probably came from a deeply embedded memory, a trauma from some years ago.

'You're not scared of being down here are you?' she asked gently.

Dash shook his head. 'It's not that.'

'What then?'

He sighed. 'I'm in Reconnection,' he said.

'Oh.'

Of course. It made sense. The charming demeanour was common amongst people who had struggled with addiction of any kind. It was one of their many tools to try and find a place in the world where they could belong and a way of being comfortable in their own skin.

'Right,' Eliza said, keeping her voice light but interested, aware of not feeding the side of Dash that would be vulnerable to a strong emotional reaction. Those in Reconnection were extremely sensitive, moving from a state of avoidance that had manifested in whatever their specific addictive behaviour had been, into a more cohesive and integrated way of being. Too much stimulation of the wrong kind could be overwhelming, tip them back into the closed shell of avoidance.

'And um,' Dash carried on, a good sign. He was aware and articulate, and kept his hands touching Eliza's, staying connected physically. 'For me it was narcissism, getting lost in my own image so, yeah, this is a bit full on.'

Shit, Eliza thought but didn't say out loud, cursing herself at this third insensitivity gaffe for the day. Her blithe assumption that he loved being looked at now turned on its head. Being looked at was probably one of his most dangerous triggers. He'd get sucked in, seeing himself as the creatures saw him, believing that all of his worth came from his looks, seduced and also completely disempowered by this thing beyond his control.

'Okay,' she said, squeezing his fingers gently, 'we can leave. I'll just, I'll come back another time for the paw.'

The chamber walls pulsed and Eliza could hear the scrambled beginnings of impatient communications from the creatures outside, those waiting to gaze on the pretty one. She could also feel the throb of the panther's paw ebbing, diminishing in strength; whether because the Al-Chem was carrying it further away, into this underwater labyrinth or – cold fear rolled through her – because the panther's life force was draining away, she couldn't tell.

'Come on,' she said, louder this time and firm. She had to see this situation for what it was and take control. She led Dash to where the cruiser was in rest mode, its amber light a soft glow in the cool, blue surrounds.

Dash squeezed her hands in return. 'I'll be fine, we've come this far. You were scared too. I mean thank you, for the offer, but I'm okay. Let's do it.'

Eliza hesitated, words of protest forming on her tongue, but she could sense the shift in Dash and he was right. They were on equal footing now, both moving through deep fear in order to carry out this action which, now started, they wanted to see all the way through to completion.

'All right partner,' she said, smiling genuine, from her heart, for the first time that day, 'let's do it.'

Eliza left Dash standing relaxed and determined in the viewing chamber. He had techniques to use from his group and individual reconnect sessions.

'You can picture my face if you want,' Eliza joked as she left, 'if you want to get a very unbeautiful image to focus on.'

Dash raised one perfect eyebrow. 'Don't be an idiot. Your beauty shines.'

Eliza flushed hot, squirming at the compliment.

'Besides which my challenge is to stay present, see what's actually right here, in my surrounds, not slip into imagination or memory. Or fantasy.'

A small, tight flutter thrilled in Eliza's core. Preparing for action always shifted her sexual vibrancy up a gear. There was no time and it was completely inappropriate but it didn't stop the swift flash of imagining Dash's lithe body up against hers and what he might feel like.

But she just grinned, jabbed him with a light, platonic punch to the arm and took off into the winding network of interconnected tunnels. She gathered all energy back into herself and focussed on following the scent of panther blood, still just strong enough to track.

If the paw had been taken as a declaration of hostility she would have to be careful as she would be known as an ally with the panthers. Her gut said otherwise. The event was so strange, targeted and specific. It didn't have the weight of past scores to settle or new wars to wage.

She tried to clear her mind as she ran, light and fast, along the narrow corridors, adjusting her direction now and then, pausing where intersections appeared to make sure she could still smell the blood. Meeting the Al-Chem with too many preconceived ideas would put up an immediate barrier to negotiations. Much like Dash she knew her best chance for success was to stay focussed in the present and deal with whatever came her way, rather than get distracted by imagined scenarios.

The walls were no longer blue, the welcoming colour of the viewing chamber had faded and while she still felt safe from the deep, black terror of the ocean, there was no comfort in the grey tones surrounding her now. Her footsteps started to fall heavier and the rhythm of her breathing lost its flow, becoming jagged. An echo of the searing pain that had ripped through her body earlier that day catapulted from skull to coccyx, pinging through every nerve and muscle. Moving through the corridor got harder, slower, like running in a dream. Her arms ached, legs wobbling now as lactic acid flooded through. Mouth parched and chest burning, how much further could she go? Would there be a point at which she should turn back – return to Dash and get them both the hell out of there?

And then she was falling.

It wasn't a bad fall, as falls went. Her stomach didn't drop away and she wondered if that was something to do with being so far under water and maybe a reason to not be so scared of the ocean after all.

Eliza bumped and floated, hitting sides of a downward slanted tunnel but not in a way that hurt. She saw a green light below that rose up towards her, or did she fall towards it? Either way, she landed, softly on her feet, golden body hair fluttering in a large room.

The green light was not garish, just the right shade and tone of emerald green. The room was circular, sparsely furnished, but sufficient, a few low wide seats to her right and to her left an office area.

Complete with desk, screens, and watching her, with a slight smile and perfect posture – Febron.

'Welcome,' said Febron.

Eliza recoiled. This was not good. She eyed Febron with caution and then took in the rest of the room properly. Yes it was a nice room, good light, well furnished, but it was also, clearly, a place where she had been lured and was now trapped. There was only one door, next to the desk. The chute from which she'd just emerged had closed over.

'I don't feel welcome,' she said.

'I can understand that,' Febron's head bobbed. Still wearing the grey robe and yellow sash, Febron's head was bare, revealing a beautiful, elongated skull and facial features both fine and wide. Those blue eyes that had glittered pale and light on land, down here were dark, almost purple. Febron's lips were a similar hue.

'I'd like to leave now,' Eliza said, 'I want to take the paw with me. I don't appreciate being tricked. If you wanted to meet with me you should have followed standard request protocol.'

Febron stood still, head cocked slightly to one side, as if curious. Other than that, no emotional response.

'I apologise,' Eliza swallowed her anger and forced herself to revert to absolute etiquette, perhaps formality would open up a more useful dialogue. 'I have not asked how you like to be referenced. I am Eliza Wild, human female, fire forged lineage, animal communications specialist.'

'I am Febron, human Non-Gen, I choose 'id' for my personal pronoun, I choose not to reveal my lineage, I am head of Research in the Grasslands council. Or rather, I was.'

The atmosphere in the room tightened, Eliza could feel the air thinning, a slow panic rising. If Febron was no longer on the council, id would follow no formal protocols. She was stuck here, under water, on her own with a person now operating outside any laws or governance.

'What do you want from me?'

'Now that the formalities are over,' Febron smiled, cool and calm, 'I agree, let us move straight to our purpose.'

'Your purpose,' Eliza corrected.

'It is a shared purpose, I think you will find.'

Febron walked behind the desk and put ids arm up to activate a screen. Eliza recognised the data that appeared – Ariki Besen's most recent findings and recommendations in his research into human-microbe communication.

Eliza's light-headedness landed with a thump. Cold hard fear dropped through her body.

Ariki's death had been no accident. If Febron had that little regard for one of the council's most respected leaders, id wouldn't hesitate to do away with Eliza. She was as good as dead.

'The council had been sponsoring Ariki's research for a long time and had been very patient. However he did not return that same level of regard and was stalling on action plans to initiate trials into human-microbe communication. As you would be well aware Eliza Wild, this is the new and possibly final frontier for humanity to fully understand our planet and the biggest breakthrough we have ever seen for potential contact with other life forms in the universe. Ariki, intelligent as he was, became confused about where his responsibilities lay.'

Febron paused, licked ids lips, and with a standard hand gesture, allowed a space in the dialogue for Eliza to fill.

'Presumably the council agreed with Ariki's progress and caution,' she said, choosing her words carefully. 'So in fact it is id – Febron – who may be confused about responsibilities, and also ethics.'

'The petty ego of one man should not interfere with the forward progress of humanity,' Febron said.

Eliza laughed. 'Ever heard of irony, Febron?' she asked, tiring of formalities now it was clear Febron was beyond any kind of reasoning.

'I see how you may interpret it that way,' Febron smiled, revealing teeth similarly long and elongated to ids smooth, white skull. 'Creatures of lesser intelligence will always fall prey to the most basic emotional interpretation of any event.'

Eliza's body hair bristled so sharply she felt the air around her harden in response.

'Before you become too agitated,' Febron continued in ids sickeningly smooth tone, 'let us move on to our next action together.'

Febron crossed in front of the desk to the curved wall and again raised an arm to activate it. Behind a dark, but transparent window, Eliza could see another room, bathed in a purple light similar to the colour of Febron's eyes and lips. Within the room appeared to be a sculpted, three dimensional landscape. She could make out a central mound and several smaller pods in a variety of shapes. They could have been based on the features of a rocky coastal outcrop, cave formations high up in a mountain range or even the figures of sleeping animals.

As Eliza stepped closer she could see that each shape was vibrating with a regular pulse, much like a heartbeat. A sigh escaped her.

'Oh!'

'Yes. They are beautiful,' Febron spoke quietly, with admiration.

'What are they?' Eliza whispered, unsure of why she was suddenly moved to tears.

'Our first successful harvest,' Febron said, 'we hope it is a representational range of microbes but it is difficult to tell. We started with a few and have been breeding them but without proper communication, as I say, it has been difficult. Up until now.'

A new kind of language was pushing into Eliza's mind, not the usual scramble of information and bursts of white noise she was accustomed to. This was like thousands of tiny bells in perfect harmony or what it might be like inside a rain drop. It was achingly exquisite and threaded through it all, an unmistakable note of sorrow. The sadness was equally as beautiful but almost unbearable in intensity.

The microbes were weeping. They were being held against their will.

Febron turned to Eliza.

She shook her head. 'I can't.'

'Oh don't be so unsure of your powers Eliza Wild. We have the greatest confidence in you.'

Eliza pulled her gaze from the microbes and fixed it on Febron, channelling as much big cat power as she could muster into her eyes and right through her body.

'I should clarify. I didn't mean I can't. I meant to say: I won't.'

Febron nodded as if expecting this answer. 'And so we come to the heart of our negotiation.'

Eliza threw her hands up. 'Nothing to negotiate. I'm not doing it.'

Febron put ids hand up to the dark window and Eliza saw how it bounced gently, reminding her that everything down here was alive, organic and connected. Then she saw a delicate trail of shining red liquid float through the purple, breaking up as it travelled into perfect, tear shaped drops. Febron had released something into the microbe's watery prison. No sooner had Eliza clocked the shimmering red trail than the echo of the day's earlier pain once again seared lightning through her body. She gasped and doubled over.

'I apologise for the pain,' Febron said, 'but it will not last. What is happening is merely part of the communications launch. We needed the panther's blood as it is so deeply connected to you. This will increase the speed and accuracy of your communication with the microbes.'

Febron's words hit Eliza like darts, piercing the pain that had now deepened, spreading inwards, reaching every fibre of her being, resonating and shaking like an internal earthquake.

'And I should mention now, that if you refuse to help us, all it takes is one touch like this,' Febron replayed the move of putting ids hand up to the dark wall, 'in the chamber where the young Besen man is now, and he will be jettisoned out into the ocean. He will implode. And I should add that unfortunately it is quite a painful path to death, not as instant or as peaceful as one might imagine.'

The temperature in the circular room had dropped. Eliza was shivering, unsure of all but one thing, she had to somehow save Dash. Had Febron cooled the room on purpose, to weaken her, knowing that her metabolism, like the big cats she spent so much time with, functioned best in hot climates? Or was it a result of the blood being released, somehow jeopardising her own life force?

'The Al-Chem who procured the paw has this final task to perform in her contract with me. She is approaching the viewing chamber as we speak.'

Febron moved through the room slowly, walking behind Eliza and back to the desk. Her dizziness and disorientation increased. Febron clicked ids fingers as if recalling a small, but important detail about their 'negotiation'.

'One final thing: the nature of the wound inflicted on your animal friend is such that it will continue bleeding, slow but steady. Should anything here go remiss, well, the Al-Chem will not be able to return to land and ensure her paw is returned or an appropriate healing solution is administered.'

Strong as Eliza's impulse was to run at Febron and tear the smarmy Non-Gen ids own unhealable wound, mention of the panther brought back what she had learned in her Blood Trials, and in all the years hence. In situations of immense pressure or confusion, decide on the single most important priority and do everything possible to achieve that goal.

Free the microbes. Save Dash. Rescue the panther.

Shit, that's three. The most important one, the most important one, the most important one. Shit. Three. And one of them probably impossible. Free the microbes. Save Dash. All right, mother fucker, two it is.

Eliza banished the vision of the panther's face from her mind and pushed down the cracking sorrow swelling in her heart. There was no way to save the animal but two out of three would have to do. She straightened from her doubled over position, stood tall, lowered her centre of gravity and looked dead into Febron's eyes.

'I'll do it,' she said, 'I'll communicate.'

She chose her words carefully, knowing she had to be careful not to lie. Being effective in any kind of battle could only come from truth.

Febron smiled, actually looking delighted, as if they were about to embark on a magical adventure together.

'If I may ask one favour?' Eliza said.

'Of course,' Febron spread ids hands, the epitome of openness and reason.

Eliza licked her lips, ran the hastily devised script in her head, then spoke:

'When the Al-Chem arrives in the viewing chamber can you please allow her entry and then, if possible, open the chute I came down in, or another similar portal?'

'Why?'

'Because she actually touched the panther, if my energy can link to hers it will make for much faster and clearer communication.'

Febron did not rush to answer, but inhaled and then exhaled slowly. The green light in the room flickered and Eliza sensed some extra level of security was being activated. She didn't move, stayed calm, tried to relax her mind and body, stay present, deal only with information that was immediate, not drift into speculation or fear.

'As you wish,' Febron said.

A shaft of cold air and blue light opened above Eliza's head, stripping breath and composure for a moment. Febron was asserting that id was in control. She nodded her thanks and refocused her energy.

Free the microbes. Save Dash.

With the chute open to the viewing chamber, Eliza could hear the hubbub of the gawking sea creatures who, by the sounds of things, were having a merry old time feasting their deep sea eyes – or whatever they used for seeing down at these depths – on 'the pretty one'. She couldn't tell how Dash was. Human mind communication was not something she'd ever mastered or had any interest in.

Eliza turned her full attention to the babble and chatter of the sea creatures and interrupted as politely as she could.

Forgive any rudeness for this moment. My business here will detain me longer. I will not be leaving.

I respectfully submit to you that the pretty one now be permitted to leave. He is ready to return to the surface and the cruiser will take him.

I thank you for your assistance and trust this adjustment to our negotiation is satisfactory.

Eliza then alerted the cruiser to enter active mode.

Febron snapped ids fingers.

'When will you begin?' ids sharp question.

'I will commence with formalities,' Eliza said, 'introductions and etiquette.' She paused, pointedly. 'They will not trust me if I rush straight into demanding answers of them.'

She moved closer to the dark window, so it looked like she was communicating with the microbes not – as was actually happening – with the sea creatures hovering outside Dash's chamber.

Febron nodded, reluctant, but clearly able to see the wisdom of this.

The babbling had eased up above and words were coming through. Eliza strained to hear and make sense of them.

We have heard your submission. We will consider it.

Impatience ripped through Eliza, a burning anxiety, tightening of muscles, rise of bile from her gut. She could only borrow so much time.

I appreciate your response. And I politely request a swift decision.

The high pitched bells of the microbes had joined the choral smorgasbord transmitting to her exhausted mind. They knew something was going on and were asking for an explanation.

'When you are ready,' Febron added ids cold, silky tones to the cacophony, 'I have initial questions pertaining to planetary origins with which to commence.'

Jesus H Christ! This slipped out in multiple languages before Eliza could stop it. Oh fuck, hopefully she hadn't inadvertently offended any deeply religious sea slug that happened to be listening.

Are you in pain?

Eliza smiled, a laugh exploding at this unexpected and oddly caring query from the sea creatures.

'They are amusing you?' Febron asked.

Eliza shrugged, 'Just a little banter.'

'The time for pleasantries must cease,' Febron asserted, adding, 'the Al-Chem is now within the viewing chamber with Besen. She awaits my orders. One touch.'

Who has entered the room with the pretty one?

Eliza offered a brief answer, that the Al-Chem was there to monitor Dash's departure.

Are these orders from you?

No.

Febron seized Eliza by the arm and steered her towards the desk. 'Now, Eliza Wild, they must surely be ready for some initial correspondence.'

On the screen above words hovered: invasive, brutal, clumsy questions designed only to get answers not to foster any kind of actual communication. She asked the sea creatures:

Have you come to a decision yet?

We cannot abide by your request.

Words swam. Eliza dulled the communication channel, knowing protest would be futile, not wanting to accidentally say anything from her cloud of helpless fury that might make things worse for Dash.

She'd failed. So much for her negotiation skills. Nothing left now but to focus on the microbes.

She turned her attention fully to the microbes, trying to sound calm and reasonable, like a human they might want to communicate with, not one almost violent with rage.

How can I best help you?

The reply was jumbled and difficult to understand. The language of the microbes was the most strange and foreign she'd ever heard. All she could pick up were random words and she wasn't even sure she had them right.

Blood ... Release ... Push

They needed more blood? She'd be happy to provide it – either her own or Febron's, but what then?

Blood ... Release ... Push ... Repeat

Fresh blood?

Wall ... Push ... Repeat

The panther's blood, Febron had released it into the microbe chamber by pushing on the malleable wall. Id had threatened Dash's life with the same technique. So id and the Al-Chem could somehow penetrate these viscous walls. Eliza figured the move would have to come from Febron, that her pressing the wall alone wouldn't have the same results. Id had some kind of connection with the organic structure of this place.

Do you mean that if we push on the wall again that will help
you all escape?

She heard a surge in the singing, a positive swell.

Wall ... Push ... Repeat ... Yes.

Eliza nodded, buying more time, looking around the room for inspiration. How could a room have so little in it? There was nothing she could see to use as a weapon or even a method of distraction.

Febron watched her closely. She couldn't ask id to touch the window without raising suspicion. Maybe she didn't have to. All they were asking was for the action to be repeated.

Eliza turned her focus inwards. She gathered the grief and sorrow balled deep within her and rolled it in the white rage still simmering at the sea creature's heartless response to her request. As trained, she built the core up with cold determination, not emotion, and then let it expand.

The energy pushed its way out through her skin and shimmering bristles, spreading all the way to her finger tips and up to the crown of her electric blue dyed hair. Her body vibrating now, she launched herself at Febron, grabbing id in a head lock, using the vice grip she'd learned during her Blood Trials. She swept Febron up, one hand around ids throat, the other supporting ids body, taut with terror it made the perfect battering ram. She knew she had only one shot at this, while Febron was in shock and vulnerable, before id had a chance to raise any alarm or security measure. Giving voice now to her howl, she propelled herself off the floor.

The green light flickered then shattered with an eye-splitting force. A great shaking swept through the room, hurling Eliza from ceiling to floor. She kept her hands locked around Febron and felt ids body crack, once at the neck and again at the arm, which had been flailing, trying to lash out and break free. She couldn't get her bearings, had no idea if the wall to the microbe chamber had been permeated in any way, or if this was some kind of defensive mechanism that would just tear her apart and achieve nothing more.

Febron slipped from her grasp.

'Febron!' she hollered, trying to recall the correct language of retribution, 'you have contravened both law and nature and for that you must be punished.'

The words escaped her mouth and got sucked into the green flashing vortex her body was spinning in. Had Febron heard? Would it make any difference or was this a futile final act?

Her words spun and seemed to get louder, stronger, the voice of many, a powerful chorus chanting.

> You have contravened both law and nature and for that you
> must be punished.

Then she saw it. A creature twice the size of the room, ink black with what looked like a thousand glowing eyes, wings spread wide and phosphorescent tail whipping through the darkness towards her.

Jesus H Christ, the words hurled out this time in every language she knew.

An almighty shudder as she was sucked towards the creature.

Not quite.

It was the chorus of hundreds...

But your saviour for today.

Was that sea creature humour? She laughed, politely, hoping to encourage, do anything, to delay the moment of imminent impact. Her mouth was open, caught in surprise, as all external sensation left her and she was enveloped in a velvet nothingness. No light. No sound. No air. Was this it? Death?

A bump, a jolt, she slipped through a membrane. Bloody hell, could rebirth be that quick? Where was she going to come out, and as what? And she felt a familiar body, warm and strong.

'Ouch!'

What?

'Dash?'

'Yes, it's me and that – ouch! – soft place where you've planted your elbow, is my testicles.'

'Shit. Sorry.'

Eliza wriggled to readjust, opened her eyes, saw the amber glow of the cruiser. She was inside it. Had Dash managed to get in and penetrate the walls to rescue her? She was about to ask when a rushing sound, like a fierce flood, roared past them. Her stomach clenched and lungs contracted. Then came a popping sensation, fireworks or electro-candy exploding, then nothing. The cruiser once again floated in the calm black of deep water and she heard a few final words:

> *We could not abide by your request because we had to attend*
> *to Febron's breaking of both law and etiquette.*
> *The premises have been destroyed.*
> *The microbes are free.*
> *We honour your negotiation with us.*

We thank you; myself and the pretty one.

Thanks are not necessary. But they are appreciated.

May I ask...

Eliza figured she could push for one cheeky question.

Did we just get swallowed up by a giant black ray?

Affirmative.

And did it, did we, I mean, how did we—

You passed through its digestive canal and were expelled.

Okay. So they'd literally been shat out into the sea. Some rescue.

'What are they saying?' Dash asked.

'I'll tell you later.'

Dash prodded Eliza's back. 'Tell me now, we nearly just died together, I think a certain level of intimacy has been reached.'

Eliza laughed, thought, then spoke. 'They said you're not just pretty. They said I'm lucky to know you because you are also brave. And good.'

'Bullshit,' Dash said.

'It's not. It's absolutely true.'

'Whatever. And for what it's worth, ditto.'

Eliza let her body start to melt into a state of relaxation. The cruiser would take them safely home. Then something soft and sad clicked over deep in her heart.

'We mourn her passing, honour her life and seek to uphold her spirit,' she murmured the words of mourning, felt the warm sting of tears on her face.

'The panther?' Dash asked.

'Yes.'

He reached up and squeezed her hand, then repeated the mourning mantra.

They travelled in silence then for some time, allowing the sadness of the unwarranted and violent death to have its moment.

'We don't need to dwell,' Eliza said eventually. 'It is appropriate now to re-focus our energy on the here and now, our own lives. There will be a proper ceremony for her once I arrive back in the Grasslands.'

Dash released her hand. After a few moments he was humming again. This time, a cheesy pop song, something with a strong dance beat that he tried – badly – to replicate by beat boxing.

'Wow, you're really spectacularly bad at that,' Eliza said.

'I know,' he sighed, 'good thing I'm so handsome hey, doesn't matter that I'll never be a pop star.'

'Very lucky,' she agreed.

'Oh and by the way,' Dash said.

'What?'

'I'm active non-sexual – by choice.'

'Right.'

She hadn't actually suggested it as yet. 'You're not a Mind-Prober are you?' she asked, suddenly worried she was warming to a person who could potentially get inside her brain

'What? No. God no. I really, literally, have almost zero skills.'

'Good,' Eliza said, a bit too enthusiastically.

'Yeah thanks. Anyway, it's just that I know sex is one of your things and you're all kind of like, "yeah I have all this excess energy and it's part of me" and anyone around you is part of it too. But like you said about me and my charm, I'm not interested in you and your sexual energy – at all. Just so we're clear.'

'Clear,' said Eliza, 'probably a good thing in fact. I mean if we're going to work together, you know, put all our combined energy into that.'

'And are we?'

'World's not perfect yet is it. There's plenty of work to be done.'

She allowed the echo of the panther's words to enter her mind and ripple down through her body. It was her duty, in light of the panther's death, to step into a role of greater responsibility. More than that, it was what she now wanted.

'You up for it, party boy?'

'We'll see.'

Outside the world around them morphed from black to blue and then began to shimmer with thousands of tiny fish and forests of coral and visitations from transparent jelly creatures and cruising sharks and rays. So many life forms, managing to co-habit, keep their environment healthy and sustainable for all.

Eliza was glad to be heading up towards sunlight and solid ground. But she was glad she'd got to spend time down here. Mourning the panther would be a slow and painful process, a loss she might never fully recover from. But her world had been shaken up and turned around in the most unexpected way. A baptism not of fire, but of water – lots of very fucking deep and dark water – that she could tell marked a threshold into a different kind of life. One where she could use all she'd been taught and was now ready to enact, to try and keep making the world a better place, one step and one word at a time. And – the biggest surprise of all – one where it just might be a human she would slowly, surely, learn to trust and maybe even come to like.

'Don't get cocky,' she said out loud, to Dash, as if he'd been party to her train of thought, warning both herself and him from getting to close too soon.

'Who, me?' he replied, and started up the beat boxing again.

Eliza cracked up laughing which set Dash off. So they were both giggling, that stupid, red-faced, can't control it kind of little kid giggle, as the cruiser broke the surface of the ocean and lifted them up into the wide, clear sky.

TANSY RAYNER ROBERTS

Death
at the
Dragon Circus

Kurt Frostad sat in the window seat of the train, his sister Inga's head pillowed in his lap. 'Law enforcement,' he suggested.

Inga's expression did not move, but she raised one slender calf in the air, pointing her foot. 'Pole dancer.'

'You or me?'

'We both have the legs for it, sunshine. But as the person least likely to snap and break the neck of a drunken customer – you.'

He tugged at a lock of her ice-blonde hair. It was too short to pull properly. Three cities ago, they had walked into a salon as partners, and walked out as siblings with white hair and blue eyes. He was still getting used to it. 'Fireman. I could be a fireman.' He looked down at his notebook. He hadn't bothered to write any of the suggestions after 'law enforcement.'

Kurt and Inga were not their real names, just as ice-white was not a natural hair colour for either of them. They were brother and sister, according to their passports, and that was also new but in a comfortable way. It made sense of the intimate, platonic friendship they shared these days.

Back when her hair was dark and his was sandy brown and they murdered people for money because it was the thing they both did best in the world, they had been amazing in bed together, wild and angry and completely ruined for anyone else.

All that had burned out long ago, and he hadn't even thought of her that way since they became Kurt and Inga. 'Sister' was the right word. It meant that they were family, and that was all either of them needed.

Crossing a body of water didn't make it less likely that their enemies would come after them, but it sure as hell felt better to do it, so they kept travelling south until they ran out of rivers.

After the ferry across the strait to Tintellegra, they found another train and chose south again, so far south that the winds picked up cold and grey around the windows.

Inga wore a white silk shirt and the necklace she had bought herself after the hair salon. She had never before owned a piece of jewellery that wasn't part of a disguise or a cover. This piece was a crystal snowflake on a silver chain that sent points of light refracting around the train carriage.

Kurt's own needs were simple. He wanted a place for them both to live and work – somewhere safe, but not stale. No killing required. He had always been good with his hands, and he liked the idea of using them to make things or fix things for a change. 'Carpentry maybe,' he said, working it through in his head. 'That sort of work – it wouldn't draw much attention.'

'Tightrope walker,' said Inga, turning her cheek against his knee. 'Did you see the circus folk on the platform earlier? I'd make an *amazing* tightrope walker.'

He curled his fingers fiercely into her short white hair. 'Yeah. You would.'

'Dragon,' she said next.

'Let's stick to viable career options, shall we?'

She tugged on his wrist; he looked up.

A dragon stared through the glass of the door to the carriage. It was enormous, filling the corridor beyond the glass, all blue and silver and snout and bright gold eyes. Power thrummed through its body: a contained implosion of muscle and magic, wrapped in shiny scales.

It was as if time had stopped for everyone except the dragon.

All his life, Kurt had one skill that rose above anything else: he knew danger. He could read the danger in a room, in a person, in a situation, as precisely as someone else might understand numbers or words or art. He didn't have to think about it - his body took over, calculating the odds of every fight, every potential variable, and who was going to walk away alive.

On the rare occasion that his path crossed with someone who was capable of taking him down, an oddly blissful silence would fill his brain.

The first time he met Inga, that silence remained for two days. Even now he only had to look at her to let it wash back over him.

His instincts were generally honed for people. Magic didn't throw off his threat assessments – hell, he'd once had a dirty weekend with a fellow assassin who could turn into a snake monster when she lost her temper. He'd seen just about everything in his line of work.

Nothing had prepared Kurt's natural defences for the deep cold shock of sharing a train with a dragon.

Kurt gazed into those deadly golden eyes and heard nothing but a faint buzzing sensation in his ears.

Inga lifted herself slightly in his lap, and he knew she was reaching for a concealed weapon. Certain habits could never be left behind. Inga would fight anyone, anything, to the death without hesitation. It was the thing he loved most about her.

'I was not expecting dragons,' she breathed, her fingers digging gracefully beneath her snowy fur-lined jacket.

The dragon huffed against the glass, and a flash of dark hair shot past. A human girl shoved the door open, allowing the creature to pour itself into the carriage.

Kurt drew his feet up on the seat as the dragon stared him down with those gold, liquid eyes, then opened its jaw to release a smoky gas that smelled like eucalyptus oil.

Inga's hands were still buried in her jacket.

'Oh gods, I'm sorry,' panted the girl. She hurled herself across the neck of the dragon, trying to twist the creature back towards the door, but it was having none of her antics. 'I thought this carriage was empty.'

'Fin, what the fuck you doing?' roared a voice. A young man with muscled arms pushed his way in the carriage, leaping over the dragon's tail. All shoulders and confidence, he grabbed the back of the dragon's neck as if it was a kitten.

'It wasn't on purpose, why would I do this on purpose?' howled the girl.

'Can't let you out in bloody public,' he snapped back. 'We need to get her back to the clowns *now*, before she pops.'

The two of them wore odd garments, as if they had been playing dress-ups backstage at an opera. Leather and velvet and lace cuffs, but they smelled of greasepaint, burned feathers, raw meat. He wore more eyeliner than she did.

Still arguing, the two only stopped blaming each other when the dragon let out a snort, and a wave of heat belched out from between its teeth. All that danger wrapped up in that powerful scaly body, and Kurt had forgotten – FORGOTTEN – that dragons actually breathed fire.

The young man spoke to the dragon in a low, pulsing language unlike anything Kurt had heard before. It was more like singing than speech. The dragon moved in a long, sinuous movement, breaking eye contact with Kurt to turn towards the young man and his beautiful voice.

When it caught sight of Inga, the dragon hesitated.

'Cover your necklace, miss,' said the girl. 'Dragons like shiny things.'

Inga placed her hand over the crystal snowflake. The dragon blinked and looked away.

'Open the bloody door,' said the man, and the girl obeyed him. The three of them slid out into the corridor again as if they were all one creature – human limbs and dragon scales combined.

Inga let out a long, slow breath, relaxing. 'I've never killed a dragon,' she considered.

'Sad you didn't get the chance?' Kurt tossed back to her. His pulse was slowly returning to normal.

'Maybe a little; for the challenge.' She creased her forehead thoughtfully. 'Might have got messy.'

Kurt couldn't sit still for long after that, not with the walls of the train closing in around him.

He did what he'd done on every train journey they had taken so far on this adventure of theirs – he walked up and down the corridor, glancing in every carriage and making threat assessments. Ten minutes to half an hour was usually enough to settle his nerves, but today was a special occasion, because he couldn't get those deadly golden eyes out of his head.

It took several passes, all the way from one end of the train to the other, before he could return to Inga and bask in her stillness.

Her stillness was a work of art, and always had been.

When he neared the carriage, he realised that she wasn't alone. The dragon trainer had returned, sprawling in the seat opposite Kurt's sister with the lazy ease of a man who knew how good he looked. Inga was charming him, and allowing him to charm her: head tilted back, eyes sparkling.

She asked questions, encouraging the young man to talk about himself. It was fascinating to watch – usually it was Kurt who gave the easy smiles and connected with people while his partner held herself in reserve, waiting for a need to provide deadly violence.

They weren't those people any more. Inga Frostad, it turned out, was rather good at casual conversation. Kurt noticed her using mannerisms that she had stolen from him.

He slid the door open and leaned a hip into the doorway. 'Am I interrupting something?'

Kurt, he decided right this moment, was protective of Inga. That was realistic, right? Brothers were allowed to be dicks about pretty men in eyeliner flirting with their sisters.

Mostly, he decided to go that way because it was hilarious, the idea of anyone thinking Inga couldn't make these decisions for herself.

'You remember my brother,' said Inga, rolling her eyes as if he was embarrassing her. 'Kurt, this is Puck.'

It was the first time she had used the words 'my brother' out loud in front of anyone but Kurt, and it warmed him to his stomach.

'How's your dragon?' Kurt asked, dropping into the seat beside Inga.

She's back in the livestock compartment, chewing on a steak,' said Puck, including Kurt in his charming, showman's smile. 'Fin's practically sitting on top of her to keep her there, like she was supposed to in the first place.'

He had cleaned up some: placed a beaded cap over his too-long hair, wiped the soot off his hands and face, and shrugged a scrappy velvet jacket over those muscled arms of his. Shame to cover them up.

'Puck came to offer us circus tickets,' said Inga, glowing with what looked like genuine delight. 'I've never been to a circus before.'

'We'll be in Candle for at least another fortnight,' said Puck, holding the tickets in his fingers as a tease. 'Maybe longer.'

'Sounds as good a place as any to stop for a while,' said Kurt, reaching out his hand to take the tickets, though he was sure that Puck would rather pass them directly to Inga.

'It's a show worth seeing,' Puck assured him. 'I promise, the dragons don't get as up close and personal with the audience as you got today.' He gave them a sheepish look, ducking his head slightly. 'If my bosses find out I let Big Blue roam the train, I'm in big trouble. She's never acted like this before – we brought her along for the auditions because she's normally good as gold.'

'The show might be an anti-climax after today's encounter,' Kurt drawled, tucking the tickets into in a pocket.

'You're not going to complain, are you?' Puck begged. 'We're on two warnings already with the train company, and the Ringmaster will blow her stack. She was against Fin and me coming along with the crew to audition trapeze artists in Tintellegra, but there's no point in seeing performers if we don't know how they handle dragons.'

'We won't tell anyone,' said Inga, with a gentle laugh. She had been practicing her laugh for the entire journey, and Kurt was never going to get used to *that*. The person she had been before never laughed.

Puck's eyes flicked between the two of them, as if he couldn't quite figure them out. If they couldn't act normal enough to fool a carnie kid, what hope did they have? 'Business or pleasure in Candle?' he asked, with an extra stress on 'pleasure' that made Kurt want to laugh at him. Was he trying to flirt with both of them? Boy had no idea what fire he was playing with.

'I'm a dancer,' said Inga smoothly. 'My company closed, and so...' she shrugged in her pretty fur-lined collar. 'Now we are travelling, my brother and I.'

Puck's eyes widened. It was the most honest expression Kurt had seen on the kid's face so far. 'Don't suppose either of you know what to do with a trapeze?'

Inga tilted her head. Kurt knew what that look meant. He had last seen it when he said, jokingly, a lifetime ago: 'You can't actually strangle a man with a satin ribbon, can you?' It was her Considering the Possibilities face.

'I could build one for you,' Kurt said, more forcefully than he had intended, but he was damned if he'd come out of this with nothing but 'the dancer's brother' as his cover story. 'But I don't think that's what you had in mind.'

The kid, it turned out, had a Considering the Possibilities face just as blatant as Inga's. 'If you're looking for work, ask for me when you come by the Big Top,' he said. 'Not being scared of dragons is top of the list, when we're looking for new artists, or crew.'

The door to the corridor slammed open. A short, surly man stood there, brimming with tension. 'Puck,' he growled. 'Fin needs you now. We figured out what's wrong with Blue.'

All the flirt fell off Puck's face, and he leaped for the door, his coat flapping behind him as he ran.

'Oh,' said Inga. 'We are *totally* going to the circus.'

'Is it the dragon?' Kurt asked. 'Or the dark-eyed boy with the wicked smile?'

She poked him in the chest with a finger that felt decidedly sisterly. 'You liked the dragon.'

Well, sure. He hadn't had an adrenalin high like that since the last time he threw them both out a third floor window to avoid being shot. 'I liked the dragon,' he admitted.

Inga looked happy. Was that a thing with her now? Maybe it was like the necklace – she tried on several dozen 'happy' expressions before finding the one she liked.

'We'll fit right in with the freaks,' Kurt added, to see if he could make her smile disappear.

Inga and her smile were relentless. 'We'll see.'

The Frostads stood against the wall in the station, watching the other passengers from their train disembark. They carried a small rucksack each, and nothing else. There was a lot to be said for travelling light.

By unspoken agreement, they waited for the crowd to dissipate before they made a move. Neither of them liked to have a lot of people at their back, especially in a new city.

Kurt sensed the wrongness before he even saw the bloke – the same surly, short fellow who had summoned Puck to deal with Blue. He looked like circus folk, wrapped up in a buttoned purple coat and a bright striped scarf despite the warmth of the afternoon. But there was something moving inside his coat.

'Stop, thief! STOP HIM!' howled a voice from further back on the platform. Kurt was already moving when he registered that the voice belonged to Puck. He lurched forward and, as if by accident, collided directly with the man in the scarf.

The purple coat burst open, and several small, gleaming creatures fanned out into the air. Dragons, Kurt realised, staring in surprise at the buzzing wings and tiny huffs of smoke coming out of perfectly formed nostrils. Baby dragons. He didn't even know dragons had babies. Didn't they emerge fully-grown from like, volcanoes or something?

Puck slammed into the purple coat man from behind, knocking him to the ground. He reached his hands up and – sang.

It was a different song to the one he had used in the carriage, but it was in the same language, foreign and melodic. As Kurt watched, transfixed, the baby dragons swooped down and nestled themselves back into Puck's arms. All but one, a little green thing that had decided it liked Inga better. It dipped and nuzzled at her face, making her laugh.

Not a fake laugh, for practice; a genuine laugh. Kurt knew then that if Inga wanted dragons in her life, he would walk over fire to give her dragons.

Suddenly the baby green nipped hard at the sparkling snowflake crystal that Inga wore about her neck. Seizing its prize, it flew up high over the station roof.

Inga's smile fell off her face. She hurled herself up the side of the station shelter as if the walls were not completely smooth and without handholds. She ran lightly along the edge of the roof and leaped into empty air, catching the baby green before it flew out of range. She tumbled as she fell back down to the platform, landing on her smartly buttoned boots.

So much for not drawing attention to themselves.

Inga brought the baby green back to Puck and handed it over by the scruff of its neck, having already reclaimed her necklace. 'Yours, I believe,' she said, not even breathing hard.

'You'd be brilliant on the trapeze,' Puck blurted out, staring at her as if he had never seen anything like it.

Inga looked pleased. 'Of course I would.'

'No, seriously. I gave you my card, right? We need a trapeze artist. Like, now. Today.'

Inga glanced over at Kurt. He was careful not to let anything show in his face – not approval, not disapproval. Her own face dimmed slightly. 'I'll think about it,' she said.

Kurt's first impression of the city of Candle was all gum trees and dust. The wind was dry and gritty and swept through the streets like it wanted to flay the skin from their bones. He and Inga made their way through the city centre and past the warehouse district to find the wide, dusty showground where the Dragon Circus pitched its tents.

On their way, Kurt kept an eye out for affordable boarding houses, in case the circus option didn't work out.

'I see what you're doing,' Inga said serenely, not even glancing in his direction.

'Every backup plan needs a backup plan,' he replied, hoisting his pack higher on his shoulder.

The circus was bigger than he had expected. Not just the Big Top (a massive sprawl of bright canvas painted with silhouettes of dragons in flight) but a surrounding carnival of games and amusements. Beyond that were the caravans, trailers and tents belonging to the circus folk. It was like a city in its own right.

A large, stout metal fence provided security, with muscular crew in cheerful, distracting costumes taking note of anyone who entered. Clowns, mostly. Intimidating, surly clowns.

'We don't open until three,' grunted one of them, stepping in Kurt and Inga's way as they approached.

Inga's body language softened, as she prepared to charm him.

'Hey, you made it,' broke in another voice, and Puck in his beaded cap and flapping patched velvet jacket ran to them both, ushering them past the clowns. 'Great timing. I want to introduce you to the Birds of Paradise.'

Kurt assumed he meant more dragons, or possibly actual birds, because circuses were full of exotic animals, right? Puck led Inga straight into the Big Top.

It was empty, with banks of seats clean and ready for the night's show. A swooping motion caught Kurt's eye, and he looked up to see a feathered shape fluttering above, and then another.

There were two of them: slender men with sleek muscles, wrapped in costumes of tight blue satin and wide, wire-framed wings. The wings dripped with colour: aqua and orange and green. Every toss and tumble that they made across the swooping trapeze swings brought out a new colour in the layers of false satin feathers.

Inga tipped her head back and stared at them both. Kurt could see her calculating how to copy those moves. It wasn't hugely different to the acrobatics required in their previous profession.

'Cicero, Cato!' Puck called up into the air. 'Come meet a new friend.'

'We're working!' yelled one of the birds – the one with pale skin and a shock of red hair. His voice was surprisingly deep for such a slight man. 'Do you know how long it's going to take to cut all our routines down to duets?'

'If this works, you won't have to!' Puck shouted back.

That caught their attention. The dark-skinned bird with a roughly shaven head dropped first, letting go of the trapeze and falling several feet before he caught another rope, one hidden in the folds of the tent, and all but floated down to the floor.

The red-haired bird was slower to follow, but no less graceful. They stood beside each other, heads tilting in identical movements as they examined both Inga and Kurt.

'So creepy when you do that,' Puck muttered. 'This is Inga Frostad. She flew with dragons at the train station this morning. I think she could learn Molly's set.

'Cato, Cicero,' he added, tapping the black man on the head, and then the white. 'Their usual partner eloped with the Assistant Grip, and these two have trouble thinking in anything but triangles.'

'Why couldn't you sub in one of the performers you already have?' Kurt asked, his arms folded across his chest.

Cicero turned a cool look on him. 'Because we hate everyone,' he said.

Cato elbowed his larger partner in the ribs. 'The best aerialists already have their own acts,' he corrected in a far more friendly voice.

'Also that.'

Inga smiled, dropping her pack and laying her white fur jacket on top of it. Her clothes were not completely inappropriate for trapeze work – she liked to wear loose, soft trousers and shirts that she could fight in, if violence became necessary. The pretty coat and the jewellery had disguised the practicality of her basic outfit.

The birds of paradise surveyed her thoughtfully.

'Costumes would have to be taken in,' said Cato. 'Molly had more boob and hip to her.'

'How fast can you climb a wall?' Cicero asked Inga directly.

Inga smiled. 'With or without hand holds?'

It took half an hour for Cato to fall in love with Inga, and perhaps another 15 minutes after that for Cicero to go the same way.

Kurt sprawled across a couple of seats in the Big Top, watching as the two of them danced around her in the air. Inga had mastered their simplest three-way flying routine, and was extending herself further.

She was holding back some of her abilities. But her effortless grace and ruthless flexibility worked for her.

Puck didn't stay to watch, but kept dropping back in to check on their progress. 'She's not bad,' he noted as Inga leaped from Cato's hand to Cicero's, across the wide expanse of empty air. 'Fearless is hard to fake.'

Kurt smirked to himself. 'She's not faking.'

Cicero was light in the air – as if a puff of that dry, dust-laced city wind might carry him away. Cato was more solid, moving like a knife through silk. They tossed Inga from one perch to another with a practiced confidence.

Inga picked up their moves and cues and then developed whole new moves of her own, forcing the Birds of Paradise to follow or be left in her dust.

This was it. Kurt had lost her to the circus. *First there were dragons and now they've taught her to fucking fly. No coming back from this. She's found her retirement plan.*

'Your sister's good,' said a calm voice just behind his ear. It was all Kurt could do not to react, to turn his hands into weapons and drop the invader to the floor in an instant. How did he get so distracted that he allowed a stranger that close to him without realising it?

He glanced back over his shoulder as if it didn't even matter to him who might be sitting a couple of rows behind him in the stands.

An ordinary-looking man, maybe 40 years old, in faded work clothes. Nothing special. He didn't have the smell of greasepaint on his skin that marked just about everyone else around here.

'She was good an hour ago,' Kurt said slowly. 'She's moved up to spectacular.'

'We'll see,' said the man with a shrug, and looked Kurt over, weighing up his potential too.

Kurt had clients like this, who tried to stare through him like they could see his insides, as if that would somehow make sense of his skill-set. He turned his back on the other man, returning his attention to his air-dancing sister.

Puck charged into the Big Top as if someone had shouted 'Fire!' He skidded on the sawdust, and slowed with a guilty expression on his face as he caught sight of their observer. 'Gaffer,' he gasped.

Gaffer? That was ominous. Kurt glanced around to reassess the man, from his shabby work clothes to his much-mended boots. Was he the one who made the decisions around here?

The Gaffer's face was flat. 'Something you want to share, Puck?'

'I found us a replacement for Molly on the train,' said Puck, nervousness spilling over. 'The trapeze artists in Tintellegra were useless, but we – I mean, quite by chance – Inga Frostad. This is her brother.' He stared frantically at Kurt, then back to the gaffer as if he wanted the ground to swallow him. There was something strange going on here. 'Frostad, this is Mr Brennan, the circus manager.'

Brennan didn't acknowledge Kurt as part of the conversation. 'On the train?' he demanded of Puck. 'Not at the auditions, then?'

'It was a funny thing,' Puck said and launched into the story of the dragon snatchers, and Inga's leap of rescue.

The Gaffer cut Puck off halfway through. 'Was this before or after Blue gave birth to half a dozen baby dragons?'

Puck swallowed. 'We met the Frostads before anyone knew about the babies. It really was a coincidence.'

'Coincidence like one of my best clowns turned out to be a fucking traitor who stole the baby dragons from us first chance he got?' Brennan growled.

'Rusty was always a bit dubious,' Puck blurted out. 'He can't have planned it, though. We would never have taken Blue on the train any if us knew she was pregnant.'

'So what do we do with this bloke, if his sister becomes our new Bird of Paradise?'

Kurt gritted his teeth, angry at being talked over like he wasn't even here.

'We need an extra Grip,' Puck suggested. 'He says he's good at fixing things.'

The Gaffer gave a scoffing laugh. 'Her yes, him no,' he said sharply and walked out of the Big Top.

Kurt didn't acknowledge the apologetic look in Puck's eyes. He was watching Brennan the Gaffer walk away. Under those shabby work clothes, he had the stance of a soldier, and held himself like he knew where all the weapons were.

'I'll talk him around,' Puck said.

'Don't bother,' Kurt said. He got to his feet, stretching. 'Tell Inga I'll be back later. I'll find us a place to stay in the city.'

'She'll be expected to live on site, when she joins us,' said Puck.

Kurt gave him a wide, thoroughly nasty grin. The kid didn't deserve it, but he wasn't in the mood to go easy. 'You think I give a damn what you people expect?'

He let Puck scurry out ahead of him, waited to catch Inga's eye, and motioned to let her know that he was going, for now.

She gave him a brief nod, and returned her intense concentration to Cato, Cicero and the dance of the air.

Oh, yeah. He'd lost her to the fucking circus.

Kurt was in a filthy mood, and the last thing he needed right now was a guided tour as to why exactly he failed to impress Puck's precious boss. So of course when he made his way out of the Big Top, the first thing he heard was their half-whispered conversation.

'They're good people, Gaffer,' Puck pleaded. 'You know how hard it is to find crew who don't freak out about the dragons, and the audition was a bust. Inga's our only chance to replace Molly this week. If we don't make room for her brother, she might walk. Since when do we turn down new muscle?'

If there was anything guaranteed to make Kurt feel the ache of every bone he'd ever broken, it was hearing a kid like Puck refer to him as 'new muscle'.

Brennan gave a sharp laugh. 'Since when? Since we found ourselves up to our ears in an accidental goldmine of baby fucking dragons. Every show in the country will be after them, not to mention private collectors and the gangs and anyone else looking to make a fast buck. Rusty proved that we can't trust our own right now, let alone strangers.'

Puck groaned. 'I didn't think of that.'

'It's my job to think about this shit, and your job to say yessir,' the Gaffer snarled. 'We're not taking on new crew, even if we get down to our last carpenter and the ballerinas have to haul tent ropes. Biceps and bright blue eyes and 'good with dragons' is exactly the type they would use to get in undercover with us. We can't afford to let our guard down until the babies are big enough to defend themselves.'

Kurt had heard enough. He kept walking until their voices disappeared into a low murmur behind him. He skirted around some argumentative clowns and a couple of carnies laden down with a crate of flashy costume props, and finally made it to the metal fence. It was in disrepair, for an outfit so concerned with the possibility of dragon theft. There was a place behind some scrubby bushes where part of the fencing had curled up, and it was large enough for a couple of lads to squeeze in – as indeed, they were doing right now.

Kurt leaned a hip against the fence, and waited for the boys to notice they had been spotted. 'Closed until three,' he said evenly, and they both scrambled back through the hole, their feet scraping on the gravel on the far side of the fence.

Yeah, in retrospect his list of possible job skills probably needed to factor in his ability to scare the fuck out of people by looking at them sideways.

Nightclub bouncer, maybe. Bodyguard. Or, based on the thugs around here, clown – though anything circus related was off the menu as far as he was concerned.

Kurt jammed the broken piece of fencing closed with his foot and propped a large rock against it. After some contemplation, he scaled the fence easily and dropped down on the far side. Better that than do the walk of shame in front of the greasepaint brigade over at the main gate.

There was a wide yard here, for automobiles and carriages. Kurt strolled along, resisting the urge to take his frustration out on any of the larger rocks strewn about the place.

He almost missed them.

A couple leaned against the fence in the shadow of a giant Dragon Circus billboard, some fella crowding in around his girl.

Kurt scuffed the ground extra hard as he walked, and saw the fella's shoulders tense. That got his attention. Now that he looked properly, they weren't kissing or cuddling at all. The man leaned in, muttering to her low, and she was pulling her face away from him. Body language was everything.

The girl was 20 years younger than the bloke, and Kurt recognised her now. She was Puck's friend, the one who had been juggling Big Blue on the train.

'Hey, Fin,' he said, calling out to her as if it was no big deal. 'Your da's looking for you, back at the Big Top.'

If he was interfering, she could let him know. Damn it all, this brother bullshit was like a virus once it got into you. He'd be protecting dames all over the place at this rate. That was going to cut into his spare time.

'Thanks,' Fin got out. She wriggled like she wanted to get away, but the bruiser had a firm grip on her shoulder.

Kurt did not like that at all.

'Take a hike, mate,' growled the bruiser.

'Yeah?' said Kurt, rolling around on his feet like he'd had a few beers and he didn't really give a shit what circus girls got up to when their daddies weren't watching. 'If you say so, mate. You know she's 15? Jailbait.'

'Screw you,' said Fin, not having to feign her outrage.

Kurt laughed. 'Seriously, kid. You're gonna get into trouble if you don't muck out the elephant stall by lunchtime.'

Fin rolled her eyes at him. Clear as day, she moved her eyes to four different points around the yard before looking back at Kurt. Four others nearby, then; good to know.

'Not going to tell you again,' said the thug, keeping his arm shoved against Fin's chest. He half-turned, snarling at Kurt with gold-capped teeth. 'Keep walking, pal.'

Fin hit him. Her hand was tiny and she barely had any power behind it apart from belligerence, but she got him in the eye good.

The bruiser squeezed her between his hands like he was going to crush her against the fence. 'You little bitch.'

'They want to use me to steal the babies!' she yelled.

Kurt had counted the shadows: he knew where the thug's friends were, and he could sense them approaching. This was going to have to happen fast. He rotated on the balls of his feet, hooked his arm around the thick neck of the arsehole that had his hands all over Fin, and flipped him to the ground with a sharp 'crack' which was the best sound he had heard all day.

'Run,' he advised Fin. The girl took off along the fence like a steam train, and Kurt followed her, circling wide to make sure he was between her and the other thugs who thundered across the yard in their direction.

It was a good fight, the closest thing to real exercise he had gotten since he became Kurt Frostad. One came flying at him from the left and Kurt spun to take him down, then disarmed him of a set of brass knuckles that came in real handy for the next one, who was bigger than the first two put together.

He ran after that; scrambling after Fin who didn't look back as she dashed to safety. Good girl.

The last two thugs, bright with gang tattoos, slammed into him in unison when he was nearly at the gate. Kurt's hands and feet took over. When he was done, the attackers lay gasping on the ground, their knives were lined up neatly along the fence line, and he had managed to work up a sweat.

When he glanced up, wiping a line of dust-caked moisture off his forehead (that turned out to be partly blood), he saw Fin hovering in the gateway, flanked by several surly clowns. She nodded at him, shaky on her feet, and disappeared into the safety of the circus ground.

Kurt gave an insulting salute in the direction of the clowns, and headed off in search of a boarding house.

Yeah, he'd had enough circus for a lifetime.

'You're an idiot,' said Inga a few hours later, when she let herself in through the window of the room Kurt had rented. Somehow she had managed to get here without the dust of the city caking itself on to her skin.

'What else is new?' Kurt grunted from where he lay on one of the narrow beds, scanning the local broadsheet for jobs. Hauling boxes and skinning fish were his best chances this week. At least the fish would need his knife skills.

Inga sat on the end of his bed, prodding him until he moved over to make room for her. 'Brennan wants to talk to you.'

'Brennan can suck my dick.'

'I don't think that's on offer,' she said archly. 'He's going to offer you a place in the crew.'

'No, he's not,' Kurt growled. 'I get it, you like the trapeze shit, that's fine. I can keep myself busy until they move on to their next city, and we'll look for something more permanent after that.'

From Inga, a silence was as meaningful as anything she had to say out loud. When Kurt felt it had gone on long enough, he glanced up to read her expression.

Damn it. 'Seriously?' he moaned. 'It's been less than a day.'

'I love it, Kurt,' she told him. 'I really do. The people are good, they're – they're outsiders too, we don't have to pretend to be normal. You should give them a chance.'

She elbowed him hard. It was the most realistic 'sister' trait she had developed so far. 'Come to the show tonight, grab some food in the services tent afterwards, and *listen* to what Brennan has to offer you.'

Kurt glared at her. Of course he was going to do what she said. Still, he could complain about it. 'He's seriously changed his mind because I beat up a couple of heavies along their fence line?'

'It proved your usefulness nicely, and Fin is the Ringmaster's daughter. Her word goes a long way.' Inga smirked. 'You impressed the clowns.'

He gave her a scornful look. 'You know if we were planning to steal those baby dragons, we would have set up a scenario exactly like that to trick the circus folk into trusting me.'

Inga cracked her back, running through a few of her favourite stretches to loosen up after her hard day of rehearsals. 'I know that and you know that. They're civilians, sunshine. They could use a little professional advice to keep the bad guys at bay.'

'Brennan's not a civilian,' Kurt growled. 'Their precious Gaffer is a lot like us. Bet you half a dollar he used to be in our line of work.'

Inga didn't look surprised. 'So why's he playing dumb?'

'I don't know, this is why I–' He gave up. 'So dinner and a show, yeah?'

Inga leaned in and kissed him solemnly on both cheeks. 'You're supposed to tell me to break a leg. It's good luck.'

'This is worse than that time we had to pretend to be opera singers,' Kurt muttered.

'I know you liked the costumes.'

The show was awful. Kurt hated it. He could see the skill involved – everyone from the clowns to the acrobats to the ballerinas and the trapeze artists themselves were nothing short of spectacular.

Inga, Cato and Cicero performed a shortened version of the usual Birds of Paradise routine, apparently, but it was clear that they were working well together. The potential for brilliance was there.

Then of course, there were the dragons. Nearly every performance involved them, whether the creatures were performing tricks at the commands of the Ringmaster, or the satin-clad pair of trainers that were Puck and Fin.

Dragons danced through the air routines, played up to the clowns, and scared the shit out of the audience by flaming brightly a little too close to the cheap seats.

Still, Kurt hated it. He couldn't pay attention to the acts, too busy reacting to the noise and smell of too many people in one place, no solid walls behind him; and potential dangers jumbling up his head and setting him on high alert.

He escaped long before the interval, fighting his way through the layers of canvas and tripping over a bunch of half-naked tightrope walkers in a flurry of powder and costume changes. Finally he found a quiet spot to stand behind the Big Top and breathe in air that didn't taste of popped corn, greasepaint and sticky hands.

'Too much for you?' asked a low voice.

Kurt glanced across and saw Brennan, still dressed like a random workman, nursing a mostly-gone cigarette through its remaining sparks.

'How do you stand it?' he asked without thinking. Great way to make an impression on a potential employer.

'I don't,' Brennan grunted. 'I don't give a crap about the performance, as long as the artists and the audience are happy. Too many other things to worry about around here.'

Kurt found that reassuring, that he wouldn't have to pretend to appreciate slapstick or dragon ballet.

'We got off on the wrong foot earlier,' Brennan said after a comfortable silence.

'Yeah, you reckon?' Kurt snorted.

'No offence, mate. It's just – if I was trying to bust open circus security, you're exactly who I'd send. That business with Fin today doesn't change that.'

'Good,' said Kurt sharply. 'It shouldn't.' Nice to know he wouldn't be working for an idiot. He risked a grin that he had been told was charming. 'I'd send me to steal your baby dragons too.'

Brennan made a huffing sound that might have been a laugh. He gave

Kurt a once-over that under other circumstances might be about a whole different kind of interest. 'Come on,' he said finally. 'Want to show you something.'

Kurt resisted the urge to ask *is it your bedroom ceiling?* 'Sure,' he said, keeping it casual. 'Whatever.'

The baby dragons were housed in a cage inside a tent, which smelled like scorched gumnuts and death warmed up. Riff, the angriest of all the surly clowns was standing guard over the tent, and didn't join them as they stepped inside. Kurt didn't blame him at all when he caught a lungful of the stench.

'Holy shit.'

'Yeah, mind your step,' said Brennan, not even joking.

'Don't they need fresh air or something?'

'They live in caves. This is their natural habitat.'

Kurt looked around at the singed fabric and the soot-stained bars. 'This is no one's natural habitat.'

Brennan folded his arms. 'My Grip is run off her feet, and doesn't have enough assistants. A new dragon pen that's secure and open to the air is on her to-do list, but it's not high up. Don't reckon she'll get to it this week.'

Ugh. 'This is you hazing the new bloke, isn't it?' Kurt accused.

Brennan gave him a look that wasn't a smile, wasn't anything really. The challenge was in his voice. 'Report to Carlotta in the morning. See if she likes you.'

'And if she doesn't like me?' asked Kurt, not keen on having to convince someone else he was worth keeping.

'Then I'm going to have to force her to admit that she's eight months fucking pregnant and should put her feet up and believe me, no one wants that conversation to happen in this lifetime. Do me a favour, Frostad, and save the charm for her.'

'I'll see what I can do,' said Kurt.

'Works for me,' said Brennan reaching out.

Kurt almost dodged away before realising it was a friendly shoulder pat and, oh, casual touching. He was going to have to get used to that in a place like this, where performers ran around in their underwear the second they got offstage, and everyone pitched in with costume and makeup and ego-stroking and chore wheels.

This was going to be like the opera all over again, only worse, because he wouldn't get to put a crossbow bolt into anyone at the end of it.

Brennan finished the shoulder pat as if he had no idea that he was blowing Kurt's mind. 'Welcome to the Dragon Circus.'

The carnival came alive after the show was done. The excited audience poured out of the Big Top and instead of going home like sensible people, they flooded the carnival, spending money like water on games and displays and food that had been cooked one too many times.

It was a security nightmare.

Kurt observed the whole mess from afar. He found a perch up high on the rigging outside the Big Top, and studied the flow of people, where they went and what they did. Eyes up high was his default position for surveillance.

The artists retreated to the campsite to eat supper and rest, though many of them returned to the carnival later on, parading around and smiling at the onlookers, still in their costumes and greasepaint.

The dragons, tired and hungry, were kept in a large roofed pen in the midst of it all; the biggest draw. Four of them: Blue, Green, Bronze and Red. No rest for them.

Puck and Fin were the only handlers allowed near the dragons during the night chaos. They fed them raw meat, gave them branches of wattle and blue gum to gnaw on for tooth hygeine, and kept them from burning the curious fingers of the onlookers.

It was a miracle that no one was killed. Still, the youngsters knew what they were doing, and all four of the dragons were finally able to curl up and sleep once the carnival was cleared, at midnight.

Kurt observed the patterns of the crew, carnies and artists as they disassembled their second, less formal show of the night, and headed for their beds.

'Everyone sleeps late,' said Inga, startling him. Of course she had danced her way up into the rigging, silent as a ghost. 'You didn't eat with us.'

'Working,' Kurt muttered.

She passed him a wrapped parcel that turned out to be a bread roll full of dripping meat and gravy. He ate without taking his eyes off the darkening carnival field.

'They didn't hire you for security,' Inga said dryly.

'I think maybe they did.' He was sure Brennan had been asking for more than a dragon pen. A cage wasn't enough to keep the babies from being stolen. Kurt needed a system, and for that, he needed to learn a hell of a lot more about dragons.

Tomorrow.

'The Gaffer gave you a mission, didn't he?' Inga said, amused.

'I don't know how to be a civilian,' Kurt confessed, wolfing the last of his food and licking his fingers clean. 'I think that's the first thing he figured out about me.'

His partner sighed and leaned into him, brushing the side of his head with a kiss. 'Come on. They've given us Molly's trailer. Sleep now, mission in the morning.'

Carnies and artists did sleep late, Kurt learned quickly. Crew did not. There was always something to work on between shows.

He left Inga sleeping in her bunk and followed a series of haphazard directions to the workshop of his new boss. The place was empty, so after a few minutes he hunted up the services tent instead, and returned with a half decent breakfast inside him to find the workshop full of Grips.

Carlotta, known to all as Grip (or sometimes The Grip, he learned later from overhearing others talk about her behind her back), was an angry woman with spiky hair, a pregnant belly approximately the size of the Big Top, and a resting bitch-face that put the entire Assassins Union to shame.

Her team was made up of Grips, Gripper and Sparks, who probably had real names, but took pride in not revealing them to the new bloke, because why make his life easier? Grippy was the one who had run off with Molly the trapeze artist.

'What do you have to offer, Frostad?' The Grip demanded of him, hands on hips.

Offering to shoot anyone who tried to steal a baby dragon probably wasn't enough.

Kurt breathed in and out again, getting his head in the game. 'Okay,' he said. 'So there are three missing bolts on the rig for the trapeze net – not enough to be a problem yet, but it has to affect the overall stability. You've got five missing seats in the highest bank, I assume because no one had time to fix them? I can make you new ones or repair the originals. The dragon pen's too damned small, and I reckon that was true two dragons ago. You're going to need to expand even more as the babies grow bigger, but the priority is the new housing for the baby dragons, which Brennan said I should handle – I'm assuming because it's a shit job and I need to prove myself. Also I dropped by the workshop earlier, and your chair squeaks.'

The Grip's mouth thinned. 'You sat in my chair?'

Kurt shrugged. 'Fella's gotta sit somewhere.'

'Maybe I like the squeak,' she said as a challenge.

'Sure.' He might be trained in lethal force in over 20 weapon grades, but he knew better than to argue with a pregnant woman holding a socket wrench.

Carlotta took Kurt's hands in hers, examined his callouses, and declared that he would be Grippo until further notice.

He considered that a win.

'You realise Brennan will shoot you out of a cannon if anything happens to those babies, right?' she added.

'I got that,' sighed Kurt.

Before he even started sourcing materials, Kurt spent a morning observing Puck and Fin with the dragons. They didn't get the artist perk of sleeping late, because dragons were up with the birds.

He questioned the kids about the needs of the babies versus the needs of the adult dragons, and was well aware that it had turned into an interrogation somewhere along the way, but they didn't seem to object.

Trouble was, neither of them had dealt with baby dragons before, so they were figuring it out from scratch as well. All they knew so far was that the adult dragons – including Big Blue, the reluctant mother – loathed the babies enough that bringing them all together in the same habitat was a bushfire waiting to happen.

Treating this as a mission was the only way to keep himself sane. By lunchtime Kurt had a rough plan, including notes and lists. He had convinced two of the other Grips to help him cannibalise a broken-down trailer that no one used any more.

'Shouldn't take more than 24 hours,' he assured Carlotta.

It took a week.

The circus embraced Inga. Whenever Kurt looked up, she was practicing her act with Cato and Cicero, flirting with Puck, laughing with the clowns, bonding with the female artists, or planning new costumes.

Kurt was used to being the charmer who smiled easily and set everyone at ease, while his partner retreated into her default mode of cool and threatening. Now Inga charmed the boys and made friends, while he worked silently and observed the circus folk from a distance.

He liked it more than he had ever imagined. All he had to do was glare every now and then, and he was left alone.

It didn't work on Fin.

Kurt had learned a lot of things about Finlay Faraday since their meeting on the train. He knew that she was 16 (he hadn't been too far off his guess), which was way too young to risk your life around fire-breathing reptiles, but what did he know? He was a professional assassin from the age of 12 so his notion of normal was a little skewed.

Fin was the daughter of Magellan, the glamorous and intimidating Ringmaster, and Serendipity, the sharp-tongued queen of costumes. Maybe having those two women in control of her life made her a little less scared of things that breathed fire.

He learned that she was brave as hell, and loyal, and stupidly reckless. He once saw her run across the back of one dragon to leap on to another, 10 feet above the ground, and almost bit his tongue to stop himself lecturing her about it afterwards. Half the tricks she proposed for Puck to add to their own act were outrageously dangerous.

Kurt had no idea why Fin would so often visit when he was mending a fence or setting up a tent – Grip called on him for daily chores along with his ongoing project of the baby dragon pen – and chatter to him about her day, and the circus, and the crowds, and the dragons.

Somehow, she felt it was completely appropriate to pour her teenage heart out to him while he banged in nails.

'Don't you have any friends your own age to talk to?' Kurt demanded once, craving five minutes of silence

Fin gave him a dirty look and said no, and after a moment's thought he realised that it was true. There were kids around, he'd seen them underfoot here and there, but most of them were much younger than Fin. There were the lads, Puck and a few others, but Kurt was pretty sure they were of an age to be drinking and screwing around and Fin wasn't there yet. She spent time with the older boys, but they weren't exactly peers.

'That must suck,' he said finally, and Fin agreed that it did. Kurt managed not to point out that however annoying the lads were, they were still a hell of a lot closer to her age than he was.

He stopped thinking of Fin's attention as an annoyance five days into the dragon pen project, when she came to him with a security concern.

'Kurt, the Gaffer's in trouble and I can't find Riff or the other clowns!'

Fin was in full stage makeup, glitter streaked through her hair. She had all five baby dragons on ribbon leashes, treated with flameproof oil. They flew above her head like bobbing balloons.

'Show me,' Kurt said, getting to his feet.

Brennan's office was a lean-to against his trailer, between the campsite and the carnival. Two heavies stood outside, and Kurt didn't have to ask their names to know that they weren't circus folk.

He walked right up to the door, Fin and the baby dragons sticking close, which was fine with him – he liked to have them in his line of sight.

One of the heavies leaned out and pushed a meaty palm against Kurt's chest. 'Our employer wants some privacy in his meeting with Mr Brennan,' he said, polite and slow.

There was a crash inside the office.

'Yeah, no,' said Kurt, and took out the fella's legs.

The other heavy grunted in surprise and lunged forward, but Kurt tripped him and gave him a hard kidney punch, then slammed his head against that of his colleague. He could see Riff and Inga charging through the carnival in their direction, so he took a chance on leaving Fin and the dragons outside while he nipped inside the office.

It was a small space, but as Kurt's eyes adjusted to the dim light he saw another two heavies sprawled on the floor, and Brennan in the corner, wiping a trail of blood from his lip.

Was it hot in here, or was it just him?

A huge man in a formal suit stood as far from Brennan as he could get, snarling threats despite his lack of back up.

'You all right in here, Gaffer?' Kurt asked cheerfully.

Brennan gave him a dirty look, as if he had been caught with his fingers in a sweet jar. 'Fine thanks, Frostad.'

'Three weeks for the payments, no exceptions,' growled the boss, and hauled his battered bodyguards to their feet before making a huffy exit.

He gave Kurt a searching look as he left.

Inga put her head in the door. 'All right to let these boys leave?' she asked casually, as if she was asking on Riff's behalf and not personally prepared to put a knife in the back of each of them.

'Fine with me,' said Brennan.

Kurt gave Inga a covert nod, knowing that she hadn't been asking the Gaffer's opinion at all. She withdrew, leaving the two of them alone.

'He recognised you,' said Brennan flatly. 'Is that going to be a problem?'

'I've not been in this city a week, he didn't recognise shit,' said Kurt. 'What was going on here? Why are they shaking you down?'

'I don't answer to you, Frostad.'

'Whatever you say, *Gaffer*,' Kurt said sarcastically. How the hell was he supposed to keep this circus safe when no one would tell him anything?

Brennan gave him a sharp look. 'Do you really think it's your responsibility to keep us all safe?'

Damn it, had he said that aloud? 'I didn't think you hired me because I'm good with carpentry tools,' he admitted.

Brennan sighed, and stepped forward so he was barely a foot from Kurt. 'I hired you,' he said after a moment's pause, 'because I used to live in Maritaur. A long time ago. I made you as the Dove and the Hammer the second you set foot in my circus.'

Kurt felt like he had been punched in the face. Maritaur. The Dove and the Hammer had worked for a crime boss there, who traded a shipload of gems and spices for six months of their services. They had been his public enforcers by day, and secret police by night. They had killed 28 people between them, in Maritaur.

Who was Brennan, that he recognised them from there?

'What is it you need us for?' Kurt demanded, furious at this revelation. They had come so far, searching for a place where no one knew the Dove and the Hammer; where no one would see them as weapons.

Brennan had a sympathetic look in his eyes, as if he knew everything boiling away inside Kurt's head. 'I need a Grip and a trapeze artist,' he said finally. 'But things are going to get worse in this city before they get better. I know you're not the Hammer any more, but if I do need extra backup around here, I want the best.'

Kurt's mind cleared at that. Brennan didn't know everything, and he wasn't asking them to be his pet assassins. Not yet, anyway.

'I have a dragon pen to finish,' he muttered, and walked out of the office.

Fin was waiting for him, her baby dragons still fluttering on their leashes. Inga stood with her, at a distance calculated to make it not look like she was playing bodyguard.

Kurt pointed a finger at Inga. 'Have you got time to give Fin self-defense training? An hour each morning?'

'I can make time,' Inga said evenly.

'Aren't you even going to ask me?' Fin objected. 'Why her, anyway? Can't you teach me?'

'Body type's wrong,' said Kurt.

At the same time that Inga said: 'He's a rubbish teacher, you'll want to kill him.'

'Hey,' Kurt protested.

Fin giggled, and handed him a baby dragon to make him feel better. 'I think I'm going to name this one after you.'

'Cranky,' said Inga, hiding a smile.

'Grumpy,' Fin decided.

The baby dragon belched a tiny ball of flame that singed the hairs off the back of Kurt's arm, and then happily licked blue paint off his hand.

Kurt was pretty sure that Inga was having sex with one of the clowns. She didn't stay in the caravan most nights, and when she returned in the mornings she was happy and mussed.

He thought it was Puck at first, and was prepared to find out exactly how young that kid was in case it was going to be a problem, but then he saw Inga leaning into Riff one night after the show, and figured he had been completely on the wrong track.

'Should I be the protective big brother about this?' Kurt asked one morning as they made tea on their little camp stove. 'All aggro about your virtue? Because that sounds exhausting.'

'Are you angry?' she asked, sounding more curious than anything.

'Nah, you're good. It's nice to see you having fun.' *You deserve it*, he didn't say, though he meant it. Inga had been quietly unhappy for so long, why shouldn't she cut loose a little?

Inga busied herself about the tea, pouring it into the tin mugs they had been issued. 'And what about you, Kurt? When are you going to have some fun?'

The thought was faintly startling. 'I have fun.'

She looked skeptical.

'I like having work to do,' he admitted. 'Being useful does it for me.'

'You can't aspire to more than useful?'

I don't deserve any more than that. I barely deserve this.

'It doesn't help that the only person I fancy in this damned circus is the bloke who writes the pay cheques. There's no way that can end well.'

Inga stared at him, and he made a face at her. 'Oh, *Kurt*.'

'Shut up, I know.'

'The Gaffer?'

'Don't make me try to explain it.'

'I don't need to,' she said, thoroughly amused. 'You have a type.'

'Don't go there,' he warned.

'You always pick the most dangerous person in a crowd. You're hunting for an equal.'

'I'm not hunting for anything!' Kurt took his tin mug off her and drank half of it down. 'He knows who we are, by the way. He knows about the Dove and the Hammer.'

Inga stilled. 'What does he want us to do for him?'

It broke his heart that her reaction was the same as his – *they know we're weapons, how are they going to use us?*

'He says all he needs is backup,' he said. 'Something heavy's brewing, something more than the giant target that the baby dragons have painted on the side of their Big Top. Mob shakedown, maybe.'

'Right,' said Inga. 'Now I have a mission too.'

Kurt gave her a grateful look. 'I didn't ask.'

She leaned in and kissed him once, on the mouth. 'You never have to ask.'

'So,' said Brennan, when the week was up. 'I asked for a dragon pen.'

'Yes, you did,' said Kurt evenly.

'And you made me a dragon caravan.'

'It works, doesn't it?'

The old trailer, past the point that humans could live in it safely, had given way like butter under a heated knife. Once Carlotta trusted Kurt (or rather, Grippo) with her tools, he was able to cut and re-weld half of the trailer into narrow metal bars.

Inside, the area that had once been a kitchenette served as a sleeping cave for the babies, padded with good chewing leaves and banksia cones, which gave way under their tiny teeth with a sound like bird skulls underfoot. The open bars enabled the dragons to be seen by as many nosy onlookers as wanted to stare.

It was wheeled which allowed them to move it easily as near or far away from the adult dragons as appropriate – and would help them transport the babies when the circus was on the move again. It had a panic cavity built into the floor where they could hide the babies from sight in an emergency, and it was highly defensible.

Thanks to Puck and a couple of his makeup artist mates, the caravan also had a mural of adorable baby dragons painted on one side, which was good, because Kurt's artistic skills were not up to that level and he was pretty sure he would never live it down if Inga knew he thought about doing that job himself.

'It works,' Brennan said finally.

That was all the feedback Kurt was going to get from the Gaffer. It would do. He'd had a solid back-pat from The Grip that morning from which he was still recovering.

In the open space above the original dragon pen, Fin and Puck were rehearsing a new trick. Fin threw herself backwards off Blue, hanging with her ankles locked around the dragon's tail. Kurt clenched his fists as the girl arched her spine and placed both hands on Puck's shoulders, only to let go of Blue altogether and flip herself into a mid-air somersault that positioned her squarely on Bronze's back.

'She's been doing that trick since she was 12,' said Brennan.

'I wasn't worried,' Kurt lied. Then, plaintively: 'She's a baby.'

'There are no children under the Big Top, Frostad. They're artists or crew or carnies.'

Kurt knew that. He wasn't an idiot.

What he was, he realised now, was far too invested in this fucking circus. It was going to break him, one way or another.

Inga's investigation had revealed a nasty history of gambling debts run up by the circus's former owner, who had been killed in an "accident" two months ago. The reason the circus hadn't moved on from Dust yet was because they were still making regular payments to several mob bosses who owned the debts.

One boss in particular – a woman known as Nadina – had been buying up the debts from the others. Her demands were ratcheting up, piling on the pressure, and until recently she had been after Brennan to give her one of the circus' dragons to pay their debt.

Now, of course, she wanted the babies.

Kurt was trying to think of a tactful way to let Brennan know how much he had discovered without getting his arse fired, when a voice interrupted the stillness of the morning. 'GAFFER!' It was Cato, his feathered costume scorched and trailing the scent of smoke behind him.

The dragons reacted to the smell, huffing their own smoke in response. Fin and Puck wrestled Blue and Bronze back into the pen.

'The Big Top's on fire!'

Brennan lurched after Cato, but Kurt hauled him back, a hand on his shoulder, ready to duck if the other man punched him. 'It's a distraction,' he hissed.

'Of course it's a fucking distraction,' Brennan shot back. 'Stay with the dragons.'

Kurt had been about to suggest the opposite, that Brennan stay here to protect the babies, but the Gaffer had a point. Only one of them would be effective in rallying the circus folk to prevent the fire from spreading, and it wasn't Kurt.

'Watch your back,' he ordered, and let his boss go.

'What do we do?' Fin asked.

Kurt looked up to see that Puck was on the verge of dashing after the Gaffer but, by a miracle, was waiting to see what he thought.

'I need you both here,' he insisted. 'The best weapons we have to protect the babies are the adult dragons, and I can't handle them without you.'

Puck nodded reluctantly. Fin glowed as if he had given her some kind of medal.

Kurt and Puck pushed the baby dragon trailer up against the side of the adult dragon pen, which got the adults riled up something fierce. That wasn't necessarily a bad thing right now.

Kurt looked around for extra weapons. He found a couple of large tent hammers discarded nearby and grinned ruefully as he weighed them in his hand.

'What's so funny?' Puck asked him.

'Private joke,' said Kurt.

The Dove and the Hammer, you'll never see them coming until they smash you in the face...

Kurt hopped up on top of the roof of the dragon trailer. He'd be lying if he said he hadn't reinforced the roof so that he could do exactly this someday.

He saw her sashaying in their direction from halfway across the carnival.

Ice-blonde and perfect: every inch the Inga Frostad that his partner had created for herself.

'That's not Inga,' said Puck in a low voice, climbing up to the roof of the trailer with Kurt. Fin joined them, hauling Bronze with her. The adult dragon perched on one side of the roof like a gargoyle about to pounce.

'Gold star to you,' said Kurt just as quietly.

'She walks differently,' Fin said, as if this was obvious.

Looked like being raised in a circus trained you up to see through disguises. Even excellent, flawless disguises.

'Who is she?' Puck asked.

'An old friend,' said Kurt, which was half right.

You always pick the most dangerous person in the crowd, Inga had said of his love life, and she wasn't wrong.

He knew whom they were up against now, at least. 'Hello, Naga,' he called out as the not-Inga drew up a short distance from them.

The intruder gave him an impatient look, tossing back Inga's bright white-blonde hair. 'Do you know how long it took me to get this shape correct to the finest detail?'

'Sorry for wasting your time,' said Kurt with half a grin. 'It's been a while, baby.'

The Naga worked the same circuit as the Hammer and the Dove. They all knew each other, the high-level professionals, even as they moved from city to city. The deadly killer you went up against in Nensk might easily be the partner you were assigned in Maritaur. You couldn't get personal about it.

The Naga had worked with the Hammer and the Dove many times, using her shape-changing skills to play any part an employer required, from murderous sex-kitten or replacement trophy wife to actual eight-foot snake monster, if the situation called for it. She was a vicious, remorseless killer, and equally ruthless (cough, amazing) in bed. She was also losing her touch if she thought she could trick him into thinking she was his sister.

'How much is this Nadina paying you?' Kurt called down. 'I can make it worth your while to walk away.'

He didn't know which of them would win in a fight between him and the Naga, not any more. If they did this here, one of them was likely to end up dead.

Inga's face shimmered, and shifted to the more prominent nose and brow of the Naga, complete with glittery hair beads and a voluminous black jumpsuit. 'You're behind the times, circus boy. This isn't any old job for me. It's my retirement plan.'

Kurt saw Brennan swing out from behind one of the nearby carnival displays, pointing an elderly shotgun at the Naga's back. 'She *is* Nadina,' the Gaffer announced. 'This one's been shaking down Dust for nearly a year now, and she thinks she can take the Dragon Circus.'

Kurt winced. Of course. Naga had always enjoyed her pets. She had a personal snake collection that was enough to make any lover think twice before rummaging in her underwear.

Now she wanted his dragons.

The Naga batted her eyelashes at Kurt, not even glancing at Brennan or his shotgun. 'Oh please, darling, for old time's sake, don't let the bad man shoot me,' she said in a baby voice.

Kurt saw her move coming, and he was too far away to stop it. 'Don't–' he said, and threw himself into the air, leaping like he was the fucking bird of paradise, working without a trapeze.

In the time it took him to slam her to the ground, the Naga had already flung a handful of sliver-thin knives behind her, straight at Brennan's chest.

The shotgun discharged, but into the air, because Brennan was on his back. Kurt couldn't see how badly the other man was wounded because he was too busy fighting the Naga.

He got in two body blows with the hammers before she disarmed him on one side with a vicious twist. They were no good for close fighting, so he flung the other hammer away and went for her throat with his bare hands, squeezing the air out of her.

Naga's shape flickered back to that of Inga, so he stabbed her in the side with his wrist-stiletto, and took some satisfaction from the blood that sprayed across the grass.

Kurt was bleeding too (she had got a knife of some kind into his upper thigh) but he pinned her wrists to prevent further damage.

'Do you really want to die today just to own a dragon?' he growled into the Naga's face – her own face again. 'They smell bad and they're hell to take care of.'

Blood blossomed on the Naga's lower lip. 'Do you want to die today to protect someone else's dragons? Look at you, domesticated as ever. You're never happy unless someone is telling you who to kill. Come work for me. We'll take all the dragons, and I'll buy you a collar and leash all of your own.'

Kurt shoved himself off her, standing up. He saw Puck and Fin crowding around Brennan's fallen body and couldn't quite bring himself to check, or to ask, if it was a *body* or if the Gaffer was still alive.

The Naga lay there, bruised and bloodied, laughing at him. He knew enough about her style not to count her out, not with the three blades she still had concealed in her sleeves, not with that look in her eye as she collected herself.

'I have a job,' he said calmly. 'For once I'm *protecting* something instead of wrecking it. You have nothing to offer me.'

He could see a crowd mobilising in their general direction, in twos and threes, gathering together. Artists and crew and carnies, all approaching with caution.

He saw Cato and Cicero. The Grip, Gripper and Grips. Magellan the Ringmaster and Serendipity the Queen of Costumes. Riff and his army of surly clowns. Inga, standing almost close enough to Riff to hold his hand.

'If you think that, you're the same idiot you always were,' breathed the Naga. 'You're a weapon, not a person. Just like me.'

Kurt knew she was going to change before she made the move. Danger awareness flooded his body, all at once.

The Naga shifted into her snake monster form, all muscles and scales and the stink of sulphur.

Still better than the smell of enclosed dragons, actually.

Spikes rose up on her arms. She could shoot them at her victim, Kurt remembered. She had threatened to do it in bed once or twice, but he had talked her out of it on the grounds that he couldn't do that thing to her with his mouth if he was perforated all over and bleeding to death.

Yeah on the whole being the Naga's opponent was better than being her boyfriend.

'I'll mount your head on my wall,' the Naga howled. 'With a bronze plaque: how the Mighty Hammer fell.'

Kurt kept his gaze steady on hers. He didn't want to let her know what he could see in his peripheral vision – Inga, his Inga, moving lightly across the grass, picking up one heavy object and then another.

'See,' he said, his voice cracking only slightly. 'That's the thing everyone always gets wrong about the Dove and the Hammer.'

The Naga gave him an odd look, her head tilting with curiosity.

Keep her distracted, just a little longer.

'Yeah,' said Kurt, grinning through dry, blood-stained lips. 'It's an easy mistake to make, if you're not paying attention. It's not like we ever corrected people. But the truth is – I'm the Dove.'

He had never seen a sight more beautiful than that of his sister, Inga Frostad, rising up behind the eight-foot snake monster with a tent-peg hammer in each hand, and death in her eyes.

'She's the Hammer,' he added helpfully, as Inga caved the bitch's head in, and kept smashing until there was a mess of blood and brains smeared across the grass.

Kurt leaned against the dragon pen, and waited until Inga was done. She stepped daintily across the mess, handed the hammers to him, and turned to face the crowd.

The circus folk stared back at her, at the blood and mess spattering her beautiful white satin-and-feathers leotard.

'Good thing we have a backup of that costume,' said Serendipity after a long moment. 'We'd better make you one in black, too – won't show the stains.'

'I told you she had the core strength to flip both of us at once,' said Cato, giving Cicero a shove. 'You said she didn't have it in her.'

Riff was grinning through his greasepaint, the first smile that Kurt had seen on a clown's face since he arrived. 'Wanna go steady?' he asked Inga.

She flicked a gob of snake flesh off her leotard. 'I'll think about it.'

'Kurt, over here,' called Fin.

As sure as he could be that the circus folk were not about to run Inga out of town for being a violent killer, Kurt went over to where Puck and Fin were helping Brennan sit up. He had several blades impaled in his chest, but he was still breathing.

'He wants *you* to get them out,' said Puck, offended he wasn't allowed to do it himself.

Kurt gave Brennan a look that was warmer than he had intended. 'Yeah?'

'I assume you have the most experience with extracting knives from people,' Brennan said sarcastically.

Kurt shrugged, and glanced back at his sister.

'He's not wrong, sunshine,' Inga said, and then went back to making out publicly with Riff the clown because apparently that was a thing she did now.

Kurt leaned over his boss, to keep this particular exchange private. 'Pride is one thing, but stupid is another,' he said in a very low voice. 'Time to move the circus on. Dust isn't going to cool down for you any time soon, so you need to get your people the hell out of here.'

Brennan glared at him. 'That was a suggestion, yes? Not the order it sounded like. Because I'm the Gaffer.'

Kurt resisted the urge to kiss him on the forehead. Instead, he removed his belt. 'You're the Gaffer,' he assured his boss, handing over the length of leather. 'Bite down on this. The next five minutes are gonna be painful.'

'We're going with them,' said Inga, that night in their caravan. 'On to the next town, and the next. We are, aren't we?'

Kurt didn't answer her.

She smacked him lightly on the shoulder. 'Talk to me.'

'They know who we are now. What we are.' He didn't say *were* because who were they kidding to pretend it was in the past tense? 'Just because they're conditioned to accept weirdos into their little family doesn't mean they're going to be okay with it.'

Fin had been giving him uncertain looks, because she knew to be afraid of him now. Kurt hadn't realised how much he liked the little hero-worship thing that the kid had going on with him until it was gone.

'I'm tired of pretending to be Inga,' his sister admitted. 'I think – this is the only way I can *become* her. A person, not a weapon. Cards on the table, all in. Surrounded by people who know how far I've come, and like me anyway.'

'Also it's your chance to explore this whole clown fetish thing,' Kurt said darkly.

She smirked. 'That too. Come on, Kurt. Let's run away with the circus.'

'One town,' he conceded. 'We'll get them safely to one more town. Maybe stick around a while to make sure there no more former assassins planning to demand dragons with menaces. Then we have our own future to build, Inga.'

'One town,' she agreed, and smiled at him as if he'd promised her the moon.

'Two towns,' he grumbled. 'That's my absolute limit.'

Inga laughed, and it was a good sound, a genuinely happy sound.

There would be time enough to think about dragons and exit strategies and how to protect a whole circus from the big bad world. Right now, Kurt was content enough to lie back on his bunk and listen to the sound of his sister laughing at him.

Clan Destine Press would like to thank
our fabulous editors, **Ruth Wykes** & **Kylie Fox**;
artist **Vicky Pratt** for the wonderful title page illustrations;
& artist **Sarah Pain** for the amazing cover art and design.

When we sent out the coded message to the cohort of Aussie
and a few Kiwi genre writers to come and play in our sandpit,
we were thrilled by the response.

We thank the 32 authors who dared to take up the challenge,
causing us to extend the *And Then...* project to two volumes.

We salute their willingness to gird the loins of their heroes,
don their many-coloured hats, lock-and-load their explodey things
and set off on adventures galorious.

In many cases our authors – for now they are *ours* – not only bent
but tripped out of their usual genres to seek action elsewhere.

And Then... was partly funded by two Indiegogo campaigns.
We would like to thank the following people for their generous support.

Amra Pajalic	Angela Lorrigan	Ann Davies	Anne Burgi
Aramanth Dawe	Bec Stafford	Bookfrivolity	Bronwennq
Catherine Heloise	Cathy Green	Cheryl Rush	Chris Bongers
Christmas Press	Claudia Colin	Danielle Kovacic	Fiona
Demet Divaroren	Diana Mumme	Diane McWhirter	Julie Bozza
Jodi Lazarou	Joelle Parrott	Julia Scott	Kath Harper
Katharine Stubbs	Kathryn Ledson	Kbmail	Kerrie Duff
Kym Poxon	L.J. Owen	Laurai	Lindymb
Lohma003	LynC	Marcus Liddle	Tim Marsh
Mary Borsellino	Moraig Kisler	Narrelle Harris	Olivia
Natalie Conyer	Pamela	Paul May	R Perry
Rachel Smith	Robin Storey	Sally Koetsveld	Tor Roxburgh
Samuel Spettigue	Sandra Wigzell	Susanne Munro	
Sandra Dusconi	silentdan2017	Tsana Dolichva	
Terry O'Connell	Therese M Noble	Leslie Falkiner-Rose	
Yael Bornstein	Read Cafe Surfers Paradise		

And Then...
the Authors

Peter M. Ball
Peter is the author of *Horn*, *Bleed*, and the Flotsam novella series. He's had short stories in *Apex Magazine*, *Eclipse 4*, and *Daily Science Fiction*.

Alan Baxter
Alan lives among dairy paddocks on the south coast of NSW, where he writes dark fantasy, horror and sci-fi, and rides a motorcycle. He also teaches Kung Fu. He is the author of: The Balance series — *Mage Sign & Realm Shift*; the Alex Caine series — *Bound*, *Obsidian* & *Abduction*; and the short story collection, *Crow Shine*.

Kat Clay
Kat is a Melbourne writer and photographer whose non-fiction articles have appeared in numerous travel magazines and academic journals. She is the author of the novella *Double Exposure*.

Emilie Collyer
Emilie writes fiction, plays and poetry. She's twice won the Cross Genre category in the Scarlet Stiletto Awards run by Sisters in Crime Australia; had stories in *Allegory* and *Cosmic Vegetable*; and her award-winning sci-fi play *The Good Girl* premiered in New York in 2016. Emilie has two collections of short fiction, *A Clean Job* and *Autopsy of a Comedian*.

Jason Franks
Jason, author of the occult rock'n'roll novel *Bloody Waters*, also writes graphic novels and comic books series including *The Sixsmiths* & *Left Hand Path*. His short fiction has been in *Aurealis*, *Midnight Echo*, *After the World*, and more. He's twice been short-listed for an Aurealis Award.

And Then...

Sulari Gentill

Sulari is author of the Hero Trilogy, a YA retelling of *The Odyssey*, and the award-winning Rowland Sinclair mysteries, that began with *A Few Right Thinking Men*. Sulari lives in her pyjamas in the Snowy Mountains foothills where she calls writing 'work' so no one will suggest she gets a real job.

Narrelle M. Harris

Narrelle is a Melbourne writer whose books include: *Witch Honour & Witch Faith*; *The Opposite of Life* & *Walking Shadows*; the Holmes/Watson romance, *The Adventure of the Colonial Boy*; and three erotic-rom series — *Talbott and Burns*, *Hammer and Tongue* and *Secret Agents, Secret Lives*. Her forthcoming supernatural thriller is *Ravenfall*.

Sophie Masson

Sophie is an award-winning author of more than 60 books for children, young adults and adults. Her most recent novels are the adult thriller, *Trinity: The False Prince*, and the YA fantasy *Hunter's Moon*.

Jason Nahrung

Jason lives in Ballarat with his author-wife Kirstyn McDermott. His passion for B-grade horror films is reflected in his gothic fiction, *Salvage* and outback vampire duology *Blood and Dust* and *The Big Smoke*.

Dan Rabarts

Dan, recipient of New Zealand's 2013 Sir Julius Vogel Award for Best New Talent, co-edited the multi-award-winning flash horror anthology *Baby Teeth — Bite-sized Tales of Terror* with Lee Murray. His short stories have appeared in numerous anthologies, magazines, ezines and podcasts.

Tansy Rayner Roberts

Tansy is a sci-fi and fantasy author, and Hugo Award winning blogger and podcaster (*Galactic Suburbia*). She is the author of: the Creature Court trilogy, *Siren Beat*, *Love and Romanpunk*, and, as Livia Day, the Café La Femme crime series. Her latest short fiction is *Fake Geek Girl*; and her serialised novel *Musketeer Space* is free on her blog.

Tor Roxburgh

Tor is a speculative fiction writer and author of 15 books, the latest an epic fantasy *The Light Heart of Stone*. She's also written 12 teen romances and two nonfiction titles. When avoiding writing, Tor runs an arts-focused homewares business, Omnibus Art Gallery, where she sells upcycled and re-upholstered furniture.

Lucy Sussex

Lucy was born in New Zealand but now lives in Melbourne. She has published widely; edited five anthologies, written five short story collections, and the award-winning neo-Victorian novel, *The Scarlet Rider*. Her latest book, *Blockbuster: Fergus Hume and the Mystery of a Hansom Cab,* won the 2015 Victorian Community History Award.

Evelyn Tsitas

Evelyn is intrigued by hybrids, art theft, Greek culture, and ambiguity in crime fiction. She has a PhD in Creative Writing and a Sisters in Crime Scarlet Stiletto Award to prove she takes her speculative research, and writing, seriously. Everything she writes has its basis in truth. Honestly.

Amanda Wrangles

Amanda won the 2009 Sisters in Crime Australia Scarlet Stiletto Award with her short story *Persia Bloom* (published in *Scarlet Stiletto: The Second Cut*). Her first novel — co-written with *And Then...* editor Kylie Fox, under the name A.K. Wrox — is the fantastical and sexy comedy, *Arrabella Candellarbra & the Questy Thing to End All Questy Things.*

www.ingramcontent.com/pod-product-compliance
Lightning Source LLC
Chambersburg PA
CBHW020416030726
47495CB00006B/1535